"You are Alouzon Dragonmaster!"

The flight through a world of twilight and mist had drained her. And now, looking at her hands, at her body, finding herself so utterly different . . .

She was in shock. She knew she was in shock, and wondered just how insane she was going to be when the shock wore off and she had to deal with a different body—and a different name.

She stood up, examined herself yet again. Strong, slender, tall. Everything she had never been before. Her voice held a dark resonance that was touched with the essence of command, and the sword at her hip, two intertwined dragons, spoke eloquently of power.

She was different, but she was strong, too. She could survive.

DRAGON SWORD

VOLUME I

BY GAEL BAUDINO

A BYRON PREISS BOOK

OMEIGA

LYNX OMEIGA BOOKS
NEW YORK

Special thanks to Cherry Weiner, Jill Bauman, Judith Stern, Leslie Skolnik, and Mary Higgins.

DRAGONSWORD

Volume 1

ISBN: 1-55802-003-9

This book is published by Lynx Books, a division of Lynx Communications, Inc., 41 Madison Avenue, New York, New York, 10010. The name "Lynx" together with the logotype consisting of a stylized head of a lynx is a trademark of Lynx Communications, Inc. The name "Omeiga" together with the logotype consisting of a stylized "O" is a trademark of Lynx Communications, Inc.

Cover painting by Walter Velez
Cover design and logo by Alex Jay
Edited by David M. Harris

Printed in the United States of America

0 9 8 7 6 5 4 3 2 1

This is for Allison, Jeff, Bill, and Sandy.
I won't forget.

DRAGON SWORD

VOLUME I

❖ CHAPTER 1 ❖

❖

THE DRAGON'S EYES COULD SHOW NO TRACE of emotion: they were no more than two balls of yellow light that peered out of a head the color of dull iron. In contrast, its voice, halfway between a thrum and a hiss, held the slightest edge of impatience as it carried softly through the curving glass walls of the paperweight and into the quiet air of the study.

"Braithwaite," it said, "you are getting old. You will die soon. You will have to choose."

Solomon Braithwaite looked up from his desk. He was not overly surprised by the bluntness of the statement, for he had heard it before, in these same uncompromising terms. "Soon? Are you giving me a date, Silbakor? Perhaps next Friday? Should I note it down on my calendar?"

"I have said before: I do not predict the future."

"You said *soon*. Why are you pressing me?"

Much as a man might fidget with his fingers, the Dragon coiled and uncoiled its body against the glass. "You will . . . have to choose."

The print on the page before him was as black and deep as if it had been chiseled into the paper. *Gueith camlann in qua arthur & medraut corruerunt . . .*

3

Arthur and Modred perished. And had the bastard son fidgeted and squirmed as he planned his treachery? "I want to know what's happening. You're edging around just like Helen did before she—"

"You must choose. You will die eventually."

"Tell me!" Solomon snapped the book closed and pushed it away. "Do you always have to drag everything out forever? *You're* the Dragon. *I'm* the Dragonmaster. Remember that."

"I will."

"So tell me."

"It is a matter of fact. You are old—"

The same equivocation. Arthur had Modred, Solomon Braithwaite had Helen, and Dythragor Dragonmaster . . . was there a traitor out there for him, too? The Dragon? "I'm not that old."

"—and I have never hidden from you the fact that you would have to find a successor. Consider: your hairline has receded, and your gray hairs are no longer confined to your temples—"

"Shut up."

Silbakor did not blink. Solomon wondered it it were capable of blinking. No, that would have been too human. Too mortal. The Dragon was neither.

But neither had the Dragon ever betrayed him. For the last ten years, the Dragon had been constancy, loyalty. Why was he speaking harshly to Silbakor? What madness was making him suspect that it would ever do him wrong?

"I haven't found anyone for the job yet," he said. He hoped that Silbakor could not read his thoughts of the past minute. "I see no reason why you have to keep interrupting me. We spoke about this last night."

"We did. To no avail."

"Have you looked at the people I have to work with? Have you seen my students? Of course you have: you're with me when I lecture. Pretty bits of manflesh, aren't they? They go on about Ambrosius and Arthur, and Vortigern and the Saxons, write up nice little papers about heroic culture, but they'd soil their pants at the thought of actually shedding some blood themselves. How about one of them, Silbakor? Would you like me to hand one the Dragonsword and tell him to go out and fight the Dremords?"

The Dragon lowered its head and stopped its thrashing. "The choice has always been yours. But choose soon: Gryylth must not be without a protector. The line must not be broken, even for an hour."

Shoving his chair back roughly, Solomon got up from the desk and went to the plate glass window. Not even for an hour, or a minute . . . probably not even for a second. He was still annoyed. Gryylth already had a protector. To speak of his replacement now seemed not only premature, but faintly cynical also.

Outside, it was dark, and the lights of the San Fernando Valley burned through air that had been washed clean by the afternoon's rain. The streetlamps danced in the heat shimmers like the campfires that had once dotted the Valley of Benardis where the wartroops of Gryylth had assembled under great, red-bearded Helkyying, and Solomon smiled quietly at the memory.

The battle had been glorious. At dawn, Gryylthan and Dremord had met face to face, challenging and being challenged in return. Weapons had been sword and shield, spear and javelin, and when the fighting had been done, the outcome had been certain: Gryylth had conquered, and the Dremords had been pushed back.

He liked that: cut and dried. To be sure, the war had been going on for a long time, and the Dremords had yet to be driven from the land, but the battles themselves had been invariably successful, and decisively so. If an understanding of his own world had eluded him, at least Gryylth was an open and honest place, with no ulterior motives, no hidden machinery, no shadowy conspiracies. Any enemies there were obvious and uncompromising.

As were friends. Vorya, and Helkyying. And now Marrget. And Silbakor the Dragon. Loyal. Friends in battle and in council. How could he blame the Dragon for doing its job?

Solomon regretted his anger. "All right," he said, turning around, "who would you say I should choose?"

For a moment, he thought that the Dragon blinked. Maybe it was something understandable after all. But, no, Silbakor never blinked. "This is strange."

"I can't make a choice myself."

"Surely there is someone."

"Silbakor, you've seen the people I know."

The Dragon's eyes had resettled into a yellow stare. "I have."

"So you understand my problem. There's no one suitable. Ten years ago, when I found you, there might have been a chance. Students and faculty were of a little sterner stuff then. But then again . . ."

The Dragon was watching him. At times, before those yellow eyes, he felt more naked than he had when Helen had turned on him, using her wifely knowledge of his frailties and weaknesses as knives and razors with which to slash him.

"But then again, I probably would have been wrong. Fairweather idealists, the whole lot of them. They knew their Karl Marx and their C. Wright Mills and their obscenities, but that was all." His voice almost caught: Helen had taken their side. "Now they're all hiding, or they've settled down to nice jobs and full lunch buckets. So much for the revolution. Good riddance." Was he talking to Helen? It annoyed him that he did not know.

"The choice was not necessary ten years ago," the Dragon thrummed softly. "It is necessary now."

"Are you saying that I'm going to die?"

"I am saying that you must choose."

Strange words from the Dragon. He thought he detected a trace of disingenuousness in its tone, but he could not be sure. Was Silbakor telling him that his death was imminent?

The diplomas on the wall. The certificate of appreciation. The photo of a younger Solomon Braithwaite in the hallowed robes of academia, receiving his doctorate on a rostrum before a weathered library of faded brick and old ivy. The portrait of Helen he should have thrown away years before but could not. Age. All age. For a moment, the study felt claustrophobic, coffin-like, as though someone were about to screw the lid down and sign to the pallbearers that it was ready.

I'm not that old. I could keep on for years . . .

A flash of yellow from the paperweight. Solomon again wondered if the Dragon could read his mind. He had never asked. He was, he admitted, afraid to know.

"I am sorry." It sounded genuinely sad.

He pretended not to have heard it. "You still haven't answered my question."

The Dragon roiled in the paperweight like a cloud of smoke. Helen had answered him. As brutally and searingly as possible. He was sorry now that he had asked.

"You have thought of all possibilities?" it said.

"All of them."

"What about your assistant, Suzanne Helling?"

Solomon had never heard the Dragon joke before, and he did not quite know how to react. He walked back across the study and peered into the paperweight. "Suzanne?" He chuckled in spite of himself. "Very good, Silbakor. A plump little earth-mother who most likely spends her time doing yoga and baking granola cookies." He leaned on his desk, laughing quietly. Oh, wonderful! Suzanne, with her big brown eyes and her dark hair worn in a style now ten years out of date. Dressed for 1980, she seemed an anachronism, as though she could only really be at home in shifts, peasant blouses, and miniskirts.

Solomon found himself looking at one of the papers he had been referencing that evening: it was in Suzanne's neat, backward-slanting handwriting. But, beside it, the picture of Helen smiled at him in sharp contrast to his memories of her. Where was Helen now? Was she well? Did she too still sleep on only one half of the bed? He reminded himself sharply that he did not care.

"She's a woman," he said abruptly.

"She is."

"She's just like those radicals I was dealing with when I found you, Silbakor. In fact, from what she's said, I think that she *was* one of those radicals."

"Like you, she has her history."

"She'd never fit in. Gryylth wouldn't accept her. In fact, I wouldn't accept her."

"She is my suggestion."

"A *woman?*" Hardening, angry, he swung round to the paperweight. "Dammit, Silbakor, what's the matter with you? She ought to be married and tending the children and the cooking pots, but instead she's shacked up with some law student—"

"She is your research assistant."

"That doesn't mean I have to approve of her! Dammit, Silbakor, you saw them back then: dirty, unwashed trash that didn't respect anything. Just like the Saxons. Just like the Dremords. How on earth Helen could have sided with them—"

There was a sudden tightness in his chest, and he stopped in mid-word and straightened up. His face felt cold. So did his arm. His right arm. His sword arm. With a quick gasp, he found his way to his chair and sat down, fumbled in the desk drawer for the pills the doctor had given him. He did not look at the label. He never had.

Painfully, he got one down, and the seizure passed slowly.

"Braithwaite?"

"You'd better not joke like that anymore, Silbakor," he said.

The skies had been clear when Suzanne had gone to bed, but during the night the clouds, gray and dull in the darkness, had moved in from the sea, and she awoke in the small hours to the sound of rain.

For a moment, she did not remember where she was. It seemed to her that everything about her— this apartment, this night alive with the pattering of rain, this man sleeping beside her—was merely another enactment of a play that had followed her from city to city, with different actors, an occasional change in the business or the props.

Her bedmate's leg was thrown over hers; his hand cupped her breast. What was his name this time? Steve? Mark? Dave? What city was this? Where was she now? She did not know. It might have been Seattle, or Akron, or Portland, or . . . or Dallas . . . No. Not Dallas. Not Dallas ever again. Her belly still cramped at the thought of the clinic, the abortion. *Now, honey, you just take these pills like it says on the bottle and call me if you have any problems.* And then she had come home and Russ had skipped out on her, taking the furniture, the money, even the car. And the rain, warm and wet, had been pattering down on the balcony just like it was now.

Slowly, she put together the lay of the light from the window, the feel of the sheets, the luminous dial of the clock by the bed: this was Los Angeles. Joe Epstein was beside her, snoring softly. Dallas was well in the past.

But the rain . . . the rain continued.

Suzanne turned over and tried to go back to sleep, tried to remember sunny skies, springtime flowers and bright green leaves, something with which to counter the rain, but all she could come up with was the May morning ten years ago that had started the play going, had given it its lines and its plot. It had begun with the mildness of early summer in northern Ohio, had ended, abruptly and brutally, with the crack of M-1s, screams, and blood pooling quickly on the dusty asphalt of a university parking lot.

She wandered among the crowds at Kent State: the students who shouted at the National Guard, the faculty members with their blue armbands who tried to moderate a confrontation that edged inexorably closer to violence, the Guardsmen themselves, who were caught in the middle of attitudes and lifestyles they did not understand.

A girl near her stuck a flower in a gunbarrel. "Flowers are better than bullets," she said to the soldier.

The strident tones of the Victory Bell shuddered through the air like a tocsin. Suzanne caught at her white cotton sweater, tried to pull her away. "You've got to get out of here," she said. "They're going to start shooting." About her, the crowds surged, expressions and words indistinct. It was a carnival, it was a Mardi Gras, it was the white face of impending death that loomed up out of pale clouds of tear gas. There was too much happening, and though this was a dream, Suzanne felt powerless to stop any of it.

But the girl nodded to her. "It's all right," she said. "You can bury me. You'll be around." And she walked off toward the parking lot. The Guardsmen marched up the hill.

She grabbed a blond man who carried a bullhorn. His hair was wild and disheveled. "Stop them!"

"Hey," he said. "This is it. This is what we've been waiting for. This is the revolution." He spoke quickly, easily, the well-rehearsed rhetoric falling from his tongue.

"They're going to kill some of us!"

"This is what we've wanted all along."

The Guardsmen reached the crest of the hill, turned, and . . .

Ten years now, and she was still dreaming of it. Even from thirty yards away, she could tell that the slim barrel of the rifle was pointing straight at her. The face of the Guardsman was, like those of his companions, indistinct, distorted by the gas mask he wore, but she felt his expression: she did not have to see it. She heard the click of the safety coming off, or maybe it was the shutter release of the student photographer next to her.

The shots had gone on for some time, the fusillade continuing in waves, rising and falling for nearly a quarter of a minute, but all she remembered, all she dreamed about, was the whine of the bullet next to her own head. It filled the air, filled the universe, and turned into the buzzing of her alarm clock.

She flinched awake with a small cry, realized again where she was, and turned off the alarm. Sitting up with her hand covering her eyes, she waited for her heart to stop pounding.

The dreams were like her migraines: they came, they went, and there was not much that she could do save sweat them out and survive. She had been surviving for ten years now.

After a while, she swallowed, took a deep breath, and prodded at the sleeping body beside her. "Up, clown," she said. "Another exciting day."

"I can sleep in," said Joe, his voice muffled by pillows. "Classes were canceled."

"Bullshit." Classes had been canceled then, too. Across the country, in the wake of the shootings, universities had closed their doors, but whether out of fear or sympathy, no one really knew. Back then, as now, there were many motives for everything, some open, some hidden.

Joe was two years younger than she, and he spoke easily of classes being canceled. Today, that casualness annoyed her, for it reminded her too much of the blond man with the bullhorn. "If you're not up in five minutes, I'm coming back with a glass of water and dousing you."

"Hey, what's the matter with you this morning?"

"Nothing."

She crawled out of bed and padded naked into the bathroom. Holding her long hair behind her with one hand, she splashed her face with water from the tap and dried off with a threadbare towel. She picked up a plastic cup and filled it, but water, whether splashed on her face or sloshed in her mouth, could not get rid of the rank horror that always accompanied the dream.

Joe was struggling out of bed in the other room, and she grabbed her robe and went into the kitchen. Her feet crunched on the unvacuumed carpet, and she kicked her way through magazines and papers that littered the floor. It was not a large apartment, and it was made smaller by the refuse left by two graduate students who were attempting to juggle classes, part-time jobs, and some kind of social life within the context of days that persisted in containing precisely twenty-four hours and no more.

Holding a saucepan of water in one hand, her feet sticking to the linoleum, she looked in vain for a clear burner on the stove. "Joe," she called, "wasn't it your turn to clean the kitchen?"

"Sorry, can't hear you." He stomped into the bathroom and slammed the door. The water in the shower came on.

She sighed, looked at the grease-stained walls. One of these days, she was going to tell Solomon Braithwaite to do his own damned research, and she was going to come home early and clean up the mess. Joe was certainly not going to do it.

But it was not the mess, really. It was the dream. It was the memory. The mess was only the emblem—and she admitted that it was a fitting one—of herself. She was soiled, so why should her home be any different? She was disorganized, fragmented. Ditto the apartment.

But she figured that, even if the mess were a metaphor of her life, she did not have to accept Joe's additions to it. This was 1980, not some medieval estate in which she was assigned the drudgery of taking care of a child-man, cleaning up after him, tending his ego, soothing his feelings . . . even though that was exactly what she was doing.

And Braithwaite was much the same. Faintly pompous, annoyingly sure that his tenure gave him the right to pronounce, not just on medieval archaeology, but on his research assistant's lifestyle, her clothing, her hairstyle; he too wanted everything, would give nothing.

At least she did not live with Braithwaite. Small consolation.

Muttering to herself, she evicted the frying pan from the front left burner and replaced it with the pot. When the water boiled, she dumped in oatmeal and turned the flame down. In the bathroom, the shower went off and the shaver went on.

She sat down on the living room carpet just as Joe exploded out of the bathroom and made a bee-line for the kitchen.

"We're having oatmeal," said Suzanne. "Leave the granola alone. I want to make cookies later."

"Just a little? I'm hungry."

"Leave it." She looked up at him dully, but there was enough of a threat in her voice to make him smile nervously and back off. He went into the bedroom to dress. "Did you leave me any hot water?" she called after him.

"Uh . . . yeah, there's some."

Which meant that there was none at all.

Still sitting, she uncrossed her legs and straightened them. The tension from the dream was threatening to turn into a migraine, and she hoped that she could head it off. The yoga sometimes helped. She stretched into her first position.

Legs over the head. Come on, Helling.

Braithwaite had probably been at UCLA back then. Or maybe Berkeley. Someone had gotten shot there, too, but Braithwaite had probably been rooting for the police. Once, she had made the mistake of mentioning that she had attended Kent State, and he had made a tactless crack to the effect that the students there should have studied more. She had held her tongue at the time. Now she wished that she had said something.

A car backfired outside, and she flinched. She rolled over on her side and found that her eyes were wet.

She had known Sandy, and had helped her feed Jeff when he showed up at her window, waving his hands and rubbing his stomach in an apologetic plea for a handout. Bill and Allison had been near-strangers to her before the shots, but she knew them well after, having participated in the intimate act of loading their bodies into the ambulances.

Blood on her hands. She had a blouse in her closet that was marked with the brick-colored spillage of ancient wounds.

"Breakfast ready yet?" Joe called.

"Give it a fucking minute, will you?"

"I've got class in half an hour!"

"I'll dump it in your briefcase." Her voice was was-pish, but hoarse with her interrupted thoughts.

He came out of the bedroom tucking in a faded shirt. "What's the matter?"

"The kitchen's a mess."

"Ran out of time. Sorry. I'll get it tonight."

"Yeah."

He stared at her, his lips pursed. "You on the rag?"

She looked up. "No, goddammit, I am not on the rag. I'm tired of waking up to a mess every day. I'm tired of taking care of you. I'm tired of you asking me if I'm on the rag."

He moved into the kitchen and lifted the cover on the oatmeal, stirred the cereal around. "Looks about done. Listen, if it means that much to you, why don't you take charge of it? I can live with almost any-thing—"

"And usually do."

He did not seem to notice. "—so it doesn't make that much difference to me. Your ruins will be around for another hour or so."

"We're doing Arthur and the Saxons."

He shrugged, hardly hearing her. "Yeah, and they'll still be dead, too."

Just eat your cereal, idiot. Get out of my hair.

Joe selected a clean dish, spooned in his breakfast, and ate it without benefit of milk or sugar. Suzanne watched as he set the unrinsed bowl down on the counter, grabbed his briefcase, and started out the door. Stopping for a moment where she sat, he patted her on the head, then bent down and kissed her. "Gotta go."

"Yeah."

"Sure you don't want to tell me what's wrong?"

"I had that dream again."

"Uh . . . oh, that." He stood uncomfortably, shifted his briefcase to his other hand. "Well, you know, things like that happen if you get involved with guns and stuff like that."

"We didn't have any guns."

"Well, you know what I mean. Quit brooding on it. Everything worked out in the end. The war's over."

Two years made a great deal of difference. As his steps receded down the walkway, she put her face into her hands.

Sol Braithwaite and Joe Epstein. Before, she had taken them one at a time. Now, struggling to put some distance between herself and the past, she had two at once. Somewhere, she had gotten the idea that going back to school would help, that the routine of classes and books would push the memories away, that research into the past would add some structure to a rapidly disintegrating present.

And yet, here she was today: dull, haggard, head-ache-ridden. Suzanne Beth Helling, B.A., graduate student. It had not worked. In spite of her efforts, she was not much different from the girl who had collapsed on the floor of an empty apartment in Dallas, her skin slick with the humid sweat of a rainy summer, her belly on fire with cramps, and her eyes nearly unseeing with pain.

Maybe that was when school had looked attractive. She could not be at all sure that, writhing on the floor, she had not cried out: *I need something. I can't go on. I've got to get out of this.*

It seemed to him that he had entered a world in which he was merely an onlooker to events, things, places for which he had no names. He himself had no name, and (though he found the thought terrifying), apparently no physical existence.

I am a sorcerer. I am not afraid of this.

He clung to the description as a desperate swimmer might catch at a twig. If he had no name, at least he had a function.

Other names came to him, though, words to describe what manifested to his eyes as though from behind a shimmering haze. He saw water. He saw mountains. He saw stone that had been poured like thick syrup to form glass-walled buildings that rose up in glittering majesty. He saw the Dragon, Silbakor . . . but tiny, and imprisoned within a glass sphere. And the pale, graying man who was with it was not Dythragor Dragonmaster . . . and yet perhaps he was.

I am a sorcerer.

That much he had, and he wrenched the vision away from the vagaries of dream and into his own hands, folded it, molded it as though it were clay, brought himself back to a place where he too had a name.

Mernyl . . . I am Mernyl.

And Gryylth was suddenly below and about him, green with grass and trees, rivers running over it and lakes reflecting the sunlight like bowls of clear water. Mountains to the west; to the east, rolling downs that marched off into the territory held by the Dremords (though he knew that that people called their lands Corrin) and thence into the sea, and from the sea to . . .

He had not come this far before, always having been held back by his own timidity, and by the workings of his counterpart in Corrin, Tireas. But today, Tireas's inward eyes were turned elsewhere, and his timidity was eclipsed by a sense of urgency that drove him beyond the white chalk cliffs and over the water to a sight that almost made him turn and flee back to his body, back to his hut in the Cotswoods.

Ahead, the world ended, and the stars floated in the void before him. Below, the sea was insubstantial, transparent, and the water dissolved into mist that rose up in wraithlike clouds.

Mernyl grappled with his fright, his physical hands clutching at his white staff of wizardry as he lay sleeping on his pallet. He knew several litanies against fear, and he was repeating one now. Worlds, he knew, were whole, complete, wrapped in air and warmed by suns. But Gryylth simply ended in an abyss, both of substance and of reason.

He was a sorcerer, though, and he forced himself to stay, to stare out at the termination of all he knew until the unreason and the longing for completion was a physical pain that ate at his chest like an unspoken grief. Only then did he withdraw.

Shaking, he turned away from the sight, turned back to the lands he knew as, rising from the misty border of matter, the sun cast its yellow light across Gryylth and Corrin. Shadows fled before it, and the land was green and golden, and huntsmen and herdsmen would awaken with the light and sally forth into the dawn. And if they happened to be Dremords, and hostile to him and to his people, that was well enough, for at least they had substance, at least they themselves were whole and complete.

Unlike their world.

His body sleeping, his soul wandering the length and breadth of his world, Mernyl floated on the energies that whispered down from the stars. Here was

Corrin. Here was Benardis, the capital, where Tarwach the king reigned with the help of his doughty brother, Darham. He did not sense that Tireas was near, and he wondered if that had something to do with the urgency that had prompted him to dare the end of the world.

The Dremords had come, it was said, from the Eastlands across the sea. But what lay on the other side of the White Sea save nothingness? Had the Dremords come from that? It was not possible. And yet the war that had raged for generations had raged so as to push the Dremords back to . . . nowhere.

A cold veil dropped across Mernyl's face, and he shuddered and slid back into his house, into his body, taking refuge in the warmth of his own blood, and the fading heat of the embers on his hearth. The knowledge he had gained was an icy sickness in his belly.

Aching, he allowed himself to surface slowly from his journey. His eyes closed, he mentally reconstructed the room about him, the rough walls of his hut, the fire, his writing table and the books and scrolls arranged neatly on the shelves behind it. The pots of herbs. The white staff of wizardry glowed faintly in his hands, its wood cool and smooth where it lay against his face.

But in that brief transition from deep trance to wakefulness, he saw something else: a sudden shaft of light struck him, warmed him as had the rising sun, seared his mind with its unutterable purity. He sat up quickly and turned, discovered that the brilliance was not confined to the rarefied worlds of dream, but was manifesting physically, in palpable and stark reality.

An arm's length from his bed, from within the

depths of a glory of gold, there shone the image of a cup out of which more light poured, flowing throughout the room like the noontide sunlight of a May morning. His eyes were dazzled, but the image was clear. A cup. A chalice. Perhaps it was all cups and all chalices, their totality intimated by this single image of containment, of nurturance, of wholeness. It was the color of a hand held up against the sun, and within its substance was a beating, as though it were alive.

Instinctively, he reached for it, but in that instant it was hidden from him, and it left behind only the pale light of morning that crept in through the cracks of his walls.

As the birdsong grew outside, finches and warblers rioting in the trees that surrounded his small garden, he found himself weeping. That the world ended in an abyss seemed a small thing now, considering that the same world that appeared so heartrendingly incomplete held within it such an emblem of wholeness. Wondering at the vision, his eyes bright with tears, Mernyl rose from his bed, his heart light in spite of the burden of the knowledge he had gained.

While he heated water on the fire, he pulled out his notebook and spread the leather covers wide. He took up and dipped a quill and set it to the whiteness of parchment pages. The ending, and the cup. He felt almost mad as he wrote, but he knew that he was not mad. The cup had told him that he was not mad.

But he had seen it: the world ended.

How could he tell King Vorya? How could he tell Dythragor Dragonmaster?

❖ CHAPTER 2 ❖

❖

LIKE THOSE WHO STOOD NEAR HER AT THE SPE-cial collections desk, Suzanne was a student, and yet she found it difficult to think of them as other than children. Their faces were too fresh, too innocent, and their voices, loud with youth, echoed off the high ceiling of the library in spite of the clerk's vain adjurations to silence.

Once she could have stood among them as an equal, but that time was years away now. She was almost thirty, and her demeanor marked her as such. Nor had the young people around her ever stopped tear gas, or felt the impact of a nightstick, either of which was enough to bring on a kind of damaged maturity that clung to one's shoulders like a shroud.

"Can I help you?" The student behind the desk caught her eye. His eyes flicked over her and she saw herself being classified as the faded, overaged hippie that she was.

"Yeah." She handed him a list. "These came in from England. I'm here to pick them up."

He glanced at the list, nodded. "Bunch of old stuff, I'll tell you. Hang on."

A couple from fraternity row was making a date

behind her, the boy tall and beefy and blond, the girl petite and pretty and in an imitation football jersey. To one side, a bearded graduate student was leafing slowly through a book on the counter, debating. A Xerox machine whined in the distance.

This place felt foreign to her. The campus as a whole was a strange land of conformity and complacency, of social games and tawdry little innuendoes. Life had become shallow and banal in the universities of the 80s.

In the 60s, the students had cared. People were poor, were discriminated against, were caught up in a world that had come to resemble nothing so much as a vast machine that took in lives as raw material and spewed out money as a product. Children were unfed, prisoners rotted in forgotten cells, the Vietnam war went on with dismaying pointlessness.

Even the Greeks and the jocks had been uneasy about it all. What was waiting for them on the other side of that diploma, anyway? A job? A messy death in a rice paddy? What else? Where did it go? What good was it all if you died too young to appreciate it, or too old to look back on anything except a life of unquestioning obedience?

Some had raised their voices in anger. A few had marched. A few had charged the police lines.

And several had died.

But there had been others, seldom seen, and never present when the tear gas had been thick and the bullets had burrowed into flesh, others who had decided to use the concern and the anger for their own purposes. Beneath their altruistic words was a drive for the same power and control that characterized the society they professed to hate. Their slogans were quick and vicious, their plans grandiose. They had incited the crowds to violence, and then they had slipped away.

This is what we've wanted all along.

"No, asshole." For a moment, she stood again on the sun-drenched commons, the Victory Bell tolling over and over in her ears as it summoned the students to protest, to betrayal, and to death. "No. That's what *you* wanted. Not us."

"Miss?"

She came back to the library. The clerk had returned. "All this stuff is pretty valuable."

"Yeah . . . I guess it would be. It's copies of the original notes and diagrams from Laycock's Cadbury excavations." He was staring at her. Old hippie. She pushed the words out through her headache. "And an original of Gildas's *De excidio et conquestu Britanniae*." She let the Latin roll off her tongue. She was no punk undergraduate. She knew what she was doing.

"Well, we've got instructions here to release it only to Dr. Braithwaite. A student won't do."

"I'm his fucking research assistant."

"Uh . . ."

"Come on, you know who I am."

"Well, yeah, but . . . " He seemed about to relent. A decade before, he might have. There had been a camaraderie among students then, one forged out of shared concerns and a horror of a society that had turned increasingly impersonal. Today, though . . . "But it's my ass if something goes wrong. I can't do it."

Behind her, the Greeks were giggling with one another. Suzanne pressed her lips together in frustration. The headache had made her temper short, and the dream had taken her back ten years. "When the revolution comes, motherfucker," she snapped, "it's gonna be your ass up against the wall, too."

His eyes widened, but she had already turned away. She knew full well that she had accomplished nothing. The rhetoric was dull now, without the bright, razor edge that had cut through so much complacency in the 60s. Her words were impotent, just like her actions.

As she descended the steps, she decided that it might be good for Braithwaite to fetch his own books. True, her job was to help him, but it would not do him any harm to run some of his own damn errands and remember what it was like to be a student who had to listen to braggart professors as they governed their miniscule fiefdoms.

She paused in the shadow of Rolfe Hall and rubbed her eyes. The headache was gaining on her, and she still had a full day ahead. More than likely, Braithwaite would blame her for the clerk's refusal, and the planning session in his office would turn into a chance for him to continue his interminable cataloging of her deficiencies.

At times, she hated him. He had money, a nice house, an old established family in New England with which he could talk about the horrid groundlings who were causing so many problems these days. When the revolution came—if it ever did—his ass would be up against the wall, too.

And yet, she could not but envy him. Safe and secure, he had weathered the troubled waters in which she herself had foundered. Where he was tenured, respected, well-known and even admired in his field, she had had difficulty convincing the UCLA registrar that Kent State classes and credits over ten years out of date could still count toward a degree in California. And when she had eventually presented herself to the graduate school with a B.A. in history, Braithwaite had all but sneered at her. "Kent State, eh?"

But she was now his research assistant. Her feet scuffing through puddles left by the night's rain, she trudged along Bruin Walk toward his office, wondering what she was trying to prove.

Ventura Boulevard took Solomon to the San Diego Freeway, and the freeway took him south and over the hills. The morning was clear, and the mountains to either side were green and glowing in the sun.

On the seat beside him, propped safely in a fold of the unused seatbelt, was the paperweight with Silbakor coiled inside it. Today, the Dragon looked almost relaxed. Its wings were folded, its tail wrapped about itself, and only the unblinking eyes showed that it was anything more than a sunbathing lizard.

Solomon's Buick had no trouble forging up the long pass, which was more than could be said for the Volkswagen ahead of him. Between the traffic and the Bug, he was going to be late for his first appointment. But he did not have to worry: it was just Suzanne. She would wait. She always did. She did not have much choice.

Suzanne.

He stole a look at Silbakor. The Dragon, he knew, had not been joking when it had suggested her for the Guardianship, and Solomon was baffled by its choice. Suzanne? Even if he ignored the fact that she was a woman—which Vorya and the others would most certainly not—he was revolted by the idea that Silbakor would suggest someone who had once tried to destroy the same educational system he considered it his duty to defend.

"If she were in Gryylth, Silbakor, she'd be a Dremord."

The Dragon blinked again, closed its eyes.

Fretting in the slow-moving press, he tried to keep his thoughts away from Suzanne, and wound up staring at a particular office building that rose up in mirrored splendor across the intervening miles of gray city. Helen's lawyer. That bastard was probably still doing quite well. Helen was probably still doing quite well. And Solomon was—

He gripped the steering wheel and forced himself to stare straight ahead. Solomon was doing quite well, too. Thank you very much.

His eyes were on the road, but his thoughts strayed uncontrollably to her. He had no idea what she was doing now. It had been ten years. He might pass her in the street without recognizing her.

No. He would recognize her. Without question.

It had been an excellent marriage at the outset. He and Helen had known one another since high school, and when he had volunteered to serve in Korea, she had vowed to wait. And she had. Fresh out of uniform, he had taken her to the altar, and she had pledged herself to him.

Twenty years of bliss. Well, not bliss, exactly, but a reasonable approximation. There were rocks in their road together, particularly when she strained at the bonds that held her at home, that dictated that she listen to what he said to her. Love, honor . . . and obey. She forgot occasionally, and he had to remind her. She cried in the bedroom, and then she made up. It was all very simple.

He had his teaching, and eventually his tenure, and she settled into the role of the professor's wife, smoothing the feathers that he ruffled, playing the hostess at faculty gatherings in the backyard, standing by his side when he was made full professor. When the student unrest began to roil at Berkeley, he naturally expected that she would support his views. And, for a while, she did.

The days had been different then. Tenure was not the Holy Grail. If you did your part, rubbed the right backs, held to the right opinions, you got it. He had earned his reward, and he had thereby held up his side of the marriage bargain. He had fully expected that she would hold up hers.

But something had come up. From somewhere.

Perhaps he could date her treason to a spring day in 1969, when the police, in clearing the so-called People's Park a few blocks from the Berkeley campus, had shotgunned a young man as he stood on a nearby rooftop. Helen had always been rather tenderhearted, particularly when it came to children, and she could not understand the action.

"They didn't have any guns," she had said. "Why did the police kill him?"

"He was throwing stones."

"And that's enough to be killed?"

"You don't understand, Helen."

"What if it was our son who had been shot?"

"We don't have any children, dear."

And it had gone on from there. The seeds had been planted, and Helen had slowly grown more secretive, more sullen. Their arguments had taken a more political turn, and to his surprise, Helen had shown herself exceedingly adept at countering his opinions, growing as clever with words as the radicals she defended. Frequently, he had found it necessary to shout her down.

Changing lanes, he grimaced, shook his head. He had, in many ways, acted no better than had the students who had disrupted his classes with their slogans and leaflets. But grappling for arguments with which to counter her sudden burst of treacherous logic, he had found his hands empty of all save a sense of rightness and of tradition. No, he could not argue rationally, but neither could a martyr so defend his choice of death over falsehood.

Perhaps his bullying had been justified, though, for Helen had refused to listen to reason. She had given him no choice. She had violated the vows she had made to him with as much intent as he had kept those he had made to her.

And that lawyer, smooth and clever . . .

And the campus radicals, glib and deceitful . . .

"Braithwaite."

He nearly missed the red light at the bottom of the offramp, and the tires screeched as he pulled up short. "Dammit, Silbakor, what is it?"

"I do not wish to intrude upon your thoughts, but I felt you would want to know that the Dremords have attacked at the eastern end of the Great Dike."

"Casualties? Is it serious?"

"That is uncertain. The garrison from Dearbought turned most of the force, but a small party broke through and proceeded north."

"North?"

"Toward the Blasted Heath."

Behind him, a horn beeped. He clenched his jaw and managed to stall when he attempted to pull out. The Buick was unused to such treatment, and it complained loudly when he turned the ignition key.

The car behind swerved around him and pulled up alongside, and the young man at its wheel gave him an easy grin and a finger.

"Hey, grandpa, learn to drive. Pedal on the right." Laughing, he drove off.

Solomon muttered a curse under his breath and got the Buick started. "If we were in Gryylth," he said, "that puppy would change his tune."

He made the turn onto Sunset and headed for the campus, feeling Silbakor's unblinking gaze on him. "The Dremord sorcerer, Tireas, is with them."

"Fine. That's just fine. If the Dremords want to play with magic, then they'll lose the war all the quicker."

"I am not sure," said the Dragon. "It is possible that they have some plan."

Solomon did not reply.

The Dragon was almost hesitant when it spoke again. "I would venture to suggest that perhaps this might be a situation in which Mernyl's advice would be of some value."

First Suzanne, and now Mernyl. What was the Dragon up to? "That charlatan? Silbakor, you must be out of your mind."

"Nevertheless, I—"

"If Mernyl gets within fifty feet of King Vorya, I'll kill him on the spot. Do you understand?"

The Dragon lowered its head. "Events are proceeding rapidly. It would be best if I examined them in more detail. I will leave you now." Its black, bat wings unfolded. "I will be back shortly."

There was a moment of turbulence in the paperweight, and when it cleared, the Dragon was gone.

Mernyl now. His arm twinged as he pulled into

the faculty lot to find that someone had taken his reserved space.

The sand beneath Flebas's feet was a hellish unknown, and he was sweating as he wielded the light spade. It was a cold sweat, one born of furtive glances over the shoulder, of the knowledge that at any moment—

"Closer to the roots, Flebas." Tireas stood a few feet from him, white robed, his arms outstretched. Flebas had little understanding of sorcery, but he knew that Tireas was shielding him and the other men of Corrin from the effects of the Tree. He complied, scrabbling in the treacherous soil inches away from the matted roots.

The Tree looked unhealthy, like something out of an evil dream. Barely twice as tall as a man, it stood, squat and bulbous, its twisted branches hung with glassy fruit that flickered fitfully, as though from inner fires. The very fact that it grew here, in the Blasted Heath, was enough to make him afraid. But, this close to it, he felt its powers crawling over his skin, probing questioningly at him, toying with potentials for magic.

Something brushed against the back of his neck, and he flinched away and whimpered. A few minutes ago, it had been a rain of bats. Before that, slime dripping from his limbs. And before that, just after he and the others had entered the Heath, it was an empty feeling, one that Flebas could only describe in terms of things unfinished: a foal stillborn, a child dead of plague, the stump of an arm lost in battle.

Tireas was looking at him. "Easy, Flebas," he said softly. "I have made this place safe."

"The Tree is not safe."

"Safe enough for now. Dig. The Gryylthans know of our journey here, and word has already been sent to King Vorya. The Dragonmaster might appear soon."

The sand was light and easy to move, and the men scooped it away from the base of the Tree with broad strokes, exposing dark roots knotted like the web of a black widow. Tireas waved them back when they were done and regarded the Tree appraisingly.

Calrach approached him. "Your wish, sorcerer?"

"Bring up the wain, captain." Calrach motioned to Flebas and two others to draw up the wagon.

A whirring came out of the blank sky to the north, though Flebas could not see anything. And north was a debatable proposition here in the Heath. There were no landmarks except for those the Heath created itself, there were no directions. Likewise, distances shifted and flowed in a terrible way, and the Tree might have been a few feet, or a few miles, from the edge of the Heath. A few steps might have taken him back to a green world that he recognized, with mountains and rivers and—

"Stand clear, men of Corrin." As usual, Tireas spoke abstractedly, his attention already taken up with the task before him. Flebas and the others gathered together some yards away and watched as Tireas raised his arms and murmured commands under his breath. In response, the Tree lifted slowly from the hole, paused when its roots cleared the surface, and floated slowly toward the wagon.

Tireas was trembling. The Tree tipped. Unthinking in spite of his fear, Flebas made as though to steady it.

Calrach grabbed his arm. "No, fool. To touch the Tree is death."

Flebas shuddered. "To stay in this place for another heartbeat might as well be."

"If Tireas is right about the Tree, it will be worth it."

With an effort, Tireas regained control and lowered the Tree slowly to the wagon's high-sided bed. Shaking with fatigue, he managed to whisper: "Lash it up. And do not touch it."

The men threw ropes from one side to the other, staying well away from the Tree. Only the ropes touched it, and where they did, they seemed to writhe of themselves, changing in an eyeblink from brown hemp to green scales to branches to iridescent fur. The transformations flitted across them like rippling water.

Flebas looked for a moment and then kept his eyes on his work, fastening the ropes solidly to the bronze staples spaced around the wagon.

They were finished quickly. Calrach nodded to the sorcerer. "We will have to hurry."

"Indeed." The sorcerer seemed to be elsewhere for a moment. "I believe that Silbakor is near."

"Dythragor, too?"

"No. Just the Dragon. Watching . . ." Tireas lifted his head, scanned the white sky. "I do not see it. But it is, nonetheless, close." He gestured to the wagon tongue. "We will go."

The men seized the tongue and slowly pulled the wagon around. Tireas held up his hands as though feeling textures in the air, and at last he pointed: this way.

Flebas walked beside the wagon, his hand clutching his spear tightly, his eyes flicking from side to side. Bats, and slime, and wraiths that gripped at his heart. And what more could befall them in this frightful place?

Minutes passed. The way out seemed much longer than the way in. They crossed sand, marshes, stretches of rocky ground and thorn trees. "Almost there," said Tireas kindly. "Stay away from the Tree even when we are free of the Heath."

The men needed no prompting. Stripped, free of concealing sand, the Tree was an awful thing, tangled and twisting, the ropes that held it changing from moment to moment, lambent fire running up and down its trunk and out to the tips of its branches as though it breathed corpselight.

Another few feet, so Tireas said, and they would be free. But there came again the whirring from the north.

Calrach whirled, his hand seizing his sword. "Arms!"

Claws were already pricking at Flebas's neck, and he batted at the one-eyed thing that grappled with him. It seemed as unfinished as everything else in the Heath. Its teeth, gleaming in a yawning mouth of phosphor, were too thin, too numerous, too needlelike. Its very touch was unclean.

There must have been a score of the creatures, dropping out of the sky like great feathered spiders, pouncing on the men. Flebas killed one, then another, ripped one from the back of Calrach's head and pinned it to the ground with his spear.

But several had gone to the Tree, had chewed through the ropes, and were attempting to topple it from the wagon. The Tree was swaying, the wagon creaking. It started to fall.

"No!"

Tireas was conjuring, but there was no time. Flebas ran to the wagon, lifted his hands, caught the Tree as it overbalanced on him.

His arms did not penetrate the Tree. Instead, the Tree entered him, flowed into his bones, stung its way through his limbs. Flebas watched as his arms turned wooden, then watery. The flesh reformed in new shapes, inhuman shapes.

And the change continued. He felt the magic pour into his chest, down his legs, rise up to shroud his face in a twisting gyre of transformation. He screamed, but it was a mewling, whining sound that spewed from his altered throat.

Sand was beneath him. Sand. Hands did not touch him. The feathered things were gone.

Dimly, he saw that Tireas was leaning over him.

"Gods," someone said. "Look at his face."

He tried to speak, but he felt blood in his throat. No, not blood. Something else.

Calrach turned away from him. Tireas shook his head. "We cannot bring him with us."

"We cannot leave him."

"We cannot but leave him."

And then they were gone. Flebas felt sand beneath him, saw a faint sun creep across the sky. With limbs that were no longer his own, he began to crawl. He did not know where he was going. He simply crawled, whimpering softly, leaving a wake of pale sand stained with the bloody sweat that oozed slowly, constantly, from what had once been his body.

Whatever it was doing, the Dragon took its time. The paperweight remained empty during Solomon's short walk to the department, and when—after he nodded to Suzanne, who was waiting by the front desk—he set it down on the bookshelf in his office, it was still no more than a transparent glass sphere, uninhabited.

It was unusual for Silbakor to vanish with such a brief explanation. There had been an urgency in its last words that had made Solomon's hand itch for the Dragonsword, but without the Dragon, he was stranded in the mundane world of books and offices and ex-radical research assistants.

Suzanne knocked briefly. He had forgotten that she was waiting.

"You should have come in sooner," he muttered, but he noticed the tight lines in her forehead that meant that she was having another headache. She groped her way to the chair beside his desk and sat down.

The bookshelf was behind Solomon, and he transferred the paperweight to the desk as he drew up a chair. If the Dragon came back, he wanted to know immediately. "Did you get the materials from England?"

She winced as if anticipating a beating. "No. They wouldn't release them to me. You have to sign for them yourself."

"Damned idiots." He saw that Suzanne was eyeing him suspiciously. Suzanne. Guardian of Gryylth. Laughable. "You could have shown some gumption and pushed them. They might have given in."

"I did. They didn't."

"Hmmm." He picked up the phone, dialed the library, asked for Special Collections. "This is Dr. Braithwaite in Archaeology. I've some materials that came in on interlibrary loan." He listened as the student tried to explain, cut him short. "Yes, I know she did. You should have given them to her. I want those things sent up to my office right now."

Suzanne's eyes were clenched as though his words were directed at her.

"Do it," he said. "Now. Or I'll have you fired." He threw the handset back into its cradle. "There. That wasn't so bad, was it?"

"He was just doing his job."

He snorted. "And I'm just doing mine. Do you know, that sort of individual is exactly the kind that made Rome lose Britain? It's true. Little budding bureaucrats looking out for number one. No sense of the daring. And the Brits themselves picked up all of that. Of course, the Saxons weren't much of an alternative. They didn't care about anything except loot. But the little Roman-style bureaucrats couldn't do anything when they broke out of their territory and started to rip up the towns."

Suzanne nodded curtly, seemed to realize that she was being impolite, and made a visible effort to control herself. "Sorry, Doctor. Headache. I'll be OK."

"Sure you don't want to go home?"

She looked at him curiously, defied him and the migraine both. "What were you saying about the Saxons?"

He was testing her, and she was rising to the bait. "They were your archetypal barbarians, Suzanne. You know that: you've seen the sources. They had no conception of higher culture, and what they didn't understand, they tried to destroy. And they would have destroyed everything, too, if Arthur and Ambrosius hadn't held them off."

Suzanne shook her head. "I thought Laycock's research had torpedoed that theory. There's no evidence of widespread disruption during that period."

"Gildas recounted the destruction," said Solomon. "He had no good reason to lie. That's why I want to look at the original of the *De excidio*. There might have been a misreading of some key words that would remove all the ambiguity."

"And the Laycock stuff?"

"He was too wrapped up in his theories. I think he ignored evidence. I want to see for myself."

Suzanne clung to her point. "If the Saxons had burned everything, there'd be evidence. Boudicca left evidence, and she certainly wasn't as widespread as the Saxons."

Leave it to Suzanne, he thought, to use a woman for an example.

"Besides," she went on, "if they had been that bad, they wouldn't have settled down so readily and put their energies into building a country."

The radicals had settled down, too. Nice little jobs. Nice little families. They had raised hell and then they had been swallowed up by the very thing they had fought. "Nice little bureaucrats," he said.

The headache, he could tell, was sharpening her tongue. "Whose side are you on, Braithwaite?"

Whose side, he wondered, was she herself on? "I'm a professor at a university," he said. "I'm on the side of civilization. I always have been." His voice was flat. "I hope you understand that."

She put her hands to her temples, and nodded. But as Solomon sat back, trying to find some savor in his words, a flash of yellow from the paperweight caught his eye.

The Dragon had returned.

"Maybe you ought to call it a day, Suzanne," he said quickly. "Why don't you go home and go to bed?"

She had followed his gaze. "I didn't know you had a paperweight like that." Her voice was dull with habitual pain. "Whatever made you choose a horned toad?"

Silbakor was unmoving. Only Solomon knew that it was alive. Only Solomon could read the tension in every line of its iron-colored body. "It's not a horned toad," he found himself saying as he tried to think of a way to bring the appointment to an end. "It's a dragon. It's too thin, you see, to be a horned toad. You can see the wings, too. Now—"

"Yeah." Helling was leaning forward as if fascinated by the unblinking eyes. With a sense of rising panic, Solomon recalled how he himself had paused in the antique shop, almost hypnotized, when he had first found the Dragon.

Silbakor, what the hell are you doing?

Solomon suddenly realized that he could not hear the air conditioning in the office. The lack of the humming produced a silence like a well. Outside, the corridor had grown absolutely still.

Suzanne roused herself suddenly. "All right, Doctor. My headache's better." Her soft voice sounded over-loud.

"I think we should break for a while."

"Why? I feel fine."

The Dragon moved. "Enough. It is urgent. You must come. Gryylth is endangered."

"*Silbakor! No!*" Solomon rose quickly from the desk and seized Suzanne's arm. She was staring, wide-eyed and pale. The glass of the paperweight began to dissolve. "You've got to go, Suzanne." He put his hand on the doorknob and pulled, but the door did not yield.

The glass was gone now, and the Dragon was growing. Solomon was raging inwardly. It was not supposed to happen like this. Silbakor had always given warning before.

The office walls faded out of existence, and there was nothing beyond them but darkness. The office itself grew dim and obscure as the Dragon expanded, rearing its black head high and unfolding its bat wings in preparation for flight. Suzanne was on her feet now, looking for a place to flee. She found nothing but darkness and the Dragon.

The bright yellow eyes burned down. "Mount."

"You want to tell me what's going on, Braithwaite?" said Suzanne. There was fear in her voice, but mixed in with it was anger. She had, he recalled, faced fear before, and death. She was stronger than she appeared.

The Dragon did not move. "Mount," it said. "Suzanne Helling also."

Her fists were clenched, but she did not flinch. She looked up at the Dragon as though staring down the muzzle of a gun.

It bent its colossal head down to her level. "You need not fear, Suzanne Helling." Its voice was almost gentle. "I will not harm you. Please. Climb onto my back. Above my wings." It extended a black talon for her use as a step, and she climbed as if in a trance. "Braithwaite," said the Dragon, "you are needed."

"Will you tell me the meaning of this, Silbakor?" He found himself shouting again.

"Mount."

Feeling as if a choice had been made without his participation or consent, Solomon stepped up and took his place on the iron neck in front of his student. Without another word, the Dragon spread its wings, and they were lifted.

❖ CHAPTER 3 ❖

❖

SINCE THAT DREAM IN WHICH HE HAD SEEN land and ocean end in an abyss that faded into the stars, Mernyl had consulted his books and his scrolls and had cast the old Ogham and the new Runes. But nothing that he read gave him the slightest clue as to the meaning of that implacable termination. In fact, the silence of texts and oracles only gave him added questions to ask. Why was there no mention? Surely, sorcerers before him had dared the edges of the world. Surely someone had written it all down. His books had come from near lands and far. Why then—?

But those questions led to others. Near lands and far. What far lands were there if the world ended a few leagues off the shore of Gryylth? Where had his books come from?

Why, from his master, and from his master before him. Try as he would, though, Mernyl could not remember the name of the man who had taught him, could not, in fact, recall being taught. And while he remembered making some of his books himself—the one bound in soft calfskin, for example, he had finished just two summers ago, on the day he had heard that big Helkyying had died in battle—others, written

41

in his own hand, he knew nothing about. They might have appeared out of the air.

Lands that dropped off into nothingness, books that had no origins, a past he did not remember . . . When he heard the sound of horse hooves in the distance, he was standing in his garden, ostensibly to harvest herbs, but actually he was peering at the leaves and flowers to ascertain if they were as thin and unreal as he now felt the whole world to be.

He held his hand up to the sun, examined the color of the glowing flesh. The cup had looked like that. The cup seemed now to be the only solid, real thing in a world full of indefiniteness and enigma. And it had been a vision. What did that say about Gryylth?

The hoofbeats drew nearer, approaching at a gallop. Mernyl looked up, and clutched at his staff. He recognized the rider. Had Vorya or Dythragor finally decided to rid themselves of their annoying magician?

But the man who approached, his blond hair wild with the speed of his journey, was not particularly terrifying. If Mernyl had not known that he came from Vorya's court, he might even have found his appearance reassuring. Slender, blue-eyed, his mouth set in what was almost a perpetual smile, he waved and whooped like a boy when he saw Mernyl, and the sorcerer heard him laugh out loud.

"Greetings, master sorcerer," he said reining in at the edge of the garden. "And how is it in the realms of magic?"

"It is well, Santhe," he said, resolved to keep his knowledge to himself for the time. He noticed that Santhe had another mount with him, saddled, but without a rider. "What is the news from Kingsbury?"

Santhe looked as though he had ridden all day without a stop. His face was grimy with the dust of the road. "The news, Mernyl, is not good." His laughing eyes were shadowed for a moment. "I have seen something . . ." He pressed his lips together, shook his head. "Evil times, these," he muttered.

He was tired, Mernyl realized. Tired and spent. He must have ridden all the way from Kingsbury in the space of a day, changing horses at Bandon and Alysby. "Come," he said. "Come into my house. I do not mind playing the woman. You need food."

Santhe nodded slowly. "And ale if you have any, magician." His humor returned for a moment. "Preferably some that will not turn me into a toad."

Mernyl helped Santhe lead the horses to the stable, and then he provided fodder for the warrior himself. Santhe slumped in the high-backed chair of the main room, smiling gratefully when the sorcerer set out bread and meat and a large bowl of ale. Mernyl could feel his fatigue from across the room, but he did not press Santhe for the reason he had come. Not only did courtesy dictate that he let the man eat, but he also found that he was not anxious to know.

"My thanks, Mernyl," said Santhe when he had finished. "I wish I could now find a corner by the fire and doze off, but I am afraid that my tasks include another ride today. With you."

Mernyl felt an eyebrow lift. "Oh?"

"I spoke of evil things. The Dremords have been active. Two days ago, during a skirmish at the Great Dike, a band in the company of Tireas and a captain named Calrach broke out and moved northward. They had a wain with them, and we should have been able to trace them, but I think that Tireas did not want to be found. And sorcerers—so I have been told—have their ways."

Santhe was teasing. Mernyl smiled in return. "I, too, have heard such rumors."

But Santhe's face clouded. "They apparently entered the Blasted Heath, and they came out again, bearing something. Scouts to the north found a man . . ." He broke off, shuddered.

Mernyl pulled a chair up to the rough table, sat down, and leaned forward.

"At least, it seems to be a man, though the wretch is mutilated beyond belief. I saw him at Alysby on the way here. King Vorya had sent me to fetch you in response to the activity of Tireas, but when I saw the man, I pushed on with all the speed I could."

"Tell me."

"I . . . I think he is a Dremord, Mernyl," said Santhe. "I think he is human. I cannot be sure. He whines and shrieks like a beast, and yet his eyes . . ." He looked out the unshuttered window as if the sight of trees and flowers would dilute the memory. "I have seen battle," he said softly. "Battle was nothing in comparison."

"Where is he now?"

"He was sent on to Kingsbury."

Mernyl had shoved his chair back and was already gathering his things together, bundling them into an old pack. "I can leave as soon as you wish," he said. "But will Vorya welcome me? Dythragor Dragonmaster, as you well know, bears me little love."

"Dythragor is not here. We do not know where he is. The king sent for you." Santhe held up a ring with Vorya's token on it. "Here. If you need proof."

Mernyl glanced cursorily at the ring, but given Santhe's tale of the Dremord, he would have gone even if Vorya had been outright hostile.

As he fastened the iron buckles of the pack, Mernyl found himself staring at them. When had he bought this pack? He could not remember. And now strange workings of magic in the land, and Tireas was active. He had to go to Kingsbury. Still . . .

"Santhe," he said. "Will you give me your word that Dythragor will do me no harm if he comes to Kingsbury while I am there? In truth, I am afraid for my life if he should find me near the king."

The warrior nodded. "I know. You have my word and my protection. On my honor as a warrior of Gryylth. And there is not a man alive who can accuse me of breaking my solemn oath." His eyes twinkled. "One or two have, but they were wrong. And in any case they are no longer alive."

Laughing Santhe. Merry Santhe. On the battlefield, a hundred men had found death at his hands, and yet he always provided song and cheer at the New Year Feasts.

How many New Year Feasts had there been, though?

Putting the questions aside for the moment, Mernyl picked up his staff, bowed. "Then I am ready."

They rode through darkness, and Solomon sensed that, behind him, Suzanne was huddled into herself, terrified. He could hardly blame her, for he himself had been afraid the first time he had journeyed to Gryylth. The blackness that surrounded them was impenetrable, and beneath them was the Dragon, immense, vital, unseen. And the stillness . . .

Suzanne shivered: that might have been the only stirring in an utterly motionless universe.

But Silbakor seemed to pass through some intangible boundary and enter into an infinite twilight, as though dawn had somehow been extended in all directions, forever. He could make out the Dragon's head now, blunt, forging through this nether region of half-light like a jetliner through a thick mist. Its wings did not move, and there was no wind, but Solomon sensed its speed.

Suzanne murmured behind him. "I'm cold," she said. "I'm cold."

He might have felt sympathy for her, but he was still angry. He leaned forward over the Dragon's head. "Why did you do this?" His voice fell flat in the twilight. "You held out a choice and then you took it away. What am I, some jackass that you have to coax along with a carrot on a stick?"

Silbakor did not answer. It banked slightly and flew on.

Solomon gave up on the Dragon and chewed on the injustice until he felt a familiar warmth creeping up his arms and his legs, and a burning in his chest. He was approaching Gryylth, and he was Dythragor, and he was satisfied. For the time being, the Dragon's actions lost their sting.

Helling murmured again, but he could not make out her words. He did not care. He felt strength being poured into him, felt the lines being taken from his face. When the clouds and darkness roiled up out of the twilight ahead of the Dragon, he had to suppress an urge to throw back his head and laugh.

The clouds came forward and engulfed them. Lightning flashes sparked the gray masses into incandescence. No thunder answered, but slowly a wind arose and stripped the clouds away. Mountains were below, shining in the light of a full moon swinging high at the zenith.

Solomon looked at his hands, now strong and youthful. The Dragonsword hung at his belt, glittering in the moonlight, and his gray suit was gone, its place taken by simple leather armor. Boots encased his well-muscled legs but left them bare from knee to tunic hem.

He jerked the Dragonsword from its scabbard and

waved it over his head. "Behold, Suzanne! Gryylth! Land under my protection! Here I am Dythragor Dragonmaster, slayer of Dremords!"

Suzanne did not answer, but Silbakor sideslipped suddenly and began to descend at a sharp angle. Below, the mountains gave way to foothills and then to rolling fields.

Dythragor leaned over the Dragon's head, his long hair whipping in the wind. "Silbakor, what's going on?"

"You are needed immediately."

His conscience pricked him for a moment. "What about Suzanne?"

"Do not burden yourself."

With a quickness that fluttered his stomach, the Dragon dropped several thousand feet in a fraction of a minute, leveling out just above the highest trees. Its wings began to beat rhythmically, and Dythragor caught sight of shapes below.

One stood out unnervingly: a shadowed bulk that nonetheless glowed fitfully in the silver of a moonlit field. A white figure stood nearby and lifted an arm. Dythragor suddenly saw neither.

No matter: the Dragon was taking him elsewhere. Two men on horseback were being set upon by a band of Dremords who were unmounted but armed with spears and swords.

"Down, Silbakor!"

The Dragon obeyed, slowing its speed and sweeping in low, like a scythe. As they approached the fight, faces turned toward them, and one of the riders brandished a sword and called weakly, "Dythragor comes!"

The Dragonsword flashed with light, and Dythragor felt power surging through the blade and up his arm. As he rolled off Silbakor's back, he was already picking his points, planning his attack.

He cut the first Dremord's legs out from under him even before he had rolled upright. His unexpected appearance had put at least half the enemy to flight, but the rest, old seasoned warriors, stayed. Several sized him up and came at him, but Dythragor slashed easily through the first and second, ducked under the third's sweeping cut, and rolled two others onto the grass. The night was cold, and the Dragonsword shone brightly.

Instinct told him to whirl. The first two were wounded, but their fighting was not done. They came on again, together, but more cautiously.

Dythragor almost laughed as he crashed through their shields and slew one outright. The other struggled to keep his shield in position as the Dragonsword leaped for blood once more and impacted on its central boss. The man's arm cracked.

"Begone." Dythragor's voice was harsh. "And take the rest of your scum with you."

The man scrambled away, and Dythragor turned in time to see one of the riders drive the last of the Dremords off in the same direction.

"Hail, Dythragor Dragonmaster," he said as he turned his horse and approached. He glanced at the fleeing enemy and added cheerfully, "As usual, you arrive in time of need."

"Almost a little too late, Santhe," said Dythragor, who had noticed that the warrior was shaking with fatigue. He gestured at the cloaked figure on the other horse. "Your companion didn't seem inclined to fight. Do you travel with a woman?"

The other answered as he rode up. "I save what powers I have for appropriate times." The shadow of his hood hid his face. "I do not care for swordwork; still, I thank you for the rescue."

"Give me more credit, Mernyl," said Santhe, laughing tiredly. "I was holding them so easily that I could have fallen asleep."

"Mernyl?" said Dythragor.

The sorcerer threw back his hood. The moon flecked his black hair with sparks, and made his eyes burn in his thin face. "I said I was grateful, Dragonmaster. There is no love between us, but I can appreciate a service."

"So you're still doing your hocus-pocus." Dythragor was chagrined to find that he had actually saved the sorcerer. "I'd think that you'd still be holed up in the Cotswoods, turning frogs into newts or whatever."

Santhe glanced back and forth as though amused by the conflict. "My lord Dythragor," he said. "Mernyl was sent for by the king."

"What?" Dythragor sheathed his sword with a clatter. "After all I've done for him, Vorya turns around and wants . . .wants . . ."

"Hocus-pocus," Mernyl finished for him. His tone was icy.

"It has been two years since you last visited us, Dragonmaster," said Santhe. "King Vorya is entitled to call upon whatever resources he has. And some things have happened in Gryylth that—"

"Resources!" Dythragor clenched his jaw. Santhe was too easygoing, too accepting of everything. At times, he was not quite sure that he could trust the man. "There's nothing in Gryylth that a good sword can't handle."

"I would differ with you, Dragonmaster. It seems—"

"Enough. If there's something wrong, then it's too

important for magic. Tell King Vorya that I've returned to Gryylth and that he'll not be needing the services of this man. Tell him that I'll arrive in Kingsbury very shortly. Tomorrow morning at the latest."

"Good, my lord." Santhe still seemed amused. Dythragor scowled, but Santhe's eyes twinkled all the more, and his blond curls bounced as he nodded. "I will tell him so, but Mernyl will be expected. I dare not send him back to his home."

"Very well, take him." Dythragor glanced up, searching the sky for the Dragon. "But be certain to have a fresh horse for his return trip . . . tomorrow afternoon."

"I am gratified," said Mernyl, "that the Dragon-master will not begrudge me a luncheon."

Dythragor ignored him. Turning once, he drew his sword and saluted Santhe, then strode off into the darkness. He had suddenly remembered Suzanne Helling.

The Dragon loomed large on the other side of the fire, dwarfing the man-sized boulders behind it. "You are Alouzon Dragonmaster," it said. Its voice was urgent.

The fire warmed her where her leather armor left her skin bare, and she huddled close in, wondering if she would ever be warm again. The flight through a world of twilight and mist had drained her of heat. And now, looking at her hands, at her body, finding herself so utterly different . . .

"Alouzon."

"What is this Alouzon stuff, Silbakor?"

"Alouzon."

She was tall and strong, her skin deeply tanned. Her hair fell in a bronze mane to her shoulders. The steel cuffs on her wrists glittered in the firelight, as did the steel bosses of her armor.

She was in shock. She knew she was in shock, wondered just how insane she was going to be when the shock wore off and she had to deal with a different body and—if the Dragon had its way—a different name. "I'm Suzanne Helling."

"Maybe," said the Dragon. "But for now, here, you must be Alouzon. The land needs you."

"For what?"

"For survival."

She stood up, examined herself yet again. Strong, slender, tall. Everything she had never been before. Her voice held a dark resonance that was touched with the essence of command, and the sword at her hip, its hilt carved into the shape of two intertwined dragons, spoke eloquently of power.

I don't want power. Power kills.

But, in spite of herself, she pulled the weapon from its sheath, lifted in in the moonlight. The keen blade glowed and flickered, and the double dragons, white and black, seemed alive under her hand.

"Alouzon."

The name rang in her head. The power that flowed from the sword was a palpable thing, warm and strong, like sun-baked rocks glowing in the hot twilight of a summer evening. It picked up her thoughts as though in a hand and cradled them. She was different, but she was strong, too. She could survive. She was . . .

"Alouzon Dragonmaster," said Silbakor.

Alouzon swallowed the name as though it were a stone. She lowered her sword. The panic was gone. Maybe she had a different name, and maybe her body was unrecognizable, but her mind was her own. She still remembered Kent. She still heard the bullets. She still knew what power was all about. "OK, Sil-bakor. Whatever."

"You are strong. That is good."

"Strong?" She regarded the sword with distrust. "Yeah, sure . . ." She did not believe a word of it. The warmth continued to flow from the sword. "Where are we?"

"In Gryylth."

"Where's Braithwaite?" The bewildering changes threatened to overwhelm her again. Everything she saw made no sense. In spite of the sword, her personality was reeling, but she held to herself grimly.

The Dragon settled itself, folded its wings. It seemed relieved that she was asking questions. "Here, Solomon Braithwaite is called Dythragor. Like you, he is a Dragonmaster: that is, he holds a Dragonsword and can call me at need. I myself am bound to Gryylth and to the swords by oath."

It was all crazy, but it made some kind of sense—at least it made sense to a shocky, battered ego that was still adjusting to a body that looked as though it had been pumping iron for years. Alouzon tried to laugh, but it turned into a sob midway through. "What about—"

Motion to her right. She whirled into a guard stance, sword up and ready, eyes scanning the tall man who had stepped into the clearing. He had a sheathed sword, and he wore armor. Instinctively, she was evaluating his carriage, his posture. A warrior. She was already picking points of attack when she realized what she was doing and mentally recoiled in horror.

"Suzanne?" he said.

"Who the hell are you, mister?"

"Dythragor." He considered, added with distaste: "Braithwaite."

"*Jesus!*" She stared at him, unable to decide whether to laugh or weep. "What's going on here?" she demanded. "What's happened to . . . to me?"

"Gryylth has accepted you," said the Dragon. "You have been prepared for your tasks."

She whirled on it, resentment shouldering its way forward. "I didn't ask for this."

Silbakor regarded her with glowing eyes and said nothing.

Dythragor scowled. "I didn't ask for this either." He turned to the Dragon. "I think you've been exceeding your authority. *I* am the Dragonmaster."

Alouzon recalled that she also held that title, but she said nothing.

"My authority," Silbakor was saying, "has not been exceeded."

"All right," said Alouzon. "You can both do some explaining. What are we doing here?"

Dythragor rested his hand on the pommel of his sword, glanced sidelong at the Dragon as if expecting an impertinence. "This land is under my protection. I defend it from the incursions of the Dremords."

Her wits were coming back quickly, and Dythragor's answer stirred up unpleasant echoes of a past decade. "Defend it? How? By killing people?" The sword burned in her hand, and she knew what the answer was.

His jaw tightened, but he went on. "They're barbarians. I keep them penned up in their lands in the southeast. Eventually, I intend to force them back across the sea. Gryylth will be free then."

Alouzon stepped up to him. Their eyes were on a level, and she knew that she was as strong and as able as he. "This is nuts. Will you tell me why you had to drag me into this boyhood fantasy of yours?"

The Dragon stirred. "You were needed."

"You're out of your mind." But she caught herself suddenly, becoming aware that she was facing a beast that could not exist by any sane rules of human logic. Even reclining, Silbakor towered over her. She backed up until she found herself against a boulder. Beyond were trees and mountains: she did not know where home was. "What have you done to me?"

Dythragor lifted his head. "Silbakor—"

"Silence," said the Dragon. "Dremords approach."

From out of the darkness surrounding the clearing came a sharp, metallic, *snick*.

"Get that fire out, Silbakor."

The flames vanished with a look from the Dragon. In the moonlight, Alouzon saw men moving through the boulders. Dythragor grabbed her wrist.

"Listen, Suzanne," he said. "You've got to believe me or you'll get killed. These people want to murder us. I'll protect you, but you've got to stay behind me."

She stared at him. It was all senseless. "Murder us? But . . . why?"

He did not answer. Already, a dozen figures were slipping into the clearing. She saw the glitter of spears and swords. For an instant, the Dremords hesitated at the sight of the Dragon, then advanced.

Dythragor drew his sword, and Alouzon knew instinctively that there was no room for acrobatics. It was going to be standing fast and slugging it out. It bothered her that she knew that.

The Dremords came *en masse*, trying to force Dythragor back against the rocks with their shields. Alouzon stayed behind him, moving back as he did, and she sensed that he was searching frantically for an opening in the shield wall.

A stone shifted beneath one of the Dremords, and he lurched slightly to one side. His shield shifted and exposed an arm.

Dythragor sprang. "Gryylth!" He crashed into the gap and hacked at the exposed men. Two dropped immediately, but the others broke and reformed.

Alouzon looked around. Dythragor's momentum had carried him away from her. There were Dremords behind her now, and two more stepped in front, isolating her.

Her hand tightened on the Dragonsword. They wanted to kill her. But there had been others who had wanted to kill her, who had very nearly succeeded. These were swords, not M-1s. Her odds had actually improved.

I'm not afraid.

The warmth surged up her arm. The Dremords seemed nonplused by her presence and gave most of their attention to Dythragor. He was trying to get back to her, but as he turned, they tripped him with a spear.

"Suzanne!"

As he fell, his head struck a shield with a hollow thud. His armor saved him from a vicious cut to the shoulder, but he could not get his sword up in time to stop the return swing.

It was aimed directly at his neck.

Alouzon was moving before she knew it. Her sword interrupted the Dremord's stroke with a sharp clang, and the man grunted as she kicked him away.

Two others closed on her, but the Dragonsword guided her. She backed slightly to let a spear reach short, parried it into the ground, and broke the shaft with a sharp blow from her foot. A sword came at her, but she used her steel cuff to batter it away, knocking the weapon from the Dremord's hand. She spun, and the flat of her foot found the side of a man's head.

"Damn you, Braithwaite, move your ass!"

Dythragor came to himself in time to block another blow to his head. "Back to back," he called. "We can hold them."

Another Dremord appeared, and she slashed without thinking as she scrambled toward Dythragor. Confronted by two skilled warriors, the rest of the Dremords broke and ran.

Alouzon and Dythragor leaned on one another, panting, wary of another attack, but the disordered sounds faded, and they were left alone with the bodies of the slain. Dythragor seemed to relax.

But Alouzon realized that her sword was dripping crimson, and she remembered the quick strike that she had unleashed into something that had yielded beneath her blade. She turned. Behind her lay a dead Dremord, his throat opened from one side to the other. His blood pooled among the stones, running down among the moon-silvered rocks.

The Dragonsword was warm in her hand, and she faced Dythragor with a pale, damaged look in her eyes. "I'm no better than they were," she said hoarsely. She was not referring to the Dremords.

❖ CHAPTER 4 ❖

❖

THE DRAGONSWORD'S HOT POWER FADED
quickly, leaving Alouzon shivering with a sick horror
in her belly. The corpse of the Dremord was that of
a young man, scarcely older than those she had
known during the demonstrations of the 60s, the resemblance furthered by his long, dark hair and by
the headband he wore to keep it out of his face.

And she had killed him.

She felt as though she had been raped, used; as if
the power unleashed in that frantic, blinding instant
had taken her and made her murder against her will.
But she could not blame the Dragonsword. It had
been her hand upon the hilt. "I could have disarmed
him," she muttered. She stared into the flames of
the meager, heatless fire as though searching for
the alternatives she had lost. "I could have. I know
it."

She had said much the same thing of the Guardsmen who had marched across the campus of Kent
State. They had, she felt, no right to be there, no
more right than she had to be in Gryylth. They had
been pressed, but they had not been forced to shoot.
No, they had made that decision themselves, perhaps
when, their backs against the chain-link fence that

surrounded the football practice field, they had looked out at the distant and scattered lines of student protesters and realized that, hot and tired and frustrated though they were, they would have to brave the abuse again.

Everyone's back had been against a wall then, not just the National Guard's. By 1970, after a decade of abuse, both internal and external, the country had been exhausted. The war protests had turned sour, the disagreements over traditional and modern values had become more hostile and touched with threat, and the once altruistic and virile civil rights movement had degenerated into bitchy and arrogant militancy.

Disillusion was a wave that swept through everything, shattering belief, leaching away at ideals. And on a campus in Ohio, frantic hopes that pointed in opposite directions clashed. And there were casualties.

Alouzon Dragonmaster, once Suzanne Helling, sat as far as she could from the blood, fingering her version of an M-1, passing the night in a cloud of self-loathing. She tried to sort through what had happened to her—her physical change, the Dragon's words, the fight—but her train of thought stopped cold at the memory of the oil-smooth sword stroke that had opened the Dremord's throat. Her dreams that night were confused melanges of horror in which it was her hands that leveled the rifle, her eye that drew a bead on the long-haired student in jeans and a western shirt.

And yet, floating in the background was a golden radiance that flowed through the visions and turned them, in spite of the M-1s and the screams, into something like a hope. It did not have to be this way.

Not forever. There was death, but death was not inevitable.

She awoke at dawn, strangely comfortable in her new body, with the absurd feeling that, if there was any answer to the killings, any answer to what had become of her life, she would find it here in Gryylth, and she would find it beating with a fertile life that bespoke only wholeness. It was here. Somewhere.

As the morning grew, she again mounted the Dragon with Dythragor, and for a few minutes, at least, the young corpse was made distant. Below her, Gryylth unfolded, turning and tipping as the Dragon banked and altered its course, a green pleasant land of mountains, rolling hills, and wide, fertile fields. The moonlight had made it seem cold, but in the warm light of the sun it glowed with verdancy, and clear streams glittered like silver threads worked into a background of deepest emerald.

"Where are we going, Dythragor?"

"To Kingsbury," he said. "Seat of King Vorya, ruler of this land."

He had said little to her since the fight. She sensed that her presence in Gryylth was an annoyance to him, and that he was angry with the Dragon for having brought her. But after his swaggering and posturing, she was almost glad to be an irritant. If Dythragor, a veteran of Korea and a supporter of Vietnam, was playing soldier in Gryylth, she would be more than happy to resume her own old role and give him a dose of conscience.

King Vorya. Another version of Dythragor? "He's the ruler? I thought you—"

"I'm the protector, Suzanne." She almost winced at the name. She was Alouzon. And then she realized how far she had fallen under the spell of Gryylth.

"I can't be here all the time," Dythragor explained. "I have to give lectures in medieval archaeology at UCLA." He threw back his head and roared.

Silbakor flew on. Alouzon saw villages surrounded by farmlands: fold, fallow, and plow. She saw stone roads that crossed the land, running ruler-straight from horizon to horizon. The mountains rose and fell in the distance. In all, Gryylth seemed a pre-industrial paradise, a textbook example of heroic feudalism, but . . .

She squinted against the stiff wind of the Dragon's passage. For all its sharp-edged clarity, there was something lacking to Gryylth. Perhaps it was a question of solidity . . . but it was not solidity exactly. She decided that Gryylth reminded her of a set for a motion picture, with impressive-looking landscapes that were nothing more than the creations of a good special effects department. There was a shallowness to what she saw, a distance that provoked only muted feelings and emotions. She might have been watching a documentary on television.

But her hands had been spattered with blood. That was real. And about that her feelings were not muted.

Silbakor began to descend. Below was a flat-topped hill, almost a plateau, its sides cloaked by trees. Its wide, triangular top was occupied by a walled town made up of stout, timbered buildings with stone foundations and a scattering of wattle-and-daub huts. The whole affair might have covered some eighteen acres and was surrounded, at the perimeter of the plateau, by wood and stone defenses. Near the center stood a large hall.

"Kingsbury," said Dythragor. "Fairly impressive, eh?"

Something niggled at her memory. "That looks familiar," she said. "Where've I seen that before?"

He grimaced at her, shook his head. "When we set down, you'd best keep your mouth shut and stay behind me."

"Not another attack?" She was not sure that she could draw her sword again.

"No. Nothing like that. Just woman's place."

She did not like the grin he gave her.

The Dragon banked sharply and approached some open fields between the town and the edge of the plateau. Its huge wings flared, and they were down with hardly a bump.

People came running from the town. Some waved; others, less exuberant, merely bowed when they reached the Dragon. Alouzon heard someone shouting "Hail, Dythragor Dragonmaster!" over and over.

Dythragor jumped to the ground with the air of a showman who knew what to give the crowd. He waved, he strutted, he went up to several men and shook them by the hand. It reminded Alouzon uncomfortably of old-fashioned, political bonhomie, shallow and fake.

"My lady," said the Dragon softly, "will you dismount?" Its voice was so quiet that it might have been sounding from within the bones of her skull. Alouzon looked around and realized that the people had not noticed her presence.

"Silbakor," she said, leaning forward toward its ear, "you've got to help me. I don't belong here."

"Suzanne . . ." Her old name. She did not mind it from the Dragon. It sounded almost reassuring. "Suzanne, I believe I have chosen well. You must stay. Please."

The *please* contained a tone of supplication that, coming from the Dragon, shook her profoundly. She persevered, though. "You don't understand. I won't kill again. I can't. I've only been here a few hours, and I hate myself more than I have in the past ten years."

"Then do not kill," said Silbakor. "Please."

She could not stand to hear the pleading again. The cold sickness intruded into her belly, but she fought it down and slid from the Dragon's back.

At once, there was silence from the people of the town. They stared at her.

She stared back. The crowd resolved itself into recognizable components: soldiers, craftsmen, boys. It might have been a random sampling of a primitive town.

She looked again. There were no women. Dythragor's smirk came back to her, but she squared her shoulders. Unconsciously, her hand dropped to the hilt of the Dragonsword.

One of the soldiers roused himself. "Has the Dragonmaster brought his mate with him? Has he decided to settle among us?"

"I'm not his mate," Alouzon snapped with a vehemence that surprised even herself. Dythragor's conduct bothered her. It smacked of something unhealthy. Even now, he was striding toward her with an easy smile on his youthful face.

She read his expression. *Stay behind me.* If he read hers, he did not show it.

"Know you, people of Kingsbury," he began, but the Dragon interrupted.

"She is Alouzon Dragonmaster," it said in a thrum that did not allow contradiction.

Dythragor whirled on it. "What is this, Silbakor? What are you doing?"

"I was Alouzon last night," she said, enjoying his discomfiture.

"Why the hell didn't you tell me?"

"Because you didn't fucking ask."

Among the crowd, men were starting to laugh. Dythragor glared at them and the laughter stopped. Someone else spoke, though. "I have no wish to fight with women."

"Aye," said another.

"Where is your husband, girl?"

"Are you a midwife, or a whore?"

Dythragor silenced them with a gesture. "Give up?" he whispered to Alouzon.

In spite of her words to the Dragon, she folded her arms. Dythragor wanted her to go? Fine. He would be disappointed. "Drop dead."

The Dragon spread its wings. Each cast as much shade as a full-sized oak. "Alouzon Dragonmaster has come to aid Gryylth at great personal sacrifice. She is to be treated with the honor she deserves."

The crowd stirred. Several men shook their heads in disgust.

Silbakor's eyes were full of fire. "Understood, men of Gryylth?"

Dythragor started to protest, looked up at the Dragon, said nothing. Silbakor seemed almost wrathful.

"I have spoken," it said. Its wings began to beat, and it lifted into the air. "I will come at need."

"Silbakor!" Alouzon screamed as it dwindled into the sky. The Dragon had been her only defense, and now it was gone.

Dythragor, though, seemed to breathe easier, as though glad that it had left. "Come on. The king is expecting us."

She steeled herself again, gestured at the crowd that was now silent, watching, hostile. "Braithwaite, you'd better start making some explanations."

"There are none to be made." He stepped up to her. "You're in this all the way. You'd better behave, or you'll wind up sold off as someone's wife. Remember: I call the shots."

"Braithwaite, you—"

"The name is *Dythragor*." With that, he turned and strode off, accompanied by several of the soldiers in the crowd.

There was nothing for Alouzon to do but follow him into the muddy streets of the town. She picked her way through puddles of stagnant water and piles of refuse that she was loathe to have touch even her stout boots. In spite of the bright sun and the solid stone and woodwork, the place was squalid, but Dythragor did not seem to notice it any more than Joe Epstein saw the debris in the apartment she shared with him.

Still, there was a curious vagueness to what she saw, as though she herself did not walk these streets. People pressed from all sides, or looked up from their work, interested in the splendid figure of Dythragor and curious or alarmed about his choice of companions, but she might have been viewing a crowd scene on the six o'clock news for all the impression that the faces made on her. Even the odors of decay and excrement, ripe and pervasive, did nothing to establish the reality of the town.

But she was roused from her analysis, for a big

man blocked the street ahead. His hair was black and close-cropped, and his eyes were also black. He wore armor a little finer than that of the soldiers who were acting as escort. The party came to a halt as he greeted Dythragor with a hand clasp.

"And what's this?" he said when he saw her. "A woman?"

She sighed, but felt fear: this time there was no Dragon to back her up.

"The Dragon called her Alouzon Dragonmaster, Relys," said one of the soldiers. "It—"

"Shut up." Relys had hardly listened. He came toward her and stopped, hands on hips. "Who are you, girl?"

Her voice did not shake when she answered, which surprised her. "I'm Alouzon Dragonmaster." She stared him straight back. "And who the hell are you?"

Relys ignored her question. He turned to Dythragor. "Why does this woman not bow to me as she should?"

Dythragor shrugged. "You'll have to ask her."

Alouzon did not wait for him to ask. "Because I don't want to," she said. "I don't see anything worth bowing to."

Relys glared and lifted a hand to cuff her. The action, Alouzon noticed, was an instinctive one, as though one might slap a child for impudence.

But the blow never fell, for her sword was suddenly in her hand and steady on his throat, her body poised for the thrust. Sickened though she was by the ease with which the action had come to her, she nonetheless knew that it was saving her just as had the Dragon.

"Don't try it," she said.

Relys looked startled, then almost amused. The corners of his mouth turned down for an instant and he nodded. "Your mate, Dragonmaster?"

"You can ask me the questions, man," said Alouzon. "And, no, I'm not his mate."

There came a commotion from up the street: horse hooves splashing through the mud and a firm voice shouting, "King's peace! King's peace here at the seat of Vorya!"

The rider was tall and slender. He cantered up on a fine horse and examined Alouzon, his eyes brown and inquiring. "We do not draw weapons here, woman, particularly against the lieutenant of the First Wartroop."

Deep water, she thought, and getting deeper. But Silbakor had left, and she knew that she would have to brazen it out. "And do men of the First Wartroop run around hitting women? What kind of a place is this, anyway?"

"She would not bow to me, Cvinthil," said Relys.

"Fuck this bowing shit. I'll bow to you when you're dead."

"Peace, peace." Cvinthil raised his hands as though smoothing fur. "Relys, go and summon the wartroop. Marrget will join you later. There is much to be done now that the Dragonmaster is with us." Relys nodded to him curtly and left. Cvinthil looked down at Alouzon with doe-like eyes. "My lady," he said politely. "Would it please you to put up your sword?"

"Is someone else going to take a swing at me?"

"No. On my word as councilor of Gryylth. Please . . ." He seemed to struggle with the oddity of the words. "Accept my apology."

She sheathed the sword, relieved. She had not killed. She had drawn her sword, but she had not killed. Death was not inevitable. She had some control. She had hope. "It's OK," she said. "It wasn't your fault." She extended her hand. "Alouzon. Dragonmaster." She was actually getting used to saying it.

He took her hand in a firm grip. "Cvinthil." He straightened in his saddle, gestured ahead. "Vorya awaits."

As they continued toward the hall at the center of town, she edged up to Dythragor. "Are the women here supposed to bow to men?"

He did not look at her. He seemed angry. "Always."

"How come?"

"Because they know their place."

The land rose slightly, the mud gave way to hard, dry earth, and the street brought them to a wall and gateway perhaps twenty feet high, made of stone and roughly dressed logs. The gate was open, and Cvinthil led them into an open space in which stood a large, barnlike building with a thatched roof.

"The king's hall," Dythragor muttered to her. "You're lucky to get this far."

"Get off my back."

Before they reached the hall, though, they heard a cry from somewhere within, a whining yelp that did not sound quite human. Alouzon stiffened, and looked at Dythragor, but he seemed just as startled as she. "What is this, Cvinthil?" he said.

His large brown eyes looked haunted. "One of the reasons we are glad of your presence, Dragonmaster." He would say no more, though. He dismounted and led them in.

The room inside was well lit by wide, unshuttered windows. A door across the way gave access to interior rooms, and before it was a long dais with a simple chair of dark wood on it. The chair was empty, though a dozen or so men were standing on and about the dais.

Cvinthil drew himself up as he entered, and he gestured Dythragor and Alouzon toward the center of the room. "Hail, Dythragor Dragonmaster," he said loudly, and Dythragor brightened considerably. Alouzon raised an eyebrow at Cvinthil, who appeared to suppress a smile. "And Alouzon Dragonmaster," he added.

Dythragor went red.

Alouzon nodded to Cvinthil and crunched across the rush-strewn floor to stand by Dythragor. One of the men on the platform was already coming forward. "Once again we meet, Dythragor." He was smiling, though the lines around his eyes told of a sleepless night, perhaps two. "Let me bid you both welcome to Hall Kingsbury." He turned to Alouzon, and his expression was both teasing and friendly. "A runner informed us of the Dragon's words. We are thankful for your presence."

Alouzon smiled and nodded graciously. She was stuck here, and survival mandated that she play along. Still, she was seething inside, not so much at these strangers, and not even at Dythragor, but at circumstances and events that had brought her to Gryylth and made her kill.

The Dragon had said that it would come at need. Need would come soon if she had anything to say about it.

Santhe bowed and turned toward the dais. A white-haired man had taken the seat. His face was almost kindly. To Alouzon he looked as though he should have had the lead in a production of *Lear*.

Cvinthil and another warrior stood to either side of him. The latter seemed much like Relys: same build, same scowl, same harsh, unforgiving gaze. He was looking at Alouzon.

"My king," he said abruptly, "what is this woman doing here?"

Alouzon sighed. Not again.

"Peace, Marrget," said the man in the chair.

At the very end of the dais, well away from the others and seemingly out of place amid the glitter of weapons, was a thin man in a gray robe. He stood silently, holding a white staff, and he watched Alouzon with an ironic smile, as if they were compatriots.

The man in the chair rose as they approached. "Dythragor and Alouzon, Dragonmasters, you are welcome to Hall Kingsbury, seat of the court of Gryylth. Alouzon, you are a stranger here. I am Vorya, King of Gryylth. You have already met Cvinthil and our merry Santhe. On my left is Marrget. These three are the captains of the wartroops of Gryylth and my trusted councilors."

"My king," said Marrget.

"Peace."

"The councils of Gryylth are no place for a woman."

"Peace, Marrget. The Dragon spoke of her sacrifice." Vorya turned to Alouzon. "Our customs are obviously not yours."

She was about to tell them all exactly what she thought of them, but she realized that anger would do no good. Marrget was prejudiced, Dythragor angry, Cvinthil and Santhe and Vorya puzzled but at least willing to tolerate her presence. An outburst would simply antagonize everyone.

Meeting Vorya's gaze levelly, and with what she hoped was dignity, she folded her arms. "I understand," she said. "And I take no offense."

Dythragor had caught sight of the man in the gray robe. "Enough," he said. "Tell me now why you felt it necessary to bring this charlatan into our councils." He waved a hand at the man, who glanced at Alouzon with another smile before he faced his attacker.

Dythragor hates his guts. She liked him already.

"Dythragor Dragonmaster," he said, "I did not ask to come, so it is ill of you to use me so insultingly. I would have gladly stayed in the Cotswoods, studying, but my king called me, and I answered."

"Well, you've answered. Now you can go home."

Alouzon spoke up, keeping her tone noncommittal. "Who is this man?"

Dythragor's jaw was clenched. Where before he had seemed angry, he now appeared almost murderous. "This is Mernyl. A sorcerer, or so he calls himself."

Mernyl bowed with a gleam of a smile. "I give greetings to Alouzon Dragonmaster." He seemed to be enjoying Dythragor's discomfiture. "I regret that I will probably not be able to entertain her as is her due."

"You're damned right," said Dythragor. He looked at Vorya. "Why did you summon him?"

His tone was nothing like that used to address a monarch, and even Santhe looked dismayed. But Vorya seemed used to it, almost resigned. He shifted in his chair. "The Dremords sent a troop of soldiers into the Blasted Heath in the company of Tireas, their sorcerer. They returned to their lands bearing something. We do not know what they took."

"So?"

Vorya signed to two soldiers who stood by a curtained door. Nodding tersely, they ducked through the covered entrance. "Bring him," came the muffled shout.

While they waited, Alouzon had time to look over the assembly. Marrget still scowled at her, but Cvinthil stood with his large hands clasped before him, staring down sadly. Even Santhe's gaiety was muted. The rest were ill at ease, glancing now and again at the door.

Again, as when she had approached Kingsbury from the air, she had the feeling that she had seen all of this before, though not with a sense of *déjà vu*. Rather, the men, the building, the armor—all were made up of details that she knew, knew well, but for the present she could not say from where.

The soldiers re-entered, escorting a hunched figure draped with a piece of thin cloth. The figure stumbled as if blind, and a claw-like hand protruded from beneath the folds of the drape.

The claw was enough. Three-fingered, hairless, it seemed to be covered with scales. Alouzon took a step back, and she was not alone. But the soldiers turned the figure toward the Dragonmasters and pulled the veil off, their eyes averted.

It was a man . . .perhaps. His face was a ruin of twisted flesh and torn features that in some places seemed to be of fur, in others, skin or even stone. It was as though his entire body had been deluged with liquid fire and left to rot. But it had not rotted: it had healed, grafting to itself a patchwork of substances both alive and inert, fusing them all together so that it was impossible to say where one left off and another began.

Blind, fish-eyed, he goggled at the room, his nose and mouth joined in a ragged slit that twitched with apprehension. What hair he had grew in blasted clumps, and his voice was a tormented whimper.

"Who . . . who did this to him?" said Alouzon. She

knew now what she had heard just before she had entered the hall.

The man himself answered. Gagging on the words, choking and heaving them out, he pawed at the air with his hooked hands. "Touched it, I did . . . I did. Tireas said not to . . . told me . . . but . . . I—" He broke off in a spasm of coughing. Blood dripped from his eyes and dribbled down his face. "Can't see . . ." He gagged again.

Vorya spoke quietly. "He was found wandering to the south of the Heath. He was apparently left by his comrades. None of our physicians has been able to say what happened to him. We even brought a midwife to examine him, since they are skilled in their own ways, but she knew nothing of his plight."

"The Tree . . . the Tree . . ." The Dremord coughed again, retched up a smear of bile.

Even Dythragor and Marrget were visibly shaken by the man. Mernyl, though, had approached him, his eyes piercing, his face a mask of compassion.

"Since we could find out nothing of his condition," Vorya continued, "I summoned Mernyl."

Dythragor interrupted. "Send him away."

"The sorcerer might be able to tell us something."

"Send him away. I've told you before that I'll allow no magic if I'm to help you. It's him or me."

Alouzon stepped up. "Mernyl may be able to help him."

"My words stand."

"Give him a goddam chance! Can *you* do anything for him?"

Dythragor looked frightened, but he was covering it with rage. "No one can do anything for him. Do you understand?"

Mernyl had been examining the Dremord, his hands gentle. He was murmuring to him reassuringly. He looked up. "My king, my allegiance is to you. What is your wish, King Vorya?"

Beneath the sorcerer's words was a challenge, and Alouzon realized that Mernyl possessed a fine command of heroic politics. If Vorya capitulated to Dythragor now, he would lose face.

Vorya realized the same thing. "Dythragor Dragonmaster, I must try to aid this man, for be he friend or foe, he is now under my protection, and laws of courtesy and hospitality apply. I am sure you understand."

Dythragor said nothing. If he withdrew now, he would show himself to be mean-spirited, which was almost as bad as losing face. He shrugged indulgently. "All right. Go ahead."

The sorcerer bowed to Vorya and turned back to the Dremord. Without waiting, he grounded the butt of his staff with a sharp thump, and the white wood sprang into glowing life. Fire traced its way up and down its length, and just above his hand, the letter M glowed like sunlight.

Alouzon stared at the letter. M for Mernyl. But English? The Roman alphabet? Where was she?

Deep ruby light began spreading from the staff in slow-moving ripples, and the soldiers flanking the Dremord looked terrified. Mernyl indicated that they could retreat, and they did, quickly. The Dremord wavered where he stood, but Mernyl seemed to be supporting him with the energy from the staff.

Alouzon looked on with mixed feelings. Magic, in the world she came from, did not exist. But dragons did not exist either, and plump little hippies did not turn into strapping amazons. In spite of an instinctive disbelief, she found herself rooting for Mernyl. Maybe there was something good in Gryylth after all.

His head bent, the sorcerer allowed the light to flood the Dremord, bathing him as though in a crimson sea. Slowly, Alouzon lost consciousness of the room, of the men. Tides of energy swept back and forth, and Mernyl seemed to be fighting something that rebuffed his powers. She felt the struggle, watched it unfold in the play of light about the sorcerer and the Dremord. She stood in a world of pure will that stretched off in all directions, and there was a completion and a wholeness to what Mernyl did that stood in sharp contrast to the tenuousness of Gryylth. If Mernyl's magic was nothing else, it was real.

"Come on, Mernyl." Her voice was a whisper. "Come on."

But his energies faltered suddenly, and he stepped back, shaking his head. The light faded, and the Dremord was unchanged.

"Told you," said Dythragor sourly.

Mernyl's eyes were haunted, almost horrified. "It's not possible," he said. "Nothing can transform someone like that. Nothing. What happened to this man?"

He was dissembling, though. His failure had been real, but Alouzon knew that the sorcerer had actually formed a good idea of what had happened. She knew also that he was afraid to say anything about it.

❖ CHAPTER 5 ❖

❖

DYTHRAGOR WASTED NO TIME. STRIDING FOR-
ward, but keeping his distance from the mutilated
Dremord, he grabbed Mernyl roughly by the arm and
pulled him toward the door. Whatever the illusion
the sorcerer had used to give himself a sense of power,
it was gone now, and Dythragor had the sense that
he was laying hands on a traitor, one who would
bring an end to all that Gryylth stood for. He could
not understand why Vorya had turned again to the
counsel of superstition, but he knew that, if he could
find an excuse to take the man's life, he would be
doing the king a favor.

Just struggle a little, faggot. Just give me an excuse.

But Mernyl was passive, limp. To slay him would
have been a dishonor. Dythragor was disgusted.

Alouzon, as usual, was complaining. "Leave him
the hell alone, Dythragor."

"What? While he sells us all down the river?"

"He tried to save the man."

"He tried to pull a fast one."

Santhe murmured to Vorya. The king rose. "Dythragor," he said softly. "You are in my house."

The Dragonmaster stopped short, glaring down at
Mernyl. The sorcerer's attention, though, seemed to

be elsewhere. He reminded him of Helen: she had been similarly distracted as she wove her own fabric of deceit and betrayal. Like Alouzon, she would have sympathized with this viper. "I want him back in the Cotswoods."

"Back to the Cotswoods he will be sent, Dythragor, but as I am king, you will not harm him under my roof." Vorya turned to Mernyl. "Is it your wish to depart?"

"There is . . ." Mernyl absently rubbed the bruises that Dythragor had given him. "There is no more for me to do here, my king. I cannot fight what has happened to this man."

"Nor anything else, either," said Dythragor.

Vorya gestured to the soldiers. They took the Dremord back out of the room.

Santhe spoke up. "My king," he said cheerily. "Mernyl and I were attacked on the way here. Dythragor saved us from a . . . *prolonged* fight." His eyes twinkled. "If Mernyl is sent home alone, he might be captured."

"Oh, how terrible," mocked Dythragor.

Santhe shot him a glance. He had nettled the councilor. He was sorry for that, but, well, Santhe laughed too much. He also tolerated Mernyl. He should know better. He was like one of those junior professors at Berkeley who had been so tolerant of the dissent on campus that they had let everything go to hell.

But Santhe found his humor again and continued. "Whether we have a use for Mernyl or not, the Dremords would be encouraged by his capture. Therefore, I suggest an escort. I would be willing to provide it."

"I am honored," said Mernyl. "But do not fear for my safety. I am adept at staying hidden when I wish."

Dythragor dismissed him with a wave of his hand. "I wish you'd stay hidden more often."

"You have my permission, Santhe," said Vorya. "But you must not leave until tomorrow morning, by my command. Your journeys lie heavily on you, and you must both rest this night."

Dythragor saw Mernyl and Alouzon exchange glances. Not good. Not good at all. If Alouzon was already sympathetic to the sorcerer, an overnight stay would give them time to collaborate.

She was, he noticed, falling back into her old persona: knee-jerk radical war-protester. He wondered how far she would carry out the regression. If given the chance, perhaps with Mernyl's help, would she blow up Hall Kingsbury? Possibly. But it was much more likely that, in Gryylth, any action she might take would be speedily neutralized. She was, after all, a woman, and whether she carried a sword or not, she was going to find out what that meant.

When the magician departed, he allowed himself to relax a little. He reminded himself of his other responsibilities. There was that Dremord . . ."What did they do in the Heath?"

"That is something we do not know," said the king. "They entered, and they left with something. From the marks on the ground, they had a wain with them."

For a moment, Dythragor recalled the brief glimpse of a white-clad figure and a shadowy something that flickered. Maybe . . .

"We were hoping that Mernyl might have told us something."

Dythragor looked up in annoyance. "Well, he

couldn't. So let's have no more of that." The glimpse, he decided, had been nothing. Maybe the moonlight. "If the Dremords can go into the Heath, then so can we. We'll take a look around and find out what they did."

Alouzon was doubtful. "If the Heath did something to that man, I'm not sure it's a good place to go."

Passive, gutless woman. What's she got up her sleeve?

"He spoke of a tree," Cvinthil ventured.

"And the rest of the phalanx went in and out without harm," said Dythragor. "There shouldn't be a problem."

"Maybe Mernyl should come," said Alouzon.

"Will you get off Mernyl?" Dythragor was finding himself becoming genuinely angry. "He couldn't do anything for that Dremord: what do you think he's going to do in the Heath?"

She glared back at him. "It was a thought. OK?"

The others were looking uneasy. Marrget, though, nodded. "The First Wartroop will accompany you."

"I wouldn't ask anyone who was unwilling to enter." Dythragor looked straight at Alouzon, hoped that she took the hint. She did not.

"My men will follow orders and be glad," said Marrget. "They will be honored to fight again beside Dythragor Dragonmaster." He glanced at Alouzon. "Even if he chooses strange companions."

There was laughter. Alouzon flushed. "Go ahead," she muttered. "I didn't ask to get tossed into this."

"I didn't ask either," said Dythragor.

Vorya silenced the mirth. "We do not honor our guest. Woman she is, but Dragonmaster also, and we will show her respect." He turned to his guards. "See to it that a place is prepared for her rest."

Dythragor was alarmed. "In Hall Kingsbury? Are you sure you want to do that? What will the war-troops say when they hear that you're putting up women?"

Vorya frowned, but Cvinthil spoke. "If Alouzon Dragonmaster is willing, my household will be honored by her presence." He said it shyly, as if embarrassed.

"I accept," said Alouzon.

Cvinthil now, too? Was Alouzon making so many inroads into the power structure of Gryylth? "Won't your wife think this rather strange, Cvinthil?"

It was a gratuitous remark, and he noticed more than one look of surprise. Cvinthil, though, shrugged.

"My wife should know that I am faithful unto death," he said simply.

Alouzon followed Cvinthil into the village. The meeting continued in the hall, as Dythragor and Marrget planned for the exploration of the Heath, but her host had left, and she was glad to get away from Dythragor. Fear and uncertainty had shortened her temper, and she had felt an almost irresistible urge to strike him as he had bullied the men of Gryylth.

"Spoiled brat."

The street—path, actually—took them to lower ground where the houses and shops crowded closely together. The stagnant puddles reappeared. Mongrel dogs snapped at one another between the buildings. Boys clashed wooden swords on shields and ran into alleyways at their approach. Alouzon could see them peering out from the shadows as they passed and heard them talking in excited whispers: "*A woman.*"

Cvinthil seemed to catch himself, and he slowed so that they were walking abreast. "Forgive me, lady," he said. "I fall into our customs."

"Huh?"

"Women usually walk behind. But you are a Dragonmaster. I was being rude."

She liked this place less and less. She was thankful that she wore armor and carried a sword. She had some protection. "They just put up with this?"

Cvinthil shrugged slightly, bewildered. "No one has questioned it. Everyone seems content."

"That's weird . . ." She looked around. Gryylth had seemingly gone beyond fundamental Islam: women, veiled or not, were not even on the streets. "How do they get anything done?"

"I do not understand."

"Uh . . . buying food, shopping . . ."

"Oh, I see." His confusion dissipated. "Market day is Thursday, still two days off. Women do not usually leave their homes save for specific reasons. Today, they have no reason."

"So they just . . . stay at home."

"There are men's tasks, and women's tasks. We are all kept busy."

"Yeah." She was acutely conscious of the stares she was receiving from the men of the village. Some were outright hostile, others were examining her as though she were a prize heifer. Deliberately, she allowed her hand to fall to the hilt of the Dragonsword, and some of the stares were redirected.

"Doubtless you would be more comfortable if you could meet some of our midwives," said Cvinthil. "Their tasks call them abroad at all hours, and they are allowed by custom to live alone, without a man."

"Sure." *Silbakor, why the hell did you bring me here?*

But it was not her place to judge Cvinthil or his people. Not yet. That might come later, but for now she wanted more information, particularly about Dythragor. "Listen, Cvinthil," she said. "What's Dythragor's game?"

"Game?"

"He sure lords it up around here. And the way he tore into Mernyl—I thought he was going to kill him."

"That, I am afraid, was a possibility. The Dragonmaster has little love for the sorcerer. He has never allowed his services."

"I could tell that. Why?"

"Years ago, Mernyl was an advisor to Vorya, and had arranged a partial settlement with the Dremords. In his own way he is a good man, Dragonmaster. He is devoted to living things, and it grieved him to see so much life taken. But I think that grief blinded him to the true nature of our enemy, for the morning after the truce, as we prepared to celebrate the end of the war, word came to King Vorya that the Dremords had attacked across the Eastreach River. We had no choice but to meet force with force."

"So that was the end of it."

"Aye."

"How long ago was that?"

"Ten summers."

"Has anyone else done anything about a settlement?"

Cvinthil stopped in the middle of the street, his hands clasped behind him. He seemed to be pondering. "No," he said. "No one. But you must understand, Alouzon Dragonmaster: the Dremords are not like us. They seem to delight in destruction and disorder. They allow their women to roam freely . . ."

He noticed her eyes, shut his mouth, and considered.

"I speak of things that are well known," he managed. "There has been much destruction."

"OK." She kept her tone carefully controlled. "But all that doesn't explain why Dythragor hates Mernyl."

"I think the Dragonmaster fears for Gryylth. I think he distrusts that which is unseen and mysterious." Cvinthil's voice was calm and factual, without any of the bluster that had characterized Dythragor and Marrget. "Mernyl fell into error because of his arts, and Dythragor would keep others from sharing that fate."

Like many of the other buildings in Kingsbury, Cvinthil's house was built of stone and timber, but the squalor of the town lay less thickly over it. The path to the door had been swept recently, and some effort had been made to brighten the small garden with flowers.

The tall warrior smiled at the blooms. "My wife, Seena, planted them. You might like her, Alouzon. She is perhaps a little stronger than most of our women."

There was pride in his voice, and love. He held the door open for Alouzon, and she stepped into a large room floored with flagstones. Rushes and fragrant herbs covered the stones, and they scented the air sweetly. A small girl with a broom stared at them with big eyes, and her eyes grew bigger when she saw Alouzon. Dropping the broom, she darted out through a door, and the Dragonmaster could hear her feet pounding up the stairs. "Mama! Mama!"

"My daughter Ayya," said the warrior. "Will it please you to sit?"

She took a stool to one side of the fire. "Dythragor

made that crack about your wife, Cvinthil . . . are
you sure I'm not going to cause problems?"

"Seena will accept my will," he said.

And just then there was a soft step on the stairs,
and a woman entered. She was shorter than Alouzon,
her long hair confined in a braid that reached to the
small of her back. Her clothing was plain: a gray
smock, simple shoes. What Alouzon noticed most,
though, was the submissive hunch to her back, and
how she kept her eyes downcast as she approached
Cvinthil. "My husband," she said, standing before
him. She bowed.

"Wife."

"Ayya told me that . . . you have brought a woman
with you. Have I displeased you?" Her voice was a
monotone, as though she were afraid to ask, more
afraid to hear the answer. "Will you now turn me
out or sell me?"

"She is a guest, Seena."

Seena dropped to her knees. Alouzon was on her
feet instantly, her stomach twisting. "Cvinthil, this
is—"

"Peace." Cvinthil looked at Seena. "Wife, this is
my will: Alouzon Dragonmaster is our guest this
night, and perhaps others. You will treat her appropriately."

"How have I displeased you, master, that I am
asked to serve women?"

"You have not displeased me, my beloved Seena."
His voice was kind.

Seena lifted her eyes and met Alouzon's. Alouzon
tried to smile reassuringly, but Seena paled. "Armor,
husband? And a sword? Is she a Dremord?"

"Nay, wife. She is a Dragonmaster." Cvinthil turned
to Alouzon. "Some Dremord women carry weapons,"

he explained. "We of Gryylth have a inborn horror of something so unnatural." He realized his error. "Ah . . . unnatural for Dremords and Gryylthans, not Dragonmasters." ·

Alouzon felt as though she were playing a farce after memorizing the wrong script. "You don't have to serve me, Seena. I don't need anyone to serve me."

"Do you then join me," said Seena, "in the keeping of the house?"

"Wife," said Cvinthil, "prepare a meal. I will serve the Dragonmaster."

Alouzon heard the effort in his voice. "Look," she said, "I don't want to put you two to any trouble. I can go out and . . ." And what? Crazies in the town, Dremords in the countryside, Dythragor running around like a little kid with a big sword, and Relys and Marrget disliking her from square one: where was she going to go? " . . . and, uh, get something from the Dragon."

Cvinthil rubbed his forehead abstractedly. "Your customs are indeed different from ours," he murmured. Seena scuttled away to the pantry, casting glances back at Alouzon. She seemed more bewildered than angry, an echo of the uncertainty that Alouzon herself had felt ever since she had slid from the Dragon and discovered the changes wrought in her body.

She stumbled back to the stool, passed a hand over her strangely altered face. "I think I need a drink."

Cvinthil brought her beer in a wooden cup. It was warm, but it cleared her head. She lowered the cup and watched Seena chopping onions and leeks. Ayya was helping. The girl was plainly frightened, and Alouzon felt her brow furrow.

"I am sorry that my household grieves you, Dragonmaster," Cvinthil said softly.

She caught back the words on her tongue. She could hardly insult her host by questioning his customs. Yet the sight of Seena and Ayya shuffling across the floor, heads bent and eyes downcast, made the beer sit badly in her stomach.

She looked for something to take her mind off the woman and the girl. "What is this Blasted Heath they were talking about?"

Cvinthil settled himself on a stool beside her. He seemed glad of the change of subject. "No one goes there. Mernyl, perhaps, has dared its borders upon occasion, but it is a foolish warrior who attempts to penetrate its interior."

"You think Dythragor's wrong to go there, then? Should he take Mernyl?"

Cvinthil shook his head. "I trust Dythragor. I believe he has only the best interests of Gryylth in his heart, though he is at times rash and imperious. He and Marrget are brave men. Marrget, I believe, is braver than all of us together, and the finest captain the First Wartroop has ever had. Even old Helkyying, the previous captain, admitted that. But . . . the Heath . . ."

Seena seemed to be listening. At the first mention of the Heath, she had drawn Ayya close to her side, as though to shield the girl from harm.

"Having never been there," said the councilor, "I can only speak from hearsay. There are dark tales of panic and fear . . . and . . . and . . ." He waved his hands to signify his lack of words. "It is as though I speak of my own death when I speak of the Heath. I think of things which are not hounds baying in the night. I see the murder of those I love. I smell betrayal and dishonest thoughts of blood. I feel the murder of babes."

Seena had stopped her cooking. She was watching Cvinthil, trembling. Ayya hid in her apron. "Husband."

"Seena." Cvinthil extended his arms, and his wife and daughter came to him. Silently, he folded them in his embrace, stroked their hair comfortingly. "Seena, Ayya," he murmured. "Have I not told you that these things are confined to the Heath? They do not trouble the land because of that."

"Forgive us for intruding, husband." Her voice was muffled in his tunic, and his hand rested upon her head as lightly as a benediction.

Cvinthil looked at Alouzon. "I, too, fear the Heath."

But she hardly heard him, for in watching Seena and Ayya, she had become aware of the pouch that Cvinthil wore on his belt. The lid was of enameled copper, and it was figured with cloisonne designs of beasts and birds and men, bordered with Celtic-style knotwork. She had seen that lid before, in a photograph. The original was in a museum, and it dated from fifth century Britain.

Details suddenly crowded at her. The brooch that fastened the councilor's cloak, silver and inlaid with garnets, was strikingly British in design, as were Seena's bracelets, as was her own leather armor. She suddenly knew why everything seemed so familiar: her field of study was Arthurian Britain.

But this was Gryylth, not Britain. This was a place of magic and Dragons and bizarre transformations, not the heroic but very mundane fifth century. And more: these were real men and women, not suppositions drawn from digs and textbooks.

Where was Gryylth? What was Gryylth?

"Dragonmaster?"

She realized how hard she had been staring, and she looked away quickly. "Sorry. I . . . was thinking."

"Are you not well?"

She shook her head. "I'm . . . OK. Don't worry." She mustered a smile for Seena and Ayya. "I'm safe, really," she assured them. "I don't bite."

From the shelter of her husband's arms, Seena nodded slowly. "I believe you, Dragonmaster."

"Tell me about Gryylth," Alouzon said to Cvinthil. Fifth- century Britain? Seena made as if to rise. "No, stay. It's all right. The food can wait."

Cvinthil nodded to his wife and she, together with her daughter, snuggled back into his arms. "Gryylth is the inhabited lands of men between the seas," he explained.

"What's beyond it?"

"The sea. And mist. There is nothing else."

"Where did the Dremords come from?" The name rankled. "Do they really call themselves Dremords?"

"Actually, my lady, no. Their lands they call Corrin."

"They're Corrinians, then."

"If you will. But we have always called them Dremords."

"Where did they come from? The Dre—" No, she was not going to play along with the game. "The Corrinians."

He seemed to struggle with little-used thoughts. "They came from lands across the East Sea. As long as even the oldest among us can remember, though, they have dwelt in the southeastern parts of Gryylth, preying on us, taking our wives and daughters, murdering our sons . . ."

The young face of the man she had killed swam up out of her thoughts, blank, pale, lifeless in the unpitying light of the full moon. Like her, he was a human being. And as Suzanne Helling, a disillusioned and broken activist, Alouzon had heard enough facts warped to fit political expediency to be suspicious. There were always two sides to any war. What, she wondered, was the Corrinian view of all of this?

"They just . . . come out and murder?" she asked. "For no reason?"

"They do."

"You've seen them do this?"

"My lady, it is common knowledge."

"But, have you seen them? I mean, a totally unprovoked attack where they, like, came out and just burned down a whole village? Or did in all the crops or something?"

He was silent for some time. Then: "No, not personally."

She found herself remembering a conversation she had had with Solomon Braithwaite in his office at UCLA. He had been characterizing the Saxons as barbaric and destructive, holding to that conviction even in the face of contradictory evidence. Everyone knew the Saxons were devils. It was common knowledge.

And everyone knew that the student protesters were unwashed, commie sympathizers. Everyone knew that the Viet Cong were murdering cowards. Everyone knew that the U.S. Marines and the National Guard were squeaky-clean, patriotic, all-American boys. Everyone knew. Common knowledge.

Alouzon was beginning to handle pieces of the

puzzle, slowly examining them with the attention of a scholar, looking for patterns, fitting them together by trial and error. There was something wrong with this place, but as yet she could not say what it was. What did Britain have to do with Gryylth? Jewelry, building design, and an ongoing conflict with an invading tribe that everyone knew was savage and barbaric . . .

Dythragor probably loves all of this. But how much did he actually know about it? How much did anyone know?

A knock came to the door. "It is Kallye, the midwife," said Seena.

"We had best be away," said Cvinthil. "It is unseemly for a man to be near such things."

"You're pregnant?" said Alouzon.

Seena lifted her head. In spite of her shuffling and her bent head, there was a flicker of pride in her eyes. "I am."

It had been four years since her abortion. Her child would have been about the same age as Ayya. "Congratulations," she said, her tongue suddenly thick.

"My thanks, Dragonmaster." Seena rose and, after hesitating, bowed to her as to a man, then went to the door.

Kallye was a tall woman with dark hair that she wore loose. She had a more confident step than either Seena or Ayya, and Alouzon sensed that she made her own decisions.

The midwife bobbed her head slightly as she entered. "Gods bless," she said. Her voice was matter-of-fact. "Lord Cvinthil? Are you here? On a Tuesday?"

Tuesday. And Cvinthil had said that market was held on Thursday. English. Come to think of it, everyone in Gryylth spoke fairly modern English. Alouzon's head was almost spinning. Was she going mad?

Cvinthil was laughing. "I am guesting Alouzon Dragonmaster, Kallye. Fear not: we will depart. Is Seena well?"

"Well enough, lord. I'll see to her today, and give you word when next I see you. But I have heard of Alouzon Dragonmaster."

Alouzon shoved aside her mental vertigo. "It's probably all over town by now," she said, standing. English?

Kallye bowed slightly, but with a smile. "Gods bless."

Alouzon nodded in return. "Thanks. You too."

"We have . . ." Kallye's smile broadened. "We have few women to whom we give honor in Gryylth. How should I call you?"

She shrugged. It seemed a strange question until she remembered that proper respect was a cornerstone of heroic culture. "Alouzon is OK. Uh . . . Dragonmaster if you really want."

Kallye laughed. "I am honored to meet you, Dragonmaster." Her manner was pleasant, full of strength and humor, and she managed to give even the formal title a casual tone, as though she were addressing a friend. "I hope we can talk at a later time. At present, though . . ." She stood, waiting.

Cvinthil took the hint, gestured Alouzon to the door. The work of a midwife had nothing to with men . . . or Dragonmasters.

They had just stepped out onto the street again when they heard a voice calling: "Lord Cvinthil!" Alouzon looked off down the way and recognized one of the soldiers who had escorted her and Dythragor to the hall. He was running, dodging dogs and men, leaping over puddles. But although in coming he seemed much like a boy, in drawing near he put on a gravity that was at odds with his years. "My lord . . ." He eyed Alouzon. "And Dragonmaster. The First Wartroop rides tomorrow morning for the Blasted Heath."

"And will you be riding also, Wykla?"

He straightened. "I am a man of the First Wartroop," he said proudly. "Marrget named me so this very morning."

Cvinthil clapped him on the shoulder. "All Kingsbury knows how hard you have worked, Wykla of Burnwood. My congratulations."

"My thanks, lord. I will try to be worthy."

"I'll be going, too," said Alouzon. "Someone with some sense better be there."

Wykla looked nervous. There was obviously a second part to his message. "Dythragor Dragonmaster said . . . ah . . ."

"Go on," said Alouzon, though she knew exactly what Dythragor had said.

"He said, lady, that you were to stay behind."

"That's OK, Wykla. Alouzon Dragonmaster says that she's going. Tough shit for Dythragor."

"Lady," said Cvinthil, "perhaps it is wiser—"

"If Dythragor kicks about it, Wykla, ask him who saved him from getting spitted on a Dremord sword the first night here."

She winced at her own words. How casually she spoke of it now! Soon, she would be bragging about it all, notching her sword in neat little rows. *And how many did you kill today? Is that all? Come on, let's have a round of drinks and show off our collections of ears.*

Wykla bowed, then turned and went back towards the hall.

Alouzon felt a pang. "He's not going to get in trouble for reporting that, is he?"

"Marrget is just," said Cvinthil. "He would never fault a man of the First Wartroop for speaking the truth, unpleasant though Dythragor might find it. I only wish that . . ."

His voice trailed off, and he looked sad. Some things in Gryylth, apparently, bothered him also. Alouzon remembered the look on Vorya's face when Dythragor had ordered him to dismiss Mernyl.

"Come on," she said, taking his arm and leading him down the street. "I've got some more questions to ask you."

❖ CHAPTER 6 ❖

❖

THE LATE AFTERNOON SUN HOVERED OVER the downs that undulated off into the west, and it shone warmly on Benardis, the capital of Corrin. On the top of the hill at the center of the city, the walls of King Tarwach's lodge had been rolled back to let in the air and the light, and Darham, brother to the king, leaned against a pillar and looked out over the town that rambled down to the edge of the Long River in a confusion of thatched roofs. Behind him, Calrach was making his report, and Darham rubbed at his beard—slowly, contemplatively—as he listened.

"Tireas showed us the way out of the Heath," Calrach was saying. He gestured to the sorcerer who stood, white-bearded and white-robed, off to one side. "We were all but clear, but then we were attacked again."

Darham turned around, shaking his head. "Again?"

Tarwach sat, leaning forward, elbows on knees and chin cupped in his hands. The blue of his eyes was icy, calculating. With a gesture, he demanded an answer.

"Aye, my lord," said Calrach. "Again."

"Such is the way of the Heath," said Tireas. "It

strikes when one least expects it, and always in a way that brings terror."

"Well, it terrified me, sorcerer," said Calrach. Sweat turned his thin, blond hair into damp ringlets. "And it took Flebas from us. The creatures of the Heath toppled the Tree out of the wagon, and Flebas tried to prop it up—with his bare hands."

Even Tarwach winced at that. Tireas had told them much about the Tree. They all knew what it could do.

"It . . . changed him, my king." Calrach was pale. "I am not sure his mind was sound after that. His body was not. He was . . ." He fell silent with a shudder.

"Did he die, then?" said Darham. "Was he buried decently?"

Calrach dropped his eyes. Tireas spoke.

"He was not dead, my lord. But . . . we had to leave him."

"You what?" Tarwach stood. "You left one of my soldiers in Gryylthan territory without aid or succor? What is the meaning of this, Calrach?" The captain clenched his jaw. His shame was etched deeply in his face. "I will have an answer, sir."

"My king," said Tireas, "I must myself take full personal responsibility for the decision. Calrach acted on my orders. Much as it grieved us to leave Flebas, alas, we had little choice. We were deep in Gryylthan lands, and Vorya and his men knew of our presence. The Dragon, Silbakor, was also near."

"What of Dythragor?"

"Nay, he was not present. But given our situation, I decided that haste was of the utmost importance. Taking Flebas with us would have caused the loss of more men, perhaps the whole phalanx." There might have been tears in his eyes.

Tarwach did not speak for some time. The light from the setting sun turned his hair into a golden halo, but it did not warm his eyes at all. "I, too, am grieved," he said at last. "Manda?"

A young woman in battle leathers stepped out of the shadows. "My king?"

"See to it that Flebas's family is provided for. Bring them to me this evening. I will speak with them."

Manda bowed to him, turned to go.

"And please bring us some wine, Manda," Darham added. "I fear the news will grow grimmer as the tale unfolds."

"Immediately, lord," she said, and she was gone, her blond braid bouncing over her shoulder as she hurried off.

"Continue, Calrach," said the king. His voice was flat, toneless.

"Flebas was a man of the Third Phalanx," said Calrach softly. His mouth was set in the manner of a captain who has known defeat. "Maybe he was not the best, but he was by no means the worst. He was loyal, and his comrades trusted him."

"He will have suitable honors, captain. Whoever the gods are, they will hear his name this night. Pray, continue."

Calrach went on with his report. The phalanx had headed south, swinging wide toward the mountains in an effort to evade Gryylthan patrols. A slightly better plan, Darham considered, would have been to turn east, but then he remembered that the Gryylthan towns of Dearbought and Pounce lay in that direction, and the men there had been hardened by years of skirmishes. Calrach had made the right choice.

Even more right than was first apparent, it seemed, for Calrach began to describe another encounter, one that made Tarwach lift his head. Darham found himself dragged out of his thoughts.

"The other rider seemed to be Mernyl, the Gryylthan sorcerer," Calrach was saying. "Santhe was escorting him southward, and I judged they were making for Kingsbury."

"It seemed fitting that we attack, and I gave such orders," said Tireas. "If we could capture Mernyl, I reasoned, we would have less trouble with Gryylthan magic."

"We have very little trouble as it is," said Darham. "Mernyl is not held in great esteem by Vorya . . . or rather by Dythragor, if I understand aright."

The captain went on. "We were almost successful, but the men were worn, and Dythragor Dragonmaster appeared and drove us off. He is . . . skilled with a sword."

Tarwach examined him coolly. Then: "How many did you lose, captain?"

"Two at that encounter. I made the mistake of following the Dragonmaster when he left—on foot—and we closed in for another try. But we lost three then, and not just to Dythragor."

"To whom, then? Is the Dragon fighting now?"

"No, my king. There was a woman with him when we found him in the foothills. She wore armor like his, and she also carried a Dragonsword. She slew Lyron, the new man of the phalanx."

The news was growing grimmer indeed. Tarwach passed a hand across his face. "Two Dragonmasters? What an evil fortune!"

"And Santhe continued south with Mernyl," added Tireas.

Darham shook his head. "Doubtless, Vorya sent for Mernyl after our attack on the Dike. Dythragor

will have him sent home again. But two Dragonmasters might bring us as much sorrow as one Dragonmaster and one sorcerer."

Tireas actually smiled. "A little less, I would hope,
my lord."

Tarwach shrugged. "So you lost Santhe and Mernyl, and the Dragonmasters drove you off."

"Yes, my king. The woman fights like Dythragor."

"Were I a woman," said Tarwach, "I would be re-
luctant to strike a blow for Gryylth." Manda had returned with wine, and he took his cup from her. "Did
you hear, Manda?" he said. "There appears to be a
female Dragonmaster in Gryylth now."

Her bright eyes flickered. "I would she come to
Corrin. She might find out which side she was on."

"Could a woman accomplish much in Gryylth,"
Darham asked, "Dragonmaster or no?"

"Perhaps we are not so badly off, then," said Tarwach. "But to assume a respite would be foolish. The
second Dragonmaster might be bringing confusion
of her own to Gryylth, or maybe not. Either way, I
believe we should move quickly." He considered,
swirling his wine in its golden cup, looking out across
the broad valley where the Long River pursued its
leisurely course to the Eastern Sea. "The Tree we
have, the Circle is Gryylth's, but with Tree and Circle
both . . ." He eyed Tireas, who bowed. "Might we be
able to neutralize the Dragonmasters, sorcerer?"

"It is quite possible, my king." Tireas's attention
was suddenly focused on the question, as though he
were studying a complicated spell. "It would certainly
give us a total control of the magic of the land. And
in spite of the Dragonswords, Dragonmasters are but
human."

"And," put in Darham, "such a clear advantage

might allow us to forgo the use of the Tree. That would be a great good."

Calrach shifted his weight from one foot to the other. "I would like that, my lord. I have seen what the Tree can do."

"Please," said Tireas. "Do not assume that the Tree can only destroy. The Tree is change. All change. We must all admit that there is good change as well as bad. Flebas took the full force of the Tree into his body, unfiltered, uncontrolled. But with care, the Tree can do much for Corrin."

"I hope you are right, Tireas," said the king, "for with the presence of another Dragonmaster, I intend to hasten our move on the Circle."

"More battle, lord?" said Tireas. He shook his head, looked at the ground.

"We will strike tomorrow morning, all together," said Tarwach. "We will take the Circle, and then we will offer terms for peace. Our terms. But until we are in a position of strength, we will not settle." He nodded to those present. "Darham, Manda, give the necessary orders."

Darham nodded, and Manda bowed deeply. But the girl watched her king depart with a crooked mouth. "And will I be able to fight for my land with the King's Guard?"

"It would not be wise, Manda," Darham said gently. "Other women have fought for us, and the Gryylthan men have singled them out for particular ferocity, disregarding wisdom and even their own safety. It would be a useless sacrifice."

"Then I am no better off than a Gryylthan woman," she cried. "I might as well be tending the cooking fires for all the battle I've seen since I donned my armor."

Tireas was pale, his eyes downcast. "I would find some other way than by battle."

Manda's fists were clenched. "I would settle for battle and be glad. Gryylth owes me a debt."

"Must it be paid in blood, child?" said Tireas gently.

She whirled on him. "Aye, master sorcerer. My blood flowed for three days when Dythragor and his friend were done, and Kasi bled for four. She found refuge in home and family. I found none save in arms. I will not forget."

Darham put an arm about her, felt the hard muscles that battle training had given Manda. Tall, broad-shouldered, the daughter of a farmer family of Dubris, she was quite capable of holding her own in any fair fight. "I understand," he said.

She bent her head, fighting back the rage.

But Tireas had grown thoughtful. "I wonder . . ." He eyed Manda. "Gryylth thinks so little of its women. I wonder if there might not be a way to end all this without the loss of so much life."

"I would that one be lost," said Manda. "I do not know his name, but I know his face and the emblems on his armor. One was that of the First Wartroop. I—"

"Peace," said Tireas. "The First Wartroop . . ." He was lost in thought, his voice drifting like a leaf in a breeze. "You may have your revenge yet, Manda of Dubris. I pray that you will recognize it."

"Revenge?" Her eyes were eager.

"Some kinds are worse than others," said the sorcerer.

Marrget disdained the confinement of urban life, and he had built his small house on a low rise to the south of the hill that held Kingsbury. Standing at his front door, he could, and often did, fold his arms and look up at the town as though he were its guardian spirit. And, in a sense, he was exactly that, for Marrget of Crownhark was the captain of the First Wartroop of Gryylth, the main attack force of the land, twenty-one men who knew all there was to know about arms and battle and who had given their lives over to the defense of their people and their king.

Dythragor liked Marrget and his ways. Both man and habit were direct, straightforward, without artifice or hidden motive. Marrget embodied in his own person the qualities that made a warrior great, and he worked to foster those virtues in his men. Pride, valor, courage, he possessed them all, and in harmony with them was a clear eye and a discerning mind. Even Relys, who was perfectly willing to state that he admired no man but himself, did not balk when Marrget's evaluation of a battle plan ran counter to his own. In all, he was everything to his men: a stern father, a harsh taskmaster, an understanding counselor, and a wise leader.

And therefore he stood, Dythragor thought, in stark contrast to Mernyl the sorcerer, who knew of nothing save intrigue and mystery, and who even smiled with the expression of one who would not tell everything. Marrget was solid, bluff, alternately dour and generous, his laughter and his frowns in even proportion; but whatever expression he wore, Dythragor was always sure that it was a perfect mirror to his thoughts, that Marrget, manly and forthright, had nothing to conceal.

Tonight, Marrget's laughter was uppermost, and so was Dythragor's. The two were together in the captain's house, and they were drinking and sharing memories, for some time had passed since Dythragor had last been in Gryylth.

They spoke mostly of battle, since all their time together had been spent in fighting the Dremords. Dythragor could remember the grand strategies, the sweeping movements of armies. Marrget, on the other hand, could supply names, faces, the way Tarwach held his sword, or how Helkyying, the last captain of the wartroop, had spoken on the day of his death. He knew the name of every man who had died under his command, and he did not hesitate to recall them. "It is important to remember that we deal in lives, Dragonmaster," he said, beckoning for his slave girl to fill their cups again, "else we might be inclined to squander them uselessly. Lives unvalued are lives wasted." His gray eyes seemed to look off into the distance for a moment. "Helkyying said that once. I did not know what he meant at the time." His smile looked as though it were more of pain than of pleasure. "I learned."

The girl approached, bowed, filled their cups, bowed again, and retreated to the kitchen. Not really listening to his host, Dythragor watched her. Marrget would lend her to him if he asked, but he was never particularly interested in sex when he was in Gryylth. There was too much else to do—battles to be fought, plans to be made . . . Silbakor usually brought him to the land when there was danger, and he rarely had enough time to relax and enjoy a woman under such circumstances. He lifted his cup to Marrget. "To Gryylth."

"To Gryylth." Marrget drank, his big hand around the stem of the cup. "What say you, Dythragor?" he said as he wiped his mouth.

"Huh?"

"Do you think Helkyying was wise?"

Dythragor shrugged, tried to recall what Marrget had been talking about. "Helkyying was a good commander. Heaven knows he never wasted his men. I think he was a little miserly sometimes, though. Like that battle up near the north end of the Dike a few years back. If he'd been willing to take a little more loss, we would have driven the Dremords back that much sooner."

"But they were driven back in the end, with less loss of life."

"Sometimes I think you don't understand, Marrget." The wine was loosening his tongue, and he went on, heedless of the expression on the captain's face. "The Dremords are beasts. We don't want them in Gryylth. It's a disgrace just to have them set foot on our lands." Years before, he had felt similarly about the radicals that had invaded his campus. Them and their propaganda . . . and the university had, over his protests, actually capitulated and allowed them to pass it out on state property. Right outside the Berkeley gates!

"I was pushing for Helkyying to send in the troops," Dythragor continued. Once, he had pressed the president of the university to do the same. No one ever listened to him then, but things were different here.

Marrget chuckled, set down his cup. "It has been years now, Dythragor. I can tell you this now. It was I who advised Helkyying to hold off."

Dythragor was struck dumb for a moment. "You, Marrget?"

"Helkyying trusted me, Dragonmaster. I saw no point in losing more men. It was obvious that we would carry the day."

Marrget's treachery stung him. "And I suppose you'll be issuing feather beds to them all next thing I know?"

The captain eyed him. His eyes had turned cold, penetrating. "I was Helkyying's lieutenant at that time, as Relys is mine now. Had Relys advice to give me, I would listen to him. Helkyying listened to me, though I believe that he had already made up his mind."

"It was a bad decision," Dythragor insisted. "The Dremords should have felt the full brunt of our forces that day. Holding back only prolonged the battle. We should have smacked them good."

"But we lost less men."

"Less men, less men." Dythragor singsonged Marrget's words back at him. "That's all I hear from you, Marrget. Are you getting faint-hearted? Have you been sleeping with your slave girl too much? Are you getting womanish yourself?"

Marrget stood up, his face set. "Dragonmaster, you insult me."

The night was warm, and quiet. In the silence, Dythragor could hear the crickets chirping outside. The fire on the hearth crackled once, twice.

It's the wine, he thought. *I've had a little too much.*

Marrget was still on his feet, waiting.

"I didn't mean it that way, Marrget." It was as much of an apology as he was willing to give. It would have to do.

"What did you mean then, Dragonmaster?"

"I . . ." Dythragor thought quickly. "I think we all have to be careful about women," he said. "You and I—that one time, remember, when we rode way past the Dremord lines? We never told anyone else about those Dremord girls we found doing their washing by the river. But I'll tell you, I don't think I fought as well that day after taking them."

Marrget eyed him carefully, turning over his words. It had been an insipid apology, but Marrget shrugged and sat down. "I have never been easy in my mind about that. In fighting the Dremords, we now seem to perform the same acts of which we accuse them. I do not think the gods smile upon such things."

"There aren't any gods, Marrget. Just men with jobs to do."

"We do not know their names or their faces, Dragonmaster, but they are there."

Dythragor was almost tempted to point out that Marrget was talking like Mernyl now, but decided against it. "Look at Cvinthil, though," he said. "He dotes on that woman of his so much that I doubt he's going to be worth anything in a few years."

Marrget's eyes narrowed. Cvinthil was his friend. "Cvinthil has his opinions, Dragonmaster. As I do. As you do. I have not noticed that his advice has proved valueless to the king."

No one understood. He wondered whether Marrget was going to start listening to Alouzon's foolishness one of these days. That would certainly be the end of it. "Come on," he said. "Let's have some more wine." Maybe he would ask Marrget for the use of his slave after all.

Night. Nightmare, actually. Alouzon had been given a couch near the hearth and rich furs and linen sheets, but she was having little success with sleep. She might have called it homesickness, but that word was too tame to connote such an absolute sundering from everything that was familiar and rational; nor did it convey any of the fear she felt at being trapped in a world where her survival, minute by minute, was predicated upon quick wits, a ready sword, and social mores about which she knew nothing.

Above her, on the upper floor, she heard Cvinthil snoring softly where he lay curled up with Seena; heard also Ayya, who had finally lost enough of her shyness to talk to the Dragonmaster that night, murmur in her sleep. A horse neighed far off. A cricket had ensconced itself in some crack in the wall and was looking for a mate.

Again she drifted off, and again her dreams were twisted mazes of horror, with a bloody Dremord face staring her down from every corner. He smiled at her from above the gash in his throat, and he turned into Jeff Miller, lying on the hot asphalt of the R-58 parking lot, his blood trailing off and away, a small red river, toward the football practice field where the Guardsmen had knelt a few minutes before.

But reality was no better, for, kicked brutally into wakefulness, clutching the sheets in white-knuckled hands, she came to herself only to be faced with Gryylth, with the uncompromisingly mundane interior of Cvinthil's house: flagstone floor, stone and wicker walls, the coals of the banked fire glowing softly and flickering with stray drafts.

She shivered in spite of the warm night, swung her bare feet off the couch and felt them rustle in the herbs on the floor. Laying the sheathed Dragonsword across her knees, she put her face in her hands, tried to find tears, failed. Sorry, Alouzon. Dragonmasters don't cry. Maybe some other time.

Last night she had dreamed of Kent, too. But last night, as she recalled, there had been something else in the dream, a golden haze that lent even Jeff's mutilated body a fragment of hope, declaring unequiv-

ocally that despair was not the inevitable outcome
of faith. She had to believe that, else the bitterness
that had tracked her throughout the last decade—
visiting her with its fetid breath in city after city,
licking her face with a slimy tongue in Dallas—would
find her here also. Gryylth was horror enough; she
did not need more.

Sitting up, her face in her hands, dozing off in spite
of herself, she willed herself to see it again. There
was wholeness in the world. There was an end to the
struggle. There was a place of safety. For a moment,
it hung within her grasp: golden, beating, a life-hued
glory that beckoned to her with the smile of a mother,
or of a goddess, a chalice brimming with water in a
wasteland. But even as she stretched out an arm to
it, it fled from her sight.

She woke up with the Dragonsword in her hands,
and she pressed the cold hilt to her forehead as
though it could fill some of the aching emptiness she
felt.

The sword was her security and her lifeline. She
clung to it as though it were a lover, and she hated
herself for her weakness. She had killed with that
sword. She should throw it away. But it was all that
stood between her and utter madness, for the thought
of being in Gryylth, and being also helpless and at
the mercy of Dythragor, was intolerable.

Unsheathing the sword, she held it up. The blade
seemed to glow softly of itself. Not a trace of blood
clung to the flawless steel. "It's me and you, guy,"
she said under her breath. "Just stay with me, huh?"

Sleep was well beyond her now, and she sheathed
the sword. Rising, she pulled on the tunic that had
lain under her leather armor. As she donned her
boots, she discovered an interior sheath that held a

small, sharp knife at the ready. Silbakor, or whoever it was that had so changed her, had thought of everything. Such wonderful little lethal niceties.

The door opened silently under her hand, and she stepped out into the moonlit night. Seena's flowers had turned to shades of silver, and the garden vegetables were scattered abstractions in argent and sable.

Around her was Kingsbury, a study in fifth-century British town life, but the strange constellations and the terribly foreign face of the moon above her told her that she could not have been farther from Britain. She sensed that Silbakor had flown through other dimensions, had entered twists of the universe that should not have existed. She might be on the other side of the galaxy. If she were in the same galaxy at all.

The isolation was a spike in her heart. Could the Dragon take her home? She hoped so. And she hoped that it would, soon. How much more of this could she take?

And yet Cvinthil and Seena had, once they had become used to her, entertained her with respect and consideration. They were actually nice people, without the ulterior motives of the Dragon or the sneering contempt of Dythragor. Alouzon Dragonmaster was a guest. Alouzon Dragonmaster was treated well. And Kallye, the midwife, had been all cheer and confidence.

There were problems with Gryylth, to be sure, but it was not all horror. The firelight on Ayya's face had touched the child with all the comfort and depth of a Rembrandt, and she had giggled as Alouzon, laughing, had shown her how to make a mouse out of a scrap of cloth. Seena's shoulders had grown less hunched in the course of the evening, and she and Cvinthil had sung a song for their guest before bed.

She was making friends. She had actually laughed. She had not realized that she could still laugh.

She sighed, breathed deeply of the night. Horse piss and straw, and the darker odors of human sweat and cattle. From the distance there came the yellow smell of wheat, and the brown of fallow land. Friends. Respect. And maybe a chance of finding something that, yes, might promise the return of her soul. It was pleasant to believe that. She began to wonder whether she were, in spite of herself, in spite of everything, beginning to like this place.

In the darkness of the moonshadow beside the house, a darker shape moved, a foot scraped on a stone. Alouzon was in action before she knew it, her bootknife sliding into her hand as she stepped toward the figure. The frost-colored blade was at the man's throat in an instant, its tip pressing into the hollow of his jaw, ready to let the life out.

❖ CHAPTER 7 ❖

❖

IT WOULD BE INFINITELY MORE CONVENIENT, Mernyl decided, if affairs in Gryylth were predicated more upon trust and affirmation than force of arms. As it was, he was saddled with the latter, and the point of Alouzon's dagger was sharp, and her arms were strong.

"I give greetings to the Dragonmaster," he said stiffly, inching the words past her choke hold.

"Christ . . ." He did not understand her oath. Some god, perhaps. Did they really have names, then? "It's you, Mernyl?"

"Aye." The dagger flicked away from his throat instantly, and she slid it back into her boot with a fluid motion.

He stood back, rubbing his neck. "I see you are adapting quite well to Gryylth, my lady."

She winced noticeably at his words, an expression of genuine pain. Mernyl frowned. Alouzon was, even more than he had thought before, very different from Dythragor. "Yeah . . . don't pay me any compliments, huh?"

"As you wish, lady. If I have wounded you, my apologies."

She was shaking visibly. "I've killed too much already, Mernyl. It seems to come damned easy here. I was just starting to find some good things about this place, and now . . ." She bent her head, teeth clenched. "I could have killed you. And without even thinking."

"There has been too much war in this land," Mernyl said gently. "And you did not kill me. You held back. That was a good thing."

"Yeah . . . that's true. I didn't kill you." In the moonlight, her thick hair was silvered, her eyes glinted like steel, and the double-dragon hilt of her sword glowed white and not-white. But her thin tunic made her seem less the Dragonmaster and more the woman, and he found that he pitied her. "What are you doing out at this hour?" she said suddenly.

"I came to see you, lady. Though I am surprised that you are awake."

She half turned away as though she possessed a guilty secret. "I have . . . bad dreams." A very different person.

His staff was in his hand, and he could have, if he had wanted, pried into her thoughts. It quivered in his hand, ready to do his will, but he bade it sleep. Alouzon, he sensed, had already been violated enough. "I, too, have bad dreams sometimes," he said.

He was still rubbing his shoulder, and she noticed. "I'm . . . sorry about that, Mernyl. I hope I didn't hurt you too bad." Her voice nearly broke.

He hastened to reassure her. "It is nothing, lady. Dythragor did much worse this morning in the Hall. If anything, you startled more than hurt me."

"Yeah . . ." She looked around at the town, shadowed by the night. The full moon crawled toward the horizon. "I'm glad you showed up, though. I've been wanting to talk to you, too. You seemed to know a lot about that Corrinian at the Hall."

Corrinian? She was using the Dremords' own terms. Mernyl rather admired her for it. "I . . . know very little, my lady. That he had been badly hurt is obvious, but—"

Her words were blunt. "Mernyl, you're lying. You know. I could tell from the energies around you."

He stopped with his mouth open, the words sticking in his throat as though set about with fish-hooks. She knew. And doubtless she would also know if he lied again. He chose his words carefully. "I . . . suspect a number of things."

"So why didn't you say something at the Hall?"

"You expected me to tell everything?" He wondered if her question were rhetorical, but he was irritated nonetheless. "And who would listen to me? Dythragor? Marrget? Either would gladly use me for spear practice."

"OK, I'm sorry. But what happened? That guy was a mess."

He had not come to speak of the Tree. He wished that he were back at his house, concerned with nothing more than pure magical research. The lethal and untidy aspects of practical sorcery were leaving him dismayed. "Have you ever heard of the Tree of Creation?"

"No. What is it?"

Her answer revealed the depth of her ignorance. What was it not? "You heard mention of the Blasted Heath."

"Yeah. We're going there tomorrow morning."

Worse and worse. "The Tree grew in the Heath. I think, though, that it is no longer there. I believe that

Tireas and the Corrinian phalanx went in and took it."

"Why would they do that?"

"Control. Magic. You saw what happened to that man at the Hall."

"The Tree did that? That's . . ."

For a moment, in spite of himself, he saw a flicker of her thoughts. Blood and torn flesh. Weapons he did not understand. A keen edge of despair that had lingered over many years. He flinched away from the images. Alouzon hurt. His own heart labored for a moment.

"That's . . . monstrous," she said. "What the hell do they want with something like that?"

"The war has gone on for a long time, Dragon-master. The Corrinians are desperate."

"What is it? What does it do?"

"I am not sure." He regretted now, as he had regretted often, Dythragor's ban on the use of magic. In Corrin, Tireas worked under the patronage of King Tarwach. He had supplies, a house, an assistant, and safety. For himself, he lived in fear for his life, and he had a shabby little hut in the Cotswood Hills. He made his own books and grew his own food, but survival left little time for magic.

And now, with the possibility of the Tree being in Corrinian hands, and with puzzles and questions about the very nature of the land thrusting themselves at him from every direction, he was beginning to worry that Dythragor's prejudice might prove fatal to everything.

"As far as I know, it is an emblem and an embodiment of change," he said. "All change. My books are uncertain as to this, and I have only seen the Tree from a distance. Tireas is a brave man for having ventured so near to it." *And a lucky man to have the support of a phalanx when he did.*

"So what happened to that Corrinian?"

"An accident, I would wager. He probably went too near the Tree."

"And they're going to do that to Gryylth?"

"I do not believe that it would profit Corrin to lay waste to Gryylth. Tarwach, for all his skill in battle, would rather pursue peace, and Tireas is not one to squander life. I think . . ." Anything was possible. The land itself seemed to be a tissue of dreams. "I do not know what to think."

"So it's possible, right?" Alouzon's voice was a fierce whisper in the darkness.

"I . . ."

"Mernyl, if you're right, that Tree is staring us right in the face."

Everything was staring him in the face: the Tree added only a single pair of eyes to the throng. "Dragonmaster—"

"Cut the Dragonmaster shit. My name is Alouzon."

"What would you suggest I do? I tried to bring peace once, and I was driven away, and the war continued. At present, my hands are tied. Dythragor will kill me if I am not gone by tomorrow morning. I cannot do anything if I am dead."

"How about on your own?"

"On my own, I can do what I have always done. I can study, I can research, I can wait to be summoned." Actually, Alouzon had a point. If anything was needed at present, it was preparation and understanding. The whole land had turned into a puzzle, and he wondered if what he had found at the ends of the earth could not have some bearing on what was happening here, at its heart.

"OK." She seemed disappointed, but she added: "If I have anything to say about it, you'll be called pretty soon."

"I am afraid that I will be called whether you have anything to say or not."

Her next question took him completely off guard, and he stared at her for the better part of a minute after she asked it. "Listen, this sounds kind of crazy, but you're someone I can ask about this. Is there something here in Gryylth that . . . that heals or something like that?"

She was not talking about the Circle, for she did not even know of the Tree. Besides, the Circle sustained—it did not heal. She had to be referring to . . . something else. Had she seen it herself then? "Why do you ask?"

"'Cause . . ." She shook her head. "Aw, shit. I don't know. I told you I had bad dreams, but since I came here they're not quite so bad. There's something else in them. Like this big gold light that makes everything better. And it's not just a dream. It's real. I know it."

He had seen the Cup again, recently, but it had fled from him as it had before. He had been riding with Santhe, and he had dozed off in the saddle. This time, a woman had been holding it. Her hair was long and dark, and she was comely enough, though her round face was worn. She had lifted her head and looked at him with an expression of both unutterable weariness and illuminated hope.

"I think that there is something in Gryylth like what you describe," he said. "I do not know where." He could not dissemble. He had to tell the truth. The sacramental quality of the vision would have made any other utterance sear his tongue like a hot coal.

In the silver light, her face was lined and marked

with shadows, and with a shock, he realized her expression was that of the woman with the Cup. Weariness. Hope. "I want it," she said. "I think I need it."

Gryylth needs it too. Desperately. Even more desperately than you, Alouzon Dragonmaster. He wondered how he knew that so clearly, without any doubt, but he spoke cautiously. "I believe that the gods give what is truly needed. If what you say is true, then you will have it."

"I hope so. It's . . . right around here . . . I can feel it. I just saw it a few minutes ago. If only . . ." She cast about uneasily, as though it would appear before her. But no: it was only a vision. At least for now.

If there was a physical battle going on in the land between Gryylth and Corrin, there was also another, subtler conflict, one that pitted the complete against the partial. The world ended in an abyss, but that was as nothing to the hollowness that he saw in Alouzon. She was like a wounded thing, like the deformed man at the Hall, achingly unfinished, painfully flawed. But both levels, he knew, were somehow linked, and Alouzon Dragonmaster had come to Gryylth for much more than simple swordwork.

The land ended. The war had arisen from nothing. But the Cup . . . the Cup promised wholeness. And Alouzon was right: it was not just a dream. It was real.

The sky was lightening in the east. "You need sleep, Alouzon," said the sorcerer. "Your journey to the Heath will begin early, and you have no friends among the wartroop, if I judge correctly."

She nodded slowly. He felt, of a sudden, that he wanted to put his arms about her, to comfort her as though she were a child. But he put the thought aside.

Alouzon needed respect as much as that same child needed meat.

"To bed, then," he said. "I will see you again, fear not. And your dreams this night shall be peaceful." He smiled and thumped his staff on the ground, and felt the reality of the night change slightly in accordance with his will.

"Yeah. Thanks."

He made his way back to his room at the Hall, wrapping himself in confusion so as not to be noticed by the guards. But his confusion was inside as well as out, for his meeting with Alouzon had raised more questions than it had answered.

But what answers had he hoped to find? He had gone to Alouzon with no more definite a goal than that speech with her would be good. Therefore, whatever he had found out, he decided, was for the best. He might not understand at present, but understanding, like everything else that was wanted— whether absolution from past horror, or the unity of a golden cup—came only after time.

He slid through the gateway. He had time, he knew. But not much of it.

The sun was just beginning to melt the mist from the eastern downs when the First Wartroop, Dythragor, and Alouzon mounted up for the Blasted Heath. Dythragor scowled when he saw Alouzon supplied with a horse, but he did not press the matter, for Wykla had, with much embarrassment, delivered her remark about the Dremord sword. Marrget had chuckled dryly, and Dythragor had been forced to admit that it was true.

But he held his tongue also because he was pondering the fact that the Dragon had brought her. Regardless of his likes or his dislikes, the Dragon never did anything without a reason. And even then, it did only what was absolutely necessary.

So, it had brought Suzanne Helling to Gryylth. He still resented it.

But saddling up, checking on men and supplies, making ready to leave—the commonplaces of combat and travel—soothed him a little. The sun was bright, weapons were sharp, and if, as he took his position beside Marrget at the head of the twin columns of the wartroop, he felt a flare of annoyance that Alouzon rode on the captain's other side, he nonetheless felt a sense of power, too. With the twenty-one men of the wartroop behind him, he could march into hell itself and not fear.

The thought made him straighten up in the saddle. If what he had heard about the Heath was true, that was exactly where they were going.

The idea that such a place as the Heath even existed in his land was a dull ache that seemed to want to shade into a sense of depression. Something was roiling around in the depths of his mind, thoughts that he wanted to leave unformed, unspoken, but which, invisible and unknown, were profoundly unsettling, as though one's backyard fishpond might harbor a school of piranha.

Perhaps it would not have been a bad idea at all to have brought Mernyl. The sorcerer seemed to know his way around the unseen world. And if he could not fight the Heath with power, at least he might baffle it with his chicanery.

He started suddenly. Work with Mernyl? Never. He was surprised that the idea had even occurred to him. He seized hold of his thoughts, reminded himself of the wartroop, the long road; took a good look at the countryside, the sky. There was no room for magic in Gryylth. This was his land.

He took the reins into one hand, patted the Dragonsword with the other. He had nothing to be afraid of: the stories of the terrors of the Heath were simply stories, tales designed to frighten women and children. They had no place in a man's heart.

But the unformed thoughts roiled in the back of his mind, refusing to be banished by the sunlight and the spears and the swords. He wished that Silbakor were around: some questions needed to be asked. But to summon the Dragon for no other reason than for advice smacked of weakness. No, he would see this matter through . . . himself.

The land rose and fell in soft, feminine curves, and the road was straight and well-paved with stone. The wartroop made good progress, and though Marrget and Dythragor seemed to be interested in haste, they both appreciated the needs of men and animals. Toward noon, they called a short halt by a river.

Alouzon appreciated it also. Everything she had heard about the Blasted Heath indicated that it was no place to enter unrested. Mernyl's expression the night before had hinted at even worse possibilities than she had imagined, and she looked toward their destination with the same queasy feeling with which she had approached her first clash with the police in Washington D.C., when she and others, angry at the continuing slaughter in Vietnam, had protested Richard Nixon's election and the war in what they termed a "counterinaugural".

She had had a purpose then, cloudy and dead-end though it may have been, and it had given her the strength to sleep among strangers in an empty church miles from home, and to face the billy clubs after making a meager breakfast of peanut butter and jelly sandwiches. Today, she had no real idea why she was riding toward the Heath. She had no idea why she was even in Gryylth. Without even the comfort of a calendar or a year, she ate bread and dried meat with the men of the wartroop, washed it all down with warm beer, and cared for her horse.

She found herself grooming the beast with the same inexplicable yet intrinsic knowledge that had characterized her handling of weapons. Unlike her swordwork, though, rubbing down her horse did not make her sick. She erred upon occasion, when she thought too much about what she was doing, but the animal looked understandingly at her. She patted its neck. "I don't even know your name," she said.

Marrget was behind her, and he startled her with his loud voice. "His name is Jia," he said. "A gelding."

She made a wry face. "It figures."

Marrget patted Jia with surprising gentleness. "A fine steed," he remarked. "From the king's stables." He turned to look piercingly at her. "A great honor."

Alouzon returned the look. "I seem to keep getting honored around here," she said, "and it seems to do nothing but get people riled at me."

Marrget grinned slightly, his face softening not in the slightest. "Well, Alouzon Dragonmaster, what do you think of Gryylth?"

"Ask me later. I probably still won't know, but at least I'll have a fighting chance."

He laughed, but he stopped suddenly. "I may come to like you in spite of myself." He shook his head. "I do not know if I will accept that."

Alouzon nodded. To receive anything less than open hostility from these men was more than she could expect. Women stayed at home. Only the midwives, by necessity, had some control over their own lives, and their field of expertise was tightly circumscribed. A woman, Cvinthil had told her, could not sew a garment that might be worn into battle. She might not even touch a weapon. A woman armed was unthinkable. "I understand."

He stood, watching her, as she finished with Jia, brushing out the silky mane until it shone like the sunlight itself. "I heard that you saved Dythragor the other night."

"Yeah . . . I did that."

"A brave deed."

"I didn't want Dythragor to get killed. But I didn't want to kill that man, either."

He looked at her as she had seen him look at Wykla, the youngest man of the wartroop. *What can I make out of this?* he seemed to be asking. *Is this fighting material?* She hoped that she was not.

"We will see how you fare against the Blasted Heath," he said in a tone that she could not read. He turned and strode away to his own horse. His voice rang out: "Mount!"

They continued north, and the road went on, straight and disdainful of the natural curves of the land. Alouzon had seen this before, also: the work of Rome. But no one mentioned Rome here, and she knew that Rome was as far away as UCLA, or Los Angeles. Gryylth . . . there was something about Gryylth.

What did she think of Gryylth? She thought that it looked like a painting by Turner, with the trees and roads and hills arranged just so, a delight to the eye, but a little too well planned. And behind it all was the same sense of unreality that she had noticed before, as though Gryylth, with all its hills and mountains and trees and rivers, were a backdrop that could, at any time, be rolled up to reveal stagehands, props, rope ladders and dusty memorabilia from previous plays.

Marrget, still polite, pointed out and named some of the landmarks. To their left, the Camrann Mountains formed a high curtain wall that separated the central from the western parts of the land. Farther north, the captain explained, the wall split into the even more massive West Range and the placid slopes of the Cotswood Hills.

"Mernyl the sorcerer lives in the Cotswoods," he added.

She nodded, but had hardly heard him. She found the sight of the mountains disquieting. Night before last, in a sheltered clearing in the foothills, she had killed a man.

Marrget excused himself and moved off to speak with Relys. Dythragor had been watching her.

"No need to take it so hard," he said blandly. "You can always bow out. The Heath isn't a pleasant place, and I'm certain someone would be glad to escort you back to Kingsbury."

"I wasn't thinking of the Heath."

He did not listen. "Wykla, for instance. I don't think he's much concerned about his reputation right now."

Involuntarily, she glanced back. Wykla was trailing the wartroop by two horses' length, and his face was set and drawn as though he were riding to his execution.

"He's just a boy," she said. "Do you always have to use boys for your cannon fodder?"

"He's seventeen, and big for his age," Dythragor

returned. "He's wanted to join the First Wartroop all his life, and now he's gotten his wish. He'll make a fine soldier . . . if we can whip some of that woman's soul out of him."

Alouzon bit back her words, managed to say calmly: "You like Gryylth, don't you?"

"Like it?" He smiled as though appreciating the air, the road, the men who followed him. "I love it. I don't have to be bothered with trivia here. Everything's cut and dried. The Dremords are murdering scoundrels, and we have to get them out of the country. And I can do something about it. I can do a lot of things."

"Like killing people?"

He turned in his saddle, his young face lean and defiant. "There's a war on, girl. Or maybe you've forgotten? Funny, you've been bragging enough about that Dremord."

She looked away quickly. "It was self-defense," she said, wishing that she could believe it.

"*Erst commt die Fressen . . .*" He snorted and turned away. "Things aren't what you're used to here. War isn't a matter of politics, it's a matter of survival. You know that now. Why don't you admit it? If we don't kill the Dremords—"

She was not about to let him off, nor was she willing to listen to a lecture. "The whole thing wouldn't have come up if you'd patched up that truce ten years ago."

He was obviously taken off guard. "Who told you about that?"

"Cvinthil."

"And Mernyl, too, I suppose."

He was trying to turn the conversation. She ignored

his words. "So how come you wanted to keep fighting? Mernyl had it all wrapped up, I hear."

"Mernyl was a fool. He actually trusted the Dremords to abide by a settlement, when all they wanted was a chance to entrench themselves even further. The ink on the treaty was hardly dry when they started another battle. If a soldier hadn't run all night to warn Vorya and the wartroops, they would have woken up with their throats cut."

"And so you had your excuse." She tried to settle herself in a saddle that had no stirrups—again, a characteristic of fifth century Britain. "Ever hear of the Tonkin Gulf Incident? It was an excuse, too. Are you really so sure that the Corrinians—"

"Corrinians now! Why don't you just ride the hell on out to Benardis and join up with your friends?"

"Shut up and listen. Are you really so sure that they're no good? That they'll stab you in the back first chance they get? I suppose you're going to tell me now that they're backed by the Soviets, and that we'll find *CCCP* stenciled on all their shields. What about the domino theory, Dythragor? What's going to fall after Gryylth? Laos?"

"Goddammit, you're still the little hippie bitch, aren't you?" His fist was clenched, and he all but shook it at her. "You can't think of anything except your radical philosophy and your effete little games."

She wondered for a moment whether, if he struck, she would parry, and what kind of a riposte she would supply. Could she kill Dythragor? Could she kill anything anymore? She hoped not.

"We were trying to end a war," she said.

"Well, that's what I'm trying to do, too. And it's not going to end until we're all safe."

And what about the Tree? Who was going to be safe from that? The deformed Corrinian goggled at her out of bleeding eyes. "Safe, Braithwaite? Or dead?"

He flushed at the name. "Don't call me that here. Don't ever call me that."

Her brown eyes were flickering with anger. "What's the matter? Does it bring it all too close to home? It's OK if Dythragor Dragonmaster cuts a few throats, burns down a few villages. But simon-pure Solomon Braithwaite would never stoop to out-and-out murder, even if it was fun—"

"Are we talking about murder now? And did you have a crush on Charlie Manson like all the other little hippie sluts?"

She blinked at the accusation. "He made me sick. I cried when I heard about Sharon Tate."

"Oh, sure, you say that now. But you all thought Manson was great. The hero of the revolution. Everyone knew that."

"Everyone knew that? Like everyone knows what the Corrinians are?"

"Dremords, dammit."

"Or shall we call them commies, and get all your fantasies out in the open?"

"*They're not my fantasies.*"

For a moment, she merely regarded him coldly, as though she were pointing him out in a police line-up. She thought of saying something about the Tree, but knew that he would not believe her. Nor would he accept anything whatsoever that had to do with Mernyl. "If Corrin offered peace, Dythragor, what would you do?" she said softly.

"I'd keep fighting."

"Why?"

"I've told you why." He would not look at her. "I'm tired of telling you why. But I'll tell you that you'd better watch your step. I've worked long and hard for Gryylth, and I'll fix you good if you start undermining everything that I've done."

She did not raise her voice, but her feelings were plain. "If what you've been doing is playing comic-book hero, then I'm going to undermine real damn good."

Dythragor's face was a plaster mask. He cantered ahead a few yards, and maintained the distance.

Marrget trotted back to the head of the column. He looked at Alouzon and nodded toward Dythragor, his eyes questioning.

Alouzon kept a lid on her temper. Marrget had not done anything. It was not his fault. Besides, he had been trying to be friendly. "Dythragor's not sure if he'll accept me either," she said. The captain nodded slowly and rode up to join him.

The Dragon had brought Alouzon. Dythragor could not shake that fact out of his mind. It had brought her very deliberately, the implication being that she was going to be his successor. His successor! The idea caught at his heart. It was a grievous betrayal, as though the First Wartroop should run from a mouse.

Marrget fell in beside him, and Dythragor was thankful that his friend was near. Marrget and Dythragor. Alouzon and Mernyl. The sides were becoming clear. The stakes, though . . .

Since Silbakor had brought him here, he had accepted what was asked of him. He had enjoyed it and had grown to love Gryylth. He had never questioned the land any more than he questioned his arms or his legs, or, for that matter, his own existence.

This was a war he could believe in, like Korea. He had not carried a gun there often, being relegated to a desk job in the photo-reconnaissance department in Seoul, but he knew what the fighting was about. Everyone did. And everyone believed in it. It was none of this wishy-washy Vietnam foolishness that was doomed to failure from the start. Alouzon's SDS friends had screamed, sure, but they had screamed because they were worried about their ivory towers, their glass castles, and their precious little student deferments.

He glanced over his shoulder at Wykla. The boy had begged and pleaded for months to join Marrget's wartroop, had even gone so far as to renounce his family. Let Alouzon swallow that! It was a strong, solid civilization she was up against this time, one in which she had no foothold, one which had existed since . . . since . . .

He faltered. He suddenly realized that he did not know. He looked around quickly, as if the rolling land, unbacked by a sense of history, might suddenly dissolve.

Where was Gryylth? What was Gryylth?

Questions. She was even putting her hooks into his own thoughts. Just like Helen.

He said nothing, pressed his lips together, wished that he could vomit Alouzon out as though she were an overdose of some lethal drug.

Marrget was looking at him, his honest face full of concern. "Are you well, Dythragor?"

"Don't trust her, Marrget. Be careful of her."

"My lord?"

"Stay away from her. Everything she says is a lie."

He plainly did not understand. "She spoke of the Dremord she killed, Dragonmaster. She was not lying then. You said so yourself."

"Stay away from her!" His hands were tight on the reins. "You keep on like that, Marrget, you're going to be just like her."

Marrget's gray eyes narrowed, but he remained noncommittal. He turned his face to the distant horizon that was veiled in the soft haze of a summer day.

❖

CHAPTER 8

BANDON WAS A LARGE TOWN, LARGER EVEN than Kingsbury, that stood on the banks of the Long River and commanded the ford there. Like everything Alouzon had seen in Gryylth, it had apparently been inspired in some circuitous fashion by the civilization of fifth-century Britain, and it showed the same earth, stone, and timber fortifications that had characterized the capital.

But whereas Kingsbury had born all the marks of a seat of government at war, Bandon's declared interest was trade. Docks and wharves projected into the river, still navigable even this far from the coast, and flat-bottomed boats were still being unloaded as afternoon drew toward evening. The town wall was stout and well cared for, and Alouzon could see, on the rooftops that projected above it, evidence of paint and gilding.

" 'Tis said you can buy anything in Bandon," said Marrget. He gestured with a wide sweep of his arm. "The road from Bandon runs straight to Kingsbury, as it should. To east and to west the river is a road . . . that is, until it reaches the Great Dike that separates Gryylth from Dremord territory."

"From Corrin?"

He lifted an eyebrow at the name. "It is so. They call their country that."

"So the Corrinians hold the seaport, then."

"Aye, but that is of small consequence. We do not trade by sea."

Cvinthil had said that the world ended in mist. She had dismissed his words as superstition, but now she recalled them. "What about . . . uh . . . other countries?"

"There is Gryylth, and . . . Corrin," said Marrget. "There is nothing else."

His beliefs were a little too absurd. "Is there's nothing else, Marrget, then where did the Corrinians come from?"

"From . . ." He pursed his lips, stared off into the east. "From across the sea."

"So there's got to be something on the other side of the ocean, right?"

"Ships, I think, were dispatched to find the Dremords' home. Once. They did not return."

It did not make sense. Nothing did. "So there's nothing out there?"

"Nothing."

"So how can you—" She caught herself. She was pushing again, and Marrget, though he did not meet her eyes, was frowning. "Sorry, Marrget. I'm being rude."

"It is well, Alouzon Dragonmaster. It takes a brave tongue to admit an error, and yours seems to be . . ." He glanced at Dythragor, who was giving orders to the wartroop regarding camp. " . . . braver than most. I must tell you that I am but a soldier. My king gives me orders, and I obey them. It is not my place to ask questions about the land. Rather am I here to

give advice regarding battle and war." He smiled
thinly. "I am sure you understand."

"Has anyone asked questions like these before?"

"No one."

"Dythragor?"

He shrugged. "No one."

Crazier and crazier. "What about to the north?
What's up north?"

"There is no road to the north, Dragonmaster. The
Heath is there. No one goes to the Heath save fools."
His smile took the edge off his words, and he left her
with a nod and went to supervise his men.

The wartroop camped outside the town walls, bi-
vouacking on thin blankets that did not provide much
of a cushion against the hard ground. Alouzon was
philosophical as she unrolled her bundle: she was so
tired that she could have slept on a slab of granite.

A short distance away, Marrget and Dythragor were
talking to a man who had arrived from the town.
Gravely clad in black, he would have seemed something of a cleric, or a judge, were his eyes not as hard
and bright as a new-minted piece of money. His
words did not carry to Alouzon, but his tone and
gestures conveyed a sense of the official.

Exhausted, she paid little attention until she noticed that he was gesturing at her. Dythragor was
scowling and shaking his head, but Marrget, as usual,
seemed to be objective, as though whatever problem
now lay before him was merely another question of
proper tactics and the right kind of force.

In another minute, the captain was walking over
to her. "Will it please you to enter the town with us,
Dragonmaster?"

"What's up?"

"The Council of Bandon wishes to pay its respects to us." He laughed. "But I think that maybe the councilmen wish us to pay our respects to them. Either way . . ."

"Dythragor doesn't want me along."

"Has he changed?" The captain was in a good humor, as though he enjoyed seeing important people make themselves ridiculous over questions of status and protocol.

Despite her fatigue, Alouzon joined the others. Senon, the man from the Council, regarded her with a mixture of distaste and fortitude. His expression was that of a man who had just bitten into a sour cherry—who had, in fact, expected it to be sour and had bitten anyway. Relys, who accompanied his captain, watched Alouzon sardonically.

In Bandon, Alouzon was once again the object of interest, though, if there was hostility, it was a little more tempered than had been the case in Kingsbury. As a market town, Bandon was used to the unusual, and more concerned with commerce than with custom.

"What do they trade in here?" she asked Marrget.

"Almost everything, lady. Grain from the towns to the east. Across the mountains, the men are fine metalworkers, and they bring their wares across the passes once every six months or so. Gold, silver." He eyed her. "Slaves."

"Female, right?"

"Aye, Dragonmaster. And male too. Though if a man cannot find a wife any other way he is entitled by law to buy one. And sometimes a troublesome woman is stripped of her legal protections and finds herself on the block."

"That doesn't make me feel real good, Marrget."

"You are entitled to know the truth, lady. I am sorry if it grieves you."

Dythragor and Relys were speaking in low voices and laughing at something. Alouzon thought that she caught her name, but could not be sure. She shivered, but though the sun had dipped below the thick walls of the town, the air was warm.

Shadows were growing deeper when Senon brought them to a dark hall that was not made much brighter by a miserly use of torches. The ceiling was high and lost in echoes and the whispers of scuttling rats. At one end was a long table where the Council of Bandon was assembled, waiting for them.

Like Senon, the men were pale, their eyes hard and usurious. They glanced at Alouzon with suspicion, as though she were a contract with a blank left in it, but they ignored her for the most part. Relys they nodded to as though he were an underling. Only Dythragor and Marrget received any marked respect: the Council actually stood when they entered, and their murmured greetings blended with the indistinct scratching of the rats.

"They'd better be nice to us," Dythragor whispered to Alouzon. "We're the reason they're safe enough from the Dremords that they can concentrate on their gold."

"I'm impressed. Are these the nice little bureaucrats you were telling me about at UCLA?"

He glanced at her, annoyed, then went forward to the long, dark table and shook hands all around. Relys waited with Alouzon, plainly irritated that, in this case, he was considered no better than a woman.

"Did you and Dythragor have a good laugh?" she asked him under her breath.

He shifted uneasily. She decided to pry.

"Alouzon Dragonmaster sold as a slave," she said. "Hey, nice fantasy, huh? Betcha she's got a hot little body under that armor."

His reaction told her that she had guessed right. "I heard that you killed a Dremord your first night here," he returned.

"Yeah."

"Very good. Very good indeed."

He could not have hit back with a more painful blow if he had tried. And he had actually attempted to be complimentary.

Dythragor seemed at home with the councilmen, exchanging news, asking about trade and commerce. Again, Alouzon was reminded of politics. Here were the smoky back rooms of Gryylth, and here also were the vested special interests, the businessmen and the rich merchants who, doubtless, had turned the endless war to their advantage.

How much money from the coffers of Bandon, she wondered, had gone into the deaths of young men? By what insane logic did the universe allow a frustrated, bigoted scholar to live out his fantasies on an entire world?

The head of the Council suddenly leaned over to Senon and spoke to him as he jabbed a finger at Alouzon. "You, woman," said Senon as though translating, "step forward and explain yourself. What are you doing here?"

With the authority of the Council behind him, Senon's tone was arrogant and surly. She had heard it before, but she had grown no more used to it. She took a step forward. "I'm Alouzon Dragonmaster."

Again a whispered interchange. "You bear arms," said Senon.

The head of the Council brooded at the end of the table. In the dim light, he looked like a rat. Alouzon found herself hating him. *Have you bought your death for the day? Have you sold your slave?* "Dragonmaster," she said, addressing him directly. "Get it?"

He glared at her, returning hate for hate.

"Show some respect to the head of the Council of Bandon," said Senon.

"How about the head of the Council showing some respect to me? I thought hospitality was a virtue here."

Dythragor broke in. "Don't pay any attention to her, Kanol. She's just that way."

"Teach your woman some civilized ways, Dythragor, if you would, then," said Kanol. His voice was thick and suety.

"*Your* woman, Dythragor?" said Alouzon.

He sidled up to her. "It's easier that way. It's something they understand."

"Understand nothing. I heard you talking to Relys. What do you think you're going to do now? Claim you own me and then sell me off?"

"Will you keep quiet?"

"Hell, no, I won't keep quiet." She stepped forward, bowed curtly. "Gentlemen," she said, forcing out the politeness, "I'm sorry that you've been misinformed. I said that I was a Dragonmaster. I meant that. I'm armed because I'm here to help Gryylth."

Kanol refused even to look at her. Senon replied for him. "We need no woman's help."

"Whether you need it or not," she said, flaring, "you're stuck with it. And if Dythragor is telling you that I'm his mate, or his slave, he's lying."

Dythragor went white.

Alouzon took stock of her position, and did not

like what she found. She had a sword that she did not want to use, and she was outnumbered. She hoped desperately that she could bluff her way out of this, wished that she could simply burn the place to the ground.

"Enough," said the head of the Council. "Tend to your woman, Dythragor, and teach her some manners." He rose abruptly and left the room in a rustle of sable robes. The others filed after him.

Dythragor whirled on her. "That was stupid."

"It was true, wasn't it?"

He did not reply. Turning, he stalked out of the room. Marrget shook his head. "A brave tongue, indeed, Alouzon. But maybe a little rash?"

"I've had it with this bullshit, Marrget. I'm here, and they're going to have to deal with me. If they don't like it, tough. I'm not going to let some anthropomorphic pudding push me around."

Relys clapped her on the shoulder. "Come, Dragonmaster." She could not tell whether he used the title sarcastically or not. From what she had seen, Relys was sarcastic about everything, but she had a feeling that he actually admired her for her bluntness. "Your battle here is over."

They crossed the town through the falling shadows of evening. The streets were deserted, the shops shut up with blank, wooden shutters. The fountain in the town square sounded forlorn and hollow. Alouzon found herself wishing that she were back among the men of the wartroop, hostile though they could be. At least they were a known threat, and if Relys and Marrget were any indication, they were also open to a change of heart.

"This place gives me the creeps," she said softly as they went down an unlit alley.

"Fear not, Alouzon Dragonmaster," said Marrget. "We know the way well."

"It's not that, Marrget. It's like everyone here is out to make a buck, and they'd sell us for fishbait in a minute if they could turn a profit."

"You have characterized Bandon very well, Dragonmaster," said Relys. "My congratulations."

"Relys," said Marrget as they rounded a corner and came within sight of the gate, "is from Bandon."

"Oops."

"Nay, nay, Dragonmaster," said Relys. He was almost laughing. "For once, I agree with you completely."

When they had passed through the gate and were well out onto the fields surrounding the town, Alouzon noticed that they had been followed. Small, dark shapes crept along the grass at some distance, keeping parallel to their course. The sun was well set, the moon not yet risen, and she could make out no detail. She nudged Marrget, and the captain squinted into the night. "Children," he said.

"Girls," said Relys with some astonishment.

Alouzon thought that she understood. She told her companions to go on ahead to the camp, waited until they were out of earshot. "OK, kids," she said. "I'm here."

They came then—in defiance of custom, at risk of punishment—to see such a strange thing as an armed woman . . . a Dragonmaster at that. Awkward with the onset of puberty, yet graceful with the lithe beauty of girls, they approached her only to find themselves speechless, their questions frozen on their tongues, their forwardness turned of a sudden to abject shyness.

"Are you really a Dragonmaster?" said one finally.

"Yeah, for real. Scout's honor and all that." She sat

down on the grass and the girls gathered round. "My name's Alouzon. What can I do for you?"

In truth, she knew. They wanted to watch her, to look at her, to both satisfy curiosity and kindle a dim hope. These were, by no means, all the girls of Bandon, only a small part. Only the ones who would risk a beating to see something they desired. "How . . ." One was tall, broad shouldered, with long red hair that flickered with dull gold in the failing light. "How do you . . . live?"

"What do you mean?"

"Your father: did he let you . . .?"

"My father let me do a lot of things," she said. She wished now that there had been a few prohibitions against such things as stopping tear gas and witnessing murder.

"Oh . . ." The girl seemed disappointed. She had little to look forward to, Alouzon knew. Maybe her husband would be good to her, maybe not. She would have no say in the matter. She was property, just like her mother, just like her sisters who, gathered around Alouzon Dragonmaster this warm summer night, stared hungrily at a banquet from which they were barred.

But, as there was with the the land, there was a sense of the insubstantial to the society. Everything Alouzon had seen had told her that custom had never been questioned here, and that, when it was, it proved less than monolithic.

And it seemed that others besides Alouzon Dragonmaster were questioning.

Another spoke. "I . . . I want to be a Dragonmaster, too."

"Do you want to be a Dragonmaster, or do you just want to be free?"

She struggled with the question for a moment. "I think that only Dragonmasters can be free."

Alouzon shook her head. She, free? Carrying a Dragonsword, able to call upon reflexes and instincts that seemed at times to be more than human, she was as much a slave as if she had been sold on the block in the market square of Bandon. Moreso, perhaps.

"I think I know how you feel," she said. "I don't like it either. I'm going to see if I can't make things a little better for everyone." Would Corrin turn the Tree upon such as these? Mernyl's words came back to her: *The war has gone on for a long time, Dragonmaster. The Corrinians are desperate.*

"Can you?" said the red-haired girl. "I am promised already to a young man, and he is kind enough, but . . ."

"I'll do what I can. I can't guarantee anything, but I'm here." And what was she going to do? Picket the hall at Kingsbury? The SDS had once sent agents out to infiltrate high schools, to radicalize the students while they were still pliable, and she wondered if that was what she was doing now, giving hope where there was really none, fostering an anger that had no resolution.

But Dythragor's arrogance was a nettle in her mind, and she resolved to do something. Trapped though she might be in Gryylth, she had a great deal of work to do. She did not know what she could accomplish, but she was sure it would be something other than what would satisfy Dythragor. Maybe the Dragon had its reasons after all.

"Ho, girls! Girls of Bandon!" It was a woman's voice, calling softly from the direction of the town.

"It is Adyssa, the midwife," said one of the girls.

"Better her than my father," said another.

The midwife came through the half light. "Girls," she said, "what are you doing out here?"

The red-haired girl straightened pridefully. "Talking with Alouzon Dragonmaster."

"What? I have heard of such a person. Senon does not like her at all. Is she here?"

Alouzon stood up, extended a hand to the short, plump midwife. "Right here, Adyssa. The kids are all right, don't worry."

Adyssa's blond hair was a shimmer in the obscurity. She took Alouzon's hand. "I am honored, Dragonmaster. I saw the children sneaking through the gate, and I did not want them to find themselves in trouble, either in or outside of town."

"They came to see me. I guess I'm pretty much a curiosity here."

"Indeed."

Adyssa, like Kallye, wore her hair loose, and her manner was matter-of-fact, but friendly. But the midwife of Bandon had something on her mind, and it went beyond the adventures of the girls that night. A weight, it seemed, had been hanging in the back of her thoughts for some time, and it added a cold edge to her smile.

She eyed Alouzon for a moment, then turned to the red-haired girl. "Gelyya, take your friends back to the town. If the guards challenge you, tell them . . ." She thought, her small mouth a crooked line. "Tell them to talk to me in the morning. I will think of something."

Gelyya's face was serious. "Are you sure, Adyssa?"

"Do not worry yourselves. At need, I can talk more quickly than the best of you."

The girls moved off with a rustle of skirts, Gelyya

keeping track of stragglers. Alouzon heard them talking and giggling among themselves, but Gelyya's voice was subdued.

"I hope nothing happens to them," she said.

The midwife shrugged. "Their fathers are used to their behavior by now. Doubtless, I will have some talking to do in the morning, but . . . well . . . that is what a midwife does, it seems."

Alouzon found it comforting to be in the presence of a woman who did not shuffle about the house and cringe in fear. "Do you like what you do?"

"I am a midwife," she said, as if that explained everything. "I do not recall ever being anything else." The sense of thoughtfulness about her deepened. "Do you?"

Alouzon could not read her tone, but there was more to her question than the words indicated. "I've been lots of things."

Adyssa's eyes were on her, bright and intent. "How? How have you been other things?"

"Well . . ." She was not sure how to take her words. "Where I come from, we're a little more free in some ways."

Adyssa shook her head. "No, that is not what I mean." Her mouth worked as though she were unsure whether to speak or not. "You are a Dragonmaster," she said at last. "You have seen other lands, and you come from a place with different customs. I am sure that you understand much more than I do. That is well, for there are things about Gryylth that I have begun to question, and no one here has answers for me."

Lady, you and me both. "Like . . . like what?"

She expected that Adyssa would talk about the war,

and so she was taken aback by her subject. "This place . . . this world. I fear that there is something wrong with it."

"Wrong?"

"I do not recall being a child," she said. "I do not recall growing up. I have spoken with others, and they share my failing. This seems to me to be other than reasonable."

"I . . ." She herself remembered too much about everything. She wished that she could forget. "You've got a point, I guess."

"Gelyya, too . . ." Adyssa wrung her hands in the manner of someone grateful to at last share a frightful secret. "Gelyya has seen thirteen summers. That is well known, for she is now old enough to be married. But . . ." Her face was a pale shadow, but Alouzon could see her confusion. "I fear you will think me a fool, Dragonmaster."

"No, go ahead."

"I and the other midwives of Bandon have caught all the babies that have been born in our town. But one day, when we met all together to share knowledge, we found that no one had caught Gelyya, nor, for that matter, any of the children of the town who are older than ten years."

Alouzon shrugged. She was not following Adyssa's train of thought. "OK, so maybe your teachers? There must have been other midwives."

"No, Dragonmaster. There have been no other midwives. When we talked, we tried to remember who had trained us, who had given us our lore and knowledge, who had dictated to us the customs that require us to live celibate, to wear our hair so, to abide by certain traditional laws. We could not remember. It is . . ." Plainly, she did not want to speak, but, plainly, she had to. "It is as though the world began ten years ago."

What Adyssa was suggesting was ridiculous, but the midwife's manner conveyed her conviction, and Alouzon could not but believe her.

"There are children who are becoming men and women today," said Adyssa. "*Who caught them?*"

And the Dremords had come from across the sea . . . from lands that, apparently, did not exist. And the war: its reasons and origins were cloaked in an obscurity as deep as that which now veiled Adyssa's features.

The land . . . She had from the beginning sensed something tenuous about it, as though it were not quite real. And Cvinthil had said that it ended in mist.

She rebelled at the thought. "There must be some reasonable explanation, Adyssa. Worlds just don't begin out of thin air."

The midwife shook her head. "Doubtless you think me deranged."

"No, nothing like that. I can't give you a reason for what you're seeing, but I'm sure there must be one. Has this been bugging you for a long time?"

"Bugging me?"

"Upsetting you."

"It has, Dragonmaster. Most of the other midwives are inclined to your opinion, and therefore they give my words little weight. But, for myself . . ." She did not speak for some time. The distant glow of the wartroop's campfires flickered on her face. "I am glad that you have listened to me. The men will not listen."

"Yeah, I know." Alouzon smiled. "They never do, do they?" She felt sympathy for Adyssa, a woman as

confused about Gryylth as she herself. And Adyssa
even lived here. "I wouldn't worry about it. Just do
your work. If I find out anything, I'll let you know."

The blond woman bowed slightly. "My thanks,
Dragonmaster. Gods bless. I hope I have been no
trouble."

"No trouble at all," said Alouzon. Adyssa started
to turn away. "What gods do you worship, Adyssa?"

The midwife paused and shook her head. "We do
not know their names," she said. "We do not know
who they are or what they might be like. That lack
also afflicts me."

Adyssa's worries seemed almost comically strange,
but as Alouzon walked back toward the camp, she
found herself planting each foot deliberately, and with
care, as though she were not sure that the land would
not suddenly turn transparent and dissolve into a
mist.

His name was Turi, and he was unconcerned with
questions of existence or of history. He came weary,
and he came in the middle of the night. His face was
smeared with blood and battle, his lance nicked in
a hundred places, his horse flecked with foam and
sweating with the long miles.

He clattered along the road that led up the mountain to Kingsbury, his commotion startling the dozing
guards out of sleep. He did not care. He wanted to
be heard. He wanted to be challenged. All the better
for his mission.

At his name and his word, the guards on the road
let him by, calling loudly to their fellows farther up
to let Turi pass, that Gryylth, the king, and everything
depended upon it. Fires started up at his passage,
torchlight ruddy in the midnight darkness, and the

sound of weapons being sharpened rang like a shiver all up and down the mountain.

Turi rode on and gained the level ground at the top. The guards at the city gate knew him, and they waved him through.

Shouts started up, shouts of alarm, shouts of confusion. Turi's horse took him to the town square, to the tocsin bell that hung, brazen and ponderous, from its wooden framework. He swung to the ground, seized its heavy rope, and rang it with what strength he had left.

"Arms!" he shouted hoarsely, his throat parched and stubborn. "Arms, men of Gryylth! The Dremords are coming! They have breached the Great Dike! They make for the Circle!"

"In force, you say."

"Yes, my king. In force."

The news was grievous, especially since Dythragor and Marrget were well away to the north, and would have to be sent for. Santhe, too, was off with Mernyl.

Vorya stroked his beard, shaking off the remaining threads of sleep that still clung to his thoughts. No one was going to get very much sleep for some time to come—of that he was sure.

Turi was so spent by his ride that Vorya had ordered a chair brought for him. The soldier was plainly uncomfortable with the seeming violation of etiquette, but he had spoken bravely, telling of the devastating attack that had fallen upon the western end of the Dike at noon the previous day.

Vorya was still considering the news when Cvinthil, still tying the sash of a light robe, entered the Hall at a run. Vorya nodded to him, beckoned him to the dais, and dismissed the councilor's formalities with a wave. Matters were too urgent. With Santhe, Marrget, and Dythragor away, he and Cvinthil would have to make all the decisions alone.

To spare Turi's voice, he briefed Cvinthil himself, admonishing the soldier to correct him as to matters of detail. Turi blinked at the thought of correcting his king, but nodded slowly, listening to Vorya's account in the manner of a common soldier who suddenly finds himself thrust into councils of state.

"They have attacked in force, Cvinthil," the king concluded. "They seem to be making a concerted drive towards the Circle. Tireas has been seen well behind the lines, as have Tarwach and Darham. If ever there was a real fight to the death at hand, this is it."

Cvinthil pondered. "The Circle? Are you sure?"

"Unless they make for Kingsbury, lord," said Turi. "But the course of the attack pushed toward the southwest, and Harrlan, the captain of my wartroop, made his judgment based upon that."

"If Tireas is with them, Cvinthil, I can see that their objective might well be the Circle. Tireas is concerned with magic and sorcery. The Circle would be his natural goal."

"What would he do there, my king?"

"Nay, I know not. If Mernyl were still in our confidences, we might have a better idea, but as things are . . ." The Circle had no direct tactical qualities to it other than that its construction made it defensible. But, like any man or woman of Gryylth, Vorya knew instinctively that the Circle was important, and that it embodied the stability and the continuance of the land.

For a moment, he wondered how he knew that. Mernyl had never said anything about it. He could not remember ever having been told. Strange . . .

Dreams. Broken sleep. He pushed the inconsequential thoughts aside and returned to the task at hand.

He regretted that Dythragor had sent the sorcerer away. The Dragonmaster's decisions in that matter had seemed over-hasty—more the product of personal prejudice than of careful thought—and Vorya was chagrined that he had, through custom, allowed so much of the government of the land to slip into Dythragor's hands when the Dragonmaster was present. Mernyl was gone, and the First Wartroop, and Marrget, and Santhe. Not a good position, not good at all.

"I would raise the countryside, Cvinthil," said the king. "Send messengers to all parts of Gryylth. The muster will be here at Kingsbury, as soon as possible. No later than day after tomorrow."

"What of the garrisons at the Dike?"

Turi spoke. "My lord Cvinthil, the garrisons are no longer at the Dike. Despite their best efforts, they have been pushed back."

"Are they holding at all?"

"Somewhat, lord. They are at least slowing the advance."

"We will send men with all possible expediency," said Vorya. "Cvinthil, what say you? Have you anything to add?"

"The question of Mernyl, my king."

The doe-eyed councilor was right. If Tireas was involved, Mernyl's presence would be of some help, even if he could provide nothing more than additional information. "Santhe will not laugh if he is sent back again to fetch the sorcerer."

"Send someone else then, my king. I only make the suggestion."

But Tireas had not been seen working any magic. From Turi's report, the attack was on a purely mundane level. Sorcery was not involved. And in any battle, Dythragor was the man to have.

"I think," said Vorya, "that we will not summon Mernyl for now. We need Dythragor, and the Dragonmaster will not help us if Mernyl is present."

"What of Alouzon?"

"She is a puzzle. I do not know. Regardless, Cvinthil, Dythragor, Marrget, and the First Wartroop must be summoned. Will you—"

Cvinthil did not wait for the order. "I will go and be glad, my king."

First light was not far off: the sky was graying already. "See if you can convince Alouzon to help us, Cvinthil," said Vorya. "She seems friendly towards you, and I fear we will need her."

"She is a woman, my king. Do you think that . . ."

Vorya shrugged, feeling cold. The Dremords wanted the Circle, and Dythragor was acting willful. He decided that it was time to take a hand in governing Gryylth, Dythragor or no Dythragor. "The Dragon brought her," he said, "just as the Dragon brought Dythragor. I think, perhaps, that we must accept Alouzon Dragonmaster for what she is, for whatever she has to give us."

❖ CHAPTER 9 ❖

❖

THE STAR OF DAVID THAT SANDY WORE around her neck flashed silver in the morning light as she and Suzanne ate bagels, cream cheese, and apples for breakfast. Her roommates were sleeping in, and the big house was quiet except for the gurgling of the coffeemaker and the barking of the dog that lived down the street. Kent as a whole seemed subdued today, a small Ohio college town, nothing more, suburbs and business district shaking off the excesses of a weekend of disturbances—rioting on Friday, burning on Saturday, the arrival of the National Guard on Sunday—trying to rise this Monday morning and face the day with something approaching equanimity.

Sandy had morning classes, but there was time for breakfast and coffee with Suzanne. Since she had left the confines of the dormitories, she had, in Suzanne's opinion, fairly blossomed: an already likable girl becoming more likable with freedom and a chance to set her own schedules and priorities. Sandy worried about being an old maid, but everyone knew that she would eventually marry, and everyone knew also that it would be a storybook relationship, giving and taking throughout the years, loving as passionately as her large heart was capable.

She's going to die today . . .

Suzanne stared at her hands, cupped now around a mug of coffee. How did she know that? There was unrest on the campus, and the Guardsmen had arrived, but everyone knew that they would never shoot at anyone. Tear gas, maybe; bullets, no.

The clock on the wall said eight-thirty. The calendar's days had been crossed out up to the fourth of May. 1970.

1970?

She kept her thoughts to herself, but a kind of a panic was welling up inside her like a spring suddenly flooding into a mine. Sandy was going to . . .

"And then there he was again," Sandy was saying as she laughed about Jeff Miller's latest appearance. *"Just truckin' on by. Just truckin' on by,* he said."

"So, uh, what did you do?"

"What we always do." She smiled warmly. "We fed him."

Outside, the morning unfolded like a yellow flower. Suzanne helped herself to more coffee, feeling her presentiment growing. The hot liquid burned her mouth when she drank. "You going to the rally at noon?"

"I'm not sure. Is it still on? You know, Governor Rhodes read the riot act and everything."

"Did he?"

"Well, I *think* he did."

"No one told anyone in the dorms about it."

Sandy shrugged. "Who is to say, then?" The phrase was an old joke, and she uttered it now in the appropriately mournful tones. But her dark brown eyes were serious.

Suzanne had spent the night penned up in the Tri-Towers dorms, a prisoner of the confused curfew laws that had descended upon both the campus and the city. Along with a crowd of other students, she had been chased into the buildings by a squad of National Guardsmen who were, themselves, apparently unsure of the legal status of the situation. "They meant business last night. I saw bayonets."

"I wish that everyone could just sit down and talk." A crease of worry had appeared between Sandy's eyes. She looked at her watch. "I've got class, Sue. I have to go."

"Don't worry, I'll clean up."

Sandy gathered up her books, slung her purse from her shoulder, pulled a strand of dark brown hair free of the strap. A clock radio went on upstairs, WKSU playing the Doors' "The End."

Sandy waved, smiled, and headed out the door. Cvinthil met her on the sidewalk, and they talked together for a moment before the councilor and the student went off, holding hands.

Suzanne touched her face. She felt cold, in spite of the early spring sunshine, but her perceptions were clear.

I'm dreaming. Aren't I?

She was not sure. Upstairs, Sandy's roommate was rising, stumping across the hall to the bathroom, running the shower, flesh bare to the cascade of water that pummeled it like so many bullets. The Doors were still playing.

"*The killer awoke before dawn, he put his boots on . . .*"

The fourth of May. 1970. Sandy was . . .

Her mind almost blank, Suzanne piled the breakfast dishes into the sink and ran for the door.

"*. . . and he walked on down the hall . . .*"

In contrast to the faint transparency of Gryylth, Kent State was hard and definite. The black squirrels glinted in shades of gun metal as they frisked from tree to tree, and the breeze rose and fell mechanically, predictably, uncompromisingly. Equally hard and equally definite were the Guardsmen, the tanks, the armored personnel carriers—the shadows they cast were solid, as though chiseled out of jet, or burned into the ground.

Suzanne ran down Summit Street, crossed into the campus by McGilvrey Hall, and headed for the Student Union. For a moment, she stood on Blanket Hill, the classic lines of Taylor Hall, columned and windowed, rising up on one side of her as though to defy the burned-out hulk of the ROTC building that lay some tens of yards away. She did not see Sandy.

The clock tower tolled 9 a.m., and the hill was already dotted with students who were enjoying the warm sunshine, spreading both blankets and books, turning the grassy slope into an outdoor study hall. Couples bent over papers, exchanging kisses between pages, and Solomon Braithwaite appeared among them, strolling across the commons with a stack of books about Arthur and an index of Anglo-Saxon place names. He nodded at her. "It's about time," he said, indicating the Guardsmen with a flick of his head.

"They don't belong here," she said.

"After that riot Friday night on Water Street? You bet they do, girl."

"It was hardly a riot. You want a riot? You should look at Watts or Detroit."

"And what do you say about that?" He freed a hand and pointed at the ruin of the ROTC building. "Kids just can't go around destroying public property like that."

"And you just can't go around sending kids off to

get killed in Vietnam. Or is it Cambodia, now, Braithwaite? Nixon better make up his mind, or else."

"Or else what?"

She was silent for a moment. Where was Sandy? Here she was, arguing theory, when a friend was going to die.

How the fuck do I know that?

She brought her head up suddenly, stared Solomon in the face. "Is this a dream?"

He looked at her. "What if it is? What difference does it make?" His tone was that of a father speaking to a spoiled child, indulgent, patronizing. "They'll still bury you all. And they'll do it again and again and—"

"I'm going to be out there at noon, Braithwaite."

"Fine. I'll be at my desk. Or maybe . . ." He looked over at the Guard. "Or maybe I'll borrow an M-1. Or a sword."

He started to walk away, his back straight, determined.

Fade. Shimmer. Montage of trees tossing in the breeze, students gathering on Blanket Hill (Taylor Hall behind them, a suitable backdrop), faces ranging from bewildered to angry, a hand reaching for the rope of the Victory Bell, the Guard in motion. Sounds: screams, catcalls, General Canterbury barking out instructions on a bullhorn, the incessant ringing of the bell. The sun moves in the sky from a shallow thirty-degree angle to a perpendicular ninety.

The rally to protest the invasion of Cambodia was beginning jerkily, interrupted by the efforts of the Guard to disperse it as bullhorn and Victory Bell alternated in discordant antiphony. A jeep cruised toward and away from the students, the guardsmen giving orders, the students ignoring them, tear gas blowing in frothy clouds that choked soldier and scholar alike.

Some were still trying to study. A few walked away in disgust. And there were still others who stood on the brick housing of the bell and shouted about the war.

Suzanne could not hear what they were saying. Distances—or maybe years—separated her from their rhetoric. They seemed little different from Dythragor and his strutting and haranguing, and the end of all of it was the same. The rodent-like burghers of Bandon, the fat generals who planned battles and falsified their outcomes, the swaggering and cocky professional agitators who blew into town to make trouble—no different from one another, really, all having their fingers in the bloody pie up to the elbows.

And then she saw Sandy. She had decided to come to the rally after all, but had given up as the violence built. Wiping the tear gas off her face with kleenex, she stumbled out of Johnson Hall and began crossing toward Music and Speech, where her 1:10 class was held. Her feet hit the asphalt of the R-58 parking lot with even sounds like the ticking of a clock.

Cvinthil, mild and polite, was passing out leaflets at the edge of the crowd. Vorya stood with folded arms, watching from the wide porch around Taylor Hall, his face old and lined, the peace symbol on his headband faded into an indistinguishable blur.

She was about to run after Sandy when a woman with ash blond hair caught at her sleeve. "Do you know me?" she said. "Can you tell me who I am? I caught some of the tear gas a few minutes ago, and now everything has changed." Her manner was formal, as though she were just out of the military, but her gray eyes were frank, open. She did not seem to be suffering from tear gas.

"I . . ." Suzanne peered at her. "I don't think I know you. Have you seen Allison?"

"Alouzon," the woman corrected. "I am looking at her."

It's a dream. It has to be a dream.

Jeff was running in the distance, middle fingers raised toward the Guard. "*Pigs off campus, you mother-erfuckers!*" His dark hair flashed in the clear sun, and he looked too young to be protesting a war. Just a boy, really, playing at growing up, preparing for an adulthood that he would not have.

The woman walked away, and Suzanne was left to struggle alone with this dream that was so much like reality. She bent down, touched the grass that was moist and humid with the growing heat of the day, straightened and watched the clouds of tear gas drifting across the commons as the Guard attempted to clear it of demonstrators. Gas canisters flew back and forth from the Guard to the students and back again, like shuttlecocks in a game of badminton.

It was a period piece she saw, old costumes—from miniskirts to beads and headbands—quaint and faintly ridiculous, like out-of-style clothes in faded black and white photographs of ancestors who looked out from the brittle paper with sternly bewildered expressions, facing a strange technology and a changing world.

Her steps took her away and over the hill, as she followed in the wake of the phalanxed Guardsmen. Seena and Adyssa taunted the soldiers, their clear voices carrying the thirty yards or so that separated them from the uniformed men. The ash blond woman, thin and patrician, stood off at the side. Cvinthil offered Suzanne a leaflet, the doe-eyed warrior bowing courteously as he put the paper in her hand. "For you, Dragonmaster."

"Cvinthil, what's going on?"

He smiled and gestured at the paper, then left her.

She opened it. Save for the outline of a cup, the page was blank. She looked up, stared straight into the muzzle of an M-1, but it was Dythragor's face she saw behind the sights. She heard the click of the safety coming off, or maybe . . .

The firing started, a quick shot, then a pause, then a thin spatter of reports. She saw the muzzle flash as Dythragor squeezed off a round, watched the bullet drift toward her.

A coed with hair the color of amber ran in front of her, took it square in the face, spun around and dropped onto her back, the ruin of her features examining the overly-blue sky critically, as though to comment on the weather.

Solomon Braithwaite walked off, marching with precision. The ash blond woman who did not know who she was came and knelt over the dead coed, lifted her eyes, spread her hands helplessly. Suzanne turned away from the blank horror on her face.

Down in the parking lot, Sandy was dead. Allison and Bill were dying. Jeff Miller was hardly recognizable.

" . . . *and he . . . he walked on down the hall* . . ."

Laughter, humming: the sounds that worlds make when they turn and move. Suzanne stared at the parking lot, knowing that it did not have to be this way, that other outcomes of this day had always been possible, but knowing also with the razorlike pain of certainty that this, this was the way that it was. The other potentials had been left in the past, and the world had ground massively onto this track, this path, and was even now rolling . . .

She wanted the light. She wanted the radiance. In spite of the death, in spite of the uselessness of what she had seen, there was reassurance in the world, too. She believed in the gold light, in the undeniable Presence that had intruded into her dreams before and brought with it a completion that filled the utter lack that had gaped open on this sunlit morning in May.

And as she believed, it came. Softly at first, and then with a growing brilliance as though the sun itself were reflected and redoubled from all sides, it came. Suzanne looked, saw, felt, knew the form and substance of a Cup, of a hand that held it, of the waters that welled up from it.

It was real. More real than Gryylth. More real even than her dream. Weeping, she fell to her knees, stretched out her arms. But the shooting began again, and it vanished into a glory of gold.

" . . . *This is the end, my only friend . . .the end . . .*"

Alouzon awoke with a cry. The early-morning sky was a blank, and Dythragor stood over her, grinning.

"Dreaming of the Heath?" he said.

She was too full of tears and wonder to take offense. "No," she said. "Dreaming . . ." It seemed absurd to say it, but she had to, for what she had seen was both a goal and a promise, and it was good to admit to herself what it was. Despite the horror. Despite the absurdity.

"Dreaming of the Grail," she said softly. "I've seen it. I . . . I think I can find it." The morning unfolded like a yellow flower. "I have to."

But Dythragor had already left, and her words were lost to all save herself.

❖   ❖   ❖

As Marrget had said, there was no road that led north from Bandon, but the way was not difficult. The land was still rolling, grass-clad hills set with stands of trees, watered by streams, and the horses found their way easily.

The morning and the mundane—breakfast, breaking camp, saddling the horses, moving out—did not made her doubt what she had seen during the night. If anything, the continuing anomalies of Gryylth only made the vision more real. In this dreamlike land of dragons and magic, of an incomplete past and (at best) a doubtful present, the Grail was whole, certain. She did not have to know its history or its future: it simply was, forever. And it had appeared to her.

She took that as a hope. Somewhere, there was an end to the shattered existence that formed the chronicle of her last ten years. Somewhere in Gryylth was a final burial of Kent State. She would remember those who had died there—she would always remember—but she would be able to release them from the confines of her brooding mind, from the pit of her guilt, and they, like her, would be able to go on, into whatever existence, whatever life awaited them.

She saw it still, the utter glory of the vision blinding her mind's eye as it had dazzled her in the dream. This was no artifice of a poet, a symbol in service of Christian mysticism. This was, instead, an image that reached well beyond the surface considerations of faith, one that could well encompass a world, or a universe, its healing waters shining forth in undeniable manifestation. It was real. It was wonderful. It was everything.

She realized that she was crying, and she wiped

the tears away with an arm that was bare to the shoulder save for a steel wrist cuff. Beside her, Marrget's face was inquiring. "Dragonmaster?"

"I'm OK, Marrget. I was just thinking about something." She came back to the sunlight and the green fields of Gryylth, pleasant enough all of themselves, as unnervingly attractive as a Come To England poster. And if there was a sense of the unfinished and the unreal about it, why, maybe she could do something about that. The Grail was in Gryylth, somewhere. That was good. That was very good.

She forced an embarrassed smile. "You probably think I'm some kind of witless female."

"For crying, Dragonmaster? Not so. I have myself wept over those lost in battle. There is no shame in tears, only in defeat."

Her smile turned wry. "Or in not being male?"

He started, then laughed loudly. "The Dragonmaster's tongue is as sharp as her sword, I see. If I have, without knowing, offended you, lady, my apologies. You have shown yourself to be of different stuff than ordinary women."

"Marrget, I've got my personal quirks, but underneath I'm just like Cvinthil's wife, or anyone else."

"Nay, Dragonmaster, surely you speak in jest."

"Honest, Marrget. It's just a matter of what you're allowed to do. Even Seena could be like me if she had a chance."

He grew thoughtful, his square jaw cocked, considering. The light was on his face, and his eyes were gray and open. "I have not thought of women in that way," he said.

"They're just people."

He sighed. "You bring strange thoughts to my head,

Alouzon Dragonmaster. I am not surprised that Dythragor is unfriendly toward you."

"And are you unfriendly?"

She had caught him again, and his smile was an honest acknowledgment of his admiration. "I will tell you this," he said. "If by some decree of the gods, I were fated to be woman instead of man, I would that I were a woman like Alouzon Dragonmaster."

Coming from Marrget, the words were a high compliment, and she accepted them as such. But she wished he had said more.

If by some decree of those same gods, she thought, *I had the Grail, I'd see if I couldn't make some changes around here.*

If I had the Grail . . .

They traveled throughout the day, stopping again for food and rest, then pressing on into the afternoon. The day was warm and bright, and the countryside glowed like stained glass, but Alouzon, looking ahead, saw something on the horizon that took all the color out of the land and sky and left them lifeless and gray, like a blight on the world.

Dythragor nodded at it. "The Heath."

She had known instinctively. "Do you have any idea what it really is?"

"What've you heard?" He spoke to her civilly, and his question was actually marked with curiosity.

"Stories," she said, hoping that she could learn a little from him. "Cvinthil said it was a place everyone stayed away from. Marrget said . . ." She caught herself. The captain had joked about fools, but, coming from her mouth, the words would have a different meaning. "Uh . . ."

"Something about fools, was it?" Dythragor

laughed dryly, as though his youthful appearance was only a thin layer that disguised but did not efface Solomon Braithwaite.

"Yeah, he said that."

"Marrget's got brains. I don't know why the hell I set myself up for this one, but if the Dremords went in and took something out, I want to know what it was."

She was almost inclined to say something about the Tree, but decided to keep dangerous names like *Mernyl* out of the conversation. "So . . . about the Heath . . ."

He shrugged, shook his head. "I don't know. Everything else about Gryylth I've pretty much figured out. The war makes sense—" He shot her a glance as though daring her to contradict him, but she kept her eyes on the horizon. "—and the people are the usual mix. But the Heath . . ."

They rode on in silence for some time, drawing nearer to the Heath. She had almost decided that he was going to say no more, but he spoke again.

"I have a hard time just admitting that it's there. It's like . . . like, if it's there, then there's something wrong with me."

Cvinthil had said something similar, but Dythragor's admission went deeper. The councilor of Gryylth did not like the Heath, Dythragor took its existence as a personal failing.

They rode on through a countryside that had appeared out of a painting, toward a region that had been stamped out of a piece of nightmare. And only the Grail seemed real.

"Can I ask you something weird, Dythragor?"

"Let's not start on the war again, all right?" He

seemed resigned, as though burdened with a nagging wife.

"No, nothing like that." She chose her words carefully. "Have you every had any . . . visions or anything like that? While you were here?"

He looked at her suspiciously, as though she had inquired of his vices. "What kind of visions?"

"Like . . ." It seemed faintly sacrilegious to utter a single word about it in the presence of one who would surely not believe. She wondered how she had been idiot enough to bring it up in the first place. "Like . . . of a cup."

To her surprise, he actually considered her question. "What kind of a cup?"

She blurted it out. "The Grail."

He was puzzled, and his face screwed up as though in response to a bad smell. "As in Arthur?"

"Well . . . yeah . . . kinda like that."

He reacted with distaste. "You take your fantasies pretty seriously, don't you?"

"I'm serious. I've . . . I've seen it."

He dismissed her with a snort. "You're even more of a nut than I thought."

But he was plainly afraid of something. In spite of her uncertainty, her question had struck home. "You've seen it too, haven't you?"

Now it was Dythragor who was on the defensive. "Well . . . you get all sorts of dreams once you've been in battle a few times."

"Answer me!"

He was plainly unwilling, but he answered. "Once or twice, back at the beginning. Silly stuff, really. I suppose it came from my work with the Arthurian materials."

"What did you see?"

"Oh, big gold light." He was trying to sound casual, offhand. "And a cup. Water. Like in the legend." He turned to her. "And what did *you* see?"

She did not want to say. It was holy, sacred, not to be ridiculed by such as Dythragor. "Well . . . like that . . ."

"Well, you know my opinion of it."

"Dammit, Dythragor, do you have to deny everything that you don't understand?"

Here they were again, arguing. Gryylth was faced with a Tree she could not talk about, might be helped by a Grail she could not talk about, and might be understood with the aid of a man she could not talk about. And she and Dythragor continued to butt heads over definitions and premises.

He sighed. "Everything that means anything," he said slowly, as though instructing her, "is understandable. The irrational is a refuge for inferior minds. You're a scholar. You should know that."

"Is something like war rational?"

"Back to the war now." He cast his eyes skyward, a henpecked husband.

"Is it?"

"Under certain circumstances, yes," he snapped. "Are you finished?"

She was, and she dropped back toward the rear of the columns. She noticed that Relys was in the process of giving Wykla a thorough dressing-down about some inconsequential infraction of the rules of the wartroop. The boy was near to tears, but he was holding them back mightily. Captains could cry, it seemed, but warriors were expected to be more stoic.

She did not like it, and Relys was being more cruel than she thought necessary, but the wartroop had its

ways, and Wykla had, by his presence, agreed to abide
by them. Still, Relys's actions smacked too much of
the same arrogance and disdain for anything gentle
that so marked Dythragor's behavior.

"You are a woman, Wykla," Relys was saying. "You
have a meek heart and your hands are soft. Why do
you not admit it?"

*And what the hell am I supposed to do about it? Am
I supposed to do anything at all?*

" . . . you should don a gown and keep house with
your sisters. That would suit you well, would it not?"

Once she had protested injustice, and she had been
dubiously rewarded. But she could stand it no longer.
"Relys."

"Dragonmaster?" Since she had challenged him in
Bandon, the sneer was gone from his voice.

"Is that really necessary?"

His hard, black eyes examined her for a minute,
then darted to Wykla. The young man sat stiffly on
his horse, his eyes forward.

"Perhaps not," said Relys. He considered Wykla
for a moment more. "At least for now." He nudged
his horse away and rode off to one side of the Troop.

It was nothing worse than she had seen before on
this journey. Wykla was the new man in the company: he had to expect that his place in the First
Wartroop would be, for a time, constantly challenged.
The others, seasoned warriors with a rough sense of
humor and the sure knowledge that their lives depended upon the cohesion and loyalty of the wartroop, had a right to try him.

They had done the same to Alouzon, indirectly,
watching what she did, listening to what she said;
and they had begun to acknowledge her as a companion who did her share of the work without com-

plaint, who was willing to help without being asked.
But several were looking at her now, curious, perhaps
a little suspicious of this strange woman who had
brought such a different ethic into their world. She
looked back at them, gestured broadly. "Yeah, yeah,
I know," she said, exasperated. "I'm wrong. So sue
me."

They smiled at her admission, and though there
was some head-shaking, she knew that she had de-
fused their fears for the moment. At twilight, when
she, as usual, pitched in with camp chores, they
laughed and joked with her as though she were one
of them.

To the north, though, more menacing with the fall
of darkness, was the Heath. It was a distinct shadow
in the night, thick, turgid, lit by flashes of blue flame.

She pointed it out to Marrget as the men bedded
down. "Aye, Dragonmaster. The Heath. Where we
test our mettle tomorrow." He looked pointedly to
his right, and Alouzon saw that his gaze rested on
Wykla, who was standing guard at the edge of the
firelight. "Some of us more than others."

Wykla seemed quite conscious of his captain's notice, and he straightened up quickly, holding his spear
as though to disprove Relys's words that afternoon.
Get off his back, will you? The other men, she
imagined, were just as frightened as Wykla of what
they would find in the Heath, but experience had
made them more skilled in hiding it. Alouzon said
nothing of her thoughts to Marrget, but after she bade
the captain goodnight, she picked her way among
the sleeping warriors to Wykla's side.

For a few minutes, she stood silently with him as
though joining him in his watch. Wykla eyed her
fearfully for a moment, then, when no criticism was
forthcoming, he returned to his alert stance.

"Everyone's pretty down on you, aren't they?" she said.

Wykla stiffened again, as though fearing some reproof. "I do not understand your words, my lady Alouzon."

"They don't have much respect for you. Neither does Dythragor, for that matter."

"Ah, my lady," he said. "It is well they do not. I am young, and have yet to earn respect. Putting great trust in me would be like a man making a spear out of green wood: he would not know how it might warp as it seasoned."

"How about you?"

"My lady?" His face was young, almost sweet, in the firelight, his amber hair flickering in soft waves.

"Where's your self-respect? Where's your confidence?"

He shook his head sadly. "I have nothing to have confidence in. My heart quails at the very thought of the Heath." He hung his head. "I am ashamed to say such things of myself. Particularly to such a warrior as you, who saved the mighty Dythragor."

She sighed. "I'm sorry I ever mentioned it."

"It is a matter of great honor, my lady."

Alouzon ran a hand over her unfamiliar face. If her transformation had not apparently banished her headaches, she would be getting one now. Still, she hated to think of Wykla walking into whatever the Heath contained with nothing to sustain him. "I'll be beside you when we enter the Heath tomorrow," she said abruptly.

He straightened with a gasp, his face shining. "My thanks, my lady," he said with difficulty.

Absently, she patted his shoulder. "Don't mention it. See you in the morning."

As she sought her place to sleep, she faced north

for a moment. Nearby—disturbingly so—was a blackness that blotted out the stars.

Dythragor had all of Gryylth under his thumb, but the Heath pricked at him: something he could not understand, that he could not control. "Afraid, Braithwaite?" She half-whispered it under her breath, and she knew that he could not hear.

❖ CHAPTER 10 ❖

❖

THE NEXT DAY DAWNED WARM, WITH NONE of the damp mist of the previous mornings. Dythragor took that as a good sign: no matter what the Heath held in store, a bright sun would do much to make it bearable.

But the Heath was a shadow, one that deepened as it was approached, and again he felt the turmoil of unfamiliar and unformed thoughts. He tried to reassure himself with the fact that the Heath, when viewed from a nearby rise, seemed to be only a few miles in diameter, but the sensation of wrongness increased as he rode toward the faint, indefinable change in the land's appearance that marked its boundary.

Marrget called a halt some fifty yards from it, and the men adjusted their armor, settling the thick leather cuirasses about themselves as though expecting an onslaught.

The captain edged his horse toward Dythragor. "Have you a plan, Dragonmaster?"

He eyed the Heath, looking for an enemy, but he saw nothing save for a change in the color of the grass as though a cloud were hiding the sun. There was no indication that there was anything frightful just ahead, but a vague apprehension was rising within him. Flashes of images crowded into his thoughts against his will, and he tried to focus only on what was visible with material eyes.

He wanted an enemy. He wanted something definite, not this insubstantial shade that lay grinning at him like a schoolyard bully. *Come on, try me. Go ahead.*

"I'd say we should keep the men together as much as we can while fanning out to see what the Dremords were doing here."

"My thoughts also, Dragonmaster."

"We don't know exactly what we're looking for."

"That is unfortunate." Marrget's smile was thin. Dythragor had seen the expression before, on the eve of many a battle. "It is difficult to look for something that someone else has already taken away."

Alouzon was trotting her horse toward them, Wykla trailing behind her like a child's pull-toy. Her presence today made Dythragor more uneasy than angry, as though there might be things in the Heath that he did not want her to see.

His horse stirred, almost shied. He looked at it sternly. "Down, sir. You will stay until I say otherwise." The animal quieted, but he could feel its tension.

"Well, lady Alouzon," Marrget said as she reined in. "It appears that you have lasted this far."

She cocked an eyebrow. "I wasn't aware that there was any doubt."

Marrget actually seemed to like her. Dythragor had noticed, too, that the entire wartroop tolerated her presence, not as an intruder, but as a guest. His horse tensed again.

"We can't take the horses into the Heath," he said abruptly.

Alouzon looked out at the shadow on the land. "Yeah. Jia's telling me he doesn't like this one bit."

Marrget agreed. "The animals are wiser than those who ride them. But we must to the Heath. If we must go on foot, then . . ." He shrugged. "I have no objection."

"Someone should look after the horses," said Dythragor.

"I seen no reason to split my wartroop," said Marrget quietly. "The horses have been trained to take care of themselves."

"What about Dremords in the area?"

"There are none. My scouts last night found a camp that has been abandoned for some time—doubtless a relic of the previous expedition—and there are no other traces."

Alouzon was nodding. "Dythragor is still looking for an excuse to leave me behind. It won't work."

"She can't come," he said quickly. "I . . ."

He had, he realized, been speaking too loudly. He caught himself and forced his hands to relax on the reins.

"I am the Dragonmaster," he said evenly. "I forbid it."

Alouzon was studying him critically. Damn, she seemed so much like Helen at times. There was no resemblance between the two, but their expressions . . .

"I'm a little old for that, Dythragor. This isn't a candy store."

"There'll probably be violence."

Her face hardened, and her voice went cold. "I've seen violence, thanks. I can handle it."

"Look here, girl . . ."

Marrget lifted a hand. "It is not well to enter a battle with ill will among the warriors," he said. "I must be so bold as to suggest that the two of you resolve your difficulties for now. I do not wish to endanger my men needlessly."

Dythragor flared. And was Marrget bucking him now? "You forget who you're speaking to."

The captain's gaze was level, uncompromising. "I know very well to whom I speak. Please do not cause me to forget it."

He was speaking formally, and there was a hint of danger in the fact that he had to constrain himself with studied politeness. Inwardly, Dythragor cursed Alouzon for having been the cause of the falling out; but he swallowed his anger, turned to the other Dragonmaster, and extended his hand.

"Alouzon," he said. She was stealing everything else from him; at least he could take the initiative in this.

She reached out and took his hand for a moment. He was startled to find that her grip was firm, strong, direct—not at all what he had expected. "OK, Dythragor. There won't be any conflict between us in the Heath."

He noticed that she had specified the location, and he grinned to show her that he understood. "None."

Marrget nodded. "It is well."

In the still air, Marrget's voice sounded flat and lifeless as he gave the order to dismount. The horses trotted off as though glad to distance themselves from the Heath. The captain watched them for a minute, then signaled the advance.

Again contrary to Dythragor's expectations, there was no definite border to the Heath. Entering it was, at first, like entering a cloud's shadow: a certain dullness came over the colors of the grass and trees. The land was still rolling and soft, but its outlines became blunted, indistinct.

Dythragor felt vulnerable on foot, as if being in contact with the ground exposed him to . . .something. He half expected that the grass beneath his boots might suddenly turn into mist, dissolve, and pitch him headlong into darkness. Or smother him in fetid vapor. The others obviously felt similarly, for in spite of the plan to fan out, they stayed close together, hands on sword hilts.

He looked up. There was no trace of the sun: the sky was a milky whiteness without feature, an opalescent swirl of half-seen, half-felt shapes that corresponded disturbingly with the thoughts that he was trying to hold down. Helen's face swam down at him suddenly, and he cringed and almost drew his sword.

Alouzon was looking at him. "What is it, man?"

He shook his head violently and pushed on, resolved to keep his eyes off the sky.

There was an undercurrent of fear among the men, a knowledge that they were in a place where they should not be, and the quiet, businesslike manner of professional soldiers changed in a few minutes to a furtive stealth.

They worked their way over the next rise and found that the grass gave way to a plain of fine sand that stretched off into the distance until it was lost in the milky haze. For a moment they stood at the crest and looked out. No one seemed willing to take the first step.

He heard Marrget talking to Alouzon, his voice a bare whisper. "I have heard it said that the Heath changes, that two men entering separately will find a different terrain. They might not even find each other."

"So how are we supposed to find out what the Corrinians did here?"

Corrinians again. That little bitch.

"I know not. We can but look, Dragonmaster."

"Yeah . . . I know . . ."

Marrget started down the slope, and the others followed. Dythragor fought with himself for a moment. Helen . . . He could not shake the thought that she was around here, somewhere, waiting for him. Maybe Silbakor had brought her to Gryylth, too. What was going on?

Alouzon murmured something under her breath, stooped, and lifted something from the sand. A spear. Parts of it, though, seemed curiously mismatched, as though the shaft was half of wood, half of something that resembled glass, with a curiously reptilian appearance overall. The tip was patched with fur that sprouted directly from the metal.

Dythragor was reminded of the deformed Dremord at Hall Kingsbury. The man was himself a crazy quilt of textures and substances.

"The style is Dremord," said Marrget, examining it gingerly, as though it held some subtle contagion. "I cannot speak for its construction, though."

"It's like that man at the hall, Marrget," said Alouzon. "Maybe this was his spear."

"That could well be."

Alouzon's eyes had narrowed. "What . . . finally happened to him, Marrget?"

The captain shook his head. "He spat blood and died shortly after you saw him, lady."

Dythragor kept his eyes off the spear. "Come on, let's go. We've got things to do. The next thing I know, you'll want to bring Mernyl into this again."

She seemed about ready to say something, but he pushed past her and stalked off across the sand. The images that fluttered across the sky persisted, so he kept his eyes downcast.

He grimaced with contempt. Clouds. If that was all the Heath had to offer, then its reputation had been greatly exaggerated. But he felt something change behind him, and when he turned around, he discovered that the endless sand was now pocked with contorted rock formations. A desert landscape. And when he turned back, he found that it lapped all the way around him, as though the scenery had prudishly waited for his back to be turned before it changed.

He could not see the wartroop or Alouzon. He was alone in a desert, abandoned by those he had thought were his allies.

"Where the hell are you?" he called. He fancied them hiding behind rocks and bushes, snickering at the sight of the great Dythragor wandering without companions. And, true, one of the scrubby trees rattled as though someone were concealed in its leaves.

He went boldly up to it, kicked the trunk with a booted foot. The tree screamed, and he found himself confronting a face inches from his own, one that smiled and mocked his predicament. He knew her. She had smiled that way before, when she, with a quick court injunction, had barred him from his own house, keeping his books, his papers, his livelihood out of his grasp, laughing as he tried to argue with the sheriffs.

"Helen!"

She spat in his face, and in a moment, his sword was in his hand and he was swinging at her, hacking at the tree, sending chunks of gray leaves and splintered bark to one side and the other. Imprisoned like a dryad within the wood, Helen bled freely, but still she smiled.

"Dythragor?"

She was standing behind him now, wearing armor like his. A sword was at her side. No matter: she would have no chance to draw it.

He rushed at her, swinging.

"Dythragor!" she cried, but he came on. Hesitating only for a moment, she slid to one side and slammed an elbow into his stomach.

He found himself on his back, struggling, with Alouzon on top of him. She was holding him down with her weight, pinning his wrists with her manly grip. Behind her, Marrget and the wartroop watched, incredulous.

"Get off me, woman," he shouted.

"Whatsamatter, Dythragor? Can't stand to be on the bottom?" She was angry, and he could not blame her.

"Get off of me." He had the feeling that he had just made a fool of himself in front of everyone, but it had all seemed so real. Helen . . . Helen was out there. He had seen her.

Alouzon let him up, and Marrget helped him to his feet. "My God," Dythragor said, passing a hand over his face. "I can't understand that."

"It is the Heath," said Marrget. "It always attacks the strongest first." There was a stony light in his eyes. "So I have heard."

Dythragor looked at them unsteadily. Disgraced. If Alouzon had not been present, he might not have minded so much. But to have *her* see. To be bested by a woman . . .

On the dim horizon, a darkness gathered . . .

. . . came closer . . .

Dythragor felt a chill wind start up, one that was pushed along by the wave of mud and slime that was suddenly towering above him like a swamp set on its edge. Stagnant water, moss, the blackened outlines of rotting trees, the flicker of marsh-lights, he saw them begin to fall on him, saw also, in the depths of a rank pool, the image of Helen's face.

With a weight as of oceans, he was dragged down into darkness, his nose and mouth plugged with muck. Gasping at fleeting pockets of air, clawing at the ooze, he saw her looking scornfully at him as she packed the last of the things awarded her by the pre-liminary settlement. The masking tape crackled and sucked as she peeled it off the roll and taped the boxes shut, and her eyes bored at him as though from out of a vat of soured love now fermented into rage.

It was a calculated, seasoned hate, one compound-ed of all her intimate knowledge of his faults, his failings, his habits, his inadequacies in bed—every-thing that only a woman who had lived intimately with him could know. And he had no place to turn. The courts were against him, his friends shunned him, his family politely declined to discuss such a tawdry thing as divorce. Only his lawyer—well paid—lent a sympathetic ear.

While outside the walls of his house, beyond the masonry of the court building, the country was going to hell, crazed students fighting with the forces of law and order, tear gas frothing across the campuses like clouds of yellow poppies.

But he was not powerless: he had the Dragonsword.

Lifting it high over his head, he waded through the slime that rose about his thighs, prepared to settle the matter at last. But the sword was growing unspeakably heavy, and, against his will, it dragged itself to the ground.

He stared. His hands were weak, womanish. Long nails, delicately manicured. Bangles on his wrists.

In his left palm was the bottle of pills that he had emptied one night when the house itself had seemed empty and the Santa Ana winds had whined dryly through the palm trees in the front yard. Everything had reminded him of Helen, and of what she had said, and of those kids just standing there, getting shot down . . .

And he . . .

"Go on. Take them," said Helen. "That's what you wanted, wasn't it?"

"They . . . they didn't kill me."

"That was a mistake. You wanted to die, didn't you?"

Trembling, he uncapped the bottle, poured the red capsules into his hand. More than enough to kill, but he had, comatose, retched up enough so that he had lived. "I lost everything . . ."

Helen came closer. "Do it, Sol. Do it right." He hesitated. "Damn it, Sol, you never could follow through on anything, you're just a weak little spineless—"

He threw the pills in her face, backhanded her. She writhed away from him, her face stretching into serpentine angles, her body assuming the form of a dragon.

It was not anything like Silbakor that he was now facing. It was a White Worm, its pallid scales nacreous in the swirling fog that surrounded it, its eyes a dark glow that shaded beyond the visible spectrum and deep into the ultra-violet. Darting at him, it twined its length about his legs, mired him in its own flesh. It stank abominably, and the sword dropped from his hands as he gagged.

"All right, Mr. Braithwaite." Old Markasham was the chairman of the department, and he had a grudge against this young man who was so belligerent in his opinions about Arthurian Britain. "Suppose you tell us why you hold such . . ." He glanced at his colleagues, and they chuckled. " . . . curious views." Here was the bad little boy of the archaeology department, come to take his doctoral orals. They had him right where they had always wanted him, and they were amused.

You spread your legs and you take it, boy. You want your precious little Ph.D? You do exactly what we tell you.

(And Marsha protested weakly as he fumbled with the fastenings of her prom gown. Her protests, though, turned to laughter when he lost control and came before he could get his pants down. She laughed at him. His father never tolerated such behavior from his mother: she had black eyes to prove it.)

"Bitches!" He found his sword and swiped at the White Worm. Its head popped off with a sound like a champagne cork . . .

(The relatives toasted the newlyweds, eyes hard and greedy for heirs, intolerant of divorce. A semen factory, that was all he was. He would show them all, would see them in hell before they got any descendants out of him.)

A little distance away, Marrget and the wartroop were facing off against a dark, woolly thing with a mouth like a dribbling, crimson slash. Their images wavered and shifted as though reflected in an unquiet pool, but he heard Marrget barking orders.

With an odor like musk, the shapeless thing advanced on the wartroop, its slit of a mouth widening to show icy fangs dripping with venom. "Marrget, I'm coming!"

But the White Worm's body was still entwined about him, and he could not budge.

"Dr. Braithwaite."

He turned to find Suzanne Helling seated at a desk beside him. A pile of books was spread out, open, before her.

"Suzanne! Help them!"

"I have some questions to ask you," she said calmly. "As your successor, I think I have a right to know. This material you wanted me to get from Special Collections: what does it have to do with Gryylth?"

"Gryylth? Why, nothing. Nothing at all."

(And the woolly thing fell on one of the men, crushing him, leaving his broken body slimed with mucous and musk. Alouzon was rushing at it, the Dragonsword bright in her hand. Suddenly aware of her, the creature fell back, but her sword leaped out and wounded it. Blood flowed freely as blank, filmy eyes peered from the rent.)

"That's all I wanted to know," said Suzanne as she made a note. "Just as I expected. Find the Tree."

"What tree? *What goddam tree?*"

"Ask your wife."

He stood, goggling at her, wrapped up to his groin in dead dragon. Suzanne faded away, leaving the books behind on the desk.

(And Marrget and the Troop battled the creature, led by Alouzon. The swords of the men seemed to do it no harm, but Alouzon's blade, wielded by a woman's hand, cut deep.)

Maddening. Just like Korea: tied down to a sterile desk job, going over photographs with a jeweler's loupe while the real action went on miles to the north. And then MacArthur wanting to invade and the petty bureaucrats holding him back. When was Solomon Braithwaite going to squeeze the trigger of an M-1?

Bit by bit, he extricated himself from the lifeless coils, hacking with his sword when he was unable to untie the knots. He ran for the wartroop and plunged headfirst through the shimmering wall. His vision exploded into yellow and silver sparks, but when it cleared, he was back on the sandy plain.

Alouzon was holding the mass of fur away from the wartroop, driving it back. "You can't have them," she was screaming. "I won't let you have them."

Dythragor made to help, but Marrget caught his arm. "What the hell do you think you're doing?"

"Our swords are useless, my lord," said Marrget. "Only Alouzon Dragonmaster can oppose the beast."

"So she's made a woman of you, too," he snapped. "Ever since she came here you've been sweet on her."

Marrget stepped back from him suddenly, his eyes hot with the insult. "By my sword," he said, "if you were not Dythragor Dragonmaster, I would have your life for that."

Turning, he took a running start and threw himself on the creature that was trying to catch Alouzon in a flow of impure blood. He succeeded only in deflecting the attack onto himself. Moving to save him, Alouzon tripped, fell.

An unfamiliar voice shouted: "Forward!" Stupidly standing without anything to do, Dythragor saw Wykla lead the wartroop in a charge. The men surrounded the beast, waving swords, distracting it as Alouzon gained her feet and swung. The thing opened up with a reek as of rotting vegetables.

Dythragor stared up at the milky sky. He felt numb. He could hardly think. Above him, he saw Helen laughing and he looked away. A strange woman with long, dark hair and robes of silver and sable caught at her arm. "Come on," she said softly. "It's time to give this up. You have to. It's killing you."

"Who are you?"

"I'm your wife. Come on. Let's go."

His wife? "Leave me alone. You want to feed me those pills again?"

Her face was gentle, almost virginal. She looked vaguely familiar, but she was not Helen. "I can learn, you can learn. Come."

He shook her hand off, and she left without protest. He sat down and put his face in his hands, forgetting, for the moment, his sword and his duty.

The sound of battle subsided, and he looked up and saw that the woolly thing was gone. Alouzon was getting up after another tumble, rubbing a shoulder. Two men were dead. Another lay injured, tended by Wykla.

The sky showed him pictures, but he did not understand them. His memory was confused, and he hardly knew his own name. Solomon? Dythragor? What was he? How many things had he been since he had first drawn breath? Since he had first heard his parents arguing through the muffling presence of a closed and locked door? Since he had sat at a desk in Seoul, wondering what it would be like to kill a man? So many things to be. So tiring.

He rose and walked toward the others, his dragging

sword furrowing the dry sand with its point, a meandering track in a featureless waste.

Alouzon saw him first, and noticed the glazed look in his eyes. Marrget glanced at him, scowled, and went to help Wykla with the wounded man.

"Marrget, he's hurt," she said, calling him back.

"Hurt? My lady, there is not a mark on him."

"Maybe not, but he's screwed up pretty good." She stopped Dythragor and searched his face. "Dythragor?"

"Why did you laugh at me?"

"Dythragor, come out of it." Her shoulder was bothering her, and the musk of the woolly thing was still a rank odor at the back of her throat. She was not inclined to be gentle with him, but she held her temper in check. "Come on, man."

"And the mud. You did it, Helen. You did it all."

She shook her head, frustrated. Gryylth defied explanation, but she was beginning to put together a few pieces of Solomon Braithwaite's personal history. A bad marriage, a messy divorce. They could happen to anyone, but he seemed to take them more personally than most.

Marrget handed her a skin of water and she splashed some over Dythragor's face, giving his cheeks a few quick slaps for good measure. Slowly, he came to himself. "What tree?"

The question chilled her. "Look, Dythragor, what's your problem?"

"I saw you. You told me about a tree. What did you mean?"

"I . . ." She hesitated. Dythragor had been acting hopelessly irrational for the last few minutes, and she had no intention of setting him off again. "All I know is that you fell down, out cold, and then something that looked like an MCP's nightmare jumped up out of the sand. Now you're asking about a tree." She looked at Marrget. "The Heath, I suppose."

The captain's anger had cooled. "The Heath, my lady." He turned to Dythragor. "My apologies."

"No, don't apologize," Dythragor said quickly. "Don't do that. I don't know what's happening out here, but you didn't do anything wrong."

Alouzon used some of the water to rinse the musky slime from her arms. She was mildly surprised that she had not been hurt worse, for the creature had fallen on her with all its weight. It had crushed one of the men with the same action, but she had come off with nothing more than a sore shoulder. The effect of the Dragonsword, more than likely.

The wounded man's injuries were minimal: he appeared to have had the wind knocked out of him, nothing more. In a few minutes, he was on his feet, a little shamefaced, but essentially well. The dead men had been stretched out together, their sightless eyes regarding the shimmering sky.

She turned away, tried to compose herself. The coed in her dream had looked at the sky in much the same way.

"Shall we go on?" said Marrget.

"This is a bad place," said Dythragor. "The wartroop should stay together. Marrget and I will search further."

"The lady Alouzon appears to have some power here, my lord. Perhaps it would be wise . . ."

In response, Alouzon nodded and stepped beside the captain. Dythragor was outnumbered, and he nodded curtly.

"Relys, you are in command," said Marrget, and the three moved off, swords drawn. The air was fairly clear at ground level, and they had no difficulty keeping the wartroop in sight.

Alouzon assumed that they were moving toward the center of the Heath, but without landmarks, she could not tell for sure. They might have been anywhere, headed in any direction. Perhaps it did not matter. The Heath was a convoluted anomaly in an anomalous world: nothing prevented it from violating physical law even more flagrantly than the land that contained it.

They came suddenly upon a pit that gaped in the sand like a lanced boil. It was perhaps ten feet across and as deep as a man was tall, but it did not seem at all natural, and when Marrget found a spade lying nearby, Alouzon knew what it had once held.

Dythragor walked around the perimeter of the pit. He seemed distracted, almost dizzy. If Alouzon did not know of his chronic addiction to bravado and glory, she would have suspected that he was on the verge of running away.

"You mentioned a tree," she said cautiously. "Did you have anything . . . specific in mind?"

"I saw you at school. You said: *Find the tree.*"

"It's . . ." She examined the pit. Mernyl had told her something about the Tree, and everything she saw was fitting the pattern. "It's about big enough to hold a tree."

"A tree of fair size," said Marrget. "But in this desert place?" He lifted his eyes to check on the wartroop, and Relys raised a hand in salute. Satisfied for the moment, he looked to Dythragor, waiting.

Dythragor shrugged impatiently. "We can assume that. But don't ask me what they intend to do with it."

Alouzon risked a little more. "Maybe we should ask Mernyl about this. He . . . might know something."

His response was as she expected. "You can leave that charlatan out of this affair. This is too important."

"Maybe it's too important to leave him out of it," she insisted. "That night we spent in Kingsbury, he told me about something called the Tree of Creation. He said that the Tree was responsible for what happened to that Dremord back at the Hall."

"Grails . . . and Trees now. What did I tell you about the irrational?"

The Heath around her, and two men dead by a *vagina dentata*: she nearly laughed out loud. "Maybe you haven't noticed, Dythragor, but this entire country runs on irrationality. Magic. Hocus-pocus. Call it what you want."

"Give me a break."

She decided to risk it all. "Can you tell me why everyone speaks English here?"

He stood, stunned. "English?"

"English is an Indo-European language." She punched out the words like a drop forge. "It took a special set of circumstances for it to evolve. But everyone speaks it here in Gryylth, and it's fairly modern English at that. You call that rational?"

"We don't bring magic into this. Leave it. Mernyl is an idiot, a stupid man who nearly sold Gryylth down the river. There's no room for him here."

"Come off it, Dythragor," she said. "I backed down before because I was new here and didn't know enough about the place. But not now. This place is crazy down to the bedrock. Nothing fits. Everything I know tells me that it couldn't have evolved naturally." She stopped, thought, turned to Marrget. "I mean no insult to you, Marrget. This is just a matter of theory."

He shook his head. "Do not stay your words for me, lady. I do not understand most of them in any case."

She went back to Dythragor. "I mean what I'm saying. Have you looked at your sword?"

He glanced at it. "So?"

"It's Celtic, straight out of fifth-century Britain. You can find its mate in any textbook on the subject. Where's Britain from here, Dythragor?"

Breathing hard, he sheathed the weapon with a sharp clang. "Leave it. Drop it. I don't want to hear it. Leave Mernyl out of it, leave your damned academics out of it, leave your antiwar sentiment and your hippie philosophy out of it. Dammit, this is Gryylth. This is *my* country. The only thing standing between you and a job scrubbing pots is the Dragon's word, and if you keep pushing, that won't hold."

The Dragonsword was heavy in her hand. Something more than Silbakor's word kept her from the scullery. It was a satisfying knowledge, but she was ashamed to think of it.

"OK," she said. "Fine. We found a pit that might have held a tree, and we've got a couple of corpses. What's next?"

"The Dremords have something in mind," said Dythragor. "They'll probably attack soon. We'll return to Kingsbury and gather the wartroops. We'll strike first." He looked at her, jaw set, eyes unyielding. "Do you have any objections?"

"You know I've got objections," she said. She turned and started back toward the wartroop, her spine straight and, she hoped, accusing.

❖ CHAPTER 11 ❖

❖

THEY WENT OUT THE WAY THAT THEY WENT in, but they went out with two bodies. Marrget himself hoisted one of the corpses onto his shoulders and, his back unbent, walked slowly along, leading his wartroop through the plain of sand. Their footsteps were still visible, leading impossibly off into what seemed to be infinite distances, but before they had traveled fifty yards, the dull grass and trees of the Heath's outskirts were once again about them, and the horses were in the distance.

Dythragor walked slightly apart, as though to demonstrate that he was not afraid of anything more befalling him. But he was acutely aware that the men of the wartroop were not concerned with him. Their thoughts, instead, were on the companions that they had lost, and on Alouzon, who had done her best to save them all, while Dythragor . . .

He kept his eyes straight ahead, feeling resentment and grief behind him, recalling Marrget's words: *It is important to remember that we deal in lives, Dragonmaster, else we might be inclined to squander them uselessly.*

What had he expected to accomplish, he wondered, in the Heath? If his goal was to waste lives, then he had succeeded very well. If, however, he had wanted to help Gryylth, he had failed miserably. Maybe he should have questioned Mernyl: the wartroop might have been spared a trip and the loss of two of its warriors.

"He should have told us," he muttered. "Why didn't he tell us at the Hall?"

Unthinkingly, he mounted his horse, but Marrget informed him that their start would be delayed while the men of the wartroop buried their comrades. The captain spoke carefully, but did not attempt to conceal his feelings about the unnecessary deaths.

Dythragor gave no indication that he noticed. He nodded curtly and remained on his horse, apart, during the half hour or so that it took to raise mounds over the bodies.

He noticed that Alouzon was helping, and that her help was welcomed.

When the graves were done, Marrget and the rest stood around them, bowed their heads briefly. The captain unsheathed his belt knife, made a shallow cut in his wrist, and let the blood fall on the graves. "Awake and live again someday," he said.

"Awake and live again," repeated the men.

Lives unvalued were lives wasted, but if the actions of the First Wartroop were any indication, then these two lives had not been wasted.

The wartroop mounted. Dythragor turned his horse away and moved out across the rolling land. His head pounded heavily, as though he were keeping himself going on one hour's sleep and three pots of coffee. He had slept soundly the night before, but the Heath had drained him.

"Trees," he snorted. Maybe he should have listened to Alouzon before he dismissed her idea. Now, if he asked her directly, he would be admitting that he was wrong. He could not face that. "What the hell do they want with a tree?"

Marrget was riding alongside now, his gray eyes scanning the horizon. His face was set, guarded.

"What do you think, Marrget?" he asked suddenly. "Do you really think there was a tree growing in the Heath?"

The captain glanced back at the twin columns of the wartroop, his expression that of a father reading battle reports in the morning paper, seeking news of his sons. "I admit that it does not seem likely that a tree would grow there. Still . . ." He looked back at the wartroop again.

Alouzon was at the end of the columns, riding beside Wykla. She would not hear. "Marrget," Dythragor said with some hesitation, "I'm sorry about the men. If I had known that it was going to be like this, I would have gone alone."

"We would not have known of the Tree if you had." Marrget was trying to ease the blame, but his words stung. With a brief nod, the captain moved off, slowed, and began speaking with his men, making his way down the columns slowly as the wartroop continued southward. Dythragor could not hear what he said, but his tone held a manly gentleness, and he supposed that they were remembering the fallen.

Awake and live again . . . What did that mean? They did not even know the names of their Gods, and here they were, praying for an afterlife. He himself had never given much thought to such things—Helen had been the religious one—but he had always supposed that something happened after death. But here in Gryylth . . .

He had no idea. He had never asked.

His hand went to the hilt of the Dragonsword. Celtic. Fifth-century Britain. Alouzon was absolutely right. Now that she had pointed it out to him, he recognized it well. And he was recognizing other things, too: the armor, the designs of boss and buckle, of saddle and spear, even the double dragons of his own sword hilt, were in the best British style, with just a hint of Roman flavoring to it.

"I'll figure it out, Alouzon," he said softly. "There's an explanation for all this. I know there is. And you can take your magic and shove it up your cute little ass."

Alouzon was tired, and as she rode, she stared at Jia's mane as though she could lose herself in sleep amid the sun-warmed hair. Burying the men had reminded her of the Dremord she had killed—killed and left unburied. She and Dythragor had not even taken the time to raise a heap of stones over him, and, in this strange place, she wondered if it were not necessary to throw a handful of soil over a corpse in order to release the soul.

Marrget was beside her, trotting along in silence. He did not speak until she lifted her eyes. "Are you well, my lady?"

He was making the rounds of his warriors, giving encouragement and kind words. With a start, she realized that he now included her needs among those of his men. "I'm OK, Marrget. I'm sorry."

"It is a soldier's life to be prepared to die. Hedyn and Yyarb knew that. And it is a captain's to witness it. Still . . . I would we had not visited this place." He nodded to her. "You are indeed a warrior, my lady. Forgive my earlier words. And . . ." He looked pointedly at Wykla. "And I am proud to say that all the men of my wartroop are valiant."

He gave the boy a grin, flicked his reins, and moved off under a sun that had passed the zenith.

"Well, Wykla," said Alouzon, "I think you're in." But he was working his mouth, unable to make a sound. "Hey, this is an honor. This is what you've been waiting for, isn't it?"

"Then you must always ride with us, my lady," he managed. "I did it for you."

"Oh, boy . . ." Wykla was stiff on his horse, as though terrified of the magnitude of his admission. Alouzon resolved to be gentle: the boy certainly could not be faulted for having emotions. "Uh . . . Wykla . . . you know, I'm not really available for . . . uh . . . relationships. I've got my hands full as it is."

Privately, she was almost amused. Would Joe Epstein have led a charge on a ravening vulva? Not bloody likely. Wykla was generous and loyal. Suzanne Helling, she decided, had rotten taste.

"Relationships, my lady?"

"Like . . . uh . . . love . . ."

"Love? Oh, no, my lady. You are too pure and noble for the likes of any of us." He lifted his head proudly. "My service is meager, but I offer what I have."

Pure and noble? What would he say if he knew about the string of faceless men and nameless cities that she had unrolled from the blood of Kent? What about her abortion? Would he still think so highly of her if he met Joe and discovered that Alouzon Dragonmaster slept with a nerd?

"Christ," she muttered. "This is crazy."

Wykla looked wounded. "My lady?"

"Nothing. Never mind. I'm proud of you for what

you did in the Heath, and I'm grateful to you for saving me." It came to her that she had never thanked the photographer at Kent State. When the shooting had started, he had thrown himself on her, knocking her to the ground. Like Wykla, he had saved her life.

I wouldn't be here today otherwise. She looked up. Some of the men of the Troop met her eyes, nodded. And Marrget thought of her as a warrior. *Jesus. Maybe it would have been better.*

Dythragor suddenly raised his hand and the columns halted. At the top of the next rise was a man on horseback, riding hard toward them.

Alouzon gave Wykla a pat on the shoulder and went up to the front of the line. "Marrget," said Dythragor. "Dremord?"

The captain squinted. "No, my lord. Unless my eyes are very bad, it is Cvinthil."

Marrget gave the order to proceed, and they met Cvinthil at the bottom of a shallow valley. Alouzon saw that his eyes were red with dust and lack of sleep. He looked as though he had been riding for days.

"Cvinthil! What news from Kingsbury brings you so far?" Marrget's question was abrupt and official, but his tone was laden with worry. He obviously feared the worst.

"Dremords," said Cvinthil hoarsely. Marrget muttered a curse and handed him a water skin. Cvinthil drank, poured a little over his face. "They have attacked," he said, his voice stronger for the drink. "They have broken through the southwest end of the Great Dike. They make for the Circle."

"When?" cried Dythragor.

"The day before yesterday, at dawn. Turi of the Fourth Wartroop reached Kingsbury with the message that evening."

"Turi is a good man," said Marrget. "Hahle of Quay trained him. I am sorry he came with such ill news. What of the garrison? The Fourth Wartroop?"

"The Dike is lost, Marrget. The phalanxes drive for the Circle."

Dythragor seemed to be calculating. Alouzon wished that she had a map. "We won't have time to make for Kingsbury," he said. "We should head for the Circle ourselves."

"Well," said Alouzon, "you got your battle. Satisfied?"

He whirled on her. "Woman, another remark like that and you will make your own way. Gryylth is at stake. My people are in danger. If you won't fight, then you can go on to Kingsbury alone."

She had seen it before: his eyes were hot and his face was set. The fit was on him. "OK, whatever you want. I've killed my man, and I won't do it again."

"You'd leave Gryylth to the Dremords," he said, as though he had caught her perjuring herself.

"I'd find another way than this."

"Yeah, like some antiwar demonstrations? You'll have a hard time with that sort of shit in Kingsbury. They don't just use tear gas here."

She almost spat at him. "They didn't at Kent, either."

Cvinthil spoke up, his voice conciliatory in spite of his fatigue. "King Vorya awaits the muster at Kingsbury."

"Then I'll join him there," said Alouzon.

"And what? Sign a petition?" Dythragor laughed harshly. "You'll betray us in our beds the first chance you get."

He was a little rash in his insults, and Alouzon sensed the resentment of the wartroop. His unas-

sailable position had eroded since he had left Kingsbury.

She turned to the captain. "My regrets, Marrget. I
can't help you with this." She expected deprecation
from him, but it did not come. He gazed at her
thoughtfully.

"Go your ways, my lady Alouzon," he said. "I do
not believe you will betray us. I have been fighting
the Dremords for as long as I can remember, and
sometimes, when my men die about me, I too wish
that there might be another way, that I might fight
no more." He shook his head and looked suddenly
around. "I speak more freely than I ought. You have
done strange things to me, my lady."

Dythragor turned to Cvinthil. "Will you ride with
us?"

"Alas," he said, "my horse and I are overspent. I
will accompany Alouzon Dragonmaster to Kingsbury
. . . if she will allow it. There we are gathering the
last of the militia to reinforce the defense of the Circle. The countryside has arisen. Fight without fear:
we will come."

Marrget smiled grimly, as he had at the border of
the Heath. "We always fight without fear." He turned
to Dythragor. "My lord? Shall we ride?"

"I go ahead of you," said Dythragor. He straightened, drew his sword and brandished it, and the polished blade caught the afternoon sun and flashed
bright beams across the ground. "*Silbakor!*" he cried.
"*I call you! By your oath to Gryylth, I call you!*"

And a soft voice thrummed in Alouzon's head: "I
come."

She felt like screaming. She had been wanting Silbakor's presence for days, and all she had needed to
do was lift the Dragonsword and ask. But she found

the idea that she alone could summon something like the Dragon to be rather overwhelming, as though she could tell an ocean to come and go at her whim.

She touched the hilt of her sword. How much power did she have here?

From the south came a gust of hot wind, and the sun dimmed. Shading her eyes, Alouzon made out a black shape against the glare. It grew, hurtling toward the ground like a falling stone. In a minute, wings flared and its descent slowed.

She touched Dythragor's shoulder. "What oath?"

"What do you mean?"

"You called Silbakor by its oath to Gryylth. What oath?"

He seemed out of patience. "I call Silbakor, and it comes. I don't know what oath the Dragon might have made. It doesn't matter. Now stay out of my hair."

Silbakor settled to the ground a short distance away. "I answer the summons," it said quietly.

Dythragor dismounted and handed the reins to Cvinthil. "Take my horse," he said to the councilor. "Yours is tired, and you need speed." Cvinthil mustered a smile.

With quick bounds, Dythragor covered the ground to the Dragon. Swinging himself onto its neck, he waved his sword once more. "The Dremords will run when they see me," he shouted. "Ride quickly, my friends, or you will find no battle."

And Silbakor unfurled its wings and rose rapidly into the air. A gust of wind, a shadow, and it was gone.

Marrget turned to the wartroop. "We must ride," he said. "Let it not be said that the First Wartroop was laggard." He offered his hand to Alouzon. "My lady, I regret you do not come with us. Your valor would stand us well."

Alouzon took his hand. "Good luck, Marrget." Wykla looked at her sorrowfully.

"It is well between us," said the captain. "We part friends." With a nod to Cvinthil, he led his men forward at a quick trot. They gained speed as they crossed a stretch of level ground, and vanished over the ridge.

Cvinthil regarded Alouzon with wonder. "The respect of Marrget of Crownhark is difficult to win."

She sighed. "Let's not keep the king waiting."

Taking the tethers of the three unmounted horses, they made their way to the south toward Kingsbury.

In spite of his words to Alouzon, Mernyl was not confident. He could research, and he could study, but how was he to do either when nothing he possessed held any information regarding the object of his inquiries? He knew about the Tree of Creation instinctively, but what mention he had found of it in his books was in his own hand, in the form of notations to passages of obscure Hebrew gematriot, glosses on Enochian sonorities, or in journal entries of the last few months. Wherever his texts came from, the Tree had arrived from someplace else, and if he was to find out anything more about it, or about the Cup, or the strange lands he had visited in dream, he would have to discover it firsthand.

He had already started the moment Santhe had brought him back to his house in the Cotswoods, for there, surrounded by the familiar and the customary, he could allow his subtler senses to roam throughout the land in search of the unusual and the strange. And he was not long in finding either, for to the south

was something that was a hot needle in the back of
his mind. As he fed Santhe and provided him with
a bed, he was wincing inwardly, torn between his
hospitality to his guest and his need to slip into full
trance so as to better comprehend what was happening.

When he did, he became aware of the attack on
the garrisons of the western Dike and he roused
Santhe in the early morning with the news. The
councilor groaned at his words, but his humor returned instantly and he laughed about feeling like a
ball tossed back and forth by an unruly lot of boys.

Santhe ate a quick meal for the road and decided
to ride directly for the battle, without returning to
Kingsbury. Even as his figure was fading into the
morning mists of the Cotswoods, though, Mernyl was
already outdistancing him, his spirit hurtling southward as his body lay, cold and still, in his own bed.

The fight was taking place entirely on the material
level, but there was a more magical component in
the background. Mernyl saw it only in fleeting images, for Tireas cloaked his workings well. Bulbous,
glowing, its fruit vitreous and sinister, it radiated a
chaos of possibilities, as though, let loose in the
world, it would stir form and substance into a boiling
cauldron of random chance, in which nothing would
be constant or stable. The man at Hall Kingsbury was
healthy and well compared with the ruin that the
Tree could bring to the land.

But Tireas, Mernyl knew, was not insane. Surely
the Corrinian sorcerer was aware of the risks involved. And then there was the Circle, the stability
of the land, to act as a balance. The two could strive
together, but utter stasis and utter change could re-

solve only in a divine tension, out of which would come healthy growth.

And if the Corrinians held both Tree and Circle? What then?

Pressed for knowledge, he meditated throughout the next day, striving for some framework into which to fit the bits and pieces of knowledge that he had. Tree and Circle: Chaos and Stasis—that made sense. But the larger pattern, the one that held as well Cup, Dragonswords, the absence of history, and the ending of earth and sky . . . that was a problem.

Gryylth was incomplete and fragmentary, and he was forced to conclude that it, in fact, did not hold all the answers. He would have to seek beyond.

That evening, as the sun set in a welter of blood, he stretched out on the floor, his staff in his hands, his body surrounded by candles to mark and honor the four directions. Incense sputtered on a coal in a clay burner, and a fifth candle flickered beside him in homage to the ways that he would travel this night, ways that involved other dimensions, other realms, other worlds.

He was afraid of what he might find, but he had to put his fear aside, for the matters at hand were infinitely more important than the cowardice of one poor sorcerer or the petty, internecine struggle of two peoples. In a moment, Gryylth was stretched out below him, bathed in sunset light, smoke from village and town drifting in soft gray plumes.

To all the gods that are, to whatever gods may hear: guide and guard me this night, for I work for all my brothers and sisters, whether they be of Gryylth or of Corrin.

He traveled to the edge of the world, and he trav-

eled beyond, to a land of tall buildings and glassy
towers, of cities that stretched on into the distance
and tattered the horizon with their gray monuments.

There was a man there, a thin man of some years,
but younger than Vorya. He had with him a glass
ball, and within the ball was Silbakor, the Great
Dragon, shrunken now to the size of a child's toy,
but alive, and thinking, and speaking. And the man,
he knew, was Dythragor Dragonmaster, though he
looked nothing like the sword-wielding warrior who
came to Gryylth to do battle with Corrin.

Reality was a confused and cratered ruin of logic
and of cause and effect, and Mernyl watched unfold
before him events that he did not want to know. He
saw the frustration and the violence in Solomon
Braithwaite, saw, clearly, the streak of cruelty that
had been nurtured by a life of inner disappointment.
With compassion—for no other response was appropriate here in these realms of the spirit—he examined the man's life and the lives of those around
him, searched for the secret of Gryylth.

And when he found it, he recoiled with a sheer
terror that sent him fleeing back to his body, heedless
of the damage that a panicked flight could wreak on
his soul. He knew only that he had found the explanation of all, and that the knowledge had been
best left alone, locked in a vault well beyond the
spheres inhabited by simple, mortal minds.

He lay for some hours in deep coma, and when at
last he stirred, his joints burning and his head on
fire with pain, he forced himself to his feet. Slowly,
he gathered together what he would need, filled his
pack again, and donned it. The sky was still full of
stars when he stumbled out of his house, his feet
seeking a southbound road.

He traveled light, for he would not be traveling long. Nor would he be returning, for he saw his imminent death marked out as unmistakably as he had seen the creation of a splinter of a world out of chaos and delirium.

"Poor Suzanne," he murmured, his eyes all but unseeing with pain. "'Twill be a longer journey for her."

Cvinthil's long ride without sleep had drained him, and although he pushed himself, he and Alouzon could not make good time. The afternoon slipped by as they rode, and evening caught them within sight of Bandon.

The councilor stared blearily at the stars and muttered under his breath.

"If you get a good night's sleep," Alouzon reminded him, "you'll reach Kingsbury sooner than if you ride all night and collapse on the way."

"Wise words, lady Alouzon," he said. "You may well counsel a starving man to eat slowly."

"Let me see if I can find you a real bed," she said. "There's no sense roughing it if there's an inn."

"In Bandon?" The river went by like oil, and the air held a muffled stillness. Even the insects were silent. A torch flared briefly on the town wall and settled into a ruddy flicker. "We will pay dearly, Alouzon."

"We're on official business. Doesn't that mean something?"

He shrugged. "It might, lady. And it might not."

But he did not protest as he followed her up to the city gate, announced herself, and asked to be shown to an inn.

The guards were suspicious, and they eyed her from the shelter of the thick stone archway. "What are you doing out?" said one who seemed to be in charge. "Are you a midwife?"

She was impatient. She had had her fill of Bandon. "No, I'm not a midwife. I'm a fucking Dragonmaster. And this man with me is Cvinthil, councilor to King Vorya. We need a place to sleep."

He looked like something straight out of a fifth-century reconstruction, down to the bronze buckles on his leather leggings. Alouzon had to remind herself that she was dealing with a person, not a museum exhibit. "Cvinthil I think I know," he said slowly, "and you too, woman. But the Council gave us no warning of guests tonight."

"There's been a change in plans, sir," she said. "War's broken out."

He nodded, and though his manner indicated that he did not believe her, he sent men running off into the town, and himself escorted them to the council chamber.

It was unchanged: the same torches, the same shadows, the same rats. Kanol showed up eventually, Senon at his side, both men dressed in informal robes as though they had come from their beds.

"You?" said Senon. "Back again? Where is the war-troop?" Kanol was talking through his lackey again, his disdain for a woman as obvious as his obesity.

"Off fighting for your skins." Alouzon grew more irritated with every question. "All we want is a place to sleep. We'll be out of your hair tomorrow morning."

Kanol examined her. His hate gleamed from his moist lips, and there was a sly, calculating look in his eyes. He whispered to Senon.

"This is somewhat . . . irregular," he said. "I am not sure that—"

Cvinthil interrupted. The councilor had ridden through the night, pushing himself and his steed to the point of exhaustion and beyond, but now he mustered his strength and stepped forward. "Kanol," he said, "I believe your charter mandates aid to the king's messengers."

Kanol was cautious, but he spoke out loud. "Aye . . . I believe it does."

"Alouzon Dragonmaster and myself are on a mission of high gravity. I must invoke your charter."

"And does the king employ women now, Cvinthil? Or is this a prize you have captured in some battle? A novelty, perhaps, for cold winter evenings?"

Cvinthil looked shocked, and he could not find words for a moment. But Alouzon found them for him: "That's a pretty low accusation, asshole. Maybe you'd like to step outside?"

Kanol blinked and glanced at Senon, who made a sour face and shook his head. The guards at the door murmured, and Alouzon put her hand to the hilt of the Dragonsword, hoping that a bluff was enough.

The councilmen conferred together in whispers. "We will honor our charter, Cvinthil," Kanol said at last. "The woman too. You shall have a room in the Black Horse Inn, courtesy of the Council of Bandon."

She did not like his tone, nor the hardness of his eyes, nor the wet gleam of his lips, but she sensed that Cvinthil was nearing collapse, and she put her hates and her anxieties aside. Nevertheless, she was seething as they rode along the cobbled streets towards the inn. "They don't hear a damned word I say, do they?"

"Ah, lady Alouzon," said Cvinthil, "Gryylth is hardly ready for such as you . . ." He fell silent. Beyond the rooftops, the sky to the south seemed darker than usual. He frowned, and the torches of their escort added years to his young features. "But it may be about time that we learned other ways."

She followed his eyes. "Could Marrget and the wartroop be down there by now?"

"Marrget would not push the men and the horses so. Only fools ride themselves to death." He smiled wryly. "No. Most likely, if the wartroop makes haste, it will arrive tomorrow afternoon or earlier, depending upon how close the Dremords have come to the Circle."

He said the name with reverence, but it meant nothing to her. She let the matter rest, though, until they had been shown to a room on the second story and had eaten.

With some food in him and something other than a horse to sit on, he was looking better. The room was warm with the summer, but the windows were wide and open to the night air. A moth fluttered in and circled the candle flame like a madcap satellite, and Alouzon heard the sound of booted feet in the courtyard.

Strange: there seemed to be quite a number of men stirring about on this quiet evening.

The councilor passed a hand across his face and sighed. "I confess that I am ready for rest, Alouzon."

"Be my guest. We've got two beds, Cvinthil."

He laughed. "Any woman but you, Dragonmaster, would be bound by law to be my wife or my concubine by now."

"You're kidding. Because we're sharing a room?"

"Aye. It is unseemly for it to be otherwise."

"Then why the hell did they just give us one room?"

"Nay, I know not."

She considered. "Could you answer a few questions

before we turn in?" She grinned. "Immoral though we are?"

He laughed out loud. "Ask, Dragonmaster. I cannot but return favor for favor."

"Tell me about the Circle. What is it?"

Some fragments of bread and cheese lay on the table between them, and Cvinthil nibbled at them tiredly as he spoke, sipping from the wine cup between thoughts. "The Circle is the foundation of the land," he said. All that is Gryylth is mirrored in its stones, not so that it can be seen, but in such a way that a hand placed on one of the fifteen central sarsens will tell more than the feel of the rock. It brings visions to those who are brave enough to sleep within its rings . . . sometimes it brings madness."

"Who built it?" A crucial question, one that stemmed not only from the curiosity of an archaeologist, but also from the doubts engendered by the statements of Adyssa, the midwife, and from the persistent sense of unreality that covered everything like a thick coating of varnish.

"My lady, I do not know. It was always here."

The moth spiraled into the flame, singed its wings, chandelled up and over, looping straight back for the deadly incandescence. On a sudden hunch, Alouzon leaned forward. "Cvinthil, how old are you?"

"Thirty-one summers, lady."

"Tell me of your boyhood."

He looked confused. "I . . . acted as a boy. I played the games of a boy. I was trained in weapons."

"Give me something specific."

By now, he looked absolutely bewildered. "I . . . I . . . cannot, my lady. I have forgotten much."

"What was your father's name?"

"Solomon."

Dythragor's name. She shook her head, perplexed. "Your mother?"

"Helen."

There was a twisting feeling in her stomach. The food and drink turned sour and began to churn. "Your grandfather? Your grandmother?"

Cvinthil looked worse and worse. "My lady, these are questions not normally asked here. I do not know their names." He was breathing heavily with fatigue, and she regretted that she had begun to grill him.

"Sorry. I needed some information."

"I regret I cannot help you."

"You'd better sleep. I'll be up for a few more minutes. See you in the morning."

"As you wish, Dragonmaster." He stumbled to his bed, rolled himself in the covers. "A question though, lady."

"Hey, fair's fair."

He shook his head at her language. "Would you have fought the Council this evening?"

"You mean, when I asked Kanol to step outside? Nah, that was an act. He hates my guts, and I hate his. But I'll be honest with you, Cvinthil: I can't stand the thought of killing. I doubt that I'll be able to fight again."

His face was a blur in the candlelight. "I . . . I am sorry to hear that. I had hoped that you might help Gryylth."

"I'll help. But I won't help like Dythragor helps."

He nodded slowly. "It is well, then." His breathing turned slow and regular, and Alouzon sat with the candle and the moth, pondering.

What she was thinking was utter madness, but she supposed that it was no more mad than magic and Dragons and what she had seen in the Heath. To further the craziness one step more and suspect that the land had existed for only ten years, only since Dythragor had first arrived, seemed an inconsequential act.

Why not? Quasi-archaic English, Celtic swords, British armor, the image of the Grail floating behind it all—it was like an indifferently researched Hollywood movie. And there was no history, no memory of anything that had happened farther back than ten years. Even some of the inhabitants were beginning to notice.

Her head hurt. She was about ready to give up when she heard the sound of someone on the stairs outside the door. And then, with an audible thump, the door was barred.

From the outside.

❖ CHAPTER 12 ❖

❖

"CVINTHIL," SAID ALOUZON, "I'M SORRY TO wake you, but I think we've got trouble."

She could hear men moving outside the door, and with her hand on the Dragonsword, her sharpened instincts told her that there were more beyond: on the stairs, and gathered in the main room below. Forty, maybe fifty. Their intentions, she sensed, were not good.

"Mmph?"

"They've locked us in."

At that, the councilor awoke fully. He rolled out of bed, picked up his sword and joined her at the door. Listening, he nodded slowly. His breathing was labored and fatigued, but adrenalin and war training were eking out his strength for the time.

"I heard a bar drop from the other side," she explained. "And I don't like the feel of this."

"Have they said anything?"

"Just mutters. Someone was laughing a minute ago. Kanol, I think."

"That bitch's whelp," said Cvinthil. "I will have his charter revoked if he is doing what I think he is. Bandon can fight the Dremords without the king's protection."

The councilor straightened, pounded on the door with the hilt of his sword. "Kanol! Councilman of Bandon! What brings you to our door in the dead of night?"

Some moments of silence, then Kanol's dry voice spoke up. "We understand that you are unlawfully cohabiting with an unmarried female, councilor. By the terms of our charter, you have agreed to abide by our laws while you are here. Therefore we must order you to give her up."

"And what the fuck do you think you're going to do with me?" shouted Alouzon.

"Cvinthil, tell your whore that she will be treated as she deserves."

Alouzon felt dizzy, sick, but a part of her mind persisted in noting that the councilman still refused to talk to her directly. "Well, at least the son of a bitch is consistent." She looked at Cvinthil. "Is what he says true? Have we agreed?"

"A doubtful question, Dragonmaster," he replied. "One that would cause some lengthy argument at a hearing before the king. As messengers, we are protected. As man and woman, we are not."

The power from her sword was burning up her arm, and her skin was tingling with energy. Suzanne Helling could worry about facts, but Alouzon Dragonmaster knew that she had to don her armor and make ready for a fight. "Do we care, Cvinthil?"

He stood, hands on hips, regarding the door. His shoulders were slumped, and his head was angled to one side in the manner of a man too long without sleep.

"Will you yield, councilor?" said Kanol from the other side of three inches of oak.

Cvinthil was still thinking.

Alouzon recognized his dilemma. "I guess I should ask it this way, Cvinthil: Do *you* care? It's your ass at stake."

He reached a resolution, straightened, and his voice rang out, deep and pitched to carry throughout the whole inn: "Know you, Kanol of Bandon, that as councilor of Gryylth I declare your actions this night to be high treason, endangering as they do the welfare of the king's messengers in particular, and of the country as a whole. Therefore, your life is forfeit as well as your charter."

She had her answer.

"I would contest your judgment, councilor." Kanol sounded unimpressed.

"On what grounds, traitor?"

"On the grounds that I have here with me fifty armed men who will do my will. You have yourself and a woman. Need I say more?"

Alouzon saw the fatigue in his eyes when he turned to her. He could not face Kanol and his men alone. "Dragonmaster? Are you prepared to fight?"

She was already pulling on her armor, trying not to think of Kent, of the dead Dremord, of the feeling that a sword made as it sliced through flesh. The men outside wanted to make a slave of her, and that terror outweighed any qualms she had.

The thought hammered against her temples in time to her pounding pulse. *They want to sell me. God-dammit, they're gonna die!*

A slow smile touched Cvinthil's face, and he laughed. "Your fate is sealed this night, Kanol. And just desserts to you!"

While the men of Bandon wondered at his words, he settled his own leathers about himself, pulled the straps tight, and helped Alouzon with buckles that she could not comfortably reach. She felt the armor ease in under Cvinthil's skilled hands, and her instincts told her that the fit was perfect, with just enough protection and just enough give. What was left of Suzanne Helling fled into the inner recesses of her thoughts, and Alouzon Dragonmaster stood, sword unsheathed, ready for battle.

The twenty-foot drop to the ground outside the window was manageable, but they both rejected that plan: there were men downstairs in the courtyard already, and once their actions became known, there would be more.

" 'Twill have to be frontal assault, Dragonmaster."

"Call me Alouzon," she said. "If you're going to fight with me, then we can at least be on a first-name basis."

He smiled like a shy boy. "Alouzon, then. But the barred door remains a problem."

She examined it. "Probably figured they could starve us into submission." She knew the door was of thick wood, but she sensed that the Dragonsword held more of an edge than ordinary steel.

Steel? She wondered for a moment. High grade steel was as rare in the fifth century as jet airplanes. Who had thought up such a thing as a Dragonsword?

Shrugging, she put the thought aside. Suzanne Helling could write a paper about it when she got back to Los Angeles. If she got back.

"The door isn't a problem, Cvinthil. You ready?"

"Aye."

"Where are the horses?"

"Fenced in the courtyard."

"OK, then we'll have to get them. That'll give us an advantage right there."

"But . . . the door . . ."

"It's not a problem." And, lifting the Dragonsword over her head, she brought it down in a two-handed strike into the door. Wood splintered and cracked as the blade plunged through the heavy planks and sliced from top to bottom. One half of the door fell back, the other sagged for a moment before she kicked it out and sent it slamming into the men on the other side. Several toppled under the impact, and several more went down a moment later as Alouzon Dragonmaster exploded through the doorway, eyes hot, sword flashing.

"Kanol, you bastard, you're dead meat!"

She did not see the councilman, but no matter: she would deal with him later. For now, her attention was occupied by the pikemen who were thrusting and trying to trip her. They surrounded her, their footing uncertain on a floor already growing slippery with spilled blood. Cvinthil fell on some from behind and freed her sword for use on the others.

Several men lay dead in the hallway, and the living were retreating and taking up a position at the top of the stairs. Cvinthil was pale as he ran at them beside Alouzon. "Bandon soldiers are soft and stupid," he muttered.

"How so?"

In reply, he skidded to a halt, seized a chair that stood in the hall, and sent it tumbling end-over-end for the soldiers. Unthinking, many took a step backward and found that the top of a flight of stairs was not a good place to stand.

Cvinthil and Alouzon were on them before they had stopped tumbling down the steps. The councilor's sword was no match for Alouzon's, but he knew how to use it, and it made men bleed and die just as effectively. Swinging as broadly as they could in the confines of the stairwell, the two hacked a path down to the common room.

If Alouzon had forgotten how it felt to kill, she was remembering now. But she had, at present, no regrets. Trapped in her room, the object of contempt, the subject of proposed slavery, she looked on the men she slashed and stabbed as having already determined their fate and their guilt. She was unconcerned with theories of pacifism or nonviolence, for she knew what these men wanted and knew that she would not give it to them. There was no choice, there was no question.

Her responses, instincts, reflexes were automatic, as though she had trained for this from childhood. And for the first time since she had lifted a sword in Gryylth, she was unutterably grateful, letting the hot power of the Dragonsword do whatever it would with her body. With calculated precision she threw herself into a soldier who blocked her path, smacked another to the floor with her steel cuff, brought her sword hilt into the face of a third before she whipped around and slew the first with the impact of a blade powered by the full force of her hips and shoulders.

She marked his expression as she had marked others: an uncomprehending blankness that shaded quickly into certainty and pain, and then oblivion. But she looked only for a instant. Others were lifting weapons against her and moving in, and Cvinthil had been backed into a corner.

And we're not even out the door yet.

"Shit!" She dropped two by cutting their legs out from under them—forehand, backhand—and seized one of Cvinthil's assailants by the hair, planted her elbow against his neck, and snapped his spine with a sudden jerk. White faces were turned to her, and

Cvinthil found an opening in which to plant a sword. In an instant, the soldiers had panicked, and they withdrew, leaving the councilor and the Dragonmaster in control of the common room.

"We're not done yet," she said.

"No, but we have made them fear us." He was shaking. Adrenalin could do a great deal for a fighter, but when it was all that was keeping one upright, it was not the best ally.

"Can you make it?" she said.

"I have no choice."

He was already stepping for the door. They heard Kanol's voice promising money to the man who killed the Dragonmaster.

"Better he should give money to the survivors of those the Dragonmaster kills," Cvinthil said. She wondered why his words did not make her wince. Once, they would have done just that. "A hard time we will have of it," he continued. "Assuming that we can reach the horses, the town gate will be manned against us."

"The horses are penned?"

"Aye."

"Tethered?"

"Nay, Alouzon. A call will bring them leaping. And they are warhorses: they can themselves fight. And they will." His hand was on the ring that served for a door pull. "Shall we?"

"Hang on." She caught her breath for a minute. Kanol was still exhorting the soldiers. "Isn't there some other way out of the inn? Something that's closer to the horses? I mean, they're *expecting* us to come out right in front of them."

He nodded, picked up a fallen man's spear and

thrust it through the ring. "I should have thought of that. You are wise, Alouzon."

"You're just tired, Cvinthil."

"Shh. If I begin thinking of beds and sleep I will be useless for anything save pike practice."

In the darkness, they found their way down a corridor that led to the rear of the large, rambling building. The owners, the help, and the other guests had apparently been warned of Kanol's plans, for the inn seemed deserted. Cvinthil's labored breathing and their hollow footsteps were the only sound.

Odors: roast beef, musty vegetables, cheese. "We're in the kitchen, I think." She tried to remember what she could of the layout of fifth-century kitchens and came up with mere scraps. Laycock and Chadwick had not excavated and analyzed sufficiently.

"Big fucking help," she muttered as she barked her knee on a wooden tub. "We're going to have to make this quick, Cvinthil. They'll be wondering about what we're doing."

"Aye." Feeling in the darkness, the councilor had found a door. With Alouzon's help, he slid the bar aside silently, cracked it open, and peered out. "We are about a score of yards from the horses," he announced in a whisper. "There are two guards on the horses, but they are more concerned with what their fellows are doing at the front of the inn."

"Hmmm. You're right."

"Right?"

She grinned. "Bandon soldiers are pretty stupid."

Cvinthil swung the door open and gave a shrill whistle just as someone began rattling the front door that he had pinned shut. Shouts, cursing.

But the horses knew the call, and they cleared the

fence with a bound. The guards tried to stop them, but Jia's hooves knocked one unconscious, and Cvinthil's mount simply rode over the other. Another whistle from Cvinthil, and the horses were heading directly for them.

"Atta boy, Jia," she whispered, throwing her arms about the familiar neck. "Are you willing to take me without a saddle?"

He was willing, and more than willing. As though sensing his mistress's danger, Jia moved fluidly and took her on his back. Cvinthil mounted also, and he sent the three extra horses ahead to charge the crowd of men that was forming at the archway that led to the streets of the town. "If we can gain the gate—"

"We'll still be up to our ass in alligators."

For a moment, he pondered the metaphor. "Well, perhaps there will be a few less alligators. Whatever they are."

The unmounted horses had been trained for impact, and they crashed into the densely packed men, toppling many, sending a ripple of disorder throughout the crowd. "At 'em, Jia," said Alouzon as she swatted his rump.

There were holes in the ranks of the men now, and with the speed of their mounts, Alouzon and Cvinthil passed through the gateway and into the streets of Bandon without having to parry a single thrust. The soldiers crowded after them, but could not keep up.

The gate of the town was not far away, and Alouzon knew that unless it could be opened quickly, the men would once more be on them. With the strength of the Dragonsword, she herself could continue to fight, but she was unsure about Cvinthil. His strength was going to give out soon, and she doubted that she would make as effective an opponent if she were burdened with an unconscious man.

Quick and to the point then. No time for dallying. They rounded the corner and found the gate closed. A torch burned in the gatehouse, but the window was covered with thick bars of iron.

Alouzon swung off Jia's back. "Yell when you see them coming. I'll get the gate open." She started running up the steps to the door, muttering to herself: "Somehow."

She tried the door and found it locked. Strangely, though, she heard the sounds of a struggle within the gatehouse. One of the combatants was Kanol, and—stranger still—from the sound of it, the other was a woman. Her voice was familiar.

"Adyssa!"

"I am trying to unbar the door, Dragonmaster!"

"You will be dead in an instant, woman," said Kanol.

"My lady, he has a sword. I have nothing."

The plump midwife would have been the underdog even if Kanol had not been armed. "You're a real brave man, aren't you Kanol?" Alouzon shouted through the window.

He did not reply. He still would not talk to her.

Two blows from the Dragonsword shattered the door, and Alouzon kicked it in and lunged after the fragments. Adyssa was in one corner of the room, holding her side. Blood was seeping out from between her fingers. Kanol stood near the turnstile that controlled the gate, his sword freshly blooded.

"I heard of Kanol's plans, my lady," said the midwife. "You were . . ." She staggered, and the blood flowed faster. "I could not let him do that to you."

Kanol faced Alouzon, sword lifted. "Come no closer."

She circled him. "Come on, man, I don't have time for this shit."

"Stay back."

"Get the fuck out of my way." She was already moving, and though Kanol had some skill, it was as nothing to the Dragonsword. He went down with a thump and a warm slithering from his opened belly.

Alouzon hauled on the turnstile and heard the chains engage. Adyssa came to her side and pulled also, and with their combined weights, the gate responded, opened, its counterbalances creaking down as the iron bars lifted into the upper levels of the gatehouse. Alouzon shot the heavy catch into place and hammered a piece of firewood in after it.

Adyssa's face was gray, her hands cold. She could barely move. Alouzon reached a hand to her. "Adyssa, you need help."

Cvinthil's cry rang from below. "Alouzon! They are coming!"

Adyssa shook her head slowly. "Nay, Dragonmaster. I am dead. I am physician enough to know a mortal wound." Her eyes blanked suddenly, and slid to the floor. Her hand fell away from her side to reveal a gash only slightly smaller than that which had felled Kanol.

"Alouzon!"

"Kanol, you son of a bitch . . ." She did not even have time to spit on him. Grabbing her sword, she ran down the steps three at a time, swung onto Jia and kicked him into a gallop. In seconds she and Cvinthil had gained the open countryside.

They let their horses run for several miles, taking shelter at last in an arm of forest that stretched out from the mountains. Cvinthil found water, and they drank, but they had no fire, nor any desire to signal their presence by making one.

Alouzon was shaking, the strain of an hour's unremitting battle falling heavily upon her physically and emotionally. She felt shocky and weak, but she told Cvinthil to sleep. "You need it more, man. I'll keep an eye out."

"You will wake me for my watch?"

"Yeah, sure," she said, but she had no intention of doing so. Tired though she was, she did not think that sleep was possible, for she saw too many dead men's faces behind her closed eyes, viewed them with too much relish.

With the Dragonsword in her hand, she sat atop a log and stared back toward the town, her ears alert for any sounds that men might make, her eyes searching for movement.

Bandon stood in the distance, a dark, huddled shape that blocked out the stars. She had killed there, but she felt no shame. If she felt anything, she realized, it was the ache of the loss of a friend.

It was not just Adyssa, though the midwife's sacrifice had touched her deeply. No, it was Suzanne Helling who had been lost. The peaceful college student was gone now, back perhaps to Kent State, where she could wander among the shades of memory, finding whatever solace she could in the remembrance of the dead, scrambling for a tainted absolution in the waters of helplessness.

Alouzon Dragonmaster was part of Gryylth now, part of the violence and the blood, and the love and loyalty too. Cvinthil had risked his life for her. Adyssa had given hers freely, had accepted her death calmly.

And they don't even know who their gods are . . .

She blinked back tears as she regarded the town with a cold loathing. "You ought to be burned down," she said. "And the ground sown with salt. And if I ever get those kids out, I just might do it."

It was not battle. It was slaughter.

Darham's sense of honor was revolted by the progress of the campaign. The garrisons at the Dike had been overpowered by surprise and by numbers, and though they continued to fight as they retreated deeper into Gryylth, they did so without food or supplies, and their morale had been devastated. Nor were the wartroops that were brought up to reinforce the defense—hastily conscripted from nearby towns, force-marched to battle, fatigued and almost useless upon arrival—any obstacle to the Corrinian phalanxes that rolled over the countryside with gathering momentum.

Easy, effortless killing. One might as well have been chopping wood. From the beginning, it was not a battle to look upon with pride, and it became less so on the afternoon of the second day, when Dythragor appeared with the Great Dragon. For a moment, it appeared that the Dragonmaster might rally the Gryylthans, for a faint cheer went up from the clumps of soldiers who had been scattered across the landscape by the latest drive of the phalanxes, and some began to reform for an advance. But a shadow fell across the land, and the cheers ceased abruptly.

By Tarwach's orders, Tireas had been waiting, holding back until his magics were needed; and as Silbakor swept in from the north, black against the blue sky, a different and more ominous blackness suddenly funneled up from behind the Corrinian lines. It rose and spread into a whirling gyre, gathered mass and potency, and, like a dark hand, batted the Dragon away as though it were a mayfly. In spite of Silbakor's efforts to bring Dythragor to the aid of his people, the Tree held it off, wrapping it in roiling clouds of unlight that flickered with pale fire, eclipsing the sun with shadow.

In the twilight cast round the battlefield by the Tree, the character of the battle changed, from slaughter to rout, from grim, single combat to a frenzied hacking. Swords flickered fitfully in the faint spill of daylight from the north, and spears flew invisibly, finding their targets by fate and chance. Men died beneath a sky that had seemingly been sealed off by a lid, and at night, the stars went unseen, their light blocked by Tireas's murk.

Through it all, Darham stayed next to Tarwach, conferring with his brother, swinging his sword when necessary to batter away the Gryylthans who attacked the Corrinian king in a desperate effort to break the momentum of the phalanxes. Tarwach was left free to give his full attention to a battle that moved constantly, that spread out like a sackful of rice dumped onto a table. The disordered ranks of men jostled and bucked at one another, Corrinian and Gryylthan losing identity as lines of combat ebbed and flowed and blended. Tarwach shouted directions, sent messengers to the phalanx captains, sometimes rode directly into a densely packed struggle to shove men bodily in the direction he wanted. His judgment—impelled by need, sharpened by the consequences of loss—was good, and the phalanxes advanced, pushing on during the day, holding positions tenaciously by night, and renewing the assault come morning.

Speed was important, for the Circle had to be won before the veteran wartroops of Gryylth could be notified and brought to the battle. Tarwach could not expect his men to endure the strain of combat indefinitely, but he had to drive them forward as quickly as he could, and therefore, the morning of the third day brought with it another command to attack.

Heavy fighting now, with groups of Gryylthan survivors banding together and throwing themselves at selected phalanxes in an attempt to slow them down, to buy time. Screams, shouts, the incessant clang of bronze and steel and iron weapons that stuck one upon another. The dead were widely scattered, strewn upon the trampled fields like a summer's sowing. Darham's horse stumbled upon a corpse, but the animal was well trained and held its footing at his word.

"Are you well, brother?" Tarwach's question was automatic.

"Better than those below me."

The Corrinians drove off another attack, and the last of the wartroops fled to the west to regroup. For the time being, the silence was broken only by cries of pain.

Tarwach called a pikeman to his side. "Tell Tireas to lift some of this endless night," he said. "Tell him I must be able to see."

"Instantly, my king." And the soldier went running to the rear.

"And what do you look for, brother?" said Darham.

"I want to know when to expect the First Wartroop. I am surprised that we have not met them yet."

"It is indeed strange." Darham strained his eyes across a rolling land that was lapped in deep twilight. In any large battle between the forces of Gryylth and Corrin, the First Wartroop was inevitably the first to arrive, the last to leave. For the best warriors of Gryylth to be so conspicuously absent now was evidence either of extreme cunning on Vorya's part or of the most woeful miscalculation.

"I cannot believe other than that this must be some kind of strategy," said Tarwach.

The sky cleared, and pale daylight flicked across the field. Darham noted that Silbakor was still fighting against Tireas's magic. It was making progress now that the darkness had abated, and he could see the flash of the Dragonsword.

He touched Tarwach's arm and pointed. "If Dythragor gains this battle, it is quite possible that we will lose ground, First Wartroop or no."

"And what of the other Dragonmaster?"

"I see only one rider." Stranger and stranger. Baffling and seemingly foolish battle plans, the absence of the crack troops of Gryylth, and now the use of only one of two Dragonmasters. "Do you suppose that, because she is a woman . . .?"

"Then why would she be in Gryylth?"

Darham shrugged. He had been fighting for two days now, his sleep fitful, broken, and of short duration. Not much longer, perhaps, and he would resemble the travel-worn neophytes that Gryylth had been sending against him. "I suppose I care not. She is not here, and that is good."

A Gryylthan warrior who had been feigning death sprang up beside Tarwach and thrust at him with his spear. Darham was on the wrong side of the king, but as Tarwach parried the weapon with his sword, his brother leaped over the horse and hewed the man in two.

Darham dragged an arm across his brow, the odor

of blood and body fluids, old and new, rank in his throat. "Valor or foolishness, I know not, brother, but I wish this were done."

Above their heads, the Tree's darkness balled itself into a fist and smacked Silbakor and its rider to the south again.

Darham watched for a minute. Dythragor was most likely livid with frustration. Well, let him be livid. Small payment it was for the damage he had done to Corrin. *Withdraw or die.* That was what he had said, over and over again, rebuffing any offer, accepting no compromise. And then there was the grief that Manda bore.

Dythragor could rot in the sky for all he cared. But the men of Corrin were another matter. "We are all tired, Tarwach," he said. "Perhaps it would be good to take a half-day's rest before we continue?"

The king debated. "I would we gain the Circle first."

"And if we drop from exhaustion once there, what good will the journey have been?"

"We must put an end to this war. We are tired now, to be sure, but are we not tired of the years of fighting? And how shall we rest from that prolonged battle save by gaining our objective?"

"But—"

In the distance, on the crest of a gentle rise, there appeared several wartroops. Darham recognized their insignia. These were no young, unblooded troops, fresh-faced and overeager to prove themselves, but rather old, skilled warriors of Gryylth, veterans of many battles, cunning and courageous opponents. Time had run out for Corrin.

And what if the First Wartroop were among them?

"I do not see Marrget," said Tarwach, as though

he had guessed Darham's thoughts. "But there will be no rest for us today, I think."

The soldier he had dispatched to Tireas returned now at a run. "The compliments of Tireas the sorcerer to the king," he gasped. "He asks that the king not engage the Gryylthans immediately."

"What?"

But the darkness spread over the sky again, dimming their view of the wartroops. With a hissing crackle, the Tree launched a bolt of black fire, its incandescence sensible more to feeling than to sight, that arced high over the phalanxes and smashed directly into the first waves of the Gryylthans. The wind was from the west, and Darham smelled burned and charred flesh.

"Behold the outcome of Gryylth's arrogant stupidity," said Tarwach. His voice was harsh. "They had their chance for a settlement, and we have been more than patient with them. Come, brother. Tireas will do his work, and then we will do ours. Perhaps we will soon have some leisure after all."

The king spurred his horse ahead, shouting for the phalanxes to form and advance.

For an instant, a flicker of sunlight glanced through the twilight, falling upon an untrampled piece of field. The grass glowed with yellow flowers as bright as Manda's hair.

Lovely Manda. Shining Manda. And if Corrin was not successful, her lot would be to crouch beside a Gryylthan cooking fire, serving a man to whom she had to bend her bright head every day.

Darham leapt onto his horse and galloped off after Tarwach. Rest or no rest, Corrin would gain the Circle.

❖

CHAPTER 13

WHEN ALOUZON DRAGONMASTER CAME once again in sight of Kingsbury, she realized why it had seemed so familiar. Cadbury Hill, in Somerset, the site of Leslie Alcock's four-year investigation into the historicity of Arthur, might have been duplicated, tree for tree and trench for trench, here in Gryylth. She did not doubt that, had she possessed aerial photographs of both hills, Kingsbury would have been distinguishable from Cadbury only in that its fortifications were exposed rather than buried.

But it was a dull recognition at best, for it was only one more peculiarity in a land rife with riddles. Her eyes swollen with a night's weeping and no sleep, she stared up at the tree-clad slopes that were wrapped now in the haze of a warm summer afternoon. Larks called, and a magpie, resplendent in its black and white livery, flitted across the road.

If there was a Grail in Gryylth—and she believed that there was—she needed it now. Added to a past filled with despair was a present saturated with violence, and she did not know whether she was disturbed more by the killings in Bandon or by her emotionless acceptance of them. Either way, the image of the life-giving, healing sustenance that flowed in such bountiful streams from the Sacred Cup drew her as though it were the promise of water in a wasteland.

And how was the Grail won? One had to go and look for it, she recalled vaguely. One had to want to look for it.

If that were the case, then her quest had already started without her even being conscious of her choice and her commitment. "OK," she said softly. "I'm here. I want it." She hung her head. "And who do I have to kill now?"

She had not said more than ten words throughout the day, and Cvinthil had grown increasingly concerned at her prolonged silence. "Alouzon? Is there something that I can do?"

They started up the road that led to the plateau. Alouzon shook her head. "Unless you can change history, I'm stuck."

The councilor did not speak at first, and together they climbed past outposts that he silenced with a gesture. "I know of your reluctance to kill, Alouzon. Yet you fought well last night, for yourself and for me. May I . . ." His tone caused her to turn, and his large brown eyes were serious. "May I call you friend?"

Gryylth was taking her to itself, was wrapping its warm, loving, blood-soaked wings about her. She reached, took his hand. "Yeah. Thanks, Cvinthil. If it weren't for you, I'd be on the block today."

"Somehow, Alouzon," he said with a nod at her sword, "I think not."

The steep road took them around the hill, and they stopped for a moment on the eastern face. Out in the distance, clinging to the horizon like a leech, was a darkness that reminded Alouzon of the Heath. But this was deeper, blacker, as though a corner of the night had caught on some projection and had torn away.

Cvinthil looked worried. "I do not like to think of our men fighting in that murk."

"Any idea what it is?"

"No. Sorcery, perhaps; though never before have I seen sorcery like that."

The Tree, she thought. It has to be the Tree. And Marrget and Wykla and the others are heading straight for it. "Come on," she said aloud, nudging Jia into a faster climb. "I think we're going to be needed there soon."

When they reached the top of the hill, they found a press of men and weapons about the village. Dust rose thickly, and there was a general sense of ill temper that was a product of heat, dirt, and the certainty of future danger. For all the noise, confusion, and clash of arms, it might have been a sham battle.

"Only the First and Second Wartroops and the garrisons of frequently attacked towns are held in readiness throughout the year," Cvinthil explained as they pushed through the crowd. "The rest, though having permanent captains who train them periodically, live the life of craftsmen and farmers. Only in times of emergency—"

"Where are your children, girl?" someone shouted at her.

Alouzon gritted her teeth, hearing in the voice the accents of a certain Kanol of Bandon. "Shove it, asshole."

"Have we come now to woman-fights?"

The men, strangers to the sight of a female Dragonmaster, looked at her suspiciously. One shook his fist at her. "Where is your husband?"

"Back, fool," returned Cvinthil. "Alouzon Dragonmaster admits no interference."

"Dragonmaster? And what trickery is this?" The speaker, a short, burly man, scowled at her, spat on the ground. "Get off that horse, girl. And give me that sword."

She was tempted to give it to him to the hilt, but she held back. Still, the Dragonsword flashed in the sunlight as it slid out of its sheath, and she brought Jia around to face her antagonist. Confronted with an armed warrior, on horseback, he seemed less inclined to dispute questions of gender.

"Look, shit-for-brains," she said, "I just got through slicing up a bunch of soldiers in Bandon who thought a lot like you, and I'm getting to the point where I don't give a damn about your little hell-hole of a country. Right now I'd just as soon castrate you as look at you. So *back off.*"

He had no chance to reply, for a moment later he was shoved to one side by one of Vorya's guards. The king and his personal soldiers were riding out from the Hall, and when Vorya saw Cvinthil and Alouzon, he hailed them gladly.

"We ride immediately," he called. "I regret that you will have no time for rest. These two hundred or so are the last of those who answered the call. The others have gone on before. The Dremords have put all their strength into this fight, and they will be difficult to stop." He gestured at the men. "These may well turn the battle."

Alouzon glared at the short man who had attempted to take her sword. He edged off and lost himself in the crowd. "Have you seen that shadow out to the east?" she said to Vorya.

"Aye, Dragonmaster. We must make haste."

"Don't you think you ought to send for Mernyl?"

Vorya looked doubtful. His brow was creased, and he was frowning as though weighing a difficult decision. The men milled about them, their captains shouting orders, forming them into lines for the march, checking their supplies. "I would not spare a man here for the journey," he said finally. "And if we summon Mernyl . . ."

"You lose Dythragor, right?"

"Aye."

"But you'd still have—" She stopped. Did she have the right to offer herself as a replacement for Dythragor? How much killing did she want to do?

Vorya seemed to understand her offer and her quandary, but he shook his head. "I would see whether Mernyl were truly necessary before I endangered a known alliance."

With a shout, he trotted his horse to the head of the columns, and in minutes, the wartroops were on the march.

When the First Wartroop arrived, Darham was almost relieved. Here at last was an end to the waiting and to the almost nonsensical Gryylthan defense. Here were Marrget and his men: any further tactics would follow more predictable patterns.

But the wartroop's appearance also signaled that the real battle was about to begin, that after several days of a fighting advance, the Corrinians' drive on the Circle had been brought to a standstill, and the best warriors of Gryylth were now arrayed against them.

"So much territory Gryylth holds that simple distance defeats us!" said Tarwach. "One would think that a small portion could be spared for Corrin."

"We are not done yet, brother," said Darham. "Tireas is still working for our cause, and if he can keep a Dragonmaster at bay, then he is surely a match for Marrget."

With a crack, the Tree flung a black bolt over their heads. It struck the ground some yards in front of the Gryylthans, ripping up the trampled grass and sending the chalky earth of the downs geysering into the air. Darham instinctively flinched at its passage: he had seen what such things did to human flesh.

Tireas had been using his bolts sparingly: he was trying to demoralize the Gryylthan defense so that more killing would not be necessary. But the Gryylthans were becoming used to his tactics, and though, when the bolts struck, they threw themselves to the ground to avoid flying stones and debris, they had apparently come to consider the bolts more an annoyance than a threat.

On the hill ahead, Marrget was giving orders, snapping out commands that were obeyed instantly. Another bolt struck, nearly at his feet, but the captain hardly glanced at it. He simply mopped the mud from his face and continued with his arrangements.

"Marrget is a brave man," Tarwach murmured. "I wish sometimes that we were not enemies." He watched the wartroops deploy, then shouted his orders. "First and Third Phalanxes to the right for flanking! Fifth and Eighth up the middle and hold your positions! King's Guard to the left!"

King's Guard would, under other circumstances, have included Manda. What, Darham wondered, was she doing now? Practicing swordwork on a wooden dummy? Or running off her frustration down by the shore of the Long River? Her skills were great, and she habitually kept a level head. He wished that she were here, but Gryylth had made its prejudices known long ago: women on the battlefield were singled out and overwhelmed by sheer weight of numbers. If they were lucky, they were killed immediately. If not . . .

Consciously, Darham relaxed a clenched jaw. Manda had already experienced the brutal attentions of Gryylth.

"Marrget and his men are without sleep," said Tarwach. "This will be an even match."

Darham hoped that his brother was right. "We cannot keep on this way."

"The sorcerer is confident," said Tarwach, "and he has something in mind, I guess. I will therefore keep my hope." The darkness clouded the sky again as the Gryylthans charged, and another bolt furrowed the ground at the feet of the vanguard, sending men toppling to the ground.

For an instant, the counterattack wavered, and the phalanxes struck.

Even though it presented an overall appearance of flatness, the land here was deeply undulating. As a result, the road was a succession of climbs and descents. Kingsbury would be hidden from sight and then would reappear farther away, as though a hand had picked it up and moved it like a chess piece.

Unlike the First Wartroop, the men Alouzon traveled with were mostly on foot, with the exception of their captains and the king. They were rough, surly, without any of the professionalism that characterized Marrget and his men, but after she took her position at the king's side, the grumbles that she had heard about women in the company faded into a dull resentment. She had yet to win these men. She was not sure that she wanted to.

But winning them was not an urgent task, for they had more to brood upon than the presence of a woman. In the distance, the darkness lay on the land like a blanket kicked to the floor by a restless sleeper. It was an imponderable mass, brooding, threatening, at times stirring like a living thing.

Vorya regarded it with unease, conferred often with Cvinthil. Alouzon heard Mernyl's name mentioned repeatedly, as well as Dythragor's.

There was no time for leisurely travel. The men were double-timed down the road in the hope of effecting some relief for those ahead. But speed took its toll, and when Vorya called a halt that evening, the soldiers slumped wearily against one another, and, not having the strength to cook, ate cold rations and slept where they had sat down in the fields.

"A pity I cannot allow them even a whole night's sleep," said Vorya. He had ordered that his pavilion not be set up in order to spare the men further fatigue, and he, Cvinthil, and Alouzon sat in the open, talking and debating plans by firelight. "I will give them until the moon is high, and then we must go on."

"When do you think we'll reach the battle?" said Alouzon.

Vorya lifted his head. The darkness was invisible at night, but the flickers of black incandescence that emanated from it told them its precise location. "Afternoon. Not until then."

Alouzon watched it for a moment. "It reminds me of the Heath."

"Tell me about that, lady," said the king. "Cvinthil told me of the First Wartroop's movements, and of

Dythragor's. He also told me of the actions of Kanol of Bandon, for which I most heartily apologize."

"Don't mention it. I had to learn eventually." She shrugged, uncomfortable with her new knowledge.

Vorya looked at her curiously. "Of the Heath, he could say nothing."

She told him in brief, omitting Dythragor's occasional ravings. It seemed unfair to expose the man's weaknesses when she had become too conscious of her own. In an effort to strengthen her recommendation that Mernyl be summoned, though, she went into some detail about the question of the Tree.

"A tree," said Vorya. "Interesting." The firelight flecked his white hair and beard with gold and crimson, and he was nodding slowly. "Before he left for the Cotswoods, Mernyl spoke in private with me. He said that he suspected the Dremords had in their possession an embodiment of most potent magic. He said that it took the form of a Tree."

"That's what he told me too," said Alouzon. "Are you sure you don't want to send for him? From what he said, that Tree can do some pretty horrible things. It did in that Corrinian at the Hall for sure."

Lightning flickered again in the distance. Vorya squinted at it. "Marrget," he whispered, "what is happening?"

But the king deferred his decision again. When the waning moon hung at the zenith, the men were awakened and the march continued with the sounds of booted feet and horses' hooves. The moon crawled down the sky, the stars wheeled overhead, and the night passed.

Stalemate.

The knowledge was like a clammy rain in the cold

morning, or like the gray smoke from the cooking fires that drifted across the troops, Corrinian and Gryylthan, sleeping and waking, as the dawn brightened the downs.

Tarwach ate quickly, his back to a fire to take the dew from his tunic. Darham had no interest in food. Tireas, called from the Tree by the king's order, sat wearily on a folding stool. The sorcerer had been at his post for many hours and had hardly slept that night. His face seemed gray against his white robes and beard, and he hung his head and groped at the plate of food in his lap with his eyes closed.

"It is not well with us," said Tarwach. "Have we lost then?"

One of the soldiers had found a stray cow, its udders full. Darham accepted a cup of milk, and he drank, cherishing the warmth. "We are in hostile territory. The enemy has only to reach out to call up more defenders. We, on the other hand, must live off our own supplies, without a roof, without a haven."

"So what do we do, brother? Go back to our lands . . ." Tarwach made a wry face. "Across the sea?"

Darham made a weary noise that was halfway between a laugh and a sob. "We have no place to go. I suppose, therefore, that we must go on. The people of Corrin at least shall know that we tried our best to preserve them . . ."

" . . .as they fall to Gryylthan swords?" Tarwach was angry. "No. We will go on, and we will win." He turned to the sorcerer. "Tireas, you have been holding back. You will have to kill in earnest now. You will have to slaughter."

"Do not torment me, my king." The sorcerer's voice was a whisper. Tireas, though he fought with immaterial weapons, was even more exhausted than the men who fought with swords and spears. "I will do what is necessary."

"You do not answer me, sorcerer." Tarwach's voice was cold. "You dissemble."

"Can I look at the passing of seasons, can I study the changes of life and love, and not be moved to kill only with great reluctance?"

"Should we lose, Tireas, we have no place to go. The killing then will be by Gryylth, and the dead will be our own people. Is that what you want?"

"Nay, lord." Tireas looked up at the young soldier who was serving him. "Bring me water, please, sir," he said. "I have no stomach for wine today." The boy nodded and ran for the supply wagons. To Tarwach he said: "I have command of the Tree, and that is a great thing. I will no longer say that it is a good thing, for as I use the Tree, so it uses me. Even now, I am not the sorcerer you knew in Benardis. And should I attempt greater potencies such as might stem this battle, I will lose more of myself. But, so be it. My people are in danger, and I will defend them."

The boy came back with a skin, and Tireas poured water over his face, then drank.

"There has been enough blood already," he said. "I pray you, King Tarwach, allow me one final chance. I confess that I quail at out-and-out killing, and therefore I have sought another way."

"You have often spoken of a plan."

"Aye. I have hesitated to give myself to the Tree as much as I would need to in order to execute it, but it seems that that course is now necessary." He stood up. "I have greater vision than your scouts, my lord. Vorya and several hundred men, and the female Dragonmaster with them, are on their way. They will arrive this afternoon. It will be a fatal blow for Corrin."

Tarwach took the news without flinching. "And therefore . . .?"

Tireas drank from the skin again, handed it back to the boy. "And therefore will I do what is necessary. Today, when the battle is thickest and you feel a humming in the air, like a swarm of bees, call a retreat of the phalanxes as quickly as you can. I will attend to the First Wartroop, and perhaps in so doing will attend to all of Gryylth."

Come morning, the darkness in the east was closer, blotting out the dawn, mocking the new day. Vorya's face was lined with strain, though Alouzon had to admire him: this was no armchair general who gave orders while sitting at home. He rode at the head of his troops, willing to share their fate.

But rests were few and too short, and the men were beginning to be affected as much by by fatigue as by the dull heaviness that had infected the air. It was a leaden feeling, like that of a humid summer day, and it turned even breathing into work.

The wind from the east picked up, carrying with it a tang of rot, as of a tide pool gone stagnant. The darkness had touched the entire sky, and the once-blue vault hung above them like a gray shroud. Alouzon sensed a change approaching.

"Cvinthil," she said abruptly, "make sure the men can get under cover fast."

There it was again: a sudden alteration in the feeling of the land, as though the faint transparency that she had come to accept as normal had increased, shuddered, and noticeably rippled.

"Something's going to happen. I can feel it."

Cvinthil's eyes flicked ahead to the darkness. "What?"

"Don't know. Something bad." She gave Jia a soft kick and trotted ahead to stay close to the king.

He greeted her warmly, but she noticed that he was deeply concerned. "The battle," he explained. "I fear that all is not well with Gryylth."

"What about Dythragor? He seems to get pretty good results."

"Nonetheless." Vorya gestured ahead. "In the face of that, I fear we are losing."

He straightened up and lifted his hand to give a signal to quicken the pace, but the darkness moved, striking like a cobra. A long, snaking tendril blasted through the air, lashing directly for Vorya's chest. The king, surprised, had barely enough time to lift his shield before it struck with a blue flash.

Instantly, the air turned to murk. Alouzon caught hold of Vorya's shoulder to keep him from toppling to the ground, but she could not see anything. There was a stench as of decay, and the horses were fighting to break away and run.

Jia was no exception. He strained against her, trying to turn around. Alouzon did not have the strength to hold the king and fight her mount at the same time. "Dammit, Jia," she shouted. "You run out on me now and I'll fix you good!"

He quieted and stood his ground, forcing Vorya's horse to hold still also. Alouzon shook the king by the shoulder. "Vorya! I can't hold you much longer."

"What?" The darkness as absolute, and a tide of confused and frightened voices was rising from behind as Vorya came to himself. "Am I blind?"

"No. It's the darkness." She turned around and

called out: "Someone light some torches." Cvinthil took up the order, and she was relieved.

In a few moments, wavering flames appeared. "My lady, the pitch burns fitfully," said a voice as uncertain as the light. She recognized it as belonging to the man who had asked her about her children.

"Better than not at all. Get some up here: the king's hurt."

Cvinthil himself appeared with a torch. Vorya looked pale. "My king?" said the councilor.

"I am well," he said. "My arm is numb, that is all."

"All, lord? That is your shield arm."

"What of it? My sword arm is sound."

Vorya's left arm had all the life of a sandbag. Shaking his head as Alouzon moved to help, he pried his shield loose from his numb fingers and threw it down, then took up the hand and tucked it into his belt.

He turned to Cvinthil. "We move on."

"In this darkness?"

"We marched in darkness last night. This is but little different. Marrget will need us now more than ever."

Rumbles from ahead. Deep rumbles, like barrels rolling downhill, or like mountains moving. Vorya lifted his head. "And what is this?"

Even in the feeble light cast by the torches, Alouzon could see that the ground was starting to lift. Large cracks appeared and widened, and trickles of sand and soil cascaded into them with a rattle. A wall began to rise ahead as the section of road occupied by the Gryylthans sank with a lurch.

The horses went wild. Even Jia reared. Alouzon gasped as she hit the stone pavement, but she reflected that, considering what was happening, it was better to be down.

A wind arose, extinguishing the torches, whipping
up to the strength of a hurricane in moments: a sudden blast of compacted air that felled those who were
still standing. Alouzon clawed for a handhold against
it, shut her eyes against the hail of sand and pebbles,
and tucked her head down as if fighting off tear gas.
She heard nothing save the sound of the driving air
that ripped and slashed at a landscape that was
embedded in the darkness like fossil fronds in pitch.

Abruptly, it was over. The wind subsided, the
darkness cleared. Alouzon unclosed her eyes and
looked up into a blue sky. The earth was still torn
and shattered, but the sun that shone on it was
friendly, and the only odor in the air was that of fresh
soil and bruised leaves.

The darkness had receded to the east. As they got
to their feet, it dwindled to a point and dissolved.

Vorya brushed himself off with his good hand. "The
attacks of the Dremords are short-lived," he remarked. He looked at his left arm in disgust. "I would
so were their wounds."

"We're not talking about weapons here," said Alouzon. "Not material ones, anyway."

He caught her meaning. "I will send for Mernyl.
My mind is made up. But we have other tasks now,
for who knows the fate of the wartroops?"

The wind had done only limited damage to the
unmounted soldiers who had not had to contend with
panicking animals. Some dislocated shoulders, some
scrapes, one or two broken bones. The few who could
not go on were sent back to the towns that lay to
the west. The rest started forward again.

The men climbed the wall that had arisen; the
horses detoured some distance into the fields on
either side in order to pass it. But beyond, the going

was smooth: the earth movements had been concentrated in the vicinity of the Vorya and the wartroops. There were cracks and pits beyond, to be sure, but few, scattered, and easily avoided.

Under the bright sky, the journey seemed to go more quickly, and the absence of the darkness gave the party less of a sense of condemned prisoners, and more that of a rescue squad. Alouzon heard someone telling jokes in the ranks, and the deep laughter of the men was a comforting sound. Her actions during the attacks had gained her respect, and some of the men were actually saluting her. She noticed, with a scholar's dogged persistence, that it was a distinctly Roman gesture.

Then they topped a rise and saw what the battle had left.

Alouzon surprised herself: she was not sickened by the sprawling heaps of dead that lay in shapeless hummocks as though bulldozed in a recreated Auschwitz. In truth, it was nothing that she had not seen before, seen and become inured to through the vitric safety of the six o'clock news. Death was the same everywhere: in Germany, in Vietnam, in Gryylth, and she discovered that, whether she confronted it as phosphorescent images in a cathode ray tube or face to face, it had, *en masse,* lost the power to move her.

Grief needed individuals. Even in Bandon there had been individuals. Here there were none. No faces to remember or to identify. Just colors and patterns laid down as though spattered by an artist. Just men—corpses of men—heaped as they had fallen, or as they had crawled together to seek some company in death.

The land was silent. There was no wind. A hundred

yards away, a few crows rose into the air. Alouzon wiped away a trickle of sweat that was threading down her cheek. She could hear the harsh breathing of the king beside her, and his voice seemed overloud as he ordered the men to look for survivors.

"The Tree," said Alouzon softly.

"Then we must concede defeat now," said Vorya, "for a sorcerer who can raise the elements against us in such a fashion cannot be stopped by mere bronze or iron."

"Mernyl?"

He shook his head. "Nor by Mernyl, I fear."

"My lord!" called Cvinthil from the far side of the valley. "We had best take the higher ground."

Vorya nodded absently and gave the signal to move. "And what of Dythragor?" he said. "Is he dead also?"

He lives, thrummed a voice in Alouzon's head.

Haul your ass back here, Silbakor, she thought. But there was no reply.

Unconsciously, she had shut her eyes when she had addressed the Dragon, and she nearly rode into Vorya, who had stopped suddenly in front of her. Drawing rein, she followed his gaze to the slope ahead.

There was a man there: bloody, filthy, but alive. Open wounds on his arms had scabbed over but lightly, and he moved with an effort as he stumbled down the slope. Only the blond curls, now matted with dirt, told Alouzon that this was Santhe. His smiles were gone. His face held nothing but shock and sorrow, and would not compromise on the slightest happiness.

He staggered forward until he reached Vorya. "My

lord," he said thickly. "I bring news of Marrget of Crownhark."

"Santhe, where—"

All his past laughter now added to the grimness that had fallen on him. This was Santhe, and yet not. Something had happened to him that went beyond the killing of men and the witnessing of death. "I learned of the breakthrough from Mernyl," he said, "and rode directly to the battle. I met my wartroop, and was leading them in a charge when . . ." He fell silent. His eyes stared at the ground, then at the sky. He became aware of Alouzon, and he flinched away for a moment before he recognized her.

"And what of Marrget? Is he alive?"

"Marrget . . . lives. The First Wartroop also." He almost collapsed, and a soldier dropped his spear and rushed forward to support him.

"Speak," said Vorya. "Are they wounded? Dying? Can we bring them relief?"

Santhe fought with his emotions and his wounds. He seemed ready to scream, unable to form coherent words. Alouzon leaned toward him to hear what he had to say, a dim sickness growing in her belly.

"My king," he said, "they are women."

❖ CHAPTER 14 ❖

❖

AT SANTHE'S WORDS, VORYA LOOKED BLANK, but only for a moment. He leaned down to the wounded man. "By the gods, Santhe, if this is your laughter speaking, you shall not speak again."

Santhe looked at him. There was not a shred of laughter left in him. Laughter was something unknown here on the fields of slaughter, with sightless eyes looking on and seeing nothing, and dead ears too full of screams to hear the joke. "My lord," he said evenly. "I speak the truth."

"Where are they?"

He gestured stiffly. "Across the ridge."

The king did not reply. Instead, he spurred his horse into a gallop and mounted the hill. Alouzon and Cvinthil stayed at his side, keeping pace with him. At the crest, they stopped, and Vorya muttered a protective oath.

Below, in a shallow valley, a group of riders stood dismounted. They bore the armor and insignia of the First Wartroop, and when they noticed that their king had come to them, they turned to face him.

It was as Santhe had said: they were all women.

One of them mounted and rode toward the king. Only the armor and the escutcheon indicated that this was Marrget, the captain. The burly warrior had become a thin young woman with ash-blond hair and a sense of fragility about her. There was a haunted, horrified leanness to her face, and she bore her body like a fresh scar.

Twelve feet from Vorya's horse, she stopped. "My lord," she said, fighting to keep her voice even, "the First Wartroop desires to lay down its arms to you, and to be dismissed from service." It was a formal request. Formality was all Marrget had left.

Vorya's jaw was set. Alouzon sensed that he was fighting some battle with himself, but she had no idea what the sides were involved. "You make your request too lightly, captain," he said at last. "I see no reason to relieve you of your duty and your oath to Gryylth. Tell your . . ." He groped for words. Marrget waited. " . . . your . . . warriors to have a care for their horses and for themselves, for battle weighs heavily on them all." His voiced seemed to fail for a moment, but he managed to continue. "When you have attended to that, I will question you as to your encounter."

Still formally, Marrget drew her sword and saluted Vorya, then rode back to her warriors. Alouzon noticed that the man she had known had not been completely effaced: the piercing eyes and proud set of the head were still evident.

If Alouzon had required individuals to make her weep, here they were. Unrecognizable, yet friends, a group of intimate strangers, their faces were distinct, each expression plain, direct, uncompromising. She wiped at her eyes, watched through a film of tears as Marrget went to her warriors and spoke to them, her voice low.

What did she say? This was no aftermath such as

the Heath had left, with two corpses that could be called dead with no equivocation. This was something else, an alteration that affected each member of the wartroop with a profundity that eclipsed the neat, tidy termination of another's life. What could she say?

The women listened, and slowly, fumbling for buckles with unfamiliar hands, they began to doff their oversized armor. Marrget was their captain, and, regardless of her form, they were loyal to her. Perhaps they even loved her. Whatever words could be said, Marrget had said them.

Alouzon wished that she had the captain's skill. Once, at Kent, she had tried to comfort the wounded and dying while they had waited through the innumerable minutes for the ambulances. But all she had found were trite and platitudinous words that exposed themselves for the lies that they were even as she uttered them.

She wanted to say something now to Marrget, to the comrades with whom she had fought and shared respect. The circumstances demanded that she say something. But she would not insult friends with those same untruths, for the circumstances also demanded honesty.

It's going to be all right.

Sure. And, by the way, you're dead.

She recoiled from the thought. No, they could not be dead. She would not allow it. She had been able to do nothing at Kent. But here, she was a Dragonmaster. She could do something.

Please say that it's going to be all right.

She might have said the words aloud. She wondered: could one pray to the Grail?

Vorya turned back down the hill to his troops, leaving the First Wartroop hidden behind the ridge. As he descended, he called Cvinthil to his side. "Find someone trustworthy to go to Mernyl with all possible speed. Have the sorcerer brought to me. Have him told whatever is necessary to insure his haste."

Cvinthil was still in shock. "And what of Dythragor's ban on sorcery?"

Beside him, Alouzon seized his arm and brought him to a halt, and stared into his face for a moment. "Fuck Dythragor," she said, and the bronze resonance of her voice seemed to clear the councilor's head. "You've got a bunch of people back there who need help, Cvinthil. Your fellow warriors."

He looked ashamed. "I am sorry, friend Alouzon. I . . ."

"It's OK, Cvinthil. Just hang in there, huh?"

She looked up at the sky. *Silbakor, where the hell are you? You better get your ass back here and quit playing around with that Marvel Comic refugee.*

At once, Silbakor's voice thrummed in her head: *I am coming.*

She glanced around, but the blue sky remained blank. "In your own good time," she muttered.

As they approached the army, she felt the massed eyes of the men watching them. Vorya rode with a studied ease, covering the strain he felt. He nodded to Santhe. "Thank you, councilor. You have done great service to Gryylth. What of your own wartroop?"

Santhe shrugged, hollow eyed. "Some eight or nine are left, some of them badly wounded."

"Like . . .?" Vorya's eyes flicked toward the ridge.

"Nay, my lord. Their injuries are from spears and flying rocks. They are some distance away, and very weak. I came to meet you."

Vorya gestured to his Guard. "Attend to them," he said. "Give them aid. Santhe will lead you."

Assisted by two soldiers, Santhe made his way

across the fields. Vorya watched him, and then turned to look back over his shoulder at the crest of the hill that hid the First Wartroop.

One of the captains of the wartroops dismounted and approached on foot. "My lord king," he said. "Is what Santhe said true?" His voice sounded thin in the late afternoon sun.

Vorya did not meet his eyes. Cvinthil conferred with a captain of the King's Guard, but the others remained silent, waiting.

Alouzon glanced back up the hill, wondering what was happening on the other side. Following orders, probably. Not thinking. That was the way it was done. After the deaths at Kent, she had gone home and cleaned house for days, occupying her mind with lesser things so that she would not see the staring eyes, the torn flesh.

Buying time. But there was always leisure eventually, always time for the fatal reflection.

Abruptly, Vorya nodded. "It is true."

The men stirred. She knew what was going through their minds: if Marrget and the cream of Gryylth, then what of themselves?

Vorya allowed no time for the thoughts. "Evening draws hard upon us," he said. "We will encamp here. My pavilion shall be to the side closest to this hill. Aside from those whom I designate, no one shall cross the ridge under penalty of death."

Cvinthil had finished his conference, and a rider dashed off to the north. The men began making camp. Vorya dismounted and went to Alouzon. "Dragonmaster," he said, "is this possible? Can sorcery do this?"

She shrugged. "I'm not surprised by anything that sorcery can do anymore."

Vorya nodded his white head. In the failing light, he looked much older. "I will see Marrget tonight, after dark. I must find out . . ." His eyes were dull, lifeless, as though he had gone blind. "Alouzon, my lady," he said, "can you . . .will you help us?"

Without thinking, she put a hand on his shoulder. "Marrget was . . . Marrget could do anything."

"Marrget still can." She hoped that she was right. "I'm surprised even less by Marrget and the wartroop than I am by magic. It's the others that you'll have to worry about."

He examined the men for a long minute. "I am afraid that this is the end of Gryylth."

The night was warm, but there was enough of a cool snap in the air to make the campfires burn brighter. Their light, though, did not reach far, and the darkness concealed the unburied dead save where a flame was reflected on a sword hilt, or a spear blade, or, dully, in a staring eye.

The men of Gryylth took what rest and refreshment they could in such surroundings, but from what Alouzon heard of their muffled conversations, they were less concerned about the slaughter than with the fate of those who remained on the other side of the hill, guarded by Vorya's pavilion and by the careful watch of his personal attendants. Even the tales brought back by the survivors of Santhe's wartroop did nothing to shift the talk to questions of mundane battle, and the undercurrent of fear ran like a steel thread throughout the entire camp.

"What do you think you will do?" said one soldier to another. "If . . . if the Dremords come again?"

"Oh, they will come . . ."

"But, what will you do?"

The moon, some days past full, was swinging mid-way to the zenith, and its light, added to that of the fires, allowed disturbing glimpses of the battlefields and the dead. But the soldiers paid no attention.

"I have no wish to be a woman."

"But—"

"I wish Dythragor were here instead of that other one. If he could face this without cowardice, then so could I."

"Maybe he will come."

Alouzon listened, then went on her way, stepping softly so that the men might not know that they had been overheard. "I'd like to punch out his lights," she muttered as she mounted Jia.

She turned his head up the slope and nodded to the guards as she passed them. Hoping that she might seem less of a threat than a man of the company, she had taken upon herself the task of fetching Marrget. The captain's conduct during the short time she had been in Gryylth had won her, unwilling though she was to be won, and if there was any way in which she could lessen the pain and shock, she was eager to find it.

At the crest, she looked down to see one small fire burning in the darkness. Dimly, she made out figures surrounding it, their gender disguised by distance and the flickering of the flames.

She started down, but had ridden only a few yards before she was brought up short.

"*Halt.*"

It was a woman's voice, high and clear, but holding nonetheless enough of a threat to make her stop instantly. "Alouzon Dragonmaster is sent by the king to request the presence of Marrget of Crownhark," she said.

A slim form stepped out from the cover of the

shadows. "You are Alouzon Dragonmaster," she said. "Pass."

The moonlight gave Alouzon a glimpse of finely molded features as she rode on. She had known the men of the wartroop by sight if not by name, but Tireas had transformed them utterly, leaving nothing unchanged. Height, weight, hair, voices—all were different. She could not recognize them. She doubted that they could recognize themselves.

When she reached the fire, the women regarded her quietly. Their oversized clothing hung on their slender frames as though they were girls dressing up in their fathers' suits, and their expressions were earnest, almost fearful. For a moment, she was reminded of the girls of Bandon—kirtles and skirts, ringlets and ponytails—their faces all the prettier for the intensity with which they regarded the armed woman who had come to them.

The thought made the sweat break out on her forehead. "Is Marrget here?"

"Behind you," came the unfamiliar voice. Marrget rode up out of the darkness. Her gray eyes examined Alouzon. "You did not have to come."

"I wanted to. For the sake of our friendship."

"I am sorry that you must associate with the vanquished." Marrget made for the ridge, and Alouzon followed.

They rode in silence, side by side, and Marrget sat stiffly and kept her gaze straight ahead, as though she were a prisoner under escort instead of a friend. In the clear moonlight at the crest of the ridge, Alouzon saw that she was wearing neither armor nor sword.

Feeling her gaze, Marrget stopped. "You could have looked better when the sun was high."

"You're unarmed."

She shrugged. "It is unseemly for a woman to carry weapons."

The bald statement was nothing more than what she would have heard from any inhabitant of Gryylth, but it struck Alouzon like a fist of ice. It had started. Marrget was a woman, and as such she was bound. The whole country could not but reinforce the devastating impact of the transformation.

But it did not have to be that way. She would not let it. She was a Dragonmaster. "I . . . I hope you don't believe that, Marrget," she said. "Have you taken a look at me?"

"Your customs are different." Marrget stared down at Vorya's pavilion. "I am not sure that I know how to bow properly to a man. Do you think . . ." Terror clawed at her face for a moment, but she mastered it. "Do you think that I will cause offense?"

"Marrget . . . don't . . . please . . ."

She blinked, shifted her eyes to Alouzon.

"You're a warrior of Gryylth."

"Do not torment me, Alouzon." She shook her head, and her long hair rustled down her back. She plucked at it. "Am I supposed to braid this?"

Alouzon felt like screaming, but she fought to form words. "You are Marrget of Crownhark."

She said nothing in reply. She turned her horse down the slope.

Vorya had pared the number of his attendants to a minimum in an effort to keep Marrget's interview as painless as possible. In his tent were, besides himself, only Cvinthil, Santhe, two trusted officers of his guard, and a scribe. Still, Marrget paused at the flap and looked around the room as though it were a trap.

"Enter and be welcome, Marrget of Crownhark," said Vorya. "Sit before me and refresh yourself. You have done hard service for Gryylth and deserve honor."

Marrget advanced to the center of the tent, and hesitated as though considering a woman's bow of subservience. She looked for a moment to Alouzon, then gritted her teeth and gave a slight nod to Vorya in the manner of a councilor acknowledging a king. "I do not know what service I have done, my king, but I am certain that it is not deserving of honor. You see that the battle is lost, and there are many dead men who, if they could speak, would tell the truth of my words."

It was all very formal, the little courtesies of heroic culture smoothing the raw edges of fear. A chair was brought for Marrget and, still with a hesitation, as though she wondered what rule of women's etiquette she was breaking, she sat. She was wearing a rough robe girt with a piece of rope, and the garment was too big for her: it gaped open at her breast. Grimly, she pulled it closed.

Alouzon filled a cup and brought it to her, but she waved it away. "My lord, you sent for me."

"I would hear something of the battle. Santhe has told me what he could. I would hear more."

Santhe nodded slowly. "I will always defer to Marrget in matters of combat," he said, his pain weakening his voice. "And in others, too." His face was worn, blasted with what he had seen, but he mustered a smile for her. "Surely, my dear comrade, you have nothing to fear from me."

Marrget bit her lip and looked down at her lap suddenly, as though suppressing tears. "My thanks, Santhe." Her thin face was soft and frail, and her hair shone in the lamplight like a swirl of gold as she began her report. "When we arrived," she said, "the slaughter had been great, but the wartroops were slowing the Dremords, and it was my opinion that the First Wartroop would turn the tide easily. The Dremords had been preparing this attack for some time, I think, gathering men and supplies in hopes of breaking through to the Circle quickly, before our forces could be brought up."

Speaking of those things that she knew, Marrget was relaxing, her voice falling into the cadences of a soldier: matter-of-fact, firm and definite. "They did not count on our strength, though, and, as I surmised, the First Wartroop held them where they were. But there was always the darkness, summoned by the unnatural sorcery of Tireas—" For a moment, she stared, shifted in her chair as though acutely conscious of her body, then plunged on.

"It looked as though clouds had gathered for a rainstorm, but these clouds brought no rain, only fear. And there was lighting that struck amid our troops, and it brought death. Still, we did not quail. A short distance from here, we planted ourselves and vowed that the men of Corrin would come no farther into Gryylthan territory." She considered, looked at her hands. "It would perhaps have been better had we given way."

"What happened, Marrget?" Alouzon kept her voice gentle.

"Early this afternoon," she continued, "there came an easing of the Dremord press, and a further darkening of the skies. The air seemed full of strange noises—a humming, or a singing—and we saw that the Dremords were bringing up a wain. In it was a tree."

She looked at Alouzon. "It seems you were right, Dragonmaster. It was a tree, but it was truly an awful one. It was as high as two men, and its trunk was gnarled, with many branches bearing withered leaves and fruit that glowed in the darkness. Tireas stood beside the wain, and he seemed to have charge of it. He placed his hands on the tree and began a conjuration."

Falling silent, she shifted in her chair again. "My body . . . went numb. I had not felt real fear in a long time, but I felt it then. It was as though serpents were crawling over me, tightening their coils. Seeing that the phalanxes were falling back, I gathered the wartroop, thinking that perhaps we could interfere with the magic."

A soldier of the King's Guard entered suddenly, followed by a man wrapped up in a thick cloak. The latter carried a pale staff, and Marrget glanced curiously at him before she continued with her tale.

"We did not stop the magic," she said. "We ran into it. The entire wartroop was unconscious for some hours, and when we came to ourselves, we became aware of the . . . changes." She clenched her jaw. "It would have been better had they killed us."

"That wouldn't have fit their plan, Marrget," said Alouzon. "They wanted you alive."

"For what? To live in disgrace?"

Vorya spoke. "No, to destroy the will of Gryylth." With his good arm he beckoned to the soldier who had entered. "You return sooner than expected."

"My king," he said, "I met him on the road. He said that he knew of our need already and had not waited for your summons."

"Mernyl?"

"I am here." The sorcerer dropped his cloak on the floor and stepped forward.

"Am I to be made the butt of a magician's fancy?" said Marrget. "Have you come to laugh at me?"

Mernyl approached her with deference. "Do I laugh

at the moon when it changes shape, captain?" He bowed deeply. "I come only to offer service, and, if possible, aid."

His voice was kind, full of compassion, and Alouzon almost turned away to hide her tears. Marrget had never liked Mernyl, but the captain, broken, defeated, was now at his mercy, and she bent her head slowly as though in acknowledgment.

"No, captain," he said gently. "Do not bow your head to me. Though you have never believed it before, I have been your friend, and I remain so now."

She lifted her eyes. "So be it."

"May I touch you?"

She considered, then nodded reluctantly. "You may."

He knelt before her and held up his hands as though she were a fire at which he warmed himself. Then, slowly, he passed his hands over her face, tracing the curve of her cheekbones, her jaw, running a thumb along her brow. He examined her hands, flexing them at finger and wrist, pressing them between his own.

After a time, he sat back on his heels and sighed. His eyes were tired, his cheeks more hollow than usual. "My thanks, captain."

"Can you heal Marrget?" said the king.

"Heal?" said the magician vaguely. "Heal? There is nothing wrong with Marrget, no hint of sickness, no taint of malady."

Marrget looked at her hands, her face pale.

"You . . . must forgive me," said Mernyl. "I have not seen anything like this before. Always, in an enchantment of shape-changing, the new semblance is but an illusion, as though a wall were daubed with mud that might run with the first rain. But there is no illusion here. Marrget's body has been remade from its very core. She is as she appears."

Marrget stiffened at the pronouns, then flared. "Perhaps you are not completely certain that it is Marrget of Crownhark who sits here in this robe. Perhaps I am a Dremord spy, a maiden done up in Marrget's armor and sent to bring you a laughsome tale."

Mernyl rose. "I have no doubt that it is to Marrget of Crownhark that I speak." He took her by the shoulders as though to convince her of her own identity. "I regret that I cannot aid you in the fashion you wish. Will you still accept me as an ally, and a friend?"

She shuddered. "Do not press me, Mernyl."

"I shall not." He released her, turned to Vorya. "Perhaps you do not appreciate what I have said, my king. If the Corrinians have this power, no one can oppose them."

"Indeed," said Vorya, "no one wants to oppose them. Since early evening, my army has shrunk by half. The men have made their way off to their homes."

"The cowards!" cried Marrget. "Desertion is a deadly crime, and now—" She broke off, looked down at herself. "And . . . who am I to say?"

Outside, there was a shout which, after a moment, was echoed and re-echoed. Alouzon finally made it out.

"Dythragor comes!"

❖ CHAPTER 15 ❖

❖

AS SILBAKOR'S WINGBEATS PULSED AT THE tent walls, Marrget looked to Alouzon, her face white. The Dragonmaster shook her head and straightened up. She tried to appear confident for the benefit of Marrget, but she knew well what was likely to happen.

Outside, there were several more shouts, Dythragor's booming answer, then the sound of a sword being sheathed and the heavy tramp of boots. The tent flap was shoved back and Dythragor stepped into the room.

Soot and ashes covered him, and grime was caked in the lines on his face and forehead, giving the semblance of added years. For a moment, Alouzon thought she caught a glimpse of Solomon Braithwaite as on old man laid out in a coffin, the burden of age upon him. But Dythragor spoke, and the illusion evaporated.

"They've slaughtered our men, and they've gained some land, but they've paid for it." His voice rasped as though with a thirst of many days, and he strode to the center of the room without noticing Marrget or Mernyl. "Three of their towns are burned—they'll get no levies there—and their crops in the southern parts of their territory are destroyed. They'll have no food this winter. They'll have to turn back."

Vorya looked at him soberly.

"Well?" said Dythragor.

"What of the battle, Dragonmaster?" said the king. "Our losses were heavy, and you have been loud in your promises of help. What of the battle?"

He seemed to grow impatient. "The wind out of the blackness pushed me far to the south and east. I did what I could."

Silence. Alouzon saw his temper building.

"I admit that burning fields is not the most noble of actions," he said. "But then, neither is the use of magic."

Mernyl had moved protectively to one side of Marrget's chair, and Alouzon now stepped to the other. The captain's hands had tightened on her robe, and the muscles of her arms, strong even in womanhood were taught and tense as she watched and listened. Her eyes said that she was frightened, but there was something else there, too, as though, under the influence of her change, she were suddenly seeing Dythragor in a new light, examining him with a head uncluttered by questions of honor and bravado. In spite of her fear and shock, she seemed almost startled by what she saw.

"You don't seem to understand," Dythragor was saying. "Because of what I did, we've got time to regroup. The Dremords will starve this winter. We can defeat them easily. We can get rid of them once and for all."

"Perhaps," said Vorya. "Yet . . . perhaps not."

There was a distinct pall over the company, one compounded equally of past death and present uncertainty. Examining the faces before him, Dythragor slowly became aware of it. Then he turned around and saw Marrget and Mernyl.

"Another woman?" he said. "And a trickster? What the hell are we coming to?" His tone had been steadily hardening, and now he whirled on the king and exploded. "Are these the counsels you're listening to? What brothel did you drag this whore out of so that you could elevate her to a position of state?"

Marrget's face was full of stunned disbelief. If Alouzon had, in the past, ever wished that the captain could be treated to a taste of a Gryylthan woman's lot, she deeply regretted it now.

"Is this your doing, Mernyl?" said Dythragor. "Not satisfied with one woman under your control, you've got to have two?"

But Mernyl stood calmly, his hand resting on Marrget's shoulder, even as Dythragor advanced on him. "My lord Dragonmaster, I have cast no spells. This is a victim of Dremord magic. It is Marrget of Crownhark who sits before you."

Marrget was shaking visibly with the strain. Dythragor stared as though he had been struck with a club. He took a few paces toward the chair and peered incredulously at the woman in it, then suddenly leaped for Mernyl.

"Liar!"

Mernyl fell back as the Dragonsword flicked out and missed him by a finger's width. With the effortless grace of a seasoned warrior, Dythragor swept in again. "You dare to insult the name of Marrget of Crownhark?"

Alouzon pulled herself out of her shock and grabbed his arm. "Dammit, Braithwaite," she yelled, "he's telling the truth."

"I've had it with your interference, bitch." He

turned on her and his stroke was aimed at her skull. Jerking out her own sword, she parried with a clang, then dropped back a step to gain room and stood between Dythragor and Mernyl.

"Back off," she said.

"The hell I will. You've been getting mighty uppity since you tore out that Dremord's throat the first night here. You think you can beat me?"

"I'm a Dragonmaster too. Stay away from Mernyl. He's telling the truth."

Vorya's guards made a motion as though to interpose, but Dythragor glared at the king. "Keep your goons off, old man."

Alouzon was already stepping in. She did not want to kill Dythragor: she was gambling that she could disarm him. His arrogance had allowed several openings to creep into his fighting technique, and the hot power of the Dragonsword, blasting through her nerves, allowed her to see them clearly.

Dragonsword met Dragonsword, and locked. Alouzon ducked to the side, snaked a leg behind Dythragor and leaned into his chest. He tripped, dropped onto his back, and she was on him instantly, pinning him. "Mernyl's telling the truth, asshole," she shouted as he flailed at her. "He was right about the Tree of Creation. The Corrinians got it out of the Heath. They can do *anything*."

Dythragor continued to struggle, his smoke-blackened face inches from her own. "Just let me up for one second, girl. I'll tan your little ass."

His words were designed to anger her and make her careless, but she was not playing. "Just listen for a fucking change, will you?" Lifting her head, she called to Vorya. "Have us pulled apart, my lord. I think I've got him."

Vorya signed to his guards, and the men seized the two Dragonmasters and lifted them up and apart. Dythragor's sword came out of his grip, spun flashing in the torchlight for a moment, then fell to the carpeted floor with a soft thump.

"You doubt Alouzon," said Vorya calmly. "I trust you will not doubt me. It is the truth."

"You'll be telling me soon that cherries grow on thorns," he returned. Vorya flushed, but the guard still held Dythragor.

"Enough," said Marrget. "I know who I am." Holding her robe closed, she rose from her chair, stood a few feet from Dythragor. "I am defeated," she said evenly. "I have been wounded grievously. I deserve no less than my present disgrace, but I am, and will remain, Marrget of Crownhark. I will not evade my dishonor with name trickery." Her eyes flashed. "Nor will I listen without protest to your insults to my king."

"Go back to your kitchen, wench. You may have bamboozled everyone here, but you can't fool me."

Marrget stood her ground. "I give you a memory: In the Heath, I stopped you from throwing your life away in battle with the beast that arose. You challenged my manhood then, and I told you that, were you not Dythragor Dragonmaster, I would have your life for that. Do you remember?"

He stared at her.

She took a step forward, her eyes bright. "I will give you another memory: Do you recall, at the Battle of Benardis, how you and I rode well behind the Dremord army and caught two maidens doing their washing at the side of the Long River? One, I recall, was as blond as Santhe, the other was dark, her hair the color of yours, Dythragor. I was never easy with our actions that day." She tossed her head, met his stare without flinching. "Perhaps I now know why."

Dythragor was pale beneath the soot when she finished. His mouth fought to form words. "M-Marrget?" His voice was dry, like the rustle of long-dead leaves.

"Aye, Dragonmaster. The entire First Wartroop is similarly afflicted."

His breathing was labored, as though only with an effort could he force the air in and out of his lungs. Pulling himself up straight, he wavered in the grip of his guard, then, with a weak shrug, pushed the man away.

Marrget watched without visible emotion as Dythragor bent, retrieved his sword, and slipped it into its sheath. He faced the captain again, searched her face, then averted his gaze as though he had found what he had sought. "Marrget?"

She stood proudly, like a patriot facing a firing squad. "It is I."

Horror grew on Dythragor quickly, and, with a sudden cry, he turned away and plunged out of the tent. They heard a horse whinny, and a moment later there were hoofbeats.

Alouzon started after him, but Marrget held her back. "Do not, friend Alouzon," she whispered. She faced Vorya again. "My king, is there anything further you wish to ask me?"

"Nay, Marrget." His voice was almost inaudible.

"Then I will return to my wartroop." She hesitated, gave a bow that held not a shred of subservience, and left.

She was walking quickly, as though she did not want company, but Alouzon followed her. Hard by the entrance to Vorya's pavilion, the Dragon waited, wings folded, head down. Marrget gave it a brief glance and went directly to her horse. Alouzon stopped for a moment, fixed it with a pointing finger. "You, I want to talk to. Later."

Silbakor sighed. "As you wish."

Marrget was already halfway up the slope by the time Alouzon was mounted. The guards let her pass as she galloped after the captain, but she managed to close the distance only at the crest.

"Marrget!"

She did not stop, but she slowed, riding stonily onward and down. Alouzon kept pace. The wartroop's guard did not challenge her. There did not seem to be a guard anymore. Something glistened on the rocks where the woman had stood, and Alouzon's belly, twisted though it was, twisted some more.

At the fire, Marrget whirled around. "Why do you follow me?" she cried. "How much do you wish to torment me? I will admit my defeat, but I will not be tormented."

"Dammit, Marrget, I'm not trying to torment you. I'm trying to help."

"And how will you help, pray?" Her eyes were cold, and her voice held a hundredweight of irony. "Can you remake us?"

Alouzon hung her head. Of course she could not. At least not physically. If there were to be any remaking, it would have to be internal: a change of belief, of attitude, an opening of the heart to other ways.

She was not sure she could do it. But she had to.

One of the women approached, touched Marrget's knee. "My captain."

"What do you wish?" Marrget did not take her eyes off Alouzon.

"My captain, seven of the wartroop are dead."

"What? More sorcery?" Marrget at last looked at the woman, searched her face. "Which are you?"

"Relys."

"Speak, Relys. How did they die? Where are they?"

"They took their own lives. Singly, they went out of range of the firelight and fell on their swords." She pointed into the darkness. "Their bodies are over there."

Marrget had kept her face carefully set in an expression of hardened fortitude, but at the news it went slack with shock. Slowly, her eyes shut tightly and she put her fists to her head as though to shield herself from the horror. She trembled. She might have been weeping.

But when at last she lowered her hands, her eyes were dry. "Who?"

Relys named them. Alouzon had known them and their faces: the full beard of one, the scars of another. But that, she reminded herself, that was all gone now. Everything familiar, everything that they could call themselves had been stripped away, to be replaced with . . .

She resolved that she would not look at the bodies. She would remember them as they themselves would have wished her to. It was all she could do for them now.

Marrget slid from her horse carefully, as though her legs might not support her, pushed herself away from the animal as though, by strength of will, she could make them. "I will go and look." She stood for a moment, staring blankly, then caught herself as though she shook a disobedient child, and went off.

Alouzon watched until she was out of sight. "Relys?"

"My lady."

Like all the rest, Relys was unrecognizable. The thick-limbed lieutenant had become a sleek girl who looked no more than eighteen. Her eyes were hard, though, set in a face that was incongruously beautiful.

"How are you, Relys?" Alouzon spoke quietly.

She shook her head. "I do not wish to die by my own hand. That is all that keeps me from following my comrades who now lie away from the fire." She ran her eyes over her soft form, weighed a breast in her hand experimentally, dropped it and shook back her hair with disdain. "So much for beauty. A pretty piece I would make on the block in Bandon, eh?"

"Don't hurt yourself, Relys."

"I said that I would not."

"Your friends used their swords. You're using words. I'll warn you: it's more painful, and a lot slower."

Relys snorted, started to walk away.

Alouzon called after her. "I noticed that Wykla was not among those that you named."

"Aye," she said, half turning. "Wykla lives."

"Where is . . ." She could not avoid the pronouns forever. Nor would it do the wartroop any good to try. Gryylth had to change. Everything had to change. "Where is she?"

Relys looked toward the fire. One of the women stirred. "H-here, my lady," she said.

The speaker was young, pretty, with amber hair that fell well below her shoulders. Her blue eyes were imponderably sad. She sat huddled by the fire as though she had been beaten.

"Wykla," said Relys. He had named the dead in the same way. "Alouzon Dragonmaster, I go to attend my captain, who inspects the . . . lucky ones."

Alouzon hardly heard her. Her attention was focused solely on the girl by the fire. "Wykla," she said softly. "I'm sorry." She got down from Jia and padded across the grass to her side. The others watched as she dropped to her knees and put her arms about her. "I'm sorry."

"My lady." She was weeping in silence, but openly, the first tears that Alouzon had seen among the war-troop. The others were impassive, their faces half blank, half stone. "I . . ."

She had to say it. The words forced themselves out. This time, though, she resolved that she would not be lying. "Wykla, it's going to be all right. I promise. One way or another, it's going to be all right." Whatever she had to do, wherever she had to go, she would make good her vow. It would be all right. Somehow.

Wykla listened to her, lifted her small hands as though Alouzon had offered her a cup brimming with a new life. But abruptly, with an inarticulate whimper, she broke down sobbing, burying her face in Alou-zon's shoulder. The grief she expressed was dragged up from deep and bitter wellsprings, and it racked her body as though it might tear her apart. Crying aloud, she in turn tore unthinkingly at Alouzon's ar-mor, and her tears mixed inseparably with her sweat as she beat herself against the thing that had hap-pened to her.

Alouzon held her, rocking her like a child as she screamed out her pain, pushing back her long hair when it threatened to choke her. She could say noth-ing more to Wykla. No endearments, no comforts, no further words of encouragement. The mere thought of such things was obscene, a trivialization of the fury of emotion that ripped and slashed at Wykla, that pushed her through pain, through agony, and into something that was at once both absolute nightmare and starkest reality.

Impaled upon such thorns, Wykla screamed, her cries those of a young woman faced with the unendurable. Alouzon, who had herself twice faced annihilations that were no less consummate for all their dissimilarities, knew that she could be no more than physical being, a simple presence that reminded the girl that the whole world was not white and raw, that held out the promise that the unendurable, accepted, might be endured.

Mercifully, Wykla spent herself quickly. Her cries became feeble, vague, and her grip on Alouzon's armor slackened and slipped away as her mind overloaded and sent her into an exhausted sleep.

With a sigh, Alouzon laid Wykla down on the grass, propping her head on a bundle of blankets. "Someone get me some water so I can wash her face," she said without looking up.

"I had hoped," came Marrget's voice, "that my warriors could take their defeat with dignity."

She was too worn to become angry. "It isn't a question of that."

"Wykla was always weak."

"Like she was in the Heath?" She looked up at the captain. Marrget stood on the far side of the fire. The angle of the light put her eyes in shadow and turned her face into a mask. Alouzon might have been conversing with a Greek tragedy. "You call that weak? She saved your ass. She's got enough guts to admit that she hurts. Maybe she's stronger than you are."

Marrget motioned to Relys. "Bring the Dragonmaster a skin of water and a cloth."

She brought them, handed them to Alouzon. Her eyes were black and hard, but their strength had turned brittle, shallow. For all her protests that she had no intention of taking her own life, Relys was slipping, just like the rest of the wartroop. Even Marrget would eventually reach her limit.

Slowly, Alouzon cleaned the salt and saliva from Wykla's face. The girl murmured in her sleep, and one hand plucked nervelessly at her short tunic, her smooth thighs, as though, even unconscious, she sought reconciliation with her body.

Alouzon wanted to sleep, to crawl under warm blankets in her own bed in Los Angeles and lie inert for hours, days, until Gryylth was far in the past. But nothing was ever in the past—Kent State, Dallas, Gryylth, whatever—for the past lay beneath the present, an underlayer of history and recollection that colored every thought and deed with the indelible hue of memory, whether sunlit or blood-spattered.

And the only way out was through.

"It's not a question of dignity anymore," said Alouzon. These were her friends. She would not let them die. Somehow, she had to find the right words. "It's not a question of dignity, or honor, or valor, or anything else." She wrung out the cloth and stood up. "What we are talking about, captain, is survival."

Marrget regarded the sleeping girl as though she stared into a mirror and saw there an overly honest reflection.

"How long do you think you can keep up this stiff-upper-lip crap?" Alouzon pressed. She allowed an edge to creep into her voice.

"I do not understand you."

"How long are you giving yourself before you join your friends over there?"

"We . . . will live."

"Like hell you will. Wykla let it out. She beat herself senseless in front of you, and you didn't do a damned thing. You just judged her. And, you know, she's probably going to do that again and again until she fights her way through to some kind of sanity. But I think she's got a chance. You, though . . ." She shook her head. "You're so fucking petrified right now I'm surprised you don't crack in two."

Marrget's mouth forced itself into a thin smile. "And so what are we to do, Alouzon Dragonmaster? Weep for our lost manhood? Wail like bereaved wives? Learn to accept our status as women, and bow and simper to our menfolk? Will you teach me now to braid my hair so that I can be properly debased?"

"It doesn't have to be like that."

"That is what women are."

"Bullshit."

Marrget spat. "You know it as well as I."

Words would not suffice. She needed action. She had to do something, and if she could not pull Marrget back, she would follow the lesson she had learned and force her onto the same path that Wykla had found: she would push her *through*.

"All right, Marrget," she said, stepping up to her. "You can get away with a lot, and you have so far. But when you start badmouthing women, you're badmouthing *me*, and I don't like it. That sort of garbage might have worked when you were lording it around in Hall Kingsbury, but it doesn't wash here. Right now, you're on my turf, lady, and you'd better get used to it."

Behind her, one of the other women was sobbing. Alouzon cringed at the sound. She was taking a terrible risk, but everything was a risk now. And, yes, Wykla *might* make it. But she was far ahead of the others, and not even finished with the worst yet.

She waited. Marrget was silent for some time, and

her eyes were fixed on Alouzon as though she held a sword and were picking a place for her first thrust. "If I have offended you, Alouzon, friend," she said, composing herself with an effort, "I am heartily sorry. I beg pardon. I can do no more."

"You'll have to do a lot more, little girl."

Marrget's fists clenched. "*By the stars, what?* What else is to be taken from us? In the span of a day we are defeated, emasculated, and made outcast. My trusted friend runs from me as though I carry plague. What now?"

"You're a captain of Gryylth, Marrget. Your land is in danger. The Corrinians will be back."

"I doubt that. It seems that the Dremords have but to wait and our army will disappear like a puddle in the sun."

"That was then, before we heard about your trusted friend's fun and games in Corrin. They might have been satisfied to wait before, but do you really think they're going to sit tight after their towns have been burned and their wheat destroyed? Really? What would you do?"

"I would . . ." Marrget stood, deliberating. She pushed her hair off her face slowly. "I would come for revenge even if victory were assured by waiting. And if they have no food . . ."

"How long do we have?"

She lapsed into mental calculations that had become automatic over the years. "One, two days."

"So you're going to have to fight." She realized that she was counseling in favor of war, but there was no choice: driven by revenge and by the need for winter food, Corrin could well slaughter everyone. "Vorya's not going to have much of an army soon. You're all he's got."

"Very good." The irony had not left Marrget's voice.

"The ideal warriors. What more have we to lose?" She snorted. "But you misunderstand, Dragonmaster. Women are not warriors."

"Yeah. You're right. I don't understand." Her vision was blurring with fatigue, but she shook it off. It had to be tonight. Anything might happen before morning: more suicides, madness, a bleak despair that could be worse than either.

"We are women," said Marrget.

"So what?"

Marrget shrugged, turned away.

The captain was breaking off the exchange. Alouzon was losing her. But she caught sight of the pile of weapons that lay at the edge of the firelight, cast off by the wartroop in an almost automatic response to the ingrained mores that said that women could not bear arms. "Then again..." She edged slowly around so that Marrget was between her and the arms. "Then again, maybe you're right. Maybe that's all you are. Women. I suppose you're built a little differently in Gryylth."

Marrget's brow furrowed.

Alouzon started her drive. "Come on, Marrget. You're just scared. You got a bellyful of battle and you finally gave up. You all gave up. You didn't become women because Tireas did it to you. You changed because that's what you all were inside. That's why you all picked on Wykla so much: you didn't want to admit it. Now you've got the right plumbing. Satisfied? Tits and ass, a sweet little pussy, and the whole thing. Relys was right: you'd make a pretty sight on the block at Bandon. Or maybe you'll want to make it legal and crawl off and get yourself a husband. I'm sure there's some big Dremord farmer out there who'd love to get between the thighs of a girl who used to be the captain of the First Wartroop."

She stepped in. Marrget stepped back, her face contorted. "You . . . *dare!*"

The other women were staring in shock. What she was saying might break some of them, but she had to take the chance. Marrget was strong, with more innate pride and valor than anyone in Gryylth. She could make it. And if she did, the chances were excellent that the others would follow. "Yeah, I dare. You always were a coward, Marrget. You stayed well out of the trouble in the Heath until Dythragor pushed you by telling you what you were. He saw it. I saw it too."

Marrget, seething, darted a glance back at the pile of weapons.

"You don't scare me, Marrget," Alouzon taunted. "Your arms are too weak to swing a bread knife, much less a sword. Hang some bangles on your wrists. Maybe you'll get up some strength if you work out with them enough." She grinned mockingly. "And don't forget to braid your hair."

It was enough. Marrget flinched as though struck. "Dragonmaster," she snarled, "you are a dead woman."

Whirling, she seized her sword. The metal shrilled as it slid from its sheath, and she brought it over her head in a sweeping arc. There was no lack of strength in her arms—the blade responded as though it were a willow wand—and with the cunning of years of combat, and the calculated anger of a skilled warrior, she drove in for the attack.

❖ CHAPTER 16 ❖

❖

I WILL NOT GO BACK THERE.

From his seat before the king, Tireas could see, in the near distance, the glow of the Tree in its wain. It had grown since it had left the loose, friable soil of the Heath, as though the diet on which it had fed— energy, passion, men's lives and souls—had fattened it like a carrion bird.

I will not go back.

One of the souls it had devoured, he knew, was his own. He was a shell now, something that went through the semblance of life's motions, ate and— sometimes—slept, spoke and defecated, wept and . . .

. . . laughed? Had he really laughed once? It seemed a strange thought. Laughter was something for men, for people who could say *Dig up this Tree,* or *We will have to leave Flebas behind.* It belonged to someone who could feel a bite of conscience at the rending of flesh, the crack of bones, the slippery convulsion of viscera dumped brutally on the ground and trampled by frenzied horses. It had no place in the heart of one whose compassion had been stripped away by the elemental desires of pure change, who could ex- perience nothing beyond a cloudy horror at the ab-

rupt transformation of an attempt to avert more
bloodshed into the white, fetid heat of mass slaughter.

Tireas wrapped his arms about himself and rocked
back and forth like a child struggling with a nightmare. He would not go back. He would not put his
hands on the Tree again. There was nothing that fate
or the gods could to that would move him. He had
given everything to Corrin and to the Tree. He had
nothing more to surrender, not even himself.

But it seemed that he would not be asked, for Tarwach was hearing reports from his forces, and there
was nothing said that did not indicate that Gryylth
was finished. Captains, soldiers, scouts who had ridden ahead and peered at the Gryylthan encampment
as the evening light died in the west—all brought
variants upon the same message.

"Simply, my king," said a tall commander, "Gryylth
does not have enough men to continue to fight. And
what few there are left are deserting."

And Tireas rocked, listening with only half of his
attention to the drone of voices.

"You saw them deserting?"

The soldier, short, young, ill-at-ease in the presence
of his king, bobbed his head emphatically, like a bird.
"With my own eyes, my liege. They were gathering
their weapons. Packing up, if you will. They went
off westward."

"Could you hear their speech?" Tarwach asked another, a scarred old veteran with a mouth set in a
perpetual grimace.

"Aye. Aye, I could, lord. They spoke of the deaths,
but mostly of the First Wartroop."

Tireas gripped himself harder, his mind a haze of
soft, rounded womanflesh forced upon unwilling

bodies and minds, the slowly dawning horror of an awakening to a loss of self, of everything familiar.

"What of the First Wartroop?"

"They are encamped separate from the rest of the army, my king."

"And what of them?"

The scout was cloaked in black, his face smeared with soot and his keen knife painted so that its gleam would not betray his presence. He indicated a fresh slash on his darkened cheek. "Women they might be, lord, and new to their station, but they fight well. This wound I had from their sentry when I was foolish enough to approach. Her womanhood has made her no less the warrior."

Darham stood next to his brother, his blue eyes showing a mixture of admiration and pity. But that was Darham: in the midst of the thickest battle, he could still maintain a compassionate fellowship with the men he fought. "And how do they fare, sir? Are they . . .?"

"Some are dead. A number have killed themselves. The rest . . ." The scout touched the slash. "I did not consider it wise to approach further."

"And Vorya's army is deserting?"

"Aye. Already it is but half of what it was." He considered, as though weighing the effect of his words. "But there is something else. The sorcerer Mernyl has been brought to King Vorya. He appears to be welcome."

Silence. Beyond the canopy hastily erected to serve as Tarwach's lodge, the campfires of the phalanxes flickered in the soft, eastern wind. The odor of woodsmoke and the murmur of men's voices fluttered in the air like the moths that circled round the torches.

Tireas felt the eyes of the king and his brother on him. He was supposed to say something. He could think of nothing to say. Nothing would make him put his hands on that trunk again, nothing could coerce him into allowing the shadowy tendrils of madness to snake across his consciousness. Nothing.

The battle was won. It would not be necessary. He clung to those thoughts. "There is little that Mernyl can do, my king," he said.

There came, from the distance, the shout of a sentry, an answering cry. A rider approached the canopy in haste. Tarwach looked up, and his guards straightened and readied their weapons. It would not be surprising if Gryylth, failing in strength, turned now to subtlety.

But the rider came armed only with a soot-streaked face and, when he had dismounted, a heavy step. He was a big, strapping man, but he was tired. "I bring greetings to King Tarwach," he said at the edge of the canopy. He bowed.

"Do I know you, sir?" said the king.

"I am a farmer of southeast Corrin, my king. I brought tribute to you last year from Rutupia. You thought the heifer was especially fine."

Tarwach considered, gestured for him to approach. "Karthin?"

"The same, my king. The war has made me turn soldier. The Eighteenth Phalanx approaches with fresh troops, but I came ahead. I fear I bear evil news."

Mernyl, and now this. No, he would not . . .

"Speak. What has happened?"

"My king, Dythragor Dragonmaster has fired the crops to the south and east of Benardis. Our wheat and barley are no more, and several villages are in ashes."

His nerves raw and bleeding, open to the faintest emotion, Tireas felt the series of thoughts and images that ran through Tarwach's mind. The crops were gone. There would be no food. And that meant that the war was not won: it would continue, with starving Corrinian against terrified Gryylthan. It would continue on, and on, and on . . .

I will not use the Tree. I will not.

But they were looking at him again. This was the time for the sorcerer to rise to his feet, lift his hands, and give some sound advice that would alleviate the crushing sense of loss and futility, that might turn the anger aside.

But the sorcerer had nothing to say. The sorcerer was not himself any more. Tireas was as far fled as Marrget of Crownhark.

It was Tarwach who rose. "By the Gods, they will pay for this."

Darham passed a hand over his face. "Adders will strike so, if trodden upon." He looked at Karthin. "Are you certain?"

"I myself watched from the vantage of the North Downs. The fields are black from Benardis to the sea."

"Dythragor, you say?"

"Dythragor."

Squatting in its wain, the Tree glowed at Tireas. *Come,* it said. *Come to me, and together we will change the world. We will make the changes endless.*

How long, he wondered, had he been looking at the Tree? Where were his wise words? Who was opening and closing his mouth? Who framed his sentences?

Tarwach stared out at the campfires as though he might take fire from them and reply to Gryylth, flame for flame. "We have no choice," he said at last.

"Gryylth has made it for us. I would rather have all of Vorya's land in ruins than allow one child of Corrin to cry for a mouthful of bread."

"Brother . . ." Darham reached out to him.

Tarwach ignored the hand. "We will rest tomorrow, and the next day we will march. If Gryylth is an adder, we will crush its head."

I . . . I will not do it.

But the Tree was calling him.

Marrget came in quickly, and Alouzon managed to get her metal cuff up in time to deflect the main impact of her drive. But the crossing of the sword caught, and before she could set her feet in response, she was tumbled over and into the grass.

She stopped herself inches from the fire, the flames stinging the hair from her arms. Rolling over and away, she found Marrget standing over her, eyes hot, face set. "Draw your sword, Dragonmaster."

Alouzon blinked at her. This was exactly what she had wanted, but for an instant, her nerves turned rubbery. Fighting? Again?

Marrget swung her sword, brought it down in a clean, precise stroke that gave her the choice of fighting or dying. Alouzon rolled, jerked out her sword, and parried. The blades rang, and Marrget examined her as she got to her feet, sizing her up for another rush.

The power of the Dragonsword was building again, hammering its way down her arm and into her brain. Nerves were quickening, muscles snapping to attention. Marrget became a target to be analyzed for weaknesses and vulnerable points, and her technique was evaluated and cataloged before Alouzon realized that the process had begun.

"My dedication and loyalty to Gryylth have been constant and spotless," said Marrget evenly, moving so as to back Alouzon against the flames. Obviously, the captain knew the power of the Dragonsword and was increasing her odds by trapping her opponent. "I will not have it insulted."

But Alouzon hardly heard her: she was busy fighting her own weapon. It was too easy to battle to the death. Marrget's technique was excellent, but it had its flaws, and the Dragonsword made her see them, urged her to exploit them. The sword wanted to kill. But Alouzon wanted it to heal.

Marrget drove in, carrying herself lithely and with a quickness that was almost hypnotic. Alouzon backed, slid to one side, and caught her in the ribs with an elbow. For an instant, Marrget staggered, and Alouzon gave the power momentary play: her foot snaked out, tripped her.

Marrget hit the dirt with a thump, but she was on her feet again without pause, rolling smoothly from the fall into a recovery, and then into a guard stance.

"Even," said Alouzon.

"You think this is a game?"

"Nope."

Alouzon attacked. Giving and taking with a lethal power that sought always to turn her actions toward death, she sidestepped in and deflected Marrget's guard, then swung hard and prayed that the captain's reflexes were good.

They were. Marrget deflected in turn and landed a backhand fist on Alouzon's jaw. She stumbled with the impact, and slashed with the hilt of her sword to break off the attack. Marrget grunted and backed away, but Alouzon felt blood trickling down her cheek.

And the fight went on. Attack, parry, smash, riposte, parry . . . Survival was a matter of blade against blade, quickness of foot, and instinct for battle. Blows came from any body part that could be swung. Weapons were anything that could damage. Attack and reply blurred into one another until they could no longer be distinguished.

Without warning, Marrget caught the Dragonsword in a sleeve of her robe, held it, and nearly tore the weapon from Alouzon's hand. Instead of pulling, though, Alouzon pushed, and her unexpected response toppled Marrget and put her on the ground as Alouzon dropped on top of her with a shoulder.

Inside, she was dancing: dancing with the power. In, out, back and forth, she let it take her, but broke away before it could make her kill. She allowed the Dragonsword to find the openings, but she herself chose when and how far to act upon them. It was a demon lover she embraced, one that filled her flesh with fire, but she steadfastly denied it full possession of her.

On their feet again, they faced off. Their movement had taken them away from the fire, and the fight continued in shadow. Blades flickered in the moonlight. Footfalls were muffled in the soft, uncrushed grass.

Gathered together by the fire, the remaining women of the First Wartroop watched. Alouzon felt their eyes as she pushed the power away again and struck for their captain. Whether they knew it or not, she was fighting for them.

It was not a matter of glory or valor. It was a matter of friendship and caring. She had knelt by the dying at Kent State, powerless, unable even to scream until the hysteria had taken her days later. Tonight, she could not scream, but she could, she hoped, heal. She could make Marrget see who she was, and what she could do; and she could pray.

Please say that it's going to be all right.

What religion worshipped a Cup? Whatever its name, its convert fought tonight beside a fire in Gryylth. She clung to the image of the healing chalice, letting it guide the hot bloodlust of her sword into something that could deal out life.

"Why don't you give up, Marrget?" she gasped as she pulled out of another flurry of exchanges. "You can't take me." Fatigue was building on both sides, but she had to press, to taunt, in order to keep Marrget fighting.

The captain was panting too, but she shook her head. "I will have vengeance." Her sword leaped. Alouzon blocked it and locked crosspieces.

Frozen suddenly, motionless, they stood straining against one another, their faces inches apart. Marrget's hard gray eyes burned out of a smooth face streaked with sweat and caked with dust. A cut in her temple oozed blood and lymph.

Alouzon planted her feet and held. In her mind, the Grail flamed alongside the power of the sword, tempering it, turning it to other ends. "What about vengeance against the Dremords?"

Marrget kicked her away, and Alouzon fell to the ground. Her breath was coming in deep, harsh gulps, her sword felt as though someone were standing on it, and she discovered that she could only pick herself half up. But Marrget did not take advantage of her weakness. The captain stared at her, sword in hand, seemingly unable to force her body into action.

They were both tired, crushed beneath a weight of mental and physical strain. For nearly a quarter of an hour they had been fighting furiously, without pause, with scarcely a chance for breath, and their reserves were nearly exhausted.

"How about it, Marrget?" Alouzon managed between pants. "You're so damned big on vengeance, and now you want to pull out of the big fight."

"I have nothing to fight for."

"Shit. You've got everything."

"I . . . cannot . . . fight." Her voice was ragged. "I *cannot.*" In spite of her words, she rushed forward and aimed a vicious cut at Alouzon's head. Still on her knees, the Dragonmaster blocked it and levered Marrget into the grass just before falling beside her.

For a minute or two, they lay still. "I just want to go to sleep," Alouzon murmured. Had she allowed herself, she could have dropped off with her hand on her sword and her head cradled on her arm, but she forced herself to her hands and knees, and crawled toward Marrget. Kneeling over her, she bent and rolled the captain onto her back. The loose robe fell open and exposed her breasts.

"Look, honey," Alouzon said, "don't give me shit about—"

Marrget swung up with both fists and punched her in the belly. Alouzon sat back on her heels and stared stupidly at her, but there was no follow-up: Marrget just panted, sucking in breaths as though she were gagging on the air.

Her robe fell off as she dragged herself up, but she paid no attention. She gripped her sword. "I am going to kill you, Alouzon Dragonmaster." She lunged.

"Goddammit, *no!*" Alouzon brought her fist down on the back of Marrget's head, and she sprawled face down into the damp grass. Teetering for a moment, Alouzon collapsed beside her.

They stared at one another as though their eyes could continue the battle. "You're not making sense, Marrget."

"I make sense enough."

"You can fight. You've been fighting me for— what?—years now." She panted, caught her breath. "You can still swing a sword."

Marrget was choking with fatigue and emotion both, and there were long moments when she could not talk at all. "I am a woman."

"Yeah. Big deal." She tried to crawl, but her body was not responding to any further commands. "So am I." She gave up and let her cheek rest on the grass.

"You do not understand."

"All I understand is that your people are going to get cut to pieces if you don't help."

Marrget pried an eye open. Her fingers twitched on her sword. "What kind of help can the likes of us give? We cannot fight."

"What the hell do you think you've been doing to me?"

She let go of the sword, pressed a hand to her face. "I am . . ." Alouzon pushed herself toward her. "A warrior of Gryylth. Say it! Dammit! Say it! *I am a warrior of Gryylth.*" Nearly toppling, she grabbed Marrget by her bare arms, shook her in cadence to the words. "*I am a warrior of Gryylth.*"

"By the stars, leave me, Alouzon. Let me die."

"No such luck. We're all stuck with this, and you're not getting out of it."

Marrget's gasping increased, and a single tear traced a path down her cheek. Her eyes stared as though they saw the life of a woman of Gryylth, as though she felt her own proud head bent unwillingly under the weight of custom. "My life . . . has been that of a warrior." She spoke in small rushes, the words tumbling over one another in their haste to get out. "If I encountered an obstacle . . . I could fight."

"You still can."

As though to indicate her body, Marrget spread her hands. "*I cannot fight this.*" Her eyes were desperate, bleak.

Alouzon could not meet her gaze. Gently, she lowered the captain to the ground. "If you can't fight it," she said softly, "you don't bother. You can't fight a mountain, or a river, so you just don't." She mustered the courage to look Marrget in the eye. "You said once that you'd wept for the men you'd lost in battle. Show some strength: cry for yourself. But don't waste your time fighting it. You're still Marrget of Crownhark. That's all you need. The rest we can take care of, one way or another."

"I . . ." Marrget shut her eyes. "I am a woman."

"Yeah." Alouzon decided to treat her words as a simple statement of fact. She spoke low, as gently as she could. "You are."

Minutes went by, and Marrget said nothing. Aside from the crackling of the distant fire, there was silence. Alouzon began to think that she had fallen asleep.

But she stirred. "I cannot fight this."

"No." Again, a statement of fact. "You can't."

"But I have no wish to die."

"That's good." She held to the image of the Grail. *Please . . .*

"Therefore . . ." Marrget lifted her head, her brow furrowed with uncertainty, looked off into the darkness as though she contemplated her future. Her mouth worked soundlessly, then, with an effort:

"Therefore I will go on. I will not continue in this fashion. I am Marrget of Crownhark: I will not grovel in the sand like an ignoble beast." She pulled herself up until she was sitting, and there was bleakness in her eyes still, but there was also the steel of an innate, prideful will. She looked down at herself, and confronted her nakedness as though it were a hostile army and she alone and weaponless. After a minute, she found her robe and covered herself. "What do you want of me, Alouzon Dragonmaster? Why do you press me so?"

"I want you and the wartroop to help fight the Corrinians."

Marrget smiled grimly in return. It was the smile with which she habitually faced a battle, and Alouzon took that as a good sign. "Thirteen women against the massed phalanxes of Corrin?" The despair was gone from her voice. There was instead a certain amusement.

Alouzon shrugged. "I'll admit, I've heard of better odds."

The other women were were clustered at the fire, still watching. They might not have moved since the fight had begun. Marrget examined them. Alouzon had seen the look before. *What can I make out of this? Is this fighting material?* "Or worse, Dragonmaster," she said after a time. "Much worse." There was a note of pride in her voice; faint, but distinct. "They are the First Wartroop."

"Can we save them?"

Marrget's gaze flicked back to Alouzon. The unspoken question was: *Can I save you?*

The captain dropped her eyes, pressed her lips together. "I can fight," she said. "You showed me that, friend Alouzon. And the First Wartroop would ride into a pit of fire if I gave them word. They will live, and they will fight. I have no laggards in my company."

They sat together in silence for some minutes. As Marrget's breathing returned to normal, the captain pulled herself up straight, as though she had sucked in strength along with the air. With a sigh, she pushed her ash-blond hair back with both hands, and she stretched like a sleeper who had awakened from a night of evil dreams to find at least a reasonably bright morning.

The wartroop's fire crackled as someone added wood to it, and Marrget rose and picked up her sword. "My warriors have need of me, Alouzon." Her voice was calm.

"You go ahead, Marrget. You can do more for them than I can. I'm going to sit here a while longer: I need the rest." Marrget looked at her, puzzled. "I'm not used to this," Alouzon explained. "Where I come from, I'm just a student."

Marrget smiled faintly. "What? In Gryylth already six days and not a fighter yet?" She turned and went toward the fire. There was grace in her movements— a sway of the hips and a set to her arms that bespoke femininity—but her back was straight, and determination was in her step. If any man were foolhardy enough to demand a bow from Marrget of Crownhark, he would get precisely what he deserved.

She moved among her women, sitting with them, talking with them, conjuring responses and even laughter. Wykla stirred at the sound of voices, and Marrget drew her to the fire and cast a blanket about the girl's shoulders with her own hands. The firelight glowed on Wykla's amber hair, and she looked to her captain with a face full of renewed hope.

Marrget's words did not carry, but her tone did, and though it bore a resemblance to that with which she had comforted the wartroop after the deaths in the Heath, there was a difference. The gruff, half-hostile affection of soldiers was eclipsed now by a sense of urgent unity. In the past, they had needed one another's presence, swords, and protection in battle, but now they needed, in addition, the kind of unconditional loyalty that would greet any temporary weakness with help and support.

Some grimaced, fetched their swords, and began to scrape together what bits of pride they could find. Others wept and were comforted. And Marrget stood among them, determined, strong, an example of what lay on the other side of despair.

Alouzon closed her eyes and sighed with as much relief as she could summon. The warriors loved Marrget. They would follow her. The emotional stability that the captain could give them might not last forever, but it was a start, something to pull them back from the abyss that had opened at their feet.

The Corrinian sorcerer had executed a very clever plan: in a society in which women were seen as valueless, he had transformed the best troops into women. What could be more psychologically devastating to Gryylth? Vorya's armies were already slipping away in fear, and, confronted with the ultimate horror, even the king might break.

Fatigue was making her thoughts wander in preparation for sleep, but she snapped awake. *Thirteen women against the massed phalanxes of Corrin,* Marrget had said. She might turn out to be right.

One thing at a time. Marrget and the wartroop had to be saved first.

When she looked back to the fire, she saw that

Marrget had the women preparing for sleep. It was the best thing they could do, she supposed, and she wished that she could join them.

In another few minutes, Marrget returned, carrying the water skin. She knelt before Alouzon. "I have wounded you."

"I can dish it out, and I can take it, too."

"Wash." She smiled and poured the water herself. Cupping it in her hands, Alouzon splashed her face. The cut on her jaw stung in protest.

She winced. "Did you get me that good?"

Marrget shrugged. "I am a warrior. When I fight, I fight well or not at all." Dampening a cloth, she swabbed at Alouzon's bruised arm. "If we had not fought as we did, I would have found less confidence in myself. You would not have been able to . . ." She shrugged again. " . . . to revive me. I have my own wounds."

"Sorry."

"I attacked first." She looked at Alouzon carefully. "There is a river nearby. We can bathe there tomorrow before we leave."

"Leave?"

"If the king will still have my counsel, I would advise him to take what soldiers he has remaining to the Circle. It is more easily defended. Mernyl may be able to help, also. With as few fighters as we have, and with the presence of the Tree, we will need what he can give us."

"What about Dythragor?"

Marrget snorted in contempt. "I judge the advice and actions of Dythragor now only by their profit to me and to Gryylth."

"Do you think we've got a chance?"

She fell silent, and seemed to be contemplating the

phalanxes that lay, encamped, somewhere to the east. "Given what they can do..." She looked at herself. "I know not, Alouzon. I fear the worst. If Mernyl can command the powers of the Circle, that might give us some hope. Otherwise, we will have to die fighting. Or hope that we are allowed to."

"Can we settle with them, do you think?"

"Settlement would mean subjection, and Corrin now has just reason to treat us with the utmost cruelty." Her mouth tightened. "I wish that Dythragor had not indulged in such foolish heroics with their grain. Such an action was not wise. I am surprised."

"I'm not."

The bluntness of her words seemed to shock Marrget, but, after considering, she nodded. "Perhaps you are right."

Sleep was tugging at her sleeve, but she had further work that night. Silbakor was just across the rise. "It's late, Marrget," she said. "Go to bed."

"Someone needs to watch."

"I'll do it. You trust me?"

Marrget took her hand, then, on impulse, put an arm about her neck. Her long hair swept along Alouzon's shoulder. "I will tell you, Dragonmaster," she murmured into her ear, "I trust you with my life." She stood up. "Wake me when the moon tells you the hours are half done. You need rest also."

"You got it."

The captain went off to the fire, and Alouzon waited for a few minutes. The wartroop slept, Vorya and his army slept . . . and probably the Corrinians slept, too. The fire burned low. She might have been the only conscious human being in a land of night and shadow.

She sat, hugging her knees, watching the failing

fire. Gryylth seemed exactly that: darkness, the unknown, the inexplicable. Where was Gryylth? What was Gryylth? Propelled by the immediacy of the threat to those she loved, the questions threw themselves at her again, and she cursed her ignorance.

If she had known more—about Gryylth, about Dythragor, about herself—lives might have been saved. As it was, she had groped blindly, trying to patch by feel and instinct the holes in Gryylth's insubstantiality. But more holes were appearing, and ahead gaped the massive rent that was the Tree.

If there was madness in her life, there was more madness in Gryylth. Only the Grail promised anything that approached the whole and the rational, and it itself was a fantasy made real.

She picked up her sword, and the stars glittered along its keen blade and on the double-dragon hilt. Of Celtic design, so magical that it could kill and heal both, it did not make sense. Nothing made any sense. But she was determined that explanations would be hers. She would demand knowledge, and whatever the consequences, she would accept it.

With both hands, she swung the sword above her head and faced the ridge. Her voice was a harsh whisper: *"Silbakor! I call you!"*

❖ CHAPTER 17 ❖

❖

ALOUZON EXPECTED AN ACKNOWLEDGMENT, but the dragon game instead. Rising above the hills on noiseless wings, it slid across the stars and glided toward her, a dark blot unlit by the hard-edged gibbous moon.

Silently, it settled to the ground before her, a living shadow. "You called me, Alouzon, my lady," it said. "I am come." There was something almost penitent in its tone, as though it were a small boy caught in a lie. It rested with its head low. Its eyes burned yellow beneath its brow ridges.

The backlog of fatigue that she had been amassing since the Heath was a wall as black and as large as the Dragon. She was tired enough that she simply wanted to kick the beast, swear at it, tell it to fly into a mountain . . . and then go to sleep. Morning was a good enough time for rational thought. No more midnight psychodrama and conversations with zoological impossibilities for Suzanne Helling, B.A. She was done.

But Suzanne was gone, and Alouzon Dragonmaster had things to do that did not include sleeping at present. Standing before Silbakor, she let the silence

build until it was pregnant with irritation, and at last
sheathed her sword with a clang.

"I think it's time you told me what the hell's going
on here," she said.

"Ask."

"Uh-uh. You tell."

The Dragon almost squirmed. "Lady . . ."

"There's a whole shitload of stuff you could have
told me right from the beginning, Silbakor, and it
would have saved me a hell of a lot of trouble and
grief."

"I—"

"Shut up and listen." Could Silbakor become angry? She was no longer concerned. Marrget had
fought because of her pride, her motives floating at
the top of her will easily stirred, easily comprehended.
But Silbakor, she sensed, had hidden agendas, among
which was one dealing with a certain Alouzon Dragonmaster, erstwhile student of medieval archaeology. For whatever reason, it needed her, and had all
along. She could afford to do a little shouting, vent
a little steam. "Marrget and the wartroop are in deep
kimchi, I cut a swath through Bandon that I still can't
believe, a woman I hardly knew died for me, most
of the men Vorya sent into battle are history, and
now Corrin has us by the fucking short and curlies
because Dythragor went out and started playing with
matches. How much of all of this did you know was
going to happen?"

"I know very little."

"Bullshit."

"My lady, you have but to ask."

The Dragon persisted in its studied, formal manner,
as though it were a voice out of a burning bush. She

would have to play its game. "OK, let's get started with the twenty questions. What the hell is Gryylth?"

"It is a land bounded by water on four sides. Most of it is under the nominal rule of King Vorya."

"I don't need geography lessons, Silbakor. What's beyond it?"

It hesitated. "There is . . . nothing beyond it."

"What? Just water?"

"No. Nothing."

Her patience, thin and stretched, buckled. "Come on, guy. You're not dealing with a fifth-century savage. I suppose now you'll tell me the whole shebang is balanced on the back of a turtle."

Silbakor did not speak. As though it had been annoyed by her tone, it lifted its head from the ground, looked at her for some time.

"Well?" In spite of all its apparent violations of common sense, Gryylth had to have some foundation in the mundane world of logic. For it to be otherwise was madness. She awaited an explanation.

She received what she did not expect. "Gryylth, as a world, is fragmentary," said the Dragon. "It exists only in part."

Alouzon stared, uncomprehending.

"Forces of prolongation that you do not understand hold it together, hold its waters upon its surface and its air about it."

She found her voice. "What's . . . what's beyond it?"

"Mist."

"Yeah, and . . .?"

"And nothingness."

After a minute of bewildered immobility, she sat down on the ground before the Dragon, picked up a handful of soil and grass, let it sift through her fingers. She half expected it to evaporate before it hit the ground. "I had to ask, didn't I?"

"Lady, I have no wish to trouble you."

"Yeah, right." It was not evaporating. That was good, for if it did, she would have to scream, and she was already feeling the claws of the irrational. "As if I haven't been troubled since I got here." She got down on her hands and knees, studied what she could of the ground. The faint transparency that she had noticed from the beginning was still evident. "OK," she said finally. "Now tell me why."

"That . . . is the way it was created."

The Dragon seemed to be choosing its words, which was exactly what Alouzon did not want. If she was to do anything to help this unfinished land, she had to know. "Created? By who? God?"

"No."

"Dammit, Silbakor, I don't have time for these games. Where did it come from?"

Unwillingly, the Dragon spoke. "From the mind of Solomon Braithwaite, who is here called Dythragor Dragonmaster." It rushed on, as though afraid that she would interrupt. "Do not judge him harshly, lady. A man or a woman may do many things in time of crisis, even unto creating a world where longed-for fantasies live."

"What . . .what you're saying is insane."

"Nevertheless."

Nevertheless. Everything was insane. Madness did indeed lurk in Gryylth, crawling in the corners of the world like a rabid dog. Alouzon's brain began putting the pieces together methodically, in spite of the fact that Alouzon herself no longer wanted to see the pattern. "We're all inside Braithwaite's mind, then?"

The Dragon shook its head. "Gryylth exists. It is an actual physical place. The stars you see above you are real suns, many with their own planets. For the most part, the physical laws with which you are familiar hold sway in this part of the universe. Gryylth is . . . an exception. It is an anomaly."

"That's putting it mildly." Her hands pressed to her head as though to hold in the thoughts that swirled through her brain. She walked away from the Dragon and stood for a few minutes at the edge of the firelight. Marrget lay near her feet, her face tranquil in sleep. She was a lovely woman, her features fine and her fingers long and tapering. A short distance away, Relys murmured, clutched at her blankets, turned over and settled down again. Wykla tossed and turned, almost cried out.

"It's gonna be OK," she whispered, knowing they did not hear, knowing also that, despite her past, despite Gryylth's origins, she would somehow fulfill her promise. The Dragon had its oath, and the Dragonmaster had hers.

She did not doubt the Dragon. It could not lie. But the idea of Solomon Braithwaite creating a chunk of a world out of his mind swamped her comprehension even as it explained everything that she had ever questioned about the land. The swords, the costumes, the buildings . . .even the bitter hostility and endless conflict between Gryylth and Corrin had their counterparts in Braithwaite's field of study. In creating Gryylth, he had reached into the world he knew best, fifth-century Britain, and had extracted the familiar, the emotional, the longed-for.

But he could not create everything, and so there were gaps and a sense of disjointedness. No one remembered their parents, past history was sketchy, and magic—the Tree, the Dragonswords, the Dragon itself—was an unmistakable undercurrent. What had not been specified had been filled in with a haze of common knowledge and unquestioned facts, eked out by a thin broth of unconscious desires and primitive beliefs that Braithwaite was loathe to claim as his own.

She returned to Silbakor. "He knows, doesn't he?"

"He does not."

She goggled. "You're letting an overgrown kid run around in a fantasy land with a big sword and no idea of what he's doing?"

"It is not my place to give advice without first being questioned. Dythragor has never asked me anything about Gryylth. He has been content to live his dream."

"Which involves killing people, right?"

"I ask that you do not judge him, lady. His wish was to fight evil. He forgot that, under many circumstances, evil is relative."

"And there's nothing beyond Gryylth?"

"Nothing save the space between dimensions, which, under certain conditions, can be filled."

Something about the Dragon's words struck her, but she was already grappling with a thought. "Then the Corrinians have always been where they are. They've got no place to go."

"True."

"Oh, Christ, the whole thing's so fucking pointless! No wonder they've been fighting like they have. I can't blame them. It's just like Vietnam. It's just like Kent State. No one understood anything. No one wanted to understand. No one listened to anybody."

She looked at the sleeping forms of Marrget and

her wartroop. Women. Casualties of a thoughtless coherence of wishes and fears, of frantic hopes that pointed in opposite directions.

This time, it was not M-1s. Or M-16s, or napalm, or mortars. This time, it was the Tree. And the Tree could do even more.

She covered her face with her hands. "They're going to attack again. And they'll be using that thing." She tried to imagine Kent all over again, but expanded, lapping everlarger like a growing pool, touched with the colors of newsreel footage she had seen of Hue and My Lai, given currency by the heaped bodies that lay on the other side of the ridge. She failed. There were no proportions in death.

"They have no choice," said the Dragon. "Their existence is threatened. If Vorya's army had been defeated and no more, they might have waited for a settlement. However, with Dythragor's actions . . ." It had no physical capability of shrugging, but the slight curve of its neck conveyed the meaning to Alouzon. "They are now pressed."

"And you might have told Dythragor what all this was about."

"Lady, he did not ask."

He had not asked: that was all the reason the Dragon needed, and its alien nature could be summed up no better. She wondered what crucial questions she herself was allowing to go unasked.

"What can we do, then?"

"I do not know. Often I have had advice to give and have not been asked. Now I am asked and have nothing to offer. The Tree that the Corrinians possess can be used in many ways. It could conceivably be wielded so as to unmake Gryylth. That would not be a wise choice."

"What is it, exactly?"

"It is called the Tree of Creation by Mernyl and Tireas. I myself do not fully comprehend it: it lies outside of my knowledge and existence. Like the Circle and myself, it was created as an integral part of Gryylth, springing directly from the unconscious of Solomon Braithwaite, and, I believe, your race."

"Archetype, then." She mused. "He doesn't like change, he doesn't like magic, he doesn't like anything that he can't control. The Heath was everything that he wanted to repress, but now there's a part of it that's loose." Silbakor, the Tree, the Circle . . . But there was something else, too, something that might actually be more important than all the rest. "What about the Grail, Silbakor? Is that real too?"

The Dragon actually looked uncomfortable. Its yellow eyes burned like suns. "It is."

"Is it just Braithwaite's, or . . ." She waited, the Dragon stared. "Don't make me pull teeth, Silbakor. Please. This means something to me."

It squirmed for a moment, as though wrestling with an answer. "It, like the Tree and the Circle, springs from the mind of your species. It is a universal. It . . ." Silbakor hesitated. "It cannot be used for war."

War? The Grail could save the whole land. The Grail could help Marrget and the wartroop. The Grail could heal Suzanne Helling. Set against its absolute wholeness, war was a paltry and puerile consideration. "I don't want it for war, Silbakor. That's the farthest thing from my mind. Where is it?"

"Within yourself."

"Don't give me metaphysics, Silbakor. It's in Gryylth. I know it. Where?"

"Within . . ." The Dragon could answer questions, but it could not volunteer information. "Within yourself." It opened its mouth again as though to speak, and Alouzon was given a glimpse of the black, obsidian-keen fangs that lay on the other side of its lips. But it said nothing.

What was the Dragon not telling her? Something important, doubtless, but she had no idea how to pry the knowledge out of it. Silbakor was not human. It hardly understood humans. How was it supposed to know what it was that she wanted?

She was left with a quest that she did not know how to begin. "OK, Silbakor, can *you* do anything?"

"I am but a balance. As was Gryylth created, so was I formed to insure its preservation."

"Cause and effect?"

"There is no cause," said the Dragon. "There is no effect. We are."

"And what if Gryylth is destroyed?"

It said nothing. Plainly unable to speak further, Silbakor closed its eyes and rested its head on the ground. Alouzon stood for a moment, frustrated, struggling with unknown questions, and then climbed onto its back and sat cross-legged between the great black wings, watching the distant fire and the uneasy sleep of the wartroop.

He had flown across the territory of the Dremords, sowing fire and destruction; he had returned to the king and found that his support had withered. Now he rode across the night-cloaked landscape of Gryylth, pressing southward, heading for no particular destination, wanting only to escape what lay behind him: the crush of men, and weapons . . .

. . . and women.

But dawn crept up on him like an assassin, and when the sky was gray and his hands were shaking, his eyes half blind with lack of sleep and the dust of the road, Dythragor turned his horse toward the town that lay a few miles off his course—which really was no course at all—looking for shelter. He might have slept outdoors, but the open sky left him feeling vulnerable, and though the stars were eclipsed by the upwelling of light that was the new day, he knew they were there, and he found their presence disquieting, as though they might, unasked, tell him what he did not want to know.

Shelter then, and a bed in a room. A roof. Shutters he could close. A door to lock. The gates of the town opened as it awoke, and he approached it, ignorant of its name, looking to hide in it as a child might pull a comforter over his head to keep out the dark.

Perhaps he had been here before: he could not remember. But the townsmen knew him, and the gate guards, a man too old for war and a boy too young to swing more than a wooden sword, jumped to their feet and saluted as he rode through. He paid no attention to them. Furtive, desperate, he rode through the half-sleeping streets that were denuded of their young men, searching for an inn.

Women were about, and he averted his gaze. One, blond and fair, looked like Marrget. Her hair was braided and she walked quickly and with her head down, a basket on her arm.

He found that he was shaking as he dismounted in the courtyard of an inn. His swagger was gone: he entered the door like a pauper. Would Marrget one day—?

"An unexpected honor, Dragonmaster," said the host. He was aged and fat, his soldiering days over. But his face was open and honest. Just what Dythragor wanted. Behind, in Vorya's tent, were Mernyl, with his secretive smiles, and Alouzon with her politics and her peacenik sympathies. Here was the solidity of Gryylth, a representative of the people he had vowed to keep safe from the Dremords. "You'll have something to eat, too?"

A meal would help. Tireas, the Dremord sorcerer, had kept him aloft for days, and when he had at last given up and turned to the firing of the crops, he had done so without pausing for rest or food.

A meal, then. And, after that, sleep. "Yes . . . yes, that's a good idea."

"How goes it with the war, if I may ask, Dragon-master? What brings you to Crownhark?"

He had turned to enter the common room, but the host's questions transfixed him like a pair of spikes. He was known and respected, and that meant that he would eventually have to say something about his anomalous absence from the battle.

And Crownhark was Marrget's town. And he had run from . . .

. . . her.

"Uh . . . it's . . ." He saw her still, sitting in a chair, lapped in a robe that was too big for her, her hair long and blond. Or maybe she was shuffling along the streets of Kingsbury, head down, a basket on her arm. *No. Not that. Never.* "It's fine. Just fine. I'm on . . . uh . . . business." His head was spinning from a combination of fatigue and lack of food, and he was suddenly afraid that Solomon Braithwaite might return and present the people of Crownhark with a bewildered, middle-aged scholar who could no more lift a Dragonsword than he could an anvil.

He thought that the host looked at him oddly, his bland face illumined from within by curiosity and doubt. Doubt. Doubt everywhere. "What the hell do you want?" Dythragor demanded. "Papers? Want to see if I'm AWOL?"

The host blinked, frightened, and gestured him into the common room with tremulous waves of his hands. "Sit yourself down then, my lord Dragonmaster. I will have food for you in a moment. Fear not: we know how to treat honored guests here, since one of our own sons has risen to command the First Wartroop of the land. Do you know him? His name is—"

Dythragor fled into the room. With most of the young male population of the land absent because of the war (killed now, he knew, or worse), the inn was quiet. There were no women visible, and the only men present were aged and weak. One was in the corner, mumbling a piece of bread and gravy. Two others were engrossed in a board game, moving pegs about from one hole to another gravely and deliberately, as though by so doing they determined the fate of worlds.

Age. Everything here was age. An old room for old men. He might just as well have been in a nursing home, having arrived between visits of the white-clad nurses and the disinterested doctors.

Solomon Braithwaite hung over his shoulder as he made his way across the room to a dark corner and sat down with his back to the wall. The gamesters did not look up—he might have been one of them— but the old, toothless codger with the bread and gravy had marked him. He stood up and hobbled toward the Dragonmaster. Dythragor tried to look occupied. He should have stayed out of towns. He should have stayed alone.

"Hail, Dythragor Dragonmaster," the old man wheezed. "I am Perni."

"Yeah." *Go away, damn you.*

The dribbling, gravy-streaked face of the old man

revolted him and made him slide his stool back until
it met the wall, but Perni paid no attention to Dythragor's discomfiture. He dragged up another stool,
spat into a corner, and settled himself gingerly. "My
bones are a little old, these days, Dragonmaster. Do
you know me?"

"Uh . . . no."

"Ah, but I think you do." He gloated with the
knowledge. "Ten years ago, I was in service of
Gryylth. I was a soldier! Think of that! I was under
Hylic, of the Fifth Wartroop, and back when that
fiend Mernyl was betraying the whole country to the
Dremords, I was stationed up by the Eastreach River."
He coughed, brought up mucus, spat it into the cor-
ner.

The host tottered in with food and drink. Dythragor looked at the tracing of spittle that wound down
Perni's chin, shuddered and left his meal untouched.
This was all that was left in the towns. The young
men lay dead under the summer sun, their bodies
picked over by the crows. "I'm . . ." An old man, living
his dreams. Pathetic. "I'm sure you served well."

"Well! I will tell you how well I served, Dragonmaster, and then you'll know what kind of reward
to give me. I have bided my time for a good number
of years now, waiting to reveal myself. Oh, youngsters
like Marrget grew up and took all the honor, but
'twas I started everything, and gave the boys a
chance." He huffed and snorted under his breath for
a moment, did not notice how Dythragor shook at
the mention of the name. "You know, I have been in
some sore straits since my heart started troubling me
a few years back."

Dythragor unconsciously felt his right arm. "I'm
sure you've been pensioned."

"I have indeed, but I want credit. And honor! There has been plenty of honor these last ten years, but all of it went to others while I stayed home with my bad heart. But I deserve it, I do, for it was I saved Gryylth from destruction." He cackled, rubbing his hands together.

Arrogant, cocksure old man. It was the beginnings of senility he was seeing, Dythragor was certain. Why else would a grown man prattle on about fantasy exploits? "I'm sure that Gryylth owes you a great debt," he said, trying to bring the conversation to a close. At his elbow, the sliced meat and bread were growing cold, the beer scumming over and turning flat. He tried not to look at the food.

"You don't believe me."

"Of course I believe you." *Now go away.*

"Tell me, Dragonmaster, why did the war not end ten years ago?"

He did not want to talk, wanted nothing more than to be away. "The Dremords betrayed the settlement," he said unwillingly. "They attacked across the Eastreach River."

"Showed they could not be trusted, eh?"

"That's it." He had not been surprised when he had heard the tale from Vorya and Helkyying. The Communists had done much the same in Korea. And the Saxons who had invaded Britain had lived by just such constant treachery.

Perni laughed, long and crow-like, tossing his head back until the cords of his withered neck stood out. "And that is true, they cannot be trusted. But no one would believe that back then, and that is where I came in."

"You . . . came in?" It was such a colloquial expression that he started, and Alouzon's remarks about English came back to him. Why English? Gryylth was not on Earth. Gryylth was . . . somewhere else. He did not know where. Somewhere.

Alouzon had infected him with her ideas. Now he was asking her questions for her. The next thing he knew, Marrget would . . .

Marrget. Sitting in the chair. Shuffling down the street . . .

He stared at Perni, finding the old man's appearance disquietingly familiar. Maybe he knew this aging rooster. Ten years? The Fifth Wartroop? No, there was more to it than that. Fascinated, his eyes held against his will, he stared the with the dawning of a horrified recognition.

Perni was preening. "You see, Dragonmaster, I knew the Dremords for the liars and the barbarians that they were. Slaves, they are. Slaves and the children of slaves. But that bastard Mernyl was going to settle, and Vorya was going to agree to it. No one else was willing to stop it. But I did."

In spite of Dythragor's efforts to deny it, the old man's features had taken on a resemblance to those of Solomon Braithwaite, and with the growth of that likeness, he began to hear his own sentiments repeated back to him in an older voice, accompanied by rheum and spittle, unmistakable.

"Everyone knows that they are barbarians," Perni was saying, "and everyone knows that it is the duty of free men to stop their advance. I expected them to attack, but when they did not, I decided that I would report an attack anyway."

Dythragor stared at him. Gryylth was . . .

"I set off at sunset, and ran all night. I arrived at Vorya's tent in the early morning and told him that the scoundrels had crossed the river. The rest you know."

Gryylth was a lie.

"Then, later, you arrived, Dragonmaster, and led us to victory. Now, what say you? Am I not deserving of a reward? Ruined my heart, I did, with that all-night run. I might still be a strong lad, might even buy a girl or two for my pleasures but for my heart."

He was feeling his own arm again, half expecting that the old pain would strike him and leave him paralyzed, unable to hold his sword. The Dremords . . . had never attacked. Gryylth had been the one to betray the treaty.

Perhaps at another time, he would have shrugged off the news. If he needed justifications for war, plenty had accumulated in the course of a decade of conflict. But he was already shaken by the slaughter of Vorya's men and the transformation of the war-troop, and now this news struck him in the face like a splash of molten lead. The foundation, the basis of the war, was a lie.

"Well?" said the old man.

"You *lied?*"

"Of course I lied, Dragonmaster. 'Twas for a good cause."

"But most of Gryylth is dead in the field!" Dythragor was on his feet, and he was shouting. The gamesters looked up, startled. The host heard his words and came running. "You old son of a bitch! You started this whole thing off ten years ago because you thought you knew better than anyone else, and you want to be rewarded? The army is slaughtered, Marrget and the First Wartroop are women, and the Dremords have the Tree. And you want money? I'll give you money!"

He might have been striking at himself. The Dragonsword came out of its sheath like oil, and the blade bit deep into the old man where his neck joined his trunk, severing bones and sinew without a sound save a soft rustle of passage, continuing on through and burying itself in the table.

Perni looked startled, but his crowing had stopped. With a gurgle, his head, shoulders, and part of his chest detached themselves, slid sideways, and tumbled to the floor. Dythragor had a glimpse of something beating within his gaping torso before that too toppled off the stool and sprawled in a heap, blood spreading like a breaking wave, frothing, spraying . . .

"Dragonmaster!"

He did not stop. Jerking the sword free, he struck again, and again, hacking at the shuddering flesh before him. But the face of Solomon Braithwaite—middle-aged, vain, impotent—continued to goggle at him from amid the shreds of red meat as his blade rose and fell, and though he splintered the wooden floor with his furious hacking, he could not banish it.

The host caught at his arm. "Stop! For the Gods' sake, stop! Perni is a fool! He is not right in his mind!"

Dythragor backhanded him and he fell into the gamesters' table, scattering the board and the wooden pegs. He brandished his sword. "Get the hell out of my way, old man. It's stay-at-home maggots like you that have turned this whole war into a shambles. I'm tired of fighting for you. You can rot for all I care."

Shoving aside tables and stools, flinging the door open, he ran to the stables, to his horse. The animal whinnied in protest as he dragged it away from a full manger and saddled it, but several swift kicks made it tractable.

He rode south. Away from knowledge. Away from thought. Away from everything.

❖ CHAPTER 18 ❖

❖

MIDWAY THROUGH WHAT WAS LEFT OF THE
night, Marrget took over the watch. The frantic
struggle was gone from her eyes, replaced now by a
kind of hollow levity, as though she had been the
victim of a particularly vicious joke. After padding
over from the fire and nodding to Alouzon, she stood
at the head of the Dragon, folded her arms as though
the beast were not there, and sighed. Her sword
gleamed at her hip, and she seemed comfortable with
it.

Alouzon had the urge to watch, in turn, the watch-
er. But Marrget did not seem to need help as much
as she needed time to herself, and the Dragonmaster
saw a familiar crease in her brow, a crooked set of
her mouth: Marrget looked as though she were debating the tactics of a difficult battle.

The next thing Alouzon knew, Marrget was prodding her awake. The sky was bluing rapidly, and the
sun, burning like a pillar of fire at the rim of the
world, sent long shadows streaking away to the west.
"Come, Alouzon. The day is reborn." Her smile soft-
ened the haggard edges of her face.

The midsummer air was tepid, and if she stamped
her feet, it was to wake herself up. She wanted more

sleep. The few hours she had been allowed had done no more than make her even more conscious of how tired she was. "How are you doing, Marrget? You look pretty good."

She shrugged. "You revived me, Alouzon. You did not cure me. I have been fighting."

"Fighting?"

Marrget shrugged again as if to indicate that her adversary was not physical, turned and strode away to the fire, flipping her hair back over her shoulder with something approximating an unconscious toss of her head. She had apparently spent at least part of her watch in providing herself with something to wear, and the tunic and trews that she now wore had been taken in quickly but carefully. She looked good in them, though somewhat like a girl dressed up in her brother's clothes.

Her voice carried to Alouzon as she woke the wartroop, parceling out morning tasks and giving orders for the day. The women responded automatically, taking shelter in the routine to which they had become accustomed, and soon the fire was built up and food was being portioned out.

Alouzon was not overly surprised to find that Silbakor was gone. Doubtless, it had its own affairs to attend to—holding an impossible world together was, more than likely, a full-time job—but she had the impression that, should she call, it would come. Her wishes were no longer given the lowest priority.

"Dragonmaster!" It was Relys's voice, she thought. "Come and eat with us!"

Breakfast was adequate, but not much more could be said of the hard bread and dried meat. It was a soldier's meal, nourishing but spartan. But, as such, it was probably better for the wartroop than a kingly

banquet, for it was yet another sign to them that their
change was outward only. They were still warriors.
They could still fight.

And they would have to.

Alouzon could not recall much of her dreams that
past night. She was mildly surprised that she had not
been visited with memories of Kent State, but the
only vision that stayed with her was that of the Grail,
hovering at the edge of thought, an indistinct but
glowing presence that warmed her as much as the
fire beside which she breakfasted with the First Wartroop. She was tired and worn, but the Grail, she
sensed, was sustaining her, as though demonstrating
a willingness to make good her words.

Yeah, kid. It's gonna be all right.

Marrget's demeanor was firm and steady. Relys
seemed to drive herself along as though her body
were an intractable horse. Wykla said little, and she
stared at her hands as she broke bread and lifted her
cup as though unbelieving that what she saw belonged to her. Her hair wandered repeatedly into her
face with her movements, and she at last seized the
ends, shaking.

"Wykla?" said Marrget.

"I . . ." Her voice caught, almost broke. "Should I
braid this?"

Alouzon almost put an arm around her. But no:
Marrget was Wykla's captain. She could handle it.

Marrget's voice was calm. "You are not married,
Wykla. There is no need."

She looked doubtful, but Marrget's tone had stea-
died her. "I am not a midwife, either."

The captain smiled thinly. "Tie it back then, Wykla,
if it pleases you. So the First Wartroop will be known
in Gryylth." She looked about, and her smile broad-

ened a trifle. "'Twill keep it out of the wine cup, at least, eh?"

Relys laughed, and some of the other women joined her. One cut a length of leather thong and tossed it to the girl, and Alouzon helped her knot it about her hair.

Whatever struggles engaged Marrget, she hid them effectively, and the wartroop responded to her strength. The women were slowly growing more assured, and if their behavior was filtered through the persisting remnants of shock and modified by their feminine voices and forms, their personalities were surfacing once more. Alouzon was beginning to recognize familiar gestures and figures of speech. They were finding themselves.

The sun was still low in the sky when Marrget and Alouzon called their horses and mounted. The captain paused at the fire to put Relys in charge of altering clothing for the Troop. "Just enough to cover everyone, lieutenant," she said. "We will make more at need. And call for sword practice. We must learn what these woman-bodies can do."

"Aye, my captain."

"And . . ." Marrget's gaze rested for a moment on a cluster of still forms that lay under blankets some distance from the fire. She bent her head for a moment, wiped at her eyes. "And bury our dead, Relys." Her voice had turned hoarse. "Give them honor. They were our comrades and our friends."

"Fear not, captain: the Gods will hear their names." For a moment, Relys's hard black eyes turned to Alouzon. "Our thanks, my lady," she said. "It seems we owe you our lives. My apologies for my ignorant jests in Bandon." She looked down at herself, touched her breast, shook her head. "And for those last night."

Abruptly, as though unsettled by her frankness, she turned away to the others.

"Do they have time for all that?" said Alouzon.

"We work quickly. We are used to making our own clothing, since custom decrees that . . ." She fell silent, seemingly torn between laughter and bewilderment. " . . . that women do not make clothing that is to be worn into battle. Garments are an unfortunate necessity, but will be but the work of an hour. Sword practice is more important."

"What about armor?"

Marrget shrugged. "Ill-fitting armor," she said, "is worse than none."

"You need something, don't you?"

"We have fought without leathers before," she said. "Perhaps one day I will tell you of the Dremord attack behind our lines that caught the First Wartroop bathing in the Long River. We fought without even clothing then." Her glance was piercing. "And we won."

A small hand touched Alouzon's knee. She looked down into a fair face set with two sad blue eyes.

"Wykla?"

"May I ride with you once again, my lady?"

Relys spoke up. "I would not be troubled, my captain. We have hands enough here."

Alouzon looked to Marrget. She nodded consent, and the girl fetched her sword and ran for her horse.

Together, they climbed the hill and halted at the crest. Marrget surveyed the camp below with tight lips, but Alouzon caught her breath, for most of it was deserted. Barely a quarter of the area staked out the night before held anything save refuse, the litter and waste left behind by frightened, fleeing men.

"Oh, Christ," she whispered. "You damned cowards."

Marrget stirred. "Is that a name of the Gods, Dragonmaster?"

"Kind of."

"Strange." Her tone was odd. "I would think that at least one would be called Alouzon."

Without waiting for a reply, she led the way down. Men stared at her, but she paid no attention. And though Wykla's face was crimson, she emulated her captain and rode casually, as if this were simply another trip to see the king, another standard, and quite mundane, report.

They entered the pavilion to find Vorya in his chair, absently rubbing his numbed arm. Alouzon doubted that he had stirred from his seat all night. Mernyl was also present, and Santhe, and a few guards. Cvinthil was not there, but she had seen him outside, giving instructions to the soldiers who remained.

Without a pause, Marrget strode to the center of the room. "Marrget of Crownhark offers fealty and service to the king of Gryylth," she said loudly and clearly. "Let not her wounds deceive you: she is as fit to bear arms as any in this land."

She approached Vorya, knelt, offered her sword. She had not faltered, not even at the pronouns.

Vorya touched the sword tiredly. "Your service is accepted, Marrget of Crownhark. Gryylth is in need."

"So I saw, my liege." She stood up. "How many do we have?"

"About seventy, counting the King's Guard," said the king bitterly. "What is left of the Second Wartroop adds another half-score. The rest melted away like frost in the sun."

"But some had only to find their wits," said Marrget. She turned. "Santhe? Can your men fight?"

The councilor stirred, and stood up. His face was still gray, his legs stiff, and he moved with some pain, but a defiant twinkle was returning to his eye. He approached Marrget, bowed. "Mernyl has healed what can be healed, my friend. We have . . . some wounds among us still. But we will take as our model for valor the First Wartroop. If there is battle, we will fight." He smiled. "We would not be thought laggards."

They stood together, facing one another. Santhe's wounds were obvious, Marrget's not. But they seemed to recognize what they shared—a bond of service, loyalty, and pain—and each searched the other's face for a sign that the old comrade was still present, that the old friendship still burned.

Without a word, Santhe opened his arms, embraced Marrget. "I am heartily glad you are still with us, my friend," he murmured into her hair. "Heartily glad."

Although Alouzon could sense Marrget's relief, her eyes were closed as if such intimate contact were nonetheless painful. "Even though . . .?"

"Even though." He stepped back, clasped her hands. "I saw too much yesterday to let such questions concern me. We have fought together before. We will fight together once again. For Gryylth."

"Aye, Santhe." Her smile was open and genuine. "For Gryylth."

He held to her hands. "But your warriors, Marrget," he said softly. "How are they?"

She glanced at Wykla, spoke without hesitating. "My women are well. They are the First Wartroop.

The best in the land." The girl was blinking back tears of pride as her captain turned back to Vorya. "I offer counsel. If we stay here, we do no more than offer ourselves to the Dremords. I would we retreat to the Circle. There we may stand and make such a defense as our numbers will permit. As for the Tree . . ." She bowed to Mernyl as to an equal. "If the sorcerer will forgive past insult from me, I would ask his assistance."

Mernyl bowed deeply in return, gripping his staff with a thin hand. "As you wish, captain, and as my king commands."

The king spoke. "And what can five score do against the might of Corrin?"

"Maybe little," said Marrget. She looked at Mernyl. "Maybe not so little."

Marrget's counsel was not as simple as it sounded. Given the condition of the army, the Circle was a good two days' journey to the southwest, and the king and his councilors had to take into account supplies and the ability of crippled wartroops to transport them. Some of Santhe's men would need an extra day or two to recover from shock. Marrget's women required time to adjust to fighting in their new forms.

But plans were made quickly, and Dythragor's absence was noticeable in the smoothness with which they were discussed. Without his constant demand for control and agreement, the captains of Gryylth were left free to explore alternatives, to accept, reject, or modify ideas. Even Marrget's sex was, for a time, forgotten, and her high, clear voice delineated pros and cons as factually as when, deeper, it had sounded at Hall Kingsbury.

Alouzon's dreams of the Grail had allowed her to

face the morning's work with some optimism, and the wartroop's partial recovery gave her hope, but she was still haunted by the specter of the Tree. And the figures that the captains were discussing were absurd: Gryylth was outnumbered by a minimum of five to one. "Look," she said at last. "Is this all you have in mind? Standing there and slugging it out?"

"What alternative do you offer, Dragonmaster?" Marrget's voice was suddenly wary.

Alouzon spoke quietly and earnestly. This was Braithwaite's fantasy, the perfect war. But all he saw was the glory. She saw people, faces, a cluster of bodies at the edge of camp. "I know this isn't going to make me real popular, but I think we should consider the possibility of settling."

Silence. Cvinthil, who had come in during the planning session, regarded her sadly. Marrget was almost hostile. Even Mernyl shook his head.

"Five to one," she said. "Have you listened to yourselves? They'll slaughter you in a direct fight. Is there any chance at all for a settlement?"

Marrget had grown heated. "So, Alouzon, we are to bow to our conquerors. Perhaps your remark about the Dremord farmer last night was not in jest?"

She shook her head. "You know why I said that, Marrget."

"They will not settle."

"Yeah, they probably won't. But it couldn't hurt to ask." She wondered suddenly if Marrget were looking forward to battle as a final proof of her abilities . . . or as an opportunity to die in combat: an honorable way out of an untenable situation.

Vorya's voice was soft, but it was heard. "The Dremords will not settle." His face was pale, as though he realized the implications of what he was saying.

"Much damage has been done over the years. There is much hate on both sides. Now, at last, they are given a chance to conquer, once and for all. Why should they consider a settlement offer as anything more than a very poor jest?"

"Ten years ago we had a settlement," said Santhe. "They did not choose to honor it: they attacked across the Eastreach River."

Braithwaite's fantasy: her life. "I know. I just had to ask."

"If there were time, Dragonmaster, I might be inclined to do as you advise." The king touched his numb arm, shook his head. "But we must retreat immediately, else questions of settlement or surrender will become moot. The Dremords are advancing: my scouts say that they are but a half-day from us. We must flee to fight as we can. I would not spare even one man—" He caught himself. "One man or one woman . . . for such an errand."

She nodded. "I didn't mean offense, Marrget."

"None taken, Alouzon. But will you hold yourself aloof from this fight? As I recall, you swore after the Heath that you would not shed blood again."

Alouzon looked to Cvinthil, who avoided her eyes. "I shed enough blood in Bandon to fill a swimming pool. A little more isn't going to matter."

"Bandon?"

"Kanol," said Cvinthil, "tried to enslave her."

"That dog! I will—"

Cvinthil interrupted. "Kanol is dead, as are many others. Alouzon's sword is keen: it is an honor to fight beside her." He bowed to her.

Alouzon touched the double-dragon hilt of her sword. "I didn't come here to give orders. I'll do what the king wills."

Marrget's eyes widened. Vorya was obviously moved. "Never before," said the king, "have I commanded a Dragonmaster." He rose unsteadily. "I am not sure whether to rejoice or mourn." He nodded to those assembled, and left the room. His guards followed.

Marrget laid a hand on her arm. "Dragonmasters have always commanded."

"No, Marrget. Get it right. *Dythragor* has always commanded." She gave a small, tense laugh. "I'm too damned afraid of getting people killed to try to tell them what to do."

"I will . . . consider what you have said, Alouzon," she said. "You are wiser than I, and perhaps, at another time . . ." She paused meaningfully. ". . . I will have much to learn from you. For now, I return to my women. We must prepare to ride." She turned to Wykla. "Do you wish to remain with the Dragonmaster?"

Surprised at the question, Wykla fumbled for a moment. "Aye, my lady . . . my captain."

"Very well." Marrget clapped a hand on her sword hilt and left the tent.

Wykla stared. "Why did she ask, Dragonmaster?"

"Because she cares, Wykla. How do you feel?"

She shrugged. "I do not wish to kill myself, my lady. And Marrget's praise . . ." She smiled painfully, squared her shoulders. "I was honored before the peers of Gryylth. That means much to me."

"Hang in there. You'll make it."

Wykla did not seem convinced, but Mernyl was coming forward. "Alouzon, I wish to speak with you. About Gryylth." His tone was urgent, but she was too preoccupied to notice.

"Yeah . . . sure . . ." Santhe was leaving, as was

Cvinthil. Outside, orders were being given, setting into motion the plans that had just been made. Marrget's horse clopped away, the sound diminishing with distance. Battle lay ahead. *Nice job, Braithwaite. Even the radical war protester can't stop it.* "What about it?"

The sorcerer had dropped his studied formality as though it were a cape. "I am grown somewhat concerned these days with its connections with Solomon Braithwaite."

For a moment, the name and its speaker did not connect. Then, with a lurch that blurred her vision, she understood. "You *know?*"

"Truly, Alouzon, I wish that I did not. But I have seen things . . ." He seemed to shudder. "It was an evil night of visions, but perhaps it was for the best. I learned. I have grown."

She was astonished by his comparative equanimity. Vorya, Marrget, and the others would have been shattered by the same knowledge. Mernyl was, instead, reflective. "So you know what a mess this place is."

He folded his arms inside his ragged sleeves. "I suppose that I pity the man," he said. "He was in great pain when Gryylth was formed. And . . ." He shook his head, smiled in spite of himself. "I suppose I show an overweening arrogance for presuming to understand and forgive the individual who created me."

Wykla was looking on without comprehension, and her young face was puzzled, almost alarmed at his words. Alouzon gave her a shake of the head to indicate that the topic being discussed was the concern of Dragonmasters and sorcerers only, that she did not have to bother herself about it. Wykla nodded, folded her arms, and stood to the side like a warrior awaiting orders.

Taking Mernyl's arm, Alouzon turned him away

from the girl. She spoke in an undertone. "I'm damned sorry you had to get involved in his problems."

Mernyl looked resigned. "If we were not involved, Alouzon, we would not exist. Unfortunately, the world after which Gryylth was modeled offers no guidance regarding certain difficulties."

"You're talking about the Tree?"

He nodded. "Tireas has used it, and he will use it again, whether he wants to or no. The Tree, being elemental and inhuman both, has its own needs, its own desires, and warps his will accordingly. I do not believe, for instance, that it was the sorcerer's intention to cause the mass death yesterday. I think the wartroop . . ."

He glanced at Wykla. The girl had lapsed into thought, her head down, her eyes troubled.

" . . . was his primary objective. The Tree turned the spell. Marrget now puts a great deal of faith in me and my powers, but I am not sure her faith is warranted."

"You can't do anything? But you're a sorcerer."

He sighed. "The power that confronts me from the Tree is unnatural—" He broke off, looked vexed. "No, unnatural is an absurd word. I must say new, and uncustomary. It can reach into the very core of being and alter it. You heard me say so at the first interview with Marrget. Such is beyond the normal powers of magic."

"But Tireas can do it."

"Tireas is using the Tree, and he has prepared for years to learn its use. I have had—what?—a week to think about fighting it."

"What about the Circle? Cvinthil told me that it was like the . . . uh . . . foundation of the land, or something like that."

"A relatively accurate description. The Circle is a

monolith of preservation, like the stone of which it is made. The Tree, however, is creation and re-creation. Constant change. When it was in the Heath, it was simply a part of Gryylth, and it caused slow changes within the natural order. But now that it has been brought out as a weapon, Tireas can do with it as he wills. Even the Circle might not be able to stand, for much of its power lies in maintaining the existence of a very fluid and, shall we say, insubstantial world."

Outside, Cvinthil was shouting orders, arranging for the destruction of weapons and materials that the severely shrunken army of Gryylth could not transport. In spite of herself, Alouzon recalled how he had stood up for her and fought beside her in Bandon.

"So . . ." She did not want to say it, but she faced the words as she had once faced the police night sticks. "So we've lost already, then?"

"Nay, not so. I am not satisfied with my own pessimism. The Tree has its power, which has been demonstrated. The Circle has its own, which is yet untried. It may be able to stand very well. But I am afraid, Alouzon, that the best we can expect is a stalemate. The Tree and the Circle are emblems of Solomon Braithwaite's mind, of the mind of our . . ." He looked vexed again, as though unsure of his terminology. "Your race."

She understood. "Mernyl, regardless of where you came from, you're one of us."

"My thanks, Alouzon. I find myself in the novel position of being the only ghost in a world of ghosts who knows he is a ghost."

"You're real."

He nodded. "Our race, then. Whether one is stronger than the other, though . . . Well . . ." He pushed open the flap of the tent. "Here. Look. Do you see?"

Sunlight spilled in, and Alouzon blinked in the

glare. Beyond the camp, beyond the still visible carnage that remained unburied, the land unrolled in greens and browns and yellows. Overhead, the sky was blue, and a lark ascended into the heights.

She understood his lesson. Change and stability. Two equal and balanced powers. They were at work everywhere, in the smallest plant, the largest mountain. This land—any land—needed both, in proper proportion, to survive.

"I might be able to hold the Tree with the powers of the Circle," he explained, letting the flap fall, "but that is all. I cannot conquer. Nor can Tireas. And the continued conflict might strain the fabric of our reality. Normally, one fights a battle with the knowledge that, regardless of any magic involved, the world will still exist come morning. At present, however, we have no such certainty."

The land could be destroyed. In one sense, she found herself confronting the idea with a sense of detachment, for, though she had been accepted by Gryylth, by its people, though she had participated in the endless shedding of blood that characterized it, she did not feel herself to be so inextricably linked with it that she would share its fate. She was from another place. She could leave.

But though her personal existence was not in question, her life, her soul, that part of her which loved and felt pity, had been caught up forever. In spite of the horror she had found in Gryylth, she had also found a fulfillment for lacks that had pursued her since that May morning in Kent. And beyond that, there was the Grail, the finding of which was becoming a nearly physical urge. In the dissolution of Gryylth, the fulfillment, the promise of final wholeness and healing, would be lost forever.

Mernyl's black eyes were compassionate. It was as

though he knew her thoughts, knew what the loss of Gryylth would mean to her. He had power, true, but within him she saw also an ocean of gentleness.

"You . . ."

"Alouzon?"

"If you know about Braithwaite," she said, "you probably know about me, too."

He nodded slowly. "Aye . . . Suzanne."

She did not mind hearing the old name, for he said it with the familiarity and the kindness of an old friend. She wondered what he had seen of her life. Probably everything. "So you know what a fuck-up I've been."

"I have seen nothing in your actions that has not been honorable. I am not the Dragon. I will give advice without being asked, and therefore I will say this: Treat yourself with as much sympathy and healing as you treat others." He indicated Wykla with a tip of his head.

"But what good is it all if the whole world goes up?" *Damn you, Braithwaite.*

"It might not."

"You don't know that."

Something about his manner said otherwise, though. Mernyl's silence was as eloquent as his words. He was not one to hold out a hope of any sort unless it were real. *It might not.*

"What aren't you telling me?"

He hesitated, and in that pause he reminded her too much of Silbakor. Choosing words. Filtering information. She wanted to scream, and her eyes threw the question at him: *Tell me!* To withhold even the slightest hope was the action of a sadist.

"If I knew for certain," he said, finally, "I would tell you. But premature words would cause irreparable harm: the loss of all."

"So you won't tell me?"

He was almost afraid. "Please, Dragonmaster, do not press me."

"I get this same shit from the Dragon!" She was shouting, unconcerned with who might hear her. Wykla started, turned wide eyes on her, and Alouzon caught hold of her temper. She was a Dragonmaster: she had to set an example, particularly to Wykla and the wartroop. Their survival depended on her stability.

But what good was her example if Gryylth was gone?

"OK, Mernyl," she said. "I'll leave it with you. You do your best, and I'll do mine. Maybe we can pull this out of the fire."

"My thanks, Alouzon."

The interview was over, and she felt drained. But she could not even afford to cry. Wrapping an arm about Wykla's shoulders, she guided her toward the tent flap. "Come on, Wykla. Let's go get you some clothes and some sword practice. Looks like we'll be hacking meat again soon. Marrget said something about a bath in a river, too."

"Aye, my lady. Although . . ." She looked at herself, held up her hands, still unbelieving. "I am not sure I can face a bath."

She tightened her grip on Wykla's shoulder. "I'll help you." She looked at Mernyl again. *There's got to be some way out of this. I promised her. I promised them all. I'm not going to let it go to hell.*

But the sorcerer stood stolidly, as though contemplating his own death. And Alouzon realized that he was.

❖ CHAPTER 19 ❖

❖

VORYA ORDERED THAT CAMP BE BROKEN THAT morning without the careful packing up and shouldering of burdens that normally characterized the movement of large numbers of men. Speed was important, and excess and unusable gear would only weigh down the soldiers that remained to him. Instead, casting aside all but what was necessary, they would travel quickly and lightly, more an expanded troop than an army, and what they left behind was burned in hastily built bonfires that sent plumes of black smoke stretching westward across the blue sky.

The dead were left unburied, for there were too many of them to attend to, even with the leisure of several days. But their constant presence throughout the night had turned them from shapeless masses of color and texture into discrete presences that, though voiceless, testified to the force of the weapon that had been turned upon them. Several corpses had been literally dismembered and scattered across tens of square yards. Others had been crushed as though heavy weights had fallen on them.

And Alouzon noticed something else about which she said nothing: though crows and ravens circled above the fallen, and occasionally alighted, they did not eat. She watched them for some time as the men assembled near the smoldering ruin of the king's pavilion, and their lack of appetite was as unsettling as it was unnatural.

"Dragonmaster? Is something amiss?"

Wykla was still with her, bathed now and in fresh garments that fitted her tolerably. Alouzon jerked her gaze away from the birds: she did not want the girl to notice. "It's nothing, Wykla. You ready to roll?"

She put her hand to her sword and nodded, forced a trace of a smile. The dry wind had taken the moisture from her hair and left it a mane of amber and gold, and if she caught it now and tied it back, she did so as though performing a common task, with unshaking hands and an air of familiarity.

But she still kept close to Alouzon, putting the Dragonmaster between herself and the curious and sometimes frightened eyes of the men who had remained loyal to Vorya throughout a terrifying night and a dubious morning. Simply in being present, though, she showed great courage, for the rest of her wartroop was still on the other side of the ridge, Marrget deeming it wise not to attempt to force matters any more than necessary.

Vorya waited at the head of the columns, Cvinthil at his side. Santhe had elected to stay with the surviving men of the Second Wartroop, and they kept to themselves, forming up at the rear of the main body as though their experiences the previous day had isolated them as effectively as had those of the First Wartroop.

The day seemed raw and unfinished, the sky achingly bright, as though the world had been worn thin with overuse and threatened now to begin to fray in sight of all. The downs, undulating to the horizon, seemed bare and lifeless despite their thick grass, and their faint transparency was a constant reminder to Alouzon that Gryylth was anything but natural, that tenuous laws and the good will of an impossible beast glued it together.

Vorya was looking at her. Time to resume the mask of competence. With Wykla keeping to her side like a golden-haired shadow, she trotted over to the king. "Gods bless, Vorya," she said.

"Gods bless, Alouzon. Is the First Wartroop ready?"

"The last I saw, they were just finishing up. They should be mounted by now." She glanced up the ridge to a slight figure just visible in the shadow of some stunted trees. She waved, and the figure waved in return. "That's Timbrin. Marrget's waiting for the order to move."

"Then I shall give it." But Vorya sat still for a moment more, his red rimmed eyes scanning the sprawled heaps of dead as though he searched for his only son.

The crows stalked among the bodies like the priests of a necropolis, their beaks shut tight as though padlocked. One cawed harshly, was answered by another. The wind was dry and warm. The odor of death was strong.

"Dragonmaster," he said desperately, in a voice low enough so that not even Cvinthil could hear. "Tell me something to cheer me. Advise me. Will Gryylth perish?"

She glanced behind for a moment. Off to one side, Mernyl was on a gray horse, his hood thrown up in spite of the heat. She could not see his face, could barely make out the glitter of his eyes.

He would not tell her what hope there was. How slight, then, was it?

"Dragonmaster?"

"You're asking me?" M-1s, and now the Tree. Gryylth might as well have been threatened with a plutonium bomb. "I told you what I thought. We can't win this war in the old way. It just won't work."

He looked frail and broken. "I see no alternative."

"Vorya," she said quietly, knowing that her words would bring little comfort. "They're dead. We lost almost *everyone* who came out here."

The king groaned at the names. "There are only aged men and small boys left in the towns. Those who could bear arms were sent ahead with haste." He swept his good arm out. "To this."

"What are you going to do about it?" She felt the cramp of guilt as she spoke, for she herself had nothing to offer, and her words could only torment an already pained old man.

He did not reply for a moment. Finally: "I will try to save the rest. I believe that fighting bravely will give them a greater chance than meek surrender." He lifted his arm to give the signal to start.

But the men were not looking at him. Their eyes were directed instead to the top of the ridge where, silhouetted against the sky, Marrget and the wartroop were waiting. They were mounted, in column, and though distance blurred details, their long hair and slender forms made it obvious that this was nothing like the First Wartroop that had set out from Kingsbury five days before.

The king lifted his sword in salute, and Marrget returned the gesture in silence, her blade flashing in the sun. "Forward, then!" cried Vorya, his voice strong in spite of the strain. "To the Circle!"

The men moved reluctantly, as though what they saw on the ridge had shaken their resolve. Only the

Second Wartroop set out briskly, and Alouzon guessed that Santhe's revitalized smile was bright enough that Marrget could see it easily, even at such a distance. She thought she saw the ash blond woman return it, but the wind gusted and her face was lost in a swirl of blond hair.

Vorya and the King's Guards rode in the lead. The rest of the force followed after, marshaled by Cvinthil. Mernyl kept his head down as though he thought of things other than the movement of the army, and he eventually straggled out so far to one side that Santhe had to ride out and bring him back.

The First Wartroop, though, did not fall into the lines, but kept a course parallel to them at a distance of some fifty yards. The women rode easily, comfortably, and Alouzon hoped that the reason she counted only ten riders was that Marrget had sent out scouts. If the women could endure these first frightening days, they might find their path smoothed. With luck, with persistence and work and change, their society might prove bearable to them.

For whether the Dremords won, lost, or settled, Gryylth as the First Wartroop knew it—as everyone in the land knew it—was going to vanish. The sanctuary created by Solomon Braithwaite in an unknown burst of obscure power was finished. He had built a world in which his dreams could live, and he had built it to be changeless. And yet it was changing out from under him.

She wondered where Dythragor was now, what he was doing. She almost pitied him. But she had other concerns.

"Wykla," she said. "Attend the king. I have to leave for a while."

"My lady, I . . ." Her eyes glanced at the big men who accompanied Vorya, swung back to Alouzon. "I . . ."

Alouzon waited. For all her girlishness, Wykla was anything but weak. During the few minutes of sword practice that she had managed to give the girl that morning, Wykla had shown herself Marrget's equal. And, driving herself as Marrget had been driven, flushed with her exertions, she had found that her body obeyed her, that it sweated and fought and gasped for air just as effectively as ever. She had smiled openly when they were through: she was a warrior still.

But her uncertainty had not been entirely banished. It was one thing for Wykla to know herself, but it was another to present herself, unsupported and female, to others. "You have to start somewhere, Wykla."

"Aye, my lady." She took a moment to gather her courage, then fell in beside Vorya. The old king nodded graciously to his new attendant and rode on, but one of his guards was staring. Wykla stared in return, her eyes large and blue in her fair face, her lips half parted in the manner of a woman confronted with something as timeless as it was incomprehensible. In a moment, she caught her breath and looked away, but Vorya's guard had already reddened and dropped his eyes. He swallowed as though something had caught in his throat, but his discomfort did not seem to be grounded in fear.

It's going to be a long haul. For everyone. Alouzon shrugged inwardly and cantered out to Marrget. "What's the story on the Corrinians?" she said. "Do you have scouts out?"

"I do." Marrget caught the additional meaning to the words and added: "Nay, Alouzon. There have been no more lives lost."

Alouzon waved to the wartroop and received a scattering of greetings in return. "How are they?" she said to Marrget.

"They are loyal to me and to you. We attempt at present to . . . ignore the changes, though that becomes difficult at times." She stared past Alouzon to the slowly moving army. Wykla's hair shone golden. "How is Wykla?"

"*Damned* good fighter."

Marrget smiled. "That is a needless statement, Alouzon. She is one of mine. I noticed though that Pas of the Guard seemed to think her attractive."

"Yeah . . . uh . . . it sure looked that way, didn't it?"

Marrget's brow furrowed, her smile departed, and she shifted in her saddle as though momentarily unsure of what to do with her body. "A strange turn of events for the First Wartroop. I am not sure how to accept this."

"Give it time, Marrget."

"Aye, Dragonmaster, that is all we can do for now." She shook herself away from the subject. "But time is not being kind to us, it seems. My scouts report that the Dremord phalanxes are closing the distance between us."

"Can we make it to the Circle?"

"We can, but only by forced march, and that will have us reaching the Circle with the spears of the phalanxes pricking our backs. Not a particularly hopeful beginning for a battle."

The Roman road lay straight as an arrow across the downs, ignoring landscape and contour, and the march of men and horses stirred a thin cloud of dust from its stone surface. Alouzon squinted into the distance. "We've got to slow them down, then."

"Aye. Could Mernyl take a hand in this?"

"I think we'd both rather do something without magic for the time being, Marrget. We'll save Mernyl for later."

"You are wise, Alouzon."

"Nah . . . I just need some reassurance that physics still works."

Marrget looked amused and puzzled both. "What do you suggest, my friend?"

The horses' hooves clopped evenly on the stone pavement, the tread of the men was measured and steady. No Roman slaves had ever built this road, since it had been created along with the rest of Gryylth, but its duplicates existed all over Europe. The Empire had used them for communication, commerce, and, most important of all, quick movement of its legions. They were an ideal surface on which to travel, and some of them were still usable in the twentieth century.

"Could we disrupt the road?" said Alouzon.

Marrget's eyebrows lifted at the thought. "With so many men," she said, "Tarwach undoubtedly finds the road invaluable."

"So what if we fuck it up real good?" Her thoughts were reverting to images of a past decade. In Vietnam, small groups of guerrillas had managed to disrupt sophisticated technologies with comparatively primitive means. Booby traps, punji stakes, pitfalls, man traps—not all would translate effectively to this temperate and open environment of rolling downs and lush grass, but the objective was to slow the Corrinians, not stop them.

The destruction of the road at key points would deprive Tarwach of his most efficient means of transport, and a thin scattering of crude but effective traps throughout the grass would make him wary of striking off across country. Quickly, she outlined the plan to Marrget. The captain listened, nodded. "That is a good idea, Dragonmaster. But I am not sure that we have hands enough to pursue it. Even under ideal circumstances, with the men . . ." She paused, sighed. " . . . and women rested and fresh, it would take time. As it is . . ."

"So what if we got more?"

"More men?"

"Uh-uh. More women." Marrget opened her mouth, but Alouzon went on. "There are villages everywhere, and I've seen some around here that can't be farther away than a half-day's quick walk. Vorya told me that there are only old men and boys left, but he's forgetting about the women because you people aren't used to thinking of them as a fighting force."

Marrget was smiling thinly. "I have . . . had my thoughts altered somewhat on that subject, Alouzon."

"I know. And you're doing just fantastic. But if I could get the women out here to help, we could screw things up good for Tarwach. We could gain . . . what do you think?"

Marrget was calculating again. "A day, maybe a day and a half. But we do not have much time. How shall we raise the women quickly enough?"

"Leave it to me." She had attempted to flense her vocabulary and her thoughts of the inflammatory but empty rhetoric she had used so casually during the antiwar years. But she had been unsuccessful: she had lapsed into it automatically when confronted by the hapless library clerk and when dealing with Dythragor. Obviously, it still lay just beneath the surface, waiting to be tapped.

If she could muster such conviction for intangibles that she could incite herself and others to brave the police and the tear gas, she could certainly fan those same flames for something as real as survival. When she had first come to Gryylth, she had received the impression that the women of the land were frightened, craven things who would shrink at the thought of leaving home. But since then she had met the girls of Bandon, who chafed under the restrictions imposed on their sex, and Adyssa, who had been willing to give her life to save a woman she hardly knew. There was fear in the women of Gryylth, but she was willing to wager that it was a brittle fear, easily chipped away under the right conditions to reveal a generous helping of steel beneath.

The massed phalanxes of Corrin lay behind, advancing, out for revenge, and with them was the Tree. She did not have much hope that she could preserve Gryylth for anything more than a few days, but given the fact that the land had only existed for ten years, a few days was a long time.

"Hang on, Marrget," she said. "I'll be back." She galloped Jia out across the downs, and the Dragonsword was a shaft of gold as she swung it over her head. She was already shouting with the voice of one used to command: *Silbakor!*

Dythragor had not slept or eaten. Neither had his horse. The animal was beginning to protest his treatment, stumbling through the forest as though blind, stopping refractorily to snatch a mouthful of herbage in spite of his rider's stubborn insistence that he continue on his way.

"Come on, dammit," he said, kicking the horse hard. "I don't have time. Move."

Move? Move where? He knew only that he was traveling south once again, that Crownhark and the mutilated body of Solomon Braithwaite lay behind him, and that, farther back, was . . .

"Come on. *Move!*"

. . . was something he did not want to think about.

A particularly violent kick brought the horse's head up, and he tried to rear, but mistreatment, hunger, and thirst had sapped his strength, and nothing more than a feeble spasm shuddered the length of the beast. Stiffly, he walked, and Dythragor could urge him into nothing quicker.

The trees fell away, and he found himself at the edge of the tidal flats that stretched out to the Isle of Mist. He had not been here before, and in light of the name of the place, he found it curious that there was no mist to be seen: the afternoon sun glowed warmly on the green hills that rose up from the wooded shores, and the air was so transparent as to seem almost unnatural.

He crossed the flats, his horse responding with a burst of enthusiasm once his hooves touched the damp mud and sand. But when he had sloshed across to the island, his lethargy returned, and he actually lay down just within the trees of the forest, his nose buried in a stream, drinking sleepily.

Dythragor swore at him, but when kicks and blows failed to stir the animal, he gave up and dismounted. Above, visible through the gaps in the leaves and branches, a white tower rose straight as a spear from the summit of the hills, glittering in the sunlight.

He blinked at it, his eyes dazzled as much by the tower as by fatigue and inner turmoil. Who lived here? It seemed a lordly place, but Vorya had certainly never mentioned anything about another king, and the nobility of Gryylth was concentrated at Kingsbury. Marrget, being from Crownhark, should certainly have known something about it, but had apparently kept silent. He resolved to ask Marrget about it if he ever saw . . .

He stood still, his thoughts moving in spite of his efforts to still them. The thought of Marrget took him back to that day at the Long River, and the scene, like a newsreel jammed in the projector, replayed itself before his eyes, although this time the girl that he forced, that he stripped and threw to the ground, bore the remade features of the captain of the First Wartroop. She was screaming, her cries weak and incoherent, her hands and arms no match for the strength of a Dragonmaster. "Marrget . . . don't . . ." he said. But his words were as brutal as his hands, and he found that he could not remember how to comfort.

He came to himself on his knees, shaking, his hands full of his own hair, his eyes shut tight against the inner vision and aswirl with phosphenes. As he staggered to his feet, the tower glinted at him mockingly, and leaving his horse by the stream, he made his way up the slope.

There was a path, and it made for an easy climb, but maze-like, it twisted back and forth as it ascended, and it seemed to Dythragor that it was more circuitous than it really had to be, for it descended almost as often as it rose and doubled back on itself unnecessarily. The day was well on into the afternoon by the time he gained the summit and stumbled across the grassy lawn toward the tower.

Scented by the sea and grass, the air was fresh and

cool, and it soothed his sleepless eyes as he went toward the door, gawking up at the polished, white monolith like a youngster approaching his first Christmas tree. In all, the tower had a strikingly modern appearance, its marble walls unfigured, its windows recessed smoothly into the stone, and he felt anomalous, even vulgar, in coarse leather armor that was stained and fragrant with the blood of the old man of Crownhark.

But in contrast to the unadorned sides of the tower, the door was not without carving. Runes and figures adorned it in expert relief, and, at head level, as though designed to ensure that he would read it, was the single word: *Listinoise*.

Lifting a hand, he traced the carved word. It seemed familiar, but like a forgotten dream, its meaning fled when he sought it. The name of the tower? But it seemed so unlike the names he encountered in Gryylth, for it seemed to have its origins more in the Latin than in the Anglo-Saxon languages.

Latin. Anglo-Saxon. There it was again, the virus that Alouzon had brought with her to Gryylth. Questions and more questions. With a violent jerk, he grabbed the pull and swung the door wide, his hand on his sword. Whoever lived here would learn to respect Dythragor Dragonmaster.

Inside, he found blank marble walls and floors, and ceilings that were lost in a luminous haze. If anything, the bareness of the interior added to the sense of modernity, and again, clad as he was in armor that, yes, seemed a part of the fifth century of his own world, and of an island called Britain, he felt that he was the anomaly, the stranger, the intruder.

He stopped with his foot on the first of a flight of stairs. Fifth-century Britain. He looked down and ex-

amined the blood-stained leather as though it had
been brought in from an excavation on Cadbury Hill,
his scholar's eyes, surfacing now within those of the
warrior, searching for, finding, details: the bronze
buckles, the saucer-brooches and fittings worked with
Celtic spirals . . . zoomorphics . . . It was impossible,
but true.

Again, he pulled himself out of the questions. Fifth-
century Britain? He might as well believe that the
world was flat.

The stairs spiraled up around the interior of the
tower and brought him to another door, this time of
apple wood, again carved. The images were confus-
ing, and to his tired eyes they writhed and capered
across the surface of the wood, prancing as though
in an endless, twining procession. Runes, animals,
faces, flowers—all tumbled and nodded, all twisted
and revolved, all glanced now and then at the strange
old man who had come to their door dressed anach-
ronistically in the armor of a bygone age, of another
world.

But he reminded himself that he was not old. It
could not be Dythragor Dragonmaster that was so
regarded by carved eyes and wooden faces. And Solomon Braithwaite lay dead on the floor of an inn,
miles away. He himself had killed him. It was just
Dythragor now, just a life of war and glory, of battle
and strength . . .

The face of the girl he had raped surfaced before
his eyes, regarded him sorrowfully, then vanished.
Her place was taken by the images of two children
who fled from burning fields, hand in hand, the boy,
by the look of him no more than four, leading his
younger sister through the flames, his face growing
older with each moment.

Then a flower, then Marrget, a woman, her hair long and flowing and free, her breasts bare. She held her head proudly as she turned to him, a cup in her hands. Her lips moved soundlessly, but he read the command:

Ask.

His hand was on the door pull, and it squirmed in his fingers as though it sought to meet his grasp. "Ask? Ask what?"

Ask.

And then she was gone into a netherworld of formless mist, of stars that shone from below the ground.

A shrieking harpy flapped its filthy wings before him, and suddenly Helen was there, her finger pointing accusingly. He did not have to read her lips: he knew what she was saying. They were almost the last words she had spoken to him, and they were replete with the hatred and contempt that had riddled their marriage and left it lifeless. She might have been— yes, she was: he could see it clearly—holding that evening edition of the *Los Angeles Times* before him as she had outside the courtroom, the screamer headlines announcing the deaths of four students in Ohio.

Are you satisfied, murderer?

Her words cut him now as they did then, and his heart twisted in his chest, his arm turned numb. But he refused to give her what she wanted, he refused to take the pills again. Spitting in her face, he opened the door and rushed into the room beyond.

It was lit with the twilight of a summer evening, the ceiling dark blue and sprinkled with silver stars, the floor a variegated carpet of browns and greens that seemed to mimic a landscape. Soothing, quiet, it seemed a sanctuary, a holy place into which the profane did not enter.

The setting sun streamed through a single window, fell upon the altar and gleamed on the embroidered threads of gold that wound through a crumpled mound of black satin. If there had been a Mystery here, it seemed that it was gone, fled. Only its veil was left. But when he picked it up he recognized with a start the blouse of Korean silk that he had brought back to Helen after his days in Seoul: the expensive, exotic gift he had given her the day before they were married.

Sacrilege. He stared at it, breathing hard, the rectilinear pictograms spelling out unknown words and sentiments, the white-plumed storks engaged in a mating dance that ridiculed both his childless marriage and the excesses of forced copulation he allowed himself in Gryylth.

"You damned bitch." His words, whispered, held an edge as brittle as glass. "Where are you?"

As in an answer to his question, the door slammed behind him, and he turned around to find that the inside of the wood was covered with a mirror, and that his own reflection—quaint and faintly absurd in the trappings of heroic culture—raged at him from out of its depths.

Footsteps pattered down the stairs outside, and he heard the door of the tower open, then close. Rushing to the window, he saw, far below, the figure of a woman running southward, her black hair flying behind her and her robes of silver and sable fluttering like the wings of a butterfly. She was not Helen, and yet maybe she was. He could no longer be sure.

"Helen!"

He caught a glimpse of a white face, and then she

was gone, vanishing into a wall of fog that was rising from the ocean that lay to the south.

Lifting his eyes, Dythragor looked out over a sea of mist. It roiled in shades of white and gray and stretched off into the distance as though it were made of twilight and shadow. The sun was setting, and the near-horizontal beams pierced it, turned it into a cloudy opal shot with sparks of fire.

The mirror penned him in the temple, but he drew the Dragonsword and lashed out at it. Reflection struck reflection, shivering the glass into fragments that imaged him from a thousand different perspectives: here he was six, watching his mother pull her collar up over the bruises his father had given her; here he was an old man, dead in his office; here again, he was Dythragor Dragonmaster, raping a Dremord girl, denying a friend . . .

The steel bit deep into the mirror, into the wood beneath it, splitting the door and leaving it hanging on its hinges. He shoved it brutally open, and a shard of glass traced a line of crimson down his palm as it showed him a picture of a young soldier examining photographs at a desk in Seoul, wondering if he would ever have a chance to kill something.

He ran down the stairs, seeding the white marble with drops of his own blood. The tower door was still open, and he ran across the grass toward the mist, following the path of the black-clad woman.

The ground dipped suddenly, the mist began, and he entered a dim landscape of ghostly trees and pale ferns. When the sun set, taking with it the last of the daylight, he was left groping by instinct, feeling his way by the touch of a trunk, or the brush of a frond across his face. The woman could have been any-

where, even behind him, and he kept his sword in
his hand, ready to slash at the slightest movement.

He followed the slope down, and the ground
turned soft beneath his boots, quaking with each step.
Lights appeared ahead, twinkling quietly, and with
a sense of relief he almost ran to meet them.

The ground grew softer, almost slippery, the footing uncertain, and as a golden light began to build
ahead of him, the faint outline of a chalice manifesting through the darkness and the mist, he tripped,
slid, and wound up face down on what he had assumed to be the damp ground of a bog, or of a sandy
shore.

But it was not a bog, nor was it sand. What lay
beneath him was a shimmering transparency, a sim-
ulacrum of earth and grass, only slightly more solid
than the projected image of a motion picture. He
could see through it; and beyond the layers of soil
and stone, which seemed to be no more than a few
feet thick, there was a nothingness that was populated
by scattered points of light.

And he realized that he could only be looking at
stars.

Ahead, the Grail hung in the black sky, just out
of reach, as though daring him to take the final step
and throw himself upon its promise. Throbbing like
a heart, golden as a summer dawn, it brimmed with
living waters that tumbled over its rim and cascaded
down into the void as though they could fill the universe.

With a cry, he turned, scrambling in soil that
seemed to want to melt away beneath his feet and
pitch him headlong into vacuum. Clawing at the half-
real grass, he worked his way back to the tower and

clung to the cold stone as though it were the only sanity in a world gone mad. He wept, screamed, his tears streaking down his face, glistening on the grass, mingling with the dew that, toward sunrise, gathered at his feet, flashing like diamonds, or like stars.

✦ CHAPTER 20 ✦

✦

ALOUZON'S VOICE GREW HOARSE FROM SHOUT-
ing, her hands scraped and raw from ringing the tocsin bell in one village after another. Silbakor could
give her speed, but even the immense bulk of the
black Dragon and its impassive, yellow eyes could
lend her no more than an air of authority. If she were
to gain the support of the women of Gryylth, it would
be by her deeds, and, more important, her words.

*I don't want you to follow me. I want you to go out
and help your men.*

The bells clanged urgently, and the Dragonmaster
shouted and gestured, digging deep into the oratory
that had lain unused since she had helped to fire the
campus protests of another world and another age.
With irony, she reflected that she was using the same
techniques, the same urgent call for change and revolution, that had so dismayed Solomon Braithwaite.
But she could not relish the triumph: these same
sentiments had led her classmates to death.

*I'm telling you this: it's not a matter of choosing
whether things are going to change. They're going to
change whether you like it or not, and all you can do
is decide which side you're on.*

The old men scoffed, and the women at first were

doubtful. Here was a stranger—and a woman at that—come now riding a Dragon as though she thought herself a hero of Gryylth, calling for them to leave their homes and (of all things!) travel across country to fight the Dremords. A clear violation of custom, taboo, and the entire context of their lives.

And if you get in the way of what's happening out there, it's going to run right over you.

Some turned away, went to their homes, and hid. Others, caught by, attracted to, this woman of power who stood atop the stone housings of the tocsin bells and declaimed sentiments that they, perhaps, in private moments, in stray thoughts, held themselves, stayed listening. Her voice was restrained and impassioned, pleading and commanding by turns, and she painted a picture of words that confronted them with the deadly scenario that was unfolding a few miles away: an army slaughtered, Gryylth on the run, the Corrinian phalanxes advancing like a wave of rage.

There's a time when the system works, and then there's a time that it starts to kill you. It's killing you right now. Even if you can't see the Dremords coming for you, believe me they're coming, and the system's helping them come. So what are you going to do about it?

And the silence would drag out, the faces of the women mirroring fright, grief, loss. Their men were no more, their husbands and sons were dead. They were defenseless. And yet, inevitably, someone—a midwife perhaps—would ask the question: "Tell us what to do, Dragonmaster."

Your lives are at stake, and all you've got to fight with is your lives. So you've got to put your bodies on the line, you've got to stop what's happening, and you've got to show the Dremords that, whether they like it or not, Gryylth isn't just going to lie down and get walked on.

They listened. Even some of the old men listened. With baskets on their arms and babies on their hips, with tools and pots and even sharp sticks, they left the villages in long straggling lines, heading for what was left of a once-proud army, bringing help to their men. By their actions, they violated custom, they ignored taboo, they shattered the brittle strictures that had hemmed them into their lives.

But they would not submit.

By the time Alouzon returned, some of the women she had harangued that morning were already within sight. The western sky was still blazing with sunset as she slid from Silbakor's back into Marrget's arms, and with what was left of her voice she told her to expect further help throughout the night.

"They are traveling after dark?" Marrget was incredulous. "What did you tell them?"

Alouzon forced a smile through parched lips. "Same thing I told you, lady." Her world spun suddenly, and she would have fallen to the ground had not Marrget caught her.

She came to herself when it was quite dark, but she judged that she had not slept long, for the waning moon had not yet risen. She was mildly surprised: she had thought that she could have remained unconscious for a week. Maybe the Dragonsword was aiding her as it had after the Heath.

For a while, though, she allowed herself the luxury of remaining among her blankets beside the fire, and with unclosed eyes, she watched the stars. The constellations were not those of Earth, but after passing night after night beneath them, she was beginning to recognize patterns and colors. Without the glare of the moon, she even saw two parallel bands of cloudy luminescence that spanned the sky: the distinctive mark of a spiral galaxy.

Maybe it was the Milky Way that so gleamed in a comforting arc. That would be nice, she thought. To be in the same galaxy with everything that she found familiar, everything that constituted her past and her present . . .

She heard the murmur of voices, male and female, the sound of spades and picks in earth, the sharpening of stakes, the grating of slabs of stone as they were lifted from the road. Marrget and Vorya, carrying out her suggestions, were overseeing the destruction of the Corrinians' most efficient means of transport and were filling the downs to either side with a scattering of simple but effective traps.

She turned over, stretched, and peered at a landscape illuminated by torchlight and populated with indistinct figures. The village women, it seemed, were doing most of the work, allowing the tired soldiers and warriors a needed rest. One laughed in the darkness, and those who were awake joined in. Cvinthil started up a song in his firm tenor, and the chorus sounded across the downs as men and women, motivated by fear and survival, worked together, finding in their work a commonality that transcended sex, custom, and world view and replaced them with a shared vision of a different life, one that—for the sake of the wartroop, for the sake of the girls of Bandon, for the sake of Gryylth and Corrin—she prayed might continue past this one night of cooperation and faith.

Afar, afar,
My love lies afar.
And who tells me he shall return

Who lies afar from me?

It was the same song that Cvinthil and Seena had sung for her, Seena's soprano riding sweetly upon her husband's countermelody. Now, though, the song came from many throats, and she heard, amid the strain, the sound of the men's line duplicated an octave higher as the women of the First Wartroop, their identities disguised by darkness and their transformation, added their old harmony in their new voices.

Footsteps approached, and someone sat down near her, sighed. Someone else stood by. "There is no need to drive yourself like an ox, child," said a woman.

"Eh?" Marrget's voice. Alouzon allowed herself another minute to drift and listen.

"You've been working like a man all evening. I've watched you."

"I believe, my lady, that we all must play the man this night."

"That is true, child. But . . ."

Alouzon stole a glance. Marrget was a few feet from her, sitting on a bundle, rubbing sore arms with dirty hands. A midwife, hair unbound, stood before her, her apron and gown stained with grass and soil.

" . . . but you are young and slender. You have had no children to strengthen you. Be easy on yourself."

"I will be easy when my work is done." Marrget's tone was friendly, but reserved.

The village women knew nothing of the fate of the wartroop, and the midwife addressed Marrget with a kind solicitousness. "I must say, though, that you are wise for your years, to take your brother's garments for yourself when you set out. What village do you come from, did you say?"

The conversation had taken an uncomfortable turn, and Marrget was suddenly cautious. "I did not say. But I am . . . from Crownhark."

"Crownhark. Hmmm. I too am from that village. Do I know you, child?"

Marrget was silent for some time. She wiped her palms on her trews, examined her hands with a crooked smile. "No, lady. You do not."

The midwife stood with her arms crossed over her apron. "Ah well, I will disturb you no more. Rest. I hope to see you in Crownhark someday. Perhaps you will come to me when you have your children. Fear not: your hips and feet tell me that your time will be easy." She looked on Marrget fondly, like a mother on a daughter. "May I know your name?"

The captain froze, and her skin was white even in the ruddy glow of the fire and the torches. Her mouth worked soundlessly for some time. "You . . ."

Even though she was surrounded by men and women, by activity and song, by voices and even occasional laughter, Marrget seemed utterly alone. For a moment, the horrified leanness returned to her face, and she stared at herself, her hands shaking.

"Child, are you not well?"

Marrget's voice was a whisper, and the words came to her lips singly, unwillingly. She would not admit weakness, but the alternative was terrible enough. "You may . . . call me Marrha."

"Gods bless, Marrha," said the midwife. "I am Nyyla. I will see you in Crownhark when times are better. I must return to my women now."

She gave Marrget a friendly nod, one woman to another, and departed, her skirts swishing on the grass. Marrget remained by the fire, her shoulders bent as though under a weight of iron. "You heard, Dragonmaster?" she said aloud, her eyes tragic. "Am I a coward then, for taking a false name?"

Alouzon got up and sat on the bundle beside her.

Tireas had taken much from Marrget, and now her falsehood had taken everything else. "You're no coward. Things are confused enough. Why add to it? You made the right decision."

"She . . . she spoke to me as though I were a woman."

"Yeah. She did." She left the obvious unspoken.

Marrget put her hands to her face and sobbed, wrenching the sorrow from someplace so deep that the release itself was an agony. She turned to Alouzon, and the Dragonmaster held her tightly as she wept, shuddering, silent, alone.

She had been for her wartroop a example and a source of strength, maintaining her equanimity in the face of a transformation so profound that it altered not only the commonplaces of appearance and gender but also the vital intangibles of perception, relationship, and social role. But, as she had held herself steady for the benefit of others, she had pushed aside her own emotions, confining her fear and horror until they tore at her heart.

And now the casual, friendly words of another woman had turned her sight inward to face the accumulated and ignored emotions. Away from the wartroop, away from the sight of all save one she had come to trust with her very soul, she wept for herself, long and deeply.

"Oh, Marrget," said Alouzon, brushing back her hair and rocking her like a child, "I think you've become a man again."

Her eyes opened, brimming with tears, unsure whether to be wounded or puzzled.

"You can cry," Alouzon said softly.

❖   ❖   ❖

The sun rose the next day on a road that, for the better part of a mile, had been essentially obliterated, and on a landscape that concealed a variety of traps and pitfalls. Only a few Corrinians might lose their lives to the hidden stakes and the deep pits, but, afterwards, the rest would be too wary to make good time.

The women left that morning, gathering their belongings and bowing, as custom dictated, to the men before they turned away from the road and set off across the downs to their home villages. But their attitudes had changed in the course of a night of hard labor, and the bows were shorter now, lighter, the acknowledgments of equals, and they were frequently returned by the men with a kind of embarrassed gratitude.

Their work had made an impression on the soldiers, and though, the village women gone, they still stared with apprehension at the First Wartroop as it mounted up a stone's throw away, the night had done much to strip away thoughts of woman's place and man's dominance. Survival and battle were the major concerns now, and when Wykla rejoined the King's Guard that morning, Pas and the others still watched her appreciatively, but they also asked her about the fighting she had done against the soldiers of Corrin, questioning her as to the tactics and the men of the phalanxes—the talk of warriors.

Marrget remained pale and shaken from her catharsis, but what reserves she possessed she had brought up and hardened, and she sat in her saddle as straight as any commander of Gryylth, her gray eyes defiant, her blond hair strangely soft and curling in the breeze. "My thanks, Alouzon, for your help."

Alouzon had been watching Mernyl, hoping for some sign that the sorcerer would share whatever hope he had found for the land. But he was keeping to himself, his hood shadowing his face, his white staff glowing faintly, even in daylight. Perhaps he was gathering his strength for what he expected to be a difficult battle.

Difficult? The whole world might end.

She felt Marrget's eyes on her. Having shown weakness, the captain was undoubtedly wondering if she were being ostracized. With a sigh, she reached out, and clasped Marrget's hand, trying to look hopeful. "We're friends, right?"

"Indeed we are."

"So what are friends for? I'll tell you, Marrget: I'm probably going to get myself good and messed up before this is all over. I hope you'll be around for me."

"Unless . . ." Marrget's expression was unreadable. "Unless death intervenes, Dragonmaster, I shall be with you."

Something about her tone. Alouzon wondered again if Marrget were looking for battle in order to die honorably. "I think I started something last night. Things seemed pretty different this morning."

"There have been changes, true. Within the army, at least." She smiled, but her eyes were still cold. "And shall I braid my hair for the townsfolk?"

There might not be anything left to braid her hair for . . . "Give yourself a break, dammit. Rome wasn't built in a day." She looked down at the road, stifled a nervous laugh. Not Rome, certainly—but Gryylth had been the work of a few hours.

"Rome?"

"Uh . . . just a figure of speech." She looked around, and realized that the Dragon was gone again. "Did you see Silbakor take off?"

"Toward midnight, Alouzon, it rose suddenly as though it had heard a call."

"Maybe Dythragor's up to something."

"I pray not. He seems to have too much talent for increasing our woes."

Again, she almost pitied the man. "Give him a break, too, Marrget."

The captain pulled herself up straight and glared at her. "My trusted comrade denies and deserts me. Shall I forgive him? Very well, I forgive him. But I need not seek out his company, nor must I be concerned with his feelings or his welfare. If he wishes to aid Gryylth, I would he submit himself to the king, so that his actions may be discussed. I am done with his imperious disregard for the safety of my people."

"Hey, Marrget, I'm sorry. Don't get down on me."

Marrget slumped on her horse. "I am overtempered today," she said. "I beg pardon."

"Don't mention it." Dythragor had behaved badly when he had seen Marrget, and he had, at one time or another, insulted almost everyone of rank in Gryylth. Gryylth was a heroic culture: Marrget was bending quite a bit just to speak of the man without cursing him. "I understand. I just wish I knew what he was doing."

"I can tell you somewhat of that, Alouzon. Nyyla, my midwife . . ." Marrget pressed her lips together, let her breath out slowly, began again. "Nyyla told me of an event in Crownhark that occurred some hours before your arrival. Dythragor appeared, riding a worn-out horse—for which, if he were a stable boy, I should have him whipped—and asked for food and lodging."

"He was in Crownhark?"

"For a short time. He did not stay. He did not even

eat. Instead, talking with a poor old fool of a man who used to be a soldier with the Fifth Wartroop, but whose brain had become addled with battle and age, he became enraged. He slaughtered the old man on the spot and fled southward."

"Jeez . . . I *thought* they were all looking at me funny when I showed up with Silbakor. I'm surprised they didn't run."

Marrget's eyes were still cold. "Perhaps they expected more sanity from a woman."

"So where the hell is he?" She straightened and looked around, as though by doing so she might catch some glimpse of Dythragor. But it was a useless gesture, for the errant Dragonmaster was far away. If he had summoned Silbakor, he could be anywhere.

From her vantage, she saw little that had not become familiar to her: the road, the army, Wykla's amber hair shining in the sun; and beyond, the rolling, grassy land. But then she looked behind. There, spreading across the horizon, was a ragged line of darkness. It mounted into the sky as though it were boiling up from a kettle, and from within it came flickers of lightning.

She had seen it before, and she had no comfortable memories regarding it. Her stomach knotting within her, she swung back to Marrget. The captain was staring at the blackness as though it were an old enemy, well known.

"Now is not the time for fear, Dragonmaster," she said. Unsheathing her sword, she brandished it, lifting her high, clear voice. "Vorya! King of Gryylth! Your enemy approaches!"

Startled faces turned in their direction, and Vorya's shout drifted back to them. "To the Circle!"

The troops began to move more quickly, Cvinthil

barking out orders that sent the men down the road at double time. Alouzon glanced back, noticed that the blackness was approaching, and wondered when it would strike.

But Mernyl was present, and Marrget's call had stirred him into action. His horse, taken off guard by his sudden resolve, reared for a moment, then turned and took him back toward the mounting shadow.

Marrget watched. "Is that sorcerer mad?"

"Haven't the faintest. But you all probably better spread out. If that thing strikes, I don't want it to nail everyone."

Marrget laughed suddenly. "Well said! Seven days in Gryylth, and a fighter at last!"

Alouzon hardly heard her last words, for she was already galloping toward Mernyl. The sorcerer had dismounted and was grounding his staff. He looked up as she approached. "Follow the army!"

"You can't fight them all, Mernyl."

"Leave sorcery to me, Dragonmaster." His voice was brusque, impatient. When she hesitated, he waved his arm. "Begone! Follow the rest. Leave this to me."

His hood fell back, and she started when she saw his face. Mernyl had been preparing for his work throughout the last day and a half, gathering his strength and raising his internal powers, and the effort had sapped him physically. She might have stared at a skull.

The intensity of his hollow eyes conveyed his demand, and, unable to argue, she left. Still, halfway to the rear guard, she stopped and looked back.

The sorcerer was standing a few yards beyond his horse, rigid, his staff upraised. There seemed to be a subtle alteration in the air about him, for his outlines shimmered as though he were wrapped in a mirage, and as she watched, the glow of his staff increased, turning slowly into a blaze of azure light.

Alouzon was transfixed. She was seeing it again: the workings of magic, the violation of everything she thought of as normal and rational. Gryylth was a world of fluidity, of the interplay of forces that made idiocy of what she knew as physical law. But perhaps that was to be expected, since Gryylth was itself a sizable anomaly in the common workings of the universe. Regardless, she watched the actions of the sorcerer as though she were a child at a circus, eyes wide with wonder, fervently wishing that the little man in the shabby robe would pull something even more splendid out of his magical hat.

And he did.

Calling out words and names in a language she did not know, he stretched as high as he could, and as his words blurred into a long, sustained scream, he reached up, seized the middle of the staff that was by now blazing with all the light of a sun and pulled it down until it was parallel with the ground.

To right and to left, a rolling wall as of ephemeral water toppled away, foaming in sparks of blue and silver. It raced into the distance, shimmering, a vast curtain of faint but potent turbulence that defied the mounting darkness as it blurred its outlines, a shield for Vorya's army.

The darkness lashed out, but it spattered off the wall in corposant sparks that smoked in the air as they dissolved. Alouzon heard a cheer from the army and a lighthearted cry from Relys: "Hail Mernyl, Sorcerer of Gryylth!"

But the army could not see Mernyl and so had no idea how much he had been weakened by his efforts. Leaning heavily on his staff, he seemed to call for his horse. But just as the animal trotted to his side, the sorcerer fell to the ground.

"*Jesus!*" Alouzon waved Vorya on and headed back to help. As she approached, a second strike from the darkness sent a noticeable concussion through the air. Jia started, but forged ahead.

She could have closed her eyes and known of the presence of the wall. Towering up, its ebb and flow of power visible as fluctuations in earth and sky, it hung like liquid glass, thick and turgid, its line of contact with the ground marked by a sheet of crimson as pure as the light of a ruby laser.

Mernyl lay a few yards from it and was attempting to get to his feet. When he saw Alouzon, his emaciated lips formed themselves into the semblance of a smile. "I am not as strong as I thought," he said, as he grasped vainly at his horse's bridle.

Keeping an eye on the shield he had created, still feeling the barrage that the Tree directed at it, she slid to the ground and helped him mount.

He struggled to hold himself up. "I must do better once we reach the Circle."

She swung onto Jia's back. "I don't like this."

" 'Twill only get worse, Alouzon."

With another glance at the wall, she led him away at a quick trot. "Why the hell doesn't he just let the armies take care of it? He doesn't have to destroy everything."

Mernyl was gasping for breath. "He is no longer quite sane, Alouzon. The Tree uses him."

A brilliant flash of light eclipsed the sun and sent shadows fleeing ahead of them. Alouzon started to turn.

"Do not look," snapped the sorcerer. "You will go blind."

Another flash. The horses shied, but the riders soothed them and continued on. "I should have made it opaque," said Mernyl. His tone was that of an artist disappointed with his work.

"How long will that thing hold?"

The ground shook slightly, and from behind came the sound of rending rock and stone. Mernyl's eyes went wide, and he kicked his horse into a faster pace. "Not long enough, I fear. And I must not squander my strength before we reach our destination."

They raced for the army as the earth vibrated beneath them. The white flashes were almost continuous now, a steady blaze of radiance that turned the landscape into afterimages burned into dazzled retinas.

Mernyl rode directly to Vorya. "How far to the Circle?"

"At least another day's ride. Perhaps a little more."

Thoughtlessly, the sorcerer looked behind. The wall was hidden by a rise in the land, but a sudden brilliant fulmination made him flinch and turn away, rubbing his eyes. "We must press on, then. I will do what I can. But, I pray you, my king: all possible speed."

They continued on throughout the day, traveling the long gray road that led toward the Circle. From behind came a continuous series of blasts and concussions that were accompanied by the blinding incandescence generated by the conflict of magical forces.

There was time for few rests, and food had to be eaten on the run. Mernyl fretted, his eyes intense, his lips tight, and though he stayed for the most part with the columns, he frequently turned back and sought high ground so as to judge the progress that

Corrin was making. In all, he seemed satisfied, but wary: the Tree seemed more hampered by the disruption of the roads and fields than by his magic.

That evening, as the army stopped to snatch a few hours of rest, he called up his spells again and threw another wall across the road. But detonations and starbursts of light made the night a poor one for sleeping, and the darkness was filled with the murmur of anxious human beings and the cries of frightened horses.

Marrget sat on the ground near a fire, hugging her knees to her breasts, and she faced the magical conflict as though wishing she could add her sword to it. "At least Tarwach's men rest no better than we this night."

"Who gives a damn about Tarwach's men?" Alouzon was almost surly. She was inextricably caught between two courses, neither satisfactory. Settlement would lead to the slaughter of her friends; battle raised the possibility that the whole world would be destroyed. And battle, it seemed, was inevitable.

"They will be tired tomorrow also. The odds will be more even." Her smile was mirthless. "Say, perhaps only five to one."

A distant ripping sound, and the earth shook.

"Gods!"

Though there were still some hours left before dawn, a dull, red glow was mounting in the east. Puffs of dark clouds mushroomed out of it, and explosions cracked across the miles.

Mernyl was already on his feet, his staff in hand. "I should have expected it: Tireas is using the Tree to open the road."

Sleep was gone for even the most fatigued now, and men and women staggered to their feet in the crimson light and turned pale faces eastward. The earth continued to quake, and the sudden shock wave that rolled away from the detonations sent one or two soldiers stumbling through the clutter of baggage and blankets as several horses broke loose and bolted away. "Dragonmaster, save us!" someone shouted, and there was fear in his voice.

She threw up her hands. "What the hell am I supposed to do? I'm a warrior, not a fucking magician." She realized what she had said. "Shit."

Mernyl set out for the king, pushing his way through clumps of gawking men. "Give me leave to ride ahead," he said to Vorya. "I have no fear that there are Corrinians ahead of us, and I must make preparations at the Circle."

Vorya scanned Mernyl's face, then looked about at his forces. "I cannot push these men and women any faster."

Mernyl was shouting above the rumbles and the confusion. "I am not asking you to drive them beyond their endurance, my liege. I want leave to ride ahead."

"What about you, Mernyl?" said Alouzon.

"What indeed?" He laughed, and she recalled his look in Vorya's pavilion. He was going to die, and he knew it. "I must go, my king. With or without your permission."

"With it, then," said Vorya. He pulled a ring from his finger and put it into Mernyl's hand. "Small honor this may give anyone in a few days, but I would you take it in token of my gratitude. I name you Councilor of Gryylth."

Mernyl slid the ring on, gave the king a bow, and sprinted for his horse, his gray robe flapping and his staff a glowing beacon. He seemed to have recovered his strength, but Alouzon recalled what his spells had done to him the day before. "I'm going with him," she said. "And . . ." She caught sight of a flash of amber hair and a questioning face. "And with your permission, I'll take Wykla, too."

Vorya nodded. "I would you stayed with us, Dragonmaster. But go. We will come with all speed."

Alouzon turned to find Marrget beside her. "I'm going ahead with Wykla."

"You have done her much good, friend. Take her. We will all meet at the Circle: the order of arrival matters not."

The lurid light from the east painted the scene with the colors of blood and fire. Alouzon gripped Marrget's hands, looking for a farewell. She recalled the captain's words: *Unless death intervene . . .* Would it? How soon? By what means?

A horse whinnied. "Dragonmaster," called Mernyl. "We must hurry."

"I'm coming." She hugged the captain. "Move your ass tomorrow, bitch," she whispered. "I'm too scared to do it all by myself."

The informality shocked Marrget, but she smiled after a moment, then roared, and her laughter followed after Alouzon as she and Wykla ran to catch up with Mernyl.

❖ CHAPTER 21 ❖

❖

THEY GAVE THEIR MOUNTS FREE REIN, GALLOP-
ing across a landscape seared by light and shaking
as though the very stones would shatter. The army,
held back by its foot soldiers, would take at least
another half day to reach the Circle. Alouzon, Mernyl,
and Wykla covered the distance in a few hours.

Just at dawn, they topped a rise that gave them a
clear view of their destination, and Alouzon, stunned,
pulled up short. She stared with disbelief at the Circle, for she might have been confronted with a ghost.

"Stonehenge!"

There it was: two outer concentric rings of stones,
one connected by lintels, the other free standing; two
inner horseshoes of individual trilithons and monoliths. But this was not the Stonehenge she had
known and studied, its trilithons fallen and weathered
with the rains and frosts of millennia, its bluestones
scattered like logs after a flood. This was new, fresh,
as though its stones had been set in place that morning and the workers had just now put away the scaf-
folding, leaving the monument gleaming in the sunlight of a new day.

Beautiful as the roots of a planet are beautiful,
awesome, ponderous, immovable, the whole con-

struction was wrapped about with a bright radiance
of power that brought tears to her eyes. Here, in this
world of abrupt change and brutal transformation,
was something she could cling to, something that
embodied preservation and constancy.

Slowly, she approached, the road taking her past
the Heel Stone and straight along the main axis. The
open ends of the interior horseshoes pointed directly
at her as she dismounted at the edge of the lawn, as
though they were open arms that would take her in
and welcome her.

And yet, for all its beauty and strength, this holy
place was but a faint echo of the Grail's ineffable
presence, a single part of a whole that subsumed
everything: Gryylth, Corrin, blood, death, resurrec-
tion . . . even the implacable transmutations of the
Tree. She handed Jia's reins to Wykla and watched
Mernyl pace to the center of the rings with his pack,
but their figures seemed transparent, ephemeral, for
she was seeing beyond the stones to the living manifestation that lay behind them. Beating with life,
overflowing with lush waters, the Grail cupped the
Circle invisibly, held it within itself, empowered it:
the dynamo of a world.

The energies and the Presence were palpable, and
she followed Mernyl into the stones with some trepi-
dation, like an orphan child brought into the palace
of a queen. She wanted to reach out and touch the
smooth surfaces of the great monoliths, to embrace
the refuge that had opened itself to her, but even if
she had forgotten what Cvinthil had said about the
stones—the visions and, yes, the madness that they
could impart—to touch seemed an act of profanation.

Stonehenge. It was impossible, but it was real.
Buried in the subconscious of Solomon Braithwaite

along with all the other knowledge, archetypes, longings, and fears, the incredible structure had appeared in Gryylth as the omphalos of the world.

Feeling as though she had entered a waking dream, she passed through the rings and entered the open area within. Mernyl was pacing off distances, his staff a bright glow, his initial scintillating out of the wood when he paused and meditated. The interior trilithons and bluestones rose up on three sides like the columns and vaults of a cathedral: peaceful, silent. Alouzon suddenly realized that the shaking and flashes of light had cut off the moment she had entered the Circle's precincts.

"Assist me, Dragonmaster," said the sorcerer. He tossed her one end of a long strip of blue cloth and told her to stand at the center of the monument. She acted as a pivot while he traced a circle on the ground. "I intend to begin by defending farther out," he said as he worked, scribing the line with the end of his staff, "but should I be driven back, I will have no time to prepare."

She only half-heard him. The sky was a blue vault over their heads, cloudless, serene, and the rings of standing stones pointed up to the heavens as though she stood in the depths of a chalice of living rock. "This . . . this has always been here?"

"Since the beginning." The sorcerer waved her silent and closed the circumference carefully, murmuring a soft chant. He straightened, and for a moment he gazed about himself appreciatively, his gaunt face softening. "You seem familiar with it."

"We've got one where I come from, too."

"Not a completely benighted world then, eh?" Mernyl's eyes twinkled as he took the end of the strip from her.

Again, she marveled at his strength. Gryylth, and everything in it, was but ten years old, and Mernyl knew himself to be the spontaneous creation of a despairing mind, but still he could smile and be glad of sunlight and stones. His expression was that of a man with a fatal task ahead of him, who nonetheless intended to do it well, and who would not let its proximity detract from the glory that surrounded him.

Wykla came into view from between the trilithons, stepping carefully as though her mere presence was sacrilege. "I took the horses to the far side of the Circle."

Her slight form appeared all the more fragile compared with the twenty-five-foot trilithons behind her, and the breeze caught her hair and ruffled it into tendrils and curls. By her looks, she might have been a girlfriend from the college years that Suzanne Helling had once known, a coed from long ago who had lived, loved, felt the first blush of dawn and sunset's lingering glow . . . and perhaps died in a rain of steel-jacketed bullets.

Mernyl's voice came to Alouzon as though from a distance. "Dragonmaster? Are you well?"

She realized that she was crying, tears running freely and unashamedly down her face. It had been a simple time then, when all questions had answers, when all problems could be solved, when there was hope that, regardless of their depth, all differences could be reconciled in the end. But those beliefs were no more sturdy than was Gryylth, and the bloodshed had ravaged them away with the impersonal precision of a razor.

She wept, not with the hysteria that had saved Wykla during the first night of her womanhood, nor with the catharsis that had restored Marrget to her humanity, but rather with a sustained, bitter grief that welled up for all the love and the beauty and the innocence that had ever been ignored, trampled, or lost in the eternal transience of people and worlds.

Eyes shut, jaw clenched, she allowed herself only a minute to plumb the aching void within her, and then she turned away from it. "I'm all right," she said at last, her voice catching. "We don't have time for me to go to pieces. You still need help, Mernyl."

He nodded, but before he bent to his pack again, he paused before her. "I saw," he said gently. "I grieve with you."

"What about Gryylth, Mernyl?" she choked. "Kent State is in the past. Gryylth is here and now. What happens to it when all this shit hits the fan?"

"I believe . . ." He watched Wykla as she crossed the open center of the monument, seemingly at one with her body, her girlish grace and her warrior's poise now combined into an emblem of newfound strength. "I believe that the gods, whatever their names, are merciful and loving. I believe that they care about the people of Gryylth and Corrin." He fixed her with a glance. "Just as you care, Alouzon Dragonmaster."

"I'm not a god."

He was silent.

"That's all you've got then? Faith?"

"Faith is a paltry thing. I have knowledge."

"Yeah . . . sure . . ."

She started to turn away, but he caught her arm. "And do you then disbelieve in the Grail?"

To disbelieve was impossible. She had seen. "That's ridiculous."

"You do not, then, simply believe. You *know.*"

"Yeah, I know."

He nodded in his strange way. "And that is Gryylth's hope."

Questions again: questions she did not know how to ask. Mernyl bent to his pack, took out a second roll of cloth, and handed it to Wykla. His face was set, his expression hidden. Alouzon had the distinct and unnerving feeling that he had just indicated that his belief and his hope rested on her.

With their help, Mernyl constructed a series of interlaced circles and triangles that surrounded and contained the large tracing he had already made. Morning lengthened into afternoon as he worked, and gradually, the lines began to assume a life of their own, shining brightly in the clear, laser light that Alouzon had seen before.

But as he was closing the final figure, the earth shook slightly, and, alarmed, he looked up to the northeast. The inner horseshoes opened out in that direction, and, beyond the outer peristyle, far beyond the Heel Stone, the darkness was gusting toward the Circle as if driven by a hurricane. "My defense is no more," he said. "The second wall has been breached."

"I hope everyone got away."

"Fear not: look."

The army of Gryylth was topping the slight rise from which Alouzon had first seen the Circle, its weapons and armor glinting in the afternoon sun. To either side of the footmen were the mounted forces: the King's Guard, Santhe's men, and, their hair streaming behind them, the women of the First Wartroop.

Mernyl came up behind her. "Ride, Alouzon," he said. "Tell them to form within the embankment but to keep the Avenue clear."

Wykla was already bringing Jia. Alouzon mounted, and the girl tried to smile. "Ride, my liege. For Gryylth."

"For Gryylth, Wykla," she returned. "When your wartroop arrives, rejoin it. Fight well."

"I fight for you, my lady." She clasped Alouzon's hand for a moment before the Dragonmaster turned her horse out along the Avenue and galloped away.

Although the disruption of the road and the surrounding fields had given the Gryylthans time to prepare for the expected onslaught, there was not much for them to do save take up positions and wait, snatching food and rest as they could. The sanctity of the Circle precincts was such that, even had there been time for defensive earthworks, no one was willing to mar the ground to make them.

But the Circle itself provided some fortifications, for surrounding the outermost peristyle of stones at a distance of about a hundred feet was a four-foot bank of earth encircled by a ditch—a formidable obstacle for the Corrinian phalanxes. Vorya stationed his warriors and soldiers behind it, but the situation still did not look good: Gryylth had a thousand feet of perimeter to defend with a little over a hundred people.

And, sweeping in from the northeast like a wave, clutching at the stainless blue with hands of jet, the darkness devoured the sky degree by degree, a constant and urgent reminder that the Gryylthans faced more than simple material weapons. From within it came the rumble of thunder, and the shadow it cast turned the day into night.

Vorya watched its progress from the rim of the bank as he massaged his useless arm. "The one battle to which I would come a whole man, and I am maimed."

Beside him, Alouzon glanced at Marrget and the First Wartroop. The women had taken up positions on the other side of the Avenue, keeping the axis of the Circle clear in accordance with Mernyl's wishes. "Others, I think, feel the same way."

At first the king did not comprehend, but he followed her eyes. Relys saluted them with an uplifted sword, her dark eyes flashing in what was left of the sunlight.

Out along the Avenue, nearly a hundred feet beyond the ditch and the bank, Mernyl stood beside the Heel Stone. If he had turned around, he would have been able to look directly into the center of the Circle, where the interior horseshoes of bluestones and trilithons opened out at him. But he did not move, nor did he appear to mind his isolation. Holding his staff level with the horizon, he stood like a monolith himself, small and puny beside the thirty-five-ton stone, barring the way as though his authority alone would suffice to keep the enemy from approaching.

A blot of darkness separated from the main mass, and, shrouded in a halo of lightning, threw itself forward. It grew rapidly, funneling itself into a glowing, black bolt, eating away at the distance to the Circle.

Vorya stiffened. He had encountered this before. His hand went to his left arm.

Behind, there was a sudden flash and a continuing glow. The Circle had turned radiant with blue fire. Light shone out through the interstices of the peristyle as though a lantern had been lit within, and Mernyl swung his staff up, holding it above his head as though in summons or in challenge.

The distance narrowed, and the bolt made directly for him. Like a striking snake, it lashed out, driving into the upraised staff with a sharp crack. But, its powers awakened, its energies invoked, the Circle flared into life, and a stream of light blasted out along the axis toward the Heel Stone. The blue and the black met at Mernyl's staff, there was a flare . . .

. . . and Mernyl stood alone again, his staff held even with the horizon. There was no trace of the bolt.

A thin chorus of cheers went up from the embankment, and Alouzon heard Marrget's shout above it all. The captain was laughing, and she saluted Mernyl with a flourish, but the sorcerer did not notice, for another bolt had appeared, this one larger than the first. It also hurled itself at Mernyl, but, as before, he neutralized it with the energy of the Circle.

Most of the sky was by now covered with darkness. Only to the extreme southwest was there an arc of blue sky to say that it was not night, but, as though to make up for that deficiency, the bolts came faster now, shouldering their way forward as though to bludgeon the frail man at the side of the Heel Stone.

Mernyl fielded them all, holding his staff over his head like a lightning rod, the energy stream from the Circle flowing into him like a river of light.

"Arms, men of Gryylth!" Vorya shouted suddenly.

Alouzon winced at his choice of words, but she did not have time to be annoyed, for the first Corrinian soldiers had appeared. Staying far away from the battle of magics, a phalanx of about twenty-five advanced in formation and ran up the bank. The men lost momentum from the climb, but they gained the top quickly.

The faces Alouzon saw were mostly young, reminiscent of the students she had known during the years of protest. Their hair was long, their eyes intense. They had been battling for days, and they were tired and worn, but they nonetheless found themselves faced with yet more fighting.

Just like the students. Just like the warriors of Gryylth.

She felt the futility mounting around her. The Corrinians had always been in Gryylth; there were no Eastlands to which they could return. The entire world had, in fact, been created with just this insoluble conflict in mind: a vehicle for the fantasy heroics of a frightened, bewildered old man. But convincing the Corrinians and the Gryylthans that their problems were all in Solomon Braithwaite's head was another matter.

Only a brief glimpse as people then, and after that she did not have time for such luxuries. Her hand was on the Dragonsword before she knew she had put it there. As the power took her, she stepped between the phalanx and Vorya, and the blade leapt from its scabbard.

"*Gryylth!*"

The cry was out of her before she knew it, and her sword was flashing. The first two Corrinians fell within moments as Alouzon ducked under their spear points and let the Dragonsword find its own way. In and out, the power glowing in her belly, Alouzon covered the defenseless left side of the king.

Vorya was holding his own, though. His good arm rose and fell mightily, and though he did not possess the graceful finesse of the Dragonmaster, those who thought that his infirmity made him an easy mark found their mistake a fatal one.

The battle lasted for a minute, and then the Corrinians retreated. On Alouzon's side of the Avenue, there had been no casualties among the Gryylthans.

"They came to test our strength," said Vorya. "Well, they know it now. Let them come."

She looked at her dripping blade and nearly became sick. *Seven days in Gryylth and not a fighter yet, thank the gods.*

Out at the Heel Stone, Mernyl was unharmed. The bolts had ceased for the time, probably because of the proximity of the phalanxes, but the sorcerer had erected a dome of force about himself that glowed like opalescent glass. The Corrinians could not touch him, and the Circle itself still pulsed with light, feeding Mernyl along the Avenue.

On the far side of the energy stream, Alouzon made out the figures of Marrget and the First Wartroop. Several were pitching a dead Corrinian down the bank and into the ditch while Santhe and his men looked on. Scarred itself by the powers of the Tree, the Second Wartroop had been the most accepting of its comrades, and the men and women were exchanging backslaps and handshakes.

She turned back to Vorya. "Your people may make it after all."

The king did not seem to hear. He was looking off beyond Mernyl's position. There, several hundred yards past the Heel Stone, the Corrinian phalanxes were massing. The ridge was thick with men. Grimly, Vorya bettered his grip on his sword.

Alouzon's nausea returned. It was going to go on and on until everyone was dead. The people would slaughter one another, and the Tree and the Circle would fight until the world, already fragile, was powdered back into dust.

She grabbed Vorya's shoulder and pointed at the ridge. "Can't you see what's going to happen?"

He shook himself free. "I see the Dremord army."

"Man, we're going to get creamed no matter what. A settlement might let *something* live."

"Do they look like men with whom we can settle?"

A terrible sense of purpose radiated from the phalanxes as they advanced slowly and methodically down the ridge. In their midst was Tarwach, the king, and his brother Darham, golden-haired giants that seemed to personify the steady, vengeful movement. Behind, the darkness gyred up and spread across the sky.

Alouzon bent her head, passed a hand across her face. Vorya laid a gentle hand on her shoulder. "Dragonmaster," he said, "I understand what you are saying." His voice was old and soft, the quiet communication between the aged and the young. "It would be a good thing if this battle did not take place, but I know well that there is no way to stop it. If we must die, we will die; and from our valiant deaths might come some compunction on Tarwach's part if, victorious, he considers the enslavement of our people. In refusing to fight, not only would we lose the chance, slight though it may be, of maintaining, but our surrender would demonstrate our weakness, and Tarwach would see no reason not to oppress us."

Unlike Dythragor's incessant preoccupation with glory and saving face, Vorya's words, though grounded in his culture's beliefs, were based on an underlying practicality. He fought because he could see no other solution. If a better way presented itself, he would consider it.

But there was none, and the phalanxes continued to advance while Mernyl stood ready at the Heel

Stone. Across the Avenue, Marrget, Santhe, and Cvinthil stood side by side with the men and women of the wartroops, weapons ready, matching the Corrinian sense of purpose with one of their own.

Alouzon moved to cover the king's left side again, though she knew that a concerted rush from so many would quickly overwhelm their position. About them, the King's Guard stood firm.

The Corrinians had almost reached Mernyl's position when he acted. With an abrupt motion, he drove the butt of the staff into the soft ground and lifted his arms. The Heel Stone flamed as though drenched in gasoline, and the power from the Circle flared along the Avenue.

Sweeping his arms out, Mernyl spread the energies around the perimeter, encircling the monument with a wall of white light that caused the darkness to leap away as though in fear. The radiance of the Circle intensified, then, and it rose in a column that pierced the roiling darkness and pushed it away to the northeast. The sun streamed down on the defenders of Gryylth.

Another cheer went up, but it was a ragged one. Most of the men and women eyed the wall of light warily, obviously wondering what was going to happen when the Corrinians reached it. Even as they watched, the energies were growing more transparent, allowing them to see the phalanxes that approached the flickering turbulence.

Mernyl's body was taught, intent. Alouzon could not believe that this was mere grandstanding.

The Corrinians reached the wall, felt it out, and, with a shouted command from Tarwach, hurled themselves against it. Red flares burst in soundless explosions at the points of contact, but the soldiers did not seem to be hurt. They were, however, held back, and when only ten or fifteen men staggered through the barrier instead of the expected hundreds, the defenders realized that Mernyl's wall was acting as as filter, allowing only a fragmentary assault.

"Considering the work of the Tree," said Vorya, "I had hoped for better from Mernyl."

"He's doing pretty good. I don't think the Circle works real well for killing, and . . ." She pointed off to the northeast, where the darkness had gathered its strength. It too was advancing. "He's got his hands full."

The king did not answer. The Corrinian forces were gathering their strength on the near side of Mernyl's barrier, collecting what men could wade through. The soldiers were tired, but they had not forgotten their purpose, and when about a hundred had assembled, they charged directly at Vorya's position.

Alouzon glanced across the Avenue, hoping for some reinforcements, but Mernyl's defense, relying on the Avenue being clear from peristyle to Heel Stone, effectively split the forces of Gryylth. A fluid defense was impossible. In order for the other captains to help, they would have to herd their warriors and soldiers all the way around the monument: nearly seven hundred and fifty feet. There was no time.

And now flashes were appearing on the other side of the Avenue. Mernyl could not do everything.

Her sword dropped a pikeman who was charging Vorya's left side. She tried not to think about what she was doing: in Bandon, her cause had been essentially just, the sides clear-cut; but here, she was merely living out Solomon Braithwaite's delusions. She hated herself for it.

Out of the corner of her eye, she saw Vorya cleaving skulls as though he were reaping crimson poppies, and she slashed at a figure that rose up in front of her, letting the power guide her. Her hand turned warm and wet and she refused to look at it.

More Corrinians were slipping through the barrier. In the daylight that had returned to the area, the red flashes of their entrance faded to a dull carnelian, and the wall turned increasingly transparent. Masses of men were pressed against it, like flies against glass. Through steady, forward pressure, they were forcing their way through.

Alouzon was almost an outside observer now, holed up in some niche of her brain, watching her body perform its lethal antics: parry, slash, stab, deflect, parry, *drive* . . . The dead rolled down the bank and into the ditch, and their living companions slipped in blood and viscera as they climbed.

She turned to find herself confronted with the Corrinian king. Tarwach towered over her by at least a foot, and he was closing on Vorya. "Not on your life, big guy," she said, and she threw herself at him. Her steel bracelet caught him on the chin and opened a vicious cut.

He turned on her, glaring. "Woman, I challenge you."

"Go to hell." He was swinging, but she stepped back suddenly and let the sword go by. Deprived of an impact, Tarwach fought with the inertia of the heavy weapon, and Alouzon had time to plant her booted foot firmly in his chest. Unceremoniously, the Corrinian king toppled off the bank and fell into the mire of his men in the ditch.

"You might think about settling, my lord," she called after him. He shook his fist at her. "I'm serious. Please . . ."

Others had taken his place, were climbing the steep

slope, were already on the bank. Facing them, she nearly fell over a body, and recognized it as that of Pas of the King's Guard.

And where was Vorya?

With the Corrinians clustering about her, she swung wildly with fists and sword, looking frantically for the king. The Dragonsword had free rein now, and with her attention diverted, it pursued its own ends, spinning her around to kill two who advanced on her, then a third and a fourth.

Don't think about it, girl. You think about it, you're going to get sick.

Her sword was slick with blood from tip to hilt by the time she found Vorya. The old king was being attacked by three. His numb arm had already been hacked deeply in several places, but he fought on, using the unfeeling flesh as a shield when he could not evade a blow.

She kicked one away while she struck at another. Vorya, free to concentrate his abilities, settled the third. The first fell back into the blades of the King's Guard and was cut to pieces.

"Your arm!" Alouzon was appalled. Bone was showing through the blood, and the flesh hung in rags.

He shook his head. "I do not feel it. I lost this arm two days ago. This is . . . a formality."

More Corrinians. "We can't keep this up."

"What do you propose?" Surrounded by battle and the dead, he actually seemed amused. His eyes held no bloodlust, only a sad fatigue, as though he were in the middle of a tedious job that he wished he could finish.

But a horn sounded from outside Mernyl's wall, and the signal was taken up by another. Tarwach was gesturing his soldiers back, and Mernyl was letting them go.

Vorya looked astonished. "What is this?"

Alouzon saw Tarwach's purpose: a hundred yards past Mernyl's position, a white-robed man stood beside a wagon. Within was a squat, glowing tree, its fruit glassy and luminous, and from its twisted branches a funnel of blackness arose, touching the sky with dark power.

The men of the phalanxes were running back, clearing the way. Mernyl stood within his hemisphere of force, staff up and ready, but now he was face to face with a strength that equaled that of the Circle.

While they watched, Tireas raised his hands and began a conjuration.

❖

CHAPTER 22

*WE SHOULD NOT BE FIGHTING ONE ANOTHER.
We should be friends.*

Darham's forearm throbbed with the cut he had
received, but lifting his eyes to the warriors who still
stood defiantly at the top of the embankment that
surrounded the Circle, he could not but admire them.
Though they were outnumbered severely, though
they had been pursued across country by a vengeful
enemy, though they faced powers that made the battles of the past seem trivial, the Gryylthans were
fighting magnificently.

He found that he was shaking. Was he getting that
old, then? Unable to take a cut in battle without
growing a little weak in the knees? He let his shoulders hunch forward experimentally as he sat on the
stool, prompting a polite but firm request from the
physician who was bandaging his arm. Straightening,
he laughed tiredly.

From his vantage, he had a clear view of the battle
to the south of the Avenue. He watched the phalanxes
shove their way through Mernyl's magical barrier and
throw themselves up the embankment. By simple
numbers, they should have had an easy time of it.

But at the top they met the swords of the First War-troop, and, repeatedly, they were toppled back into the ditch with heavy casualties.

He shook his head in wonderment. Unbelievable. Though Tireas had struck the First Wartroop with a spell that had altered the men beyond their deepest nightmares, they fought on, bravely, their skill matching—no, he had to admit it, *surpassing*—Corrin's best. Marrget herself seemed to be everywhere, a blonde fury, her gray eyes flashing as coldly as the blade of her sword. Beside her, Relys was a whirl of black hair and steel. And . . .

The physician cut another length of bandage, began adding further layers to an already sizable dressing.

And then there was that amber-haired girl, decep-tively pretty, who had slid under his guard with all the grace of a dancer and opened his forearm from wrist to elbow. He would, if he kept his arm, carry that scar to his grave, a reminder of the skill of wom-en warriors. As though Manda would ever let him forget.

His enemies were valiant. He recalled that it was Dythragor who had fired the crops, not these. And Dythragor was well known for his impetuosity and willfulness. Perhaps he had acted on his own. Perhaps there was a way out of all of this killing.

"Well, Dervyhl," he said to the physician. "Must I now learn to eat with my left hand?"

Dervyhl was a thin, desiccated man, and he eyed Darham like a mother an ill-behaved child, his mouth screwed into a frown. "If you insist on having it carved like a New Year roast, lord, perhaps you should. But, no, not this time. You will heal."

"The bandage seems overlarge."

"The blood is soaking through, lord. If I might be so bold, I would suggest that you not fight any more."

"What?"

"I would say for this battle, at least. But, knowing you, I will say for the day. And I would hope you would listen."

A big man was passing by, tottering, holding his side. Darham recognized Karthin of the Eighteenth Phalanx. The vicissitudes of battle had shifted men from one formation to another, and Darham had found himself often fighting beside the big farmer.

Farmer? Regardless of his skill with a scythe, the man knew how to use a sword. "Ho! Karthin!"

His face was ashen, and for a moment, Darham was afraid that he had been mortally wounded. But Karthin noticed his expression, shook his head. "I will live, lord Darham. 'Twas that blonde demon did this to me." He cracked a smile, almost chuckled. "I believe she has broken my ribs."

"Dervyhl," said Darham. "Attend to this man as to me."

With a sigh, the physician gestured Karthin to another stool and began examining him, prodding at his battered side.

"Marrget?"

"Marrget. Ouch!" Karthin jumped. Dervyhl mumbled an abstracted apology and went right back to his prodding. "She is amazing."

"I was reflecting that it would be far better if we were friends with these people."

"It would indeed."

Something was approaching along the Avenue. Darham did not have to look to know that it was the Tree. The cursed thing radiated unhealth like a fire radiated heat, and he could have had his head in a sack and still told of its passage.

When Tireas had first brought the Tree out of the Heath, he had been able to govern it, and though it had been a terrifying entity, Darham had been able to find nothing in its presence or use to which he could object. But since the transformation of the First Wartroop and the wholesale slaughter of the forces of Gryylth, it had acquired an aura of pain and disease that filled him with revulsion. Tireas, he was sure, was no longer quite sane. That Tarwach still condoned the use of such a deadly thing indicated only that the war had degenerated to depths that Darham was afraid to contemplate.

I would rather have all of Vorya's land in ruins than allow one child of Corrin to cry for a mouthful of bread, Tarwach had said. Judging from the slaughter and the whirlwind of darkness that rose up from the Tree, Tarwach might get his ruins. And Darham feared greatly that, in the end, there would be neither bread nor children to cry for it.

The Tree passed, swaying bulbously in its cart. Karthin watched. "The damned thing," he said. "Have the people of Gryylth and Corrin not suffered enough? It is time to end all of this."

"The wheat, Karthin . . ." Darham shrugged helplessly. Maybe he was indeed getting old. There did not seem to be much that he could do.

"We could share, Gryylth and Corrin both. I am a farmer: I know my kine and my crops. It would be a hard winter, but we could all live."

Horn calls went up, and both men could see Tarwach gesturing the phalanxes back. Tireas had taken up a position a short distance from the Heel Stone and was squaring off against Mernyl.

"This is madness, lord. Utter madness." Karthin stood up, lifted a hand to Marrget. "I would be your friend, Gryylthan!" he called, though the distance was too great for her to hear him.

Dervyhl pushed him gently back into his seat. "Captain, your side will not stand it."

"I am not a captain. I—"

Darham interrupted. "You are now, man of Rutupia. From this moment, I name you a captain of Corrin. We will fight together, no?"

Dervyhl scowled. "Fighting? I said—"

Karthin waved aside the physician's protest. "Perhaps the time has come to fight with words rather than swords," he said. He leaned over to Darham and took his hand. "You do me great honor, my lord."

"None that is not deserved, captain."

The phalanxes were still retreating, and Tireas waited beside the Tree. A shaft of sunlight fell on the women of the wartroop. The amber-haired girl was there, and, beside her, Marrget stood straight and slender. She regarded the sorcerer defiantly, as though daring him to smite her again.

"Tell me." Darham pointed at her with his bandaged arm. "What would you do if you were her friend?"

Karthin was submitting to Dervyhl's ministrations. He looked up, watched Marrget. "I would . . ." He mused for a time. "I am a rude farmer. I do not know the niceties of heroes. Perhaps I would bring her flowers."

"Flowers?"

"In hopes of a better time," he said. "Besides . . ." Marrget's sword flashed as she brandished it at the Tree. "She looks as though she could use some."

❖   ❖   ❖

Hovering by necessity between the mundane world and the magical, half in and half out of his body, Mernyl saw the Tree not as a ligneous growth in a wain, nor as the genesis of Tireas's conjuration. He was confronted instead with a staring eye of transformation, a maelstrom of ravening change. Wheels within wheels, starbursts of rank growth, a gaping mouth of bloody wounds, it rose up before him, wrapping carrion wings about the world, an embodiment of elemental force.

Even the great stone beside him was dwarfed by the titanic energies that were poised like a wave about to break. Mernyl felt isolated, alone, and the Circle, though linked with him along the Avenue, seemed altogether too distant, too remote to be of any help.

But that, he knew, was an illusion. The Circle was itself an elemental manifestation, and it stood behind him as a champion might bolster an embattled retainer. Mentally, he reached back to it, was received with an embrace that thrust into perspective the snarling images of the Tree, and was folded into arms that could have encircled the Universe.

Mernyl tightened his grip on his staff, and watched as the Corrinian sorcerer placed his hands on one half of the cosmos. The world rippled as though it were a layer of moss upon an unquiet lake, and though he knew full well that such a course would, in the end, prove futile, Mernyl fought to stabilize it with the Circle.

At one time, Tireas might have known of the insubstantiality of Gryylth, but his present actions indicated that he had forgotten. The Tree was perfectly capable of generating energies that would destroy everything, even if the Circle negated them. The negation itself would be the end.

There was one hope: Suzanne Helling. Stripped of the heroic guise that had been thrust upon her, it was the quiet, sorrowing student who held the world in her hands. Dythragor had thrown his Guardianship to the winds and left the great magics to battle to utter destruction. But if Suzanne took the Guardianship onto herself, a different set of archetypes could come into existence; and as she was conscious of their origin, she had some hope of reconciling them. Suzanne could be healed. Gryylth could be healed.

It was an urgent need, but one that lay still in the future. Beyond her hazy knowledge of the Grail, Suzanne was not even yet conscious of what she had to do, and he had been unwilling to confront her with the truth. All he could do was give her as much of a future as possible to find within herself the affections and the loyalty that had been so deeply buried on a May morning in Kent. She had made progress already. He could hope.

To all the gods that are. To whatever gods might hear.

Mernyl did not know what gods there might be, but he knew compassion. Perhaps that was enough.

"May you find your Grail, Suzanne," he whispered. "For your sake, and that of my world."

Lifting his staff, he locked himself and the Circle into combat.

As Tireas continued his conjuration, his white head bent close to the glowing trunk of the Tree, Alouzon felt fear enveloping the Gryylthan forces like a killing frost. Even Vorya had stiffened, and the old king stared at the Tree as though expecting at any moment to feel its magic burrow into his flesh and blood.

Alouzon grabbed him roughly and shook him. "Vorya!"

He seemed to fight his way out of a trance and shook his head as though to clear it. But his face was still tight. "Whatever fate comes in battle is an honorable one," he murmured.

Motion to the right of the Avenue: the First Wartroop was in action. Marrget called several women to her side, instructed them with quick words and gestures, and sent them running to the rear. Wykla was among those sent, and her hair streamed out behind like an amber oriflamme. In a moment, she and the others had disappeared around the far side of the Circle.

There was a soundless flash of lurid light, and the defenders dropped behind the embankment as a crimson tide swept out from the Tree like a surging breaker. Mernyl's hemisphere was under attack, its colors shifting as the Tree fastened upon them and forced them toward blue and violet, invisibility and destruction.

The Corrinians had either pushed their way back to their fellows or had thrown themselves face down on the ground like cast-off pieces of statuary. Between the Tree and the Circle seemed to be a no-man's-land of trampled grass, still forms, and seething crimson light. On the rise, the massed phalanxes were watching. It was an oddly silent scene—only a single, choking cry went up from one of the King's Guard.

"*No . . . no . . . no . . .*"

Alouzon turned on him, nearly cuffed him. "Shut up, you idiot, or I'll do the fucking job myself."

That silenced him. She heard the sound of cantering horses and saw that Wykla and the other women were returning to the front with the war-troop's mounts. They were spirited animals, and they did not shy at being led toward the conflict. They seemed almost eager.

Mernyl counterattacked, sending a sheet of fire up between himself and the Tree. The shaft of radiance connecting him with the Circle flared as the color shift was put to flight. The hemisphere shone pure once more.

The red flood swelled and the fire grew to combat it, but, as the battle went on, Alouzon realized that Tireas's flood and Mernyl's fire were only a side effect of something much bigger. Transparent yet palpable, insubstantial yet ponderous, the conflict grew—massless, ephemeral, immeasurably potent—neither side giving or yielding, the sorcerers' wills stretched as taught as a spring at the breaking point.

With a crack that echoed off the standing mono-liths of the Circle, the Heel Stone suddenly split from top to bottom and fell back as though shoved by a giant hand. Hot, searing wind blasted across the open space between the two armies, and Mernyl's defenses crumbled as Tireas's flood rose into the sky and turned once again to darkness.

As Alouzon watched, aghast, Mernyl lost his foot-ing and fell, tumbling over and over. Tireas kept his hands on the Tree, summoning whatever might he needed to destroy his rival.

Marrget's voice rang out: "Mount! And *forward!*"

Mernyl's wall had been broken along with his per-sonal defenses, and the phalanxes were rising, form-ing, surging toward the Circle. But Marrget and the wartroop were horsed, and even now they were charging over the embankment, across the ditch, making straight for the fallen sorcerer. The captain was leading, her sword high. Relys was close behind. So was Wykla.

Vorya stood up. "To battle!"

But the Corrinians were coming in force, Gryylth's defenses were gone, and Mernyl might be dead. Nothing was left but for the phalanxes to roll over the Circle and take it for their own. Above all was the whirlwind of darkness, an obscene stain against the blue sky, growing ever larger and gusting toward the horizon like a storm.

But there was another motion in the sky, too. Off to the north, a black speck had appeared in the blue, and Alouzon thought that she recognized it. Torn between it and the sight of the advancing phalanxes, she at last forced herself to watch until she saw that it was driving toward the Circle with great speed. It seemed to flutter, as with the beating of wings.

"*Silbakor!*"

I come.

Marrget and the wartroop had already engaged the advance line of Corrinians, which was trying to encircle the sorcerer. Mernyl was not dead, it appeared. In fact, he was trying to crawl towards the Circle, his clothing tattered and his face creased with pain.

A pikeman broke through Marrget's defense, but Mernyl had seemingly lost patience: the man was driven back by a blast of green fire. Another group attempted to interpose themselves between him and the wartroop, but when the sorcerer slashed at two with his staff, sparks coruscated the length of the white wood and the men crumbled into black ash.

The rest hesitated and drew back instinctively. Marrget sent her horse leaping to the side of the sorcerer, reached down, and dragged him up behind her.

Silbakor was by now a distinct presence in the sky,

but the Corrinians had not noticed it: their attention was on Mernyl and Marrget. The captain was slowly working her way back to the Circle with her passenger, and though the attacking phalanx sought to prevent their return, the women surrounded their captain and kept her and the sorcerer from the pikes and swords.

But they were running into difficulties. With an unhealthy sheen that itself was enough to make the wartroop's horses shy, the ground began to shift beneath their hooves, and they threatened to bolt. The firm hands of the women kept their mounts steady, but forward progress became impossible, and more Corrinians were surrounding them.

A phalanx had reached the embankment, and several ran at Alouzon. She dropped them with her eyes still on the wartroop and the Tree. Tireas could not attack directly without killing his own men, but he knew how to be subtle: slowly and methodically, he was penning the women, keeping them from escape. The soldiers could handle the rest.

But, deep in his trance, the Corrinian sorcerer could not but be startled when Silbakor blazed down out of the sky. Leveling out fifteen feet from the ground, the Dragon streaked over the Tree like a precision bomber, its turbulence raising dust, throwing Tireas to the ground, and nearly toppling the wagon.

As quick as the shadow of a bird, the Dragon was gone. It roared over the Circle and swept out to the south, its wing beats strong and sure as it gained altitude. Its passage had been sudden and unexpected, and the Corrinian host was thrown into disarray, the phalanxes fragmenting as the disruption of Tireas's working sent a noticeable shudder through the fabric of the world.

Marrget, though, was acting, using the lull in the fighting to force her way back to the Circle, leaving behind a wake of confused and bleeding soldiers. The phalanxes were too shattered to follow: Silbakor's strafing run had hit the key point in the offensive.

The speed of the Dragon was such that some time passed before it could swing around to begin another attack, and it was not yet done when Marrget brought Mernyl to the king. The sorcerer was shaken, and his forehead was bruised and cut. Blood turned the dust on his face into black mud.

"I was a fool, my liege," he said. "An utter fool. To attempt to fight the Tree at such a distance from the Circle . . . It is fortunate that we were not all killed."

Marrget looked at him over her shoulder. "You will fight from the Circle then?"

"It is the only way." His bruises were swelling, and his hands shook so that he could barely hold on to his staff.

Above, Silbakor had aligned itself and was beginning another run. The Corrinians had retreated in the face of the added threat, and even Tarwach was hesitating. While his men stood about in clumps, their eyes on the Dragon, the Corrinian king conferred with his brother and another big man, arguing loudly when they seemed to disagree with what he said.

Tireas appeared to be judging how best to deal with his new adversary. Putting his hands on the Tree again, he sent a lance of light darting up toward the Dragon. It had no effect. As Silbakor began to descend, Tireas considered, then edged the black gyre around to point directly at it.

In another minute, Tarwach was shouting orders, and the phalanxes were reforming. This time, without the distractions of sorcerers in conflict, the battle would be straightforward, sword to sword and spear to spear.

"They seek our deaths," said Vorya. "I cannot say but that, were I in their position, I would do no different. A pity we must fight. I have always thought of the Dremords as cowards and barbarians, but I see now that they are no worse than those who have sought to . . . exterminate them."

"Stupid war." Alouzon's words were replete with contempt.

"Aye, Dragonmaster. And stupid men fight it. But there is no escaping it."

The phalanxes were advancing swiftly. "My lady," came a soft voice, "Wykla of Burnwood asks leave to fight beside you." The young woman's sword was bloody, and the knuckles of her left fist were bruised and bleeding.

"You OK?"

"I fight for you, my lady."

Mernyl touched Marrget's shoulder. "Get me to the Circle, captain." His weakness was such that he nearly fell when she tugged at the reins, and he had one moment in which to nod to Alouzon. "Farewell, Dragonmaster. Remember me."

His tone struck her cold. He was going to die. He knew it. She knew it. She took a step after him, stopped, sickness rising in her belly.

Relys was shouting. "First Wartroop to the Avenue. Wykla, Marrget gave you leave to stay with the Dragonmaster. Alouzon . . ."

She looked up at her name. Relys smiled as best she could out of her hard face and lifted her sword.

"Hail, Dragonmaster," she said. She was away then, leading the Troop.

Something large and heavy nudged her, and she found that Jia was nuzzling at her arm. She took his bridle from the man who had brought him, stroked his head for a moment, then swung into the saddle. "Wykla," she said. "I'm afraid we're going to buy it."

Wykla said nothing and remounted her own horse. Her eyes told Alouzon that, having fought herself for two days, battle against five-to-one odds was nothing.

High to the northeast, Silbakor folded its wings and blasted directly into the heart of the black gyre. There was a brittle, crackling sound, as of meat burning, but the Dragon forged on, battling up the stream of unlight. Its passionless eyes glowed through the murk, and Tireas looked up and froze as he realized that it was not going to stop.

Relys's party joined with the rest of the wartroop and with Marrget at the intersection of the bank and the Avenue. With the phalanxes less than fifty yards away, Marrget led the women forward in a charge, attempting to split the attack.

Silbakor, wings spread just enough to give control, once more streaked over the Tree like a black bullet. The gyre snuffed out, the wagon toppled, and the Tree went down.

As the sky suddenly brightened, someone in the phalanxes looked back, and his open-mouthed fear communicated itself to his companions. The attack wavered. The second's pause gave Marrget and her women the purchase they needed, and the wartroop plowed into the phalanxes, scattering men and weapons with their impact. On the other side of the Avenue, Santhe led a charge with the Second Wartroop, and the Corrinian advance ground to a halt.

A low, throbbing hum arose from the Circle, as though a large generator had been switched on. Alouzon looked back to see a blue iridescence creep up the stones. The monument shimmered slightly as though half-slipping into another dimension, then solidified.

"We strike now," said Vorya suddenly. "Disorganized, they will retreat. Are you with us, Dragonmaster?"

It was Bandon all over again. Dragged away from her normal life, she had been thrown into a uniform, issued a lethal weapon, and placed in a hostile environment. Like the Guardsmen who had shot down her classmates, she was surprised at what she would do under such circumstances.

The Dragonsword was bright where it was not dripping. "I'm with you," she said. "Let's go."

With Wykla and a few others, they spurred down the bank and through the ditch. Sword up, power surging through her like a dipper of molten steel, Alouzon closed on the flank of the Corrinian army. The faces of the men ahead blurred into a single hostile entity, and she crashed through the lines.

Corrinians all around her. Swords and spears flashing.

So goddam many.

The Dragonsword moved her body like an intricate marionette, attacking, retreating, guiding Jia with knee pressure as though she had been born in the saddle. Dust went up, raised by scuffling feet and falling bodies, and her hand turned slimy with blood and brains.

Nearby, Wykla was fighting with deadly grace. Too small of stature now to meet force with force, she side-slipped rather than clashed, her sword snaking in through unguarded openings, the blades of her opponents bypassing her harmlessly.

But her horse was cut out from beneath her. Swinging Jia around to deal with spears from behind, Alouzon saw the girl go down, and she forced a way through the press to find her on her feet, ringed by arms and armor. She had caught the end of her ponytail in her teeth to keep it away from grasping hands, and her blue eyes were searching for openings.

Alouzon kicked her way through the men, riding over one who refused to move, severing the arm of another who attempted to pull her down. "I don't want to hurt you, dammit! Get the fuck out of my way!"

Wykla grabbed hold and swung up. Alouzon went out the way she had gone in. No one tried to stop her.

Vorya was galloping toward her along the fringe of the fighting. "Back to the bank," he called. "We are finished out here."

The mounted counterattack had disrupted the Corrinians once more, and when they reached the lip of the embankment, they found that only three of the King's Guard had been killed. Still, Alouzon felt the hopelessness. Three out of a hundred was a sizable loss, and there was nothing to stop the phalanxes from forming up again and advancing. As had been the case for the last ten years, the war would drag on, the atrocities mounting on both sides, fueled by the the frustration, by the uselessness of a struggle that appeared capable of burying everybody involved, and then continuing.

She looked at her hands, looked away quickly. She was part of it now, too.

Marrget and Santhe were returning, leading their warriors up the bank as Alouzon slid, shaking, from Jia's back. She returned their hearty waves with a

short, dizzy nod and turned around to find that Silbakor had settled a short distance away across the
open ground that surrounded the stones. The Dragon
was crouched in the grass, its wings folded. Standing
beside it was Dythragor.

❖ CHAPTER 23 ❖

❖

AT FIRST, ALOUZON STARED AT DYTHRAGOR numbly, her interior battle of power and sickness raging unabated, draining her of comprehension. Then, reluctantly, she pushed herself away from Jia and stumbled toward him, unsure whether she wanted to hug him or beat him senseless.

He stood, waiting for her, and she noticed that, in spite of his youth, his stature, his armor and sword, he seemed now more like Solomon Braithwaite, the scholar, than Dythragor Dragonmaster, the braggart warrior. He was shaking, and as she approached, he looked toward her as though he held a drowned child in his arms and was praying that she had brought a miracle with her.

"Suzanne," he said suddenly. "You've got to help me. You've got to explain this place."

Her old name was a drink of clear water. She had almost forgotten that she was Suzanne, that Alouzon and battle and blood were but recent arrivals. But his words were also the most human thing he had ever said to her, and she stopped short, her head clearing. "I've got to explain *what?*"

As he came toward her, she saw that his eyes were frantic, terrified. The words spilled out of him as though a wine skin had been slit. "This place. Gryylth. It's crazy. It drops off. No . . . it just vanishes. It isn't a world. It's just a piece of something."

"What did you see?"

"It's crazy."

"Answer me, dammit, I don't have time for this."

Silbakor spoke. "We have flown the length and breadth of Gryylth. We have followed the coasts, journeyed along the promontories, examined the islands and the seas. Dythragor has seen the Great Ending."

"What did you tell him?"

"He asked nothing."

She wanted to kick the Dragon between the eyes. "*You could have said something, you goddam lizard!*"

Silbakor blinked yellow eyes. Dythragor was holding his head as though it might burst. "You've got to explain. I think I'm going crazy."

The hum from the Circle rose in pitch, increased in volume. Alouzon glanced behind. The Tree was back on its wagon and was being moved slowly closer. Turning back, she took Dythragor by the shoulders and shook him until some of the blankness left his eyes. "You're not going crazy. You don't have time to go crazy."

"But, then—" Dythragor was looking past her at the glowing Tree. He seemed to become aware that there were more pressing concerns than his. "What's going on?"

"Tireas has the Tree, and he's out for blood. Mernyl's trying to cook up something that'll stop him."

The wagon halted by the remains of the Heel Stone. The Tree swayed against its ropes, then settled. "Is that what they took out of the Heath?" said Dythragor.

"That's it." Tireas appeared to be debating his next move. Tarwach approached him, but the sorcerer waved him away peremptorily. "I guess I should thank you. You saved our lives with that strafing run you did."

He shook his head. "That was Silbakor's idea, not mine. I was too far gone for decisions." The fear crossed his face again, and he went on tonelessly. "But two passes were all I could handle. When it went down on the second run, I thought someone was trying to . . . to tear my mind out of my head."

"There's a reason for that." She did not want to explain, had to, went on without stopping. "That thing out there is a part of you. It's your deepest unconscious. It's the Tree of Creation, Dythragor. In fighting it, you're fighting yourself."

He did not appear to comprehend at first, then suddenly raged. "Garbage! What is this crap you're giving me? More of Mernyl's damned fairy tales?"

She wanted to strike him. "Get off the Mernyl shit. He didn't do this. Gryylth is your baby."

He was livid, and she noticed that his leather armor was thick and crackling with dried blood. She remembered that he had slaughtered an old man in Crownhark, and held back the accusations that she wanted to throw at him.

The Dragon spoke again. "It is the truth."

Dythragor stopped, gasped. Fighting with his rage, he turned to Silbakor. "My friend," he choked. "You have never lied to me."

"I do not lie. I cannot lie."

Alouzon prodded it with her foot. "Go on," she said. "Quit waiting for questions. Tell him what you told me. I don't care if he asked you or not."

Its tail twitched like that of a nervous cat. "Gryylth

was created in its entirely on the night that your divorce was finalized. Confronted at last with the wreckage of your life, you tried to kill yourself with sleeping pills. In the resultant delirium, your unconsciousness was freed. It created a piece of a world: a land in which your enemy was plain, in which you could fight as you wished, in which you would not be bound by what you perceived as the restrictions of civilization."

Dythragor tottered, his face that of a dead man. "This is . . . this is all a dream?"

"It's real, Dythragor," said Alouzon. "I haven't been killing illusions."

"I . . . don't know. I can't believe it."

The earth quaked, and from its depths came the sound of rumbling and snapping. A bolt of green light flashed from the Tree and struck the rim of the embankment. It tore up the ground, sent chunks of turf high in the air, and began burrowing toward the Circle. But before it could dig very far, Mernyl countered.

A mountain could not have been more massive, nor a sheet of lighting quicker than the energies unleashed by the Gryylthan sorcerer. Mernyl was no longer trying to defend away from his power source. He was at the heart of it now, with his hands virtually holding the controls of the existence of the world. The Circle throbbed and the humming mounted into a roar as his counterstroke ripped into the Tree.

Alouzon pulled words from her throat: "*Everybody down!*"

The Gryylthans had no choice. The concussion was tremendous, a shimmering pressure wave that rippled through air and earth alike, throwing men and women and horses to the ground, sending them skidding across the grass. Alouzon slammed into Silbakor, and it wrapped a protective wing about her. Dythragor rolled, putting the Dragon between himself and the blast.

The echoes died away. Silence. Then a few faint groans.

Bruised and breathless, Alouzon peered out from the folds of Silbakor's wing. "Gods," she said. "*It hasn't been touched.*"

Dythragor scrambled up on the Dragon's back for a better look. "Jesus." He stiffened, drew his sword, and leapt to the ground. "They're coming, Alouzon. All of them."

She closed her eyes. It was all hopeless. "Shit."

Tireas was moving again, drawing the Tree closer to the Circle. Behind him and to either side, the phalanxes surged forward. Alouzon saw Dythragor examining them, estimating strengths, calculating battle strategies. With a shake of his head, he seemed to arrive at the inescapable conclusion. "If I made this place," he said to the Dragon, "I can change it, can't I?"

Silbakor shook its head. "It changes of its own accord. You can do nothing to alter it."

"Then . . . I've gotten us all killed."

Alouzon bristled. "Don't underestimate Mernyl."

He laughed bitterly. "Mernyl? After the things I've done, I'd be surprised if he didn't blow the whole place away just to get back at me."

"He's not like you, Dythragor." Alouzon regretted her words the moment she had said them. Dythragor seemed to sag, and a shade of pain crossed his face.

Marrget cantered over and noticed Dythragor, regarding him as though she expected him to break and run. When he only stared in return, she shrugged and turned to Alouzon. "We are forming for defense, Dragonmaster. Where do you wish to stand?"

"Doesn't matter. If I could be with you, I'd be honored."

"The honor would be mine, friend Alouzon."

Dythragor wavered. "M-Marrget?"

She turned her gray eyes on him without apology. "The same, Dragonmaster."

He swallowed and stepped forward. "If . . . if I could stand with you also . . . it would be a greater honor for me than I could decently expect."

Marrget looked off to the side, as though examining the green grass and the yellow flowers that spotted it. "You would wish to fight with women?"

"I . . . I don't wish to fight against them."

A hum was rising from the Circle again, a confused sea of voices that overlapped and blended with one another, shouting, singing, calling out. Marrget sighed. "As you wish, Dragonmaster." She started to turn her horse, thought better of it, extended her hand to Dythragor. He hesitated a moment, then took it.

"I will have your horses brought to you," she said.

Dythragor looked after her as she rode away. "I owe Marrget more of an apology than that."

"It'll have to do for now." She turned back to the Dragon. "Silbakor, can you help with this?"

"I am one with Gryylth," it said. "The land, not the people. I cannot oppose something that springs directly from the creation of the world." It fixed Dythragor with its yellow eyes. "I must tell you this, Dragonmaster. You do not ask, and yet I will tell you. You imperil yourself in attacking the Tree. Should it perish, you will die. It is a manifestation of your in-most being. Your lives are one."

"And the Circle also?"

"It is so."

The Corrinian phalanxes drew closer, following and flanking the Tree. Dythragor chose his words carefully. "Dragon, you said I would die soon. Is this what you meant?"

"I have told you before: I do not predict the future. I do not prophesy."

"If the Tree or the Circle perishes, will Gryylth end?"

"It will not, should your successor accept the Guardianship."

Alouzon blinked. "Successor?"

"One to follow after," said the Dragon. "One who will complete. One who will care."

She understood. All her unthought-of and unasked questions were suddenly answered, and the knowledge fell on her with the crushing weight of a world. "Wait a minute . . . is that why you dragged me into this?"

"Suzanne, I swear it wasn't my idea," said Dythragor.

She was not looking at him, did not hear him. "What the fuck are you trying to do to my life?" she screamed at the Dragon. "You son of a bitch, you want to get me out here all the time, make me into some kind of hero? You've already made me kill. You want more? Aren't you satisfied?"

Revolted by the thought, she sat down heavily on the ground and covered her face with her arms. She wanted to cry. She tried to cry. But her tears were gone along with a great deal more, and her eyes were still dry when she heard the sound of approaching horses and looked up to see Wykla bringing their mounts.

Wykla halted beside her, looked puzzled. "Your horse, my lady." She nodded quickly to Dythragor, as though embarrassed.

"Wykla . . ." said Alouzon. Dythragor started but did not speak. The girl appeared to be frightened by what she was seeing. "Wykla, I . . . I don't know what to do."

"My lady?" Wykla stared with wide blue eyes, and Alouzon saw the confidence draining away from her. If the Dragonmaster could not stand, then neither could Wykla, nor, more than likely, the First Wartroop.

But it's not my responsibility.

They were all looking at her now. She felt the bulk of the Dragon at her side. It was waiting. Wykla was waiting. Dythragor was waiting.

I can't let this craziness take over my life.

"My lady Alouzon?"

At last, her vision blurred, tears brimming, stinging their way down her face as though they might cleanse the madness from her life. The nimbus of the Circle became, to her eyes, a haloed glory that beat and shimmered with all the vigor of the Grail. Half dazzled, she looked up at Wykla. "I . . ."

She loved the girl. She loved them all: Vorya, his hand and arm cut to pieces, still fighting on; Marrget and Relys and the wartroop, pushing themselves toward sanity in spite of a fear that ate at their very souls; Cvinthil, the gentle warrior who held his wife and daughter tenderly and who had stood with her in Bandon. And there was Adyssa, too, the simple midwife who had dared to question her own existence, who had given her life for a woman she hardly knew.

The land, rolling and green, as fresh and bright as a new penny, holding within itself the living, breathing presence of the Grail . . .

. . . threatened with ending, termination . . .

Still, she fought. *It's crazy. I'm tired of giving. That's all I do.*

A flare burst all about them, followed by another concussion. Wykla and Dythragor fought to calm the horses, but Alouzon had fallen to the side, her face pressed now against the cool grass, yellow buttercups and dandelions, bright even in the Tree's murk, waving before her streaming eyes.

With sudden resolution, she pushed herself up and grabbed Jia's bridle. Yes, everything could end. But the Tree was still attacking along the vacant line of the Avenue, and the Corrinians were still coming on, numerous and vengeful. She understood the puzzle: what difference did it make?

Her heart caught. There was a great difference. Now there was hope, both for Gryylth and for herself. There was the Grail.

Silbakor watched her. "Suzanne Helling?"

"Later," she snapped. "I've got things to do."

Jia had been fighting Wykla, but he settled when he felt Alouzon's hand. Swinging into the saddle, she loosened her sword and touched Wykla's shoulder to reassure her. "Stay with me, warrior."

"Aye, lady."

The rim of the embankment flared into light, kindled by a flash of fire from the Circle. Mernyl was attempting to filter the ranks of attacking soldiers again, but this time, as quickly as his shield formed, it was shivered into a thousand corposant shreds by a blast from the Tree.

With a shout, the phalanxes covered the remaining ground, but they mounted the embankment only to be met head-on by the forces of Gryylth. The first wave, off-balance from the steep climb, was thrown back, the men tumbling back into their comrades and knocking them down.

The Avenue, though, was level ground, an easy entrance, and it was here that Marrget was making her stand. Disregarding the fact that the position placed the wartroop squarely within the conflict of Tree and Circle, she had led her women out to plug the gap in the defenses.

Dense, close-packed, the Corrinians surged forward along the Avenue, pushing through a gap in the ditch and bank that was not more than twenty feet wide. For the First Wartroop to have its enemies so disorganized by lack of space was an immeasurable advantage, but as Alouzon spurred Jia toward the gap, she became increasingly aware of a subtle change in the atmosphere. The air seemed electrified, and her body tingled, her hair, dusty though it was, bristling with static.

The smell of ozone hung thickly. She looked ahead and saw Tireas at work. The sorcerer seemed to be locked in a more subtle combat with Mernyl, and Alouzon doubted that he would send a blast straight into his own men.

She jumped Jia into the fray with Dythragor and Wykla directly behind her. Marrget was busy with her sword and did not look up, but a shout of "*Hail, Dragonmasters!*" rose above the tumult of shouts, screams, and the heavy clangs of sword and spear.

Alouzon killed. Her sword moved, inserted bright and withdrew dripping, lashed out and broke skulls. Jia took her where she willed as though the horse's brain was plugged directly into her own, and she killed, and killed again.

She tried not to think, but she had little success this time. Actions seemed slowed in the press, and she had time to see her foes' faces, note their individual stances, their tactics: the twisting lunge of this one, the side-step of this other. Young men, middle-aged men. She watched herself kill them.

What else can I do?

Treading on the bodies of the fallen, Jia missed his footing and stumbled. Alouzon, overbalanced, fell. The dusty Avenue came up quickly and felt like fresh concrete when she hit. She was not hurt, but when she opened her eyes, she saw, besides the startled eyes of a white-faced corpse, booted feet—and the sweep of a sword aimed at her neck.

"Damn you, Helling! Move your ass!"

Dythragor's voice roused her, and she got her feet beneath her and came up, blocking the sword and several spears with her wrist guards, slashing out with her own weapon and clearing a space for herself.

Dythragor was pushing toward her, hacking murderously through the confusion. Pikes were flashing all about her, but she was fending them off with strokes that were flavored with the cold precision of the Dragonsword. A Corrinian jumped on her from behind, trying to hold her so that others could strike. She did not hesitate. Driving her elbows back, she heard the crunch of breaking ribs, and his grip loosened. She whirled around and ripped him open.

The ozone was stronger now, and so was the tingling. She was reminded strongly of the signals that precede a lightning strike. The Dragonsword echoed the thought.

Lightning strike.

Dythragor reached her at last, a Corrinian hanging to his leg like a limpet. Alouzon beat the man away and clambered up behind. "Listen," she shouted above the noise, "we've got to get everyone off the Avenue."

"What?"

"Look at the Tree!"

The branches and leaves were enveloped in a violet glow, and Tireas was staring straight along the Avenue. For an instant, Alouzon met his gaze and was shaken by the absolute lack of anything human she saw in it. Mernyl was right: the Tree was controlling the Corrinian sorcerer.

The tingling increased, and the odor of ozone turned as thick as the haze of blood that hung in the air. Holding to Dythragor as he backed and spurred his horse through the battle, Alouzon searched the confusion for Marrget, and found her at the middle of the Avenue, surrounded by dead and dying men. Her face was smeared and grim, and blood ran down her arm from a deep cut in her shoulder.

"Marrget," Alouzon shouted, "get the women off the Avenue! The Tree!"

Marrget sliced deeply into a soldier, glanced at the Tree, turned her horse. Her clear voice rang above the clamor like a bell. "*To flanks!*"

The wartroop and the Dragonmasters forced a slow passage through the phalanxes and had barely reached the cover of the ditch when the Avenue exploded into light. With a roar, a crater opened up in the area they had just left, earth and rock hailing through the air. The Corrinians had continued to press forward into the undefended gap, and when the detonation faded, the ground was littered with torn and mutilated bodies.

Dythragor was aghast. "Doesn't he care about his own damned men?"

"I think if we'd been caught, he would have considered it worthwhile," said Alouzon.

"What a bloody waste. You don't throw lives away like that. You just . . ." He looked stricken. "You just don't."

The Corrinians had withdrawn at the explosion, and the siege had fallen off. Alouzon expected another charge from Vorya, but none came. Marrget signaled a return to the area within the embankment; Dythragor urged his horse up the slope. "We can't go on like this," he muttered.

"You got any ideas?"

He shook his head impatiently. "It's just attrition until we're all dead . . . or until the sorcerers destroy each other. Then that's it for everything."

She bowed her head. She did not want to think about the Guardianship at the moment, but it was forcing itself on her. Even now, the Tree was moving forward again, and Tireas was increasing the fury of his assault.

Mernyl knew about the consequences of a magical defeat for either side. He had, she reflected, always known. And he knew about her, about Kent State, about Solomon Braithwaite and his despair. Did he then know about the Guardianship, too? Probably. And he had kept the knowledge from her so that she would not reject it before she was so intimately involved with Gryylthan affairs that to refuse would be tantamount to the betrayal of a lover.

And he was fighting . . . and that meant that he was hoping.

Damn.

As she jumped down from Dythragor's horse, she heard a crackle and saw that Mernyl had thrown up another screen. It was promptly shattered by the Tree. She began to understand Tireas's strategy: Mernyl, engaged by the Tree, would be unable to deal with the phalanxes. Outnumbered, the Gryylthans would eventually be destroyed, and then it would be a simple matter of magic against magic.

Regardless of who won that contest, Gryylth would end. What happened to souls, she wondered, if their existence was literally negated?

She looked up at Dythragor. "You said this wasn't your idea."

Another screen, and the Tree fragmented it in a moment. "It wasn't," he said. "I'm afraid it was the Dragon that chose you."

"Why me?"

"I don't know." He spoke calmly, but sadly. The constant rage and swagger was gone. "I couldn't find anyone I thought suitable, and Silbakor was pressuring me. But I don't think it picked you out of desperation."

"You . . . you think I'm meant for this?"

He hesitated, shrugged. "All I can say is that, from what I've seen, I've made a hash out of everything. I kept the conflict up so long that the Dremords were forced into this just to preserve their lives. I can't stop it now, and there's a good chance that Gryylth might not exist because of that." He offered his hand, and she took it. "It's your choice, not mine. I won't blame you for what's happened . . . or what will."

"Don't blame yourself, either."

"Can you say that, girl? Keeping the pot on the boil for as long as I have? Any civilized, reasonable man would have moved for a settlement. My God! we *had* a settlement ten years ago, but I . . ." His face turned haunted for an instant, and his grip on her hand tightened. "I wouldn't argue with Silbakor's choice."

"Oh?" The Tree inched forward, shattered another one of Mernyl's screens.

"You seem to have done well enough with Marrget and the wartroop. I don't know what you did, but you pulled them through. I've never seen them fight so well as they have today."

"Yeah, thanks . . ." Jia had found his way back to the Circle, and now he nosed her. There seemed to be a trace of shame in the horse's eyes. "No blame on you, either, guy." She took his bridle. "Happens to all of us."

Out beyond the embankment, the phalanxes were reforming, but Mernyl was not acting at all: there was a dim humming from the rings of stones, no more. Closer to her, Vorya was conferring with Marrget, Cvinthil, and Santhe. Dythragor was joining them.

Nothing from Mernyl?

Wary of the waves of energy that rolled out from the Circle even when it was not actively fighting, she crawled into Jia's saddle and tried to find an angle at which she could see the center of the monument through gaps in the outer peristyle and the inner trilithons. Not until she had covered nearly a quarter of the circumference did she find one, and when she did she wished that she had not.

Mernyl was a wreck. Shaken by his defeat at the Heel Stone, blasted by the power of the Tree, sapped further by his exertions within the Circle, he was weak, shaking, his eyes as hollow as his cheeks. If he remained on his feet it was only because he was using his staff as a crutch.

He looked up and saw her. "I am not finished yet," he called, his voice hoarse but defiant.

She murmured to herself. "Yeah . . . but how long can you keep this up, man?"

He could not hear her. Stretching out his arms, he straightened and seemed to gather strength from the stones. Behind him, the three central trilithons, their uprights stretching over twenty feet into the air and their lintels adding further height to that, were radiant, crackling with power, shining as though they mirrored the sun that was now sinking toward the horizon.

A subterranean rumble shook the stones as though it might topple them, but the Circle held. Mernyl tottered for an instant before he braced himself with his staff. "Go, Alouzon! This is the great fight!" He swept an arm out and was lost in a shimmer as the interstices of the peristyle filled with light.

The Tree was barely ten yards from the bank now, and as she rode to join the others, Alouzon noticed that the tension in the Gryylthan ranks was back. Marrget and the First Wartroop were too visible, and the Tree was an ominous reminder of their transformation. Although the men of Gryylth no longer balked at fighting beside them, it was obvious that they did not wish to become women warriors themselves.

Energy flared at the lip of the bank, but it came from the Tree, not from Mernyl. Behind it, the phalanxes advanced through the ditch and began to climb. The Gryylthans tried to push through the shield to attack, but it was too dense, and the slope of the embankment was too treacherous.

The Circle erupted in a burst of blue, shattering the wall. Before the defenders could attack, though, it was reinstated by the Tree. Again, Mernyl struck, but the phalanxes had gained the embankment.

Slow, insidious movement. The Gryylthan forces were reduced to watching and waiting as the Corrinians advanced. As often as Mernyl destroyed the wall, it was remade, and the phalanxes had covered nearly a quarter of the distance from the bank to the outer peristyle before Mernyl changed his tactics.

The blast thrown out by the Circle shook the ground, and several women of the wartroop, though nowhere near the Avenue, were thrown from their horses. Blazing, furious, the energies drove through the wall and the advancing men, incinerating several where they stood, and struck directly for Tireas.

For a moment, the Tree was lost in an incandescence that roared into the sky like a gas explosion, rising and mushrooming and riving the darkness with light. As the sorcerer, enveloped in flame, fought for his life, his protective wall crumbled, and the defenders threw themselves on the Corrinians.

Marrget led another charge, attempting the same tactics that had disrupted the previous attacks, but this time, they were going awry. The soldiers were not acting. They stood uncertainly, eyeing the Tree which, as the flames dissipated, was once again becoming visible. Weapons hanging useless at their sides, they ignored Cvinthil's efforts to rally them. Some were even inching to the rear, leaving the wartroop isolated.

Without the foot soldiers to engage them, the phalanxes were free to turn their full strength upon Marrget and her women. Alouzon saw two fall, one dead, the other fighting to regain her horse. Ahead,

Dythragor was plunging into the phalanxes, cutting down a wide swath of men as he went to help. Cvinthil gave up on the foot soldiers and followed him, and Alouzon spurred close behind.

"Comic book hero," she muttered just before she met the first ranks. "We're all fucking comic book heroes."

She hacked her way through the lines, trying to open an escape route for the beleaguered wartroop. Dythragor was guarding the woman who had been unhorsed while she remounted. Her black hair and hard eyes offered the Dragonmaster the faintest gleam of a smile of gratitude before she was off again, fighting.

"King's Guard," Alouzon shouted as she opened the needed passage. "King's Guard to the front. Come on, dammit! Show some balls!"

Marrget and Cvinthil were bringing the wartroop through the gap, but on either side, the Corrinians were swamping the plain surrounding the Circle. Mernyl threw up shields in a desperate effort to slow the flood, but the Tree shattered them instantly.

Dythragor waved Alouzon back, gestured to Marrget, and shook his head, tight-lipped. The Circle was lost.

Abruptly, a portion of the King's Guard rallied and charged. It was a quixotic gesture at best, since there was little that ten or twelve could do against hundreds, but Alouzon guessed that they were trying to give their wounded comrades some extra time in which to escape the phalanxes.

As she watched, though, the air seemed to shimmer before them, their movements slowed down, and they began screaming as the flesh melted from their bones and the ground under their feet turned into a quagmire of white-hot magma. Tireas was using the Tree again, attacking in a manner that would confirm the Gryylthans' panic.

The wailing cries of incinerated throats filled the air, and Alouzon's anger, pent and banked and controlled with the intimate knowledge of the results of violence, was unleashed suddenly at the sight, its embers blazing up in a moment into blinding, mindless hate.

Her hand was on the Dragonsword. *Do it. Do it now.*

A Corrinian pikeman was running by, and she turned and slew him outright, snatching his weapon from his lifeless hand as he fell, his eyes wide and his throat open. It was a good spear—balanced, straight—and it seemed to come to life in her hand, become a part of her.

She poised herself on Jia's back and braced her legs. Her gaze was focused on Tireas as though through a gunsight, and had she held an M-1 instead of a spear, she would have pulled the trigger without hesitating, just as, now, she hurled the bronze-tipped shaft with all her strength, striking straight for Tireas's heart.

As it intersected the flow of energy from the Tree, it burst into flame, but its speed was such that its course wavered only slightly. Burning like a bolt from the hand of a god, it plunged through the trunk of the Tree and pierced the sorcerer's groin, spun him around, and broke his connection with the Tree. Fire licked at his robe from the burning shaft, and where there was not fire, there was blood.

But as Alouzon watched, her anger replaced by a sick horror, he was staggering to his feet, his hair blazing, his robe smoldering against his charred flesh.

As though he were dragged by unseen chains, he approached the Tree once more, his inhuman eyes fixed on Alouzon.

"Back!" cried Marrget. "Before it comes again!"

The phalanxes swept over the plain like a tidal bore. Alouzon and the others retreated, following the route of the panicked soldiers. The sun was a streaming glory in their eyes as they fled over the southwest bank and into the open countryside, leaving the Corrinians in possession of the Circle.

❖ CHAPTER 24 ❖

❖

THE EYES OF THE CORRINIAN SORCERER WERE clear, almost luminous, and when he spoke, he spoke with assurance. He sat in a chair before the king, lapped in a clean white robe, at ease, confident, poised . . . but Darham knew that he was as mad as if he had been groveling in the fields, gulping grass and howling at the night sky.

Tarwach did not notice, for he was silently raging at the terrible losses of the day. It seemed inconceivable that five score Gryylthans could have inflicted such damage on over thirty phalanxes, but after the captains had made their reports, the truth was evident. Corrin had gained the Circle, but its strength was barely a quarter of what it had been that morning.

"What do you recommend, sorcerer?" said Tarwach, breaking the silence suddenly.

Tireas shifted, pursed his lips, looked out through the open flap of the pavilion. In the distance was the Circle, glowing with light and power. Mernyl was still within, still alive, still able to summon potent energies to his aid. "We do not yet hold the Circle," he said, his voice strangely hollow.

The night was warm, and moths danced about the

415

torches. One fluttered in front of Tireas, and he lifted
a hand to bat it away. At his touch, the insect dropped
lifelessly into his lap. Darham stared, then looked at
Karthin, who was beside him. He had also noticed,
and his blue eyes had turned distrustful.

Darham ventured to speak. "The grounds of the
Circle are secure," he said. "The Gryylthans have fled.
I would say that our task is finished."

There was more—or maybe less—in Tireas's eyes
than Darham remembered. "Mernyl is still alive."

"What can he do? He is as much a prisoner as if
we held him in Beñardis."

"He can do much." The sorcerer's voice, already
hollow, deepened, turned threatening. "So long as he
lives, the Circle is not ours. So long as we do not
possess the Circle, we do not have Gryylth."

"There are many men now dead," said Tarwach,
"who gave their lives to gain the Circle. Do we not
owe them success?"

"We *have* the Circle," insisted Darham. The sorcerer held him with his black eyes. Black eyes? Had
his eyes not been gray long ago?

"We do not," said Tireas.

Something was wrong. There was a sense of the
malign about Tireas, about the entire scene: the Circle
glowing, the lightning-lit bulk of the Tree rising up
from its wain, the sprawling heaps of the dead . . . A
subtle pestilence was abroad in Gryylth this night,
and the land was waiting anxiously to see what they
would do about it.

"My brother . . ." Darham glanced at Tireas, then
ignored him. This was a decision for a king, not for
a magician. "My brother, I would propose something."

"You have my ear always, Darham."

"Do I, Tarwach?" He stepped forward, clumsily easing the loop of the sling that cradled his wounded arm. "It seems that your ear is turned more toward others these days. I feel often that I must beg for your attention like an out-of-favor courtier."

"Darham!" Tarwach half-rose from his seat. "If so, then my apologies. Speak. I listen only to you."

Darham glanced at Karthin. The captain nodded. "I would propose another way, Tarwach. The killing has gone on long enough. The dead lie thick on both sides, and there are many women in both Gryylth and Corrin who will lament the fall of their mates and sons."

As though he had guessed what Darham was going to say, Tireas opened his mouth to speak. But the king raised his hand. "Your turn will come, sorcerer. Continue, brother."

"My suggestion is simple. A settlement, now, with generous terms for Gryylth. Regardless of the past, it is a noble people we have been fighting, and far better it would be if we learned to be friends instead of enemies."

Tarwach went white, then flushed. "You would propose that? What of the dead that lie scattered from here to the Great Dike? Gods, man, they have slaughtered three quarters of the phalanxes!"

Darham put his hands on his hips, stepped forward. He did not like opposing his brother, nor was he at all reassured by the alteration in Tireas's behavior, but the senselessness of the battle had overwhelmed him. "Three-quarters? And what were we trying to do to them?"

Tarwach spluttered, at a loss for words. Tireas's

eyes bored out at Darham. "Shall we abandon our plans now?" The sorcerer intoned the words like a spell. "With the end in sight?"

"There is no end in sight, Tireas," said Darham. "Look at the reality before you. Destroying Mernyl will lead us into further enormities against Gryylth. Were Corrin so crushed, our people would nurse their wounds until they were ready to turn on their conqueror. We should expect nothing different from Gryylth."

"We can ensure that they can never rise again." The sorcerer was adamant.

"How? By killing them all?" Heedless of Tireas's ire, Darham stepped toward him, the fist of his good arm balled at his side in an effort to keep his passion from mastering him. "Could we continue to call ourselves honorable after such an atrocity? What say you?"

Tireas did not flinch. "They have killed our men."

Karthin burst out. "You bitch's whelp! You wiped out four phalanxes yourself when you threw your bolt at the First Wartroop."

The silence was deadly, but the big farmer folded his arms and stood defiantly. His was the anger of the foot soldier confronted with the grandiose plans of one who had held himself aloof from the common, messy battles of sword and spear. His disdain for the sorcerer was obvious. So recently raised to the captaincy, he could be sent back to the ranks in disgrace, but still he stood, a man of Corrin, as tall and unyielding as the king himself.

Something writhed on Tireas's lap. With quiet convulsions, the moth was quivering back to life. As Darham watched, it turned smooth and slimy, like a slug, and its iridescent skin shone with unclean mottlings as it crawled along the folds of the sorcerer's robe.

Tireas noticed and brushed it off onto the floor with annoyed flick of his wrist. It hit with a soft plop and inched toward the shadows.

Darham was shaken. This was not Tireas. This was . . . something else.

Tireas stood up. "Aye, hayseed, some of our men perished in my attack. But they knew well that their lives were at risk when they entered the fray."

The white slug writhed into the darkness.

Karthin seemed as unnerved as Darham. "The First Wartroop . . ." He stumbled over his words. "The First Wartroop still lives."

"Do you thank the Gods for that, hayseed?"

Again, Karthin did not rise to the insult. "I keep my own counsel."

"Maybe you wish to bed the pretty women, and insinuate yourself between the thighs of your enemies. Perhaps you have been unmanned, and now want to make love rather than war."

Tarwach interrupted. "This is a captain of Corrin, Tireas. Save your ire for our enemies."

Tireas's indignation was a little too calculated. "If he defends Gryylth, then he too is an enemy."

"Do you impeach my loyalty to Corrin?" demanded Karthin. The sorcerer snorted and turned away. "By the Gods, I will have an answer, sir!"

In spite of the tension in the air, Tarwach smiled. "Well said, captain. I would utter the same challenge. But I cannot say but that I agree with Tireas's desire regarding Mernyl and the Circle. Bread will be scarce this winter, and it is the doing of Gryylth."

"Dythragor Dragonmaster, rather," said Darham. "Is there a difference?"

"At one time, I would have said that there was no difference. But now . . ." The white thing had vanished, but he felt its presence. "I think that Dythragor acted on his own. Vorya would never countenance such a cowardly act."

"The deed is done. We must safeguard our own folk."

"Aye, it is done. But Karthin here says that both our peoples can yet live, and I think that is the wiser path."

Tarwach gestured to the sorcerer to sit. "Do you think me a fool, brother?" he said. There was no challenge in his voice. Rather, his tone was that of one seeking support for a difficult decision.

"Nay, Tarwach. But we differ in this matter."

"We do indeed." He rose, went to the flap, watched the Circle for a time. Energy flickered across the monoliths and trilithons. "I intend to give Tireas his way. Mernyl must die, and the Circle must be ours. I see no particularly good arguments against that course." He put his hand to his cut chin for a moment, winced, and considered. "Dythragor and the female Dragonmaster are at large, and nothing prevents the country from rising against us. Do you understand my reasoning?"

"I do. But I do not agree."

"My king," began Tireas.

"Sit down, sir!" said Tarwach.

The sorcerer sat, folded his arms, bent his head. Brooding, powerful, angry, and not quite human, he was a frightening presence in the pavilion. Even Tarwach seemed affected.

"Darham . . ." The king's tone was almost pleading. "We have always stood together."

"Forgive me, brother. I cannot do this."

"Will you help subdue Gryylth?"

Silence lengthened. Darham turned away, arms folded, eyes examining the floor. He sensed Tireas as though a bonfire burned in the tent and found that he hated what the sorcerer had become. "I will not," he said at last. "I cannot. To do so would be the action of a traitor."

Tireas spoke again. "To refuse to fight is the—"

Tarwach whirled on him, his sword sliding out of its sheath. "You forget yourself, sir. One word more and you will have spoken an insult that can only be avenged in one way." His passion had opened the cut in his chin again, and a trickle of blood wound down his throat.

Tireas watched it for a moment, as though disdainful of such overt mortality. "I have the Tree." His voice was calm, assured, cruel.

"Aye, sorcerer," said Darham. "You have the Tree. And you have the king. And you will have your fill of death this night, and tomorrow, and the next day after that." His words seared the air. "And you will enjoy it, sorcerer, because you have become as bloodthirsty as that thing out there in the wain. I sincerely believe that you would destroy all of Gryylth and Corrin for your satisfaction. Therefore, I will say good-bye."

He turned. Karthin offered his hand. Darham took it, and together they went toward the flap.

"Darham!"

"I will see you in Benardis, brother Tarwach," said Darham without turning around. "You can decide our fates then. We will be waiting for you . . .and for your judgment."

"Darham, please!"

But now the opening of the pavilion framed only

the Circle, glowing brightly, and some branches of
the Tree that writhed and snaked in the darkness.

"My king?" said Tireas.

Tarwach held his head, weeping, fighting for
words. "Go, Tireas," he whispered. "Do what you
must."

The sun had set long before, the moon had not yet
risen. Only the glow from the Circle saved the night
from absolute darkness. The standing stones shone
blue, and the interstices of the peristyle were barred
with luminescence: the sorcerer of Gryylth still lived.

"How many have we?" said Vorya. His voice was
dull. The surviving soldiers and warriors had gathered
about him, but the faces were few, too few.

Marrget spoke. "Thirty, my liege."

"Thirty . . ." Vorya sighed bitterly.

They had made a crude sort of camp in the hollow
of two hills some distance from the Circle. There,
they had eaten what food there was, rested, tended
wounds, and watched helplessly as the phalanxes se-
cured the area.

So far, there had been no further attacks on the
monument, and Tireas had not attempted to enter.
The Tree, in fact, had been taken away, and was not
even visible to the Gryylthans. Judging from their
actions, the immediate objectives of the men of Corrin seemed to be a comfortable camp and a peaceful
night. Tomorrow was soon enough to contemplate
the fate of Gryylth.

"I estimate they have about one hundred and fifty,"
Marrget continued.

"We cannot attack," said Vorya, "save to give ourselves an honorable end in battle."

"I'd hardly call that honorable," said Alouzon.

Dythragor growled under his breath. He was standing off by himself, watching the lack of activity at the Circle. He had jammed a knuckle in his mouth and was in the process of gnawing the skin off. "We've got to get Mernyl out of there."

Marrget followed his gaze. "My friend Dythragor," she said softly, "we all owe Mernyl our lives many times over. But we are powerless to repay him."

"We've got to get that damned Tree."

Alouzon sighed. The wine she had drunk to wash down the meager meal of bread and cheese now burned in her stomach as though it were vinegar. Neither she nor Dythragor had mentioned the consequences of the destruction of either Tree or Circle to the others. Nor had they mentioned the choice she faced.

Freedom, or the successorship . . . and a chance at the Grail.

Guardian of Gryylth: an escape from helplessness, from powerlessness, from the constant victimization that had come to characterize her existence since Kent State. Like Solomon Braithwaite, she had drunk her fill of despair, and now she could, if she wanted, flee to Gryylth and become the hub of an entire world.

Her right arm ached from the exertion of swinging five pounds of preternatural sword all day, and though she had washed her hands she still felt the slime of death on them. Deny it though she might, there was little difference between herself and the middle-aged professor. Silbakor had spoken of completing the world, but what kind of land, she wondered, would spring from her unconscious? She shuddered at the thought.

And yet . . . the Grail . . .

"What about raising the countryside?"

"It was raised days ago," said Marrget. "You saw the result. The few that remain are distant. It would take weeks to gather them. Once Tireas has done with Mernyl, the Tree and the Circle will be united under his control. We are conquered."

"Not if we get that Tree," Dythragor insisted.

Alouzon planted herself before him. "How? With thirty people, you want heroics again?" She wondered whether it was the hopelessness of the cause or her fear of the Guardianship that made her argue. If both the Tree and the Circle remained, even though Gryylth were enslaved, her services would not be needed in the future.

The thought was an obscenity, and she thrust it from her.

"Heroics be damned," said Dythragor. "I'm done with them. I don't want Mernyl killed."

Light suddenly flared at the Circle, and they turned to see the Tree once again approaching the rings of stones. Tireas was moving the wagon up, keeping well away from the deadly focal axis of the monument. A group of soldiers dragged a small sledge into position, and Tireas floated the Tree to it.

Alouzon noticed that he showed no signs of the damage she had inflicted on him. His hair was white and flowing, as was his beard, and he moved as though his body had never felt a trace of a wound. The wine in her belly roiled again when she compared him with Mernyl, a thin, wretched figure who used his staff as a prop to keep from falling over.

Tireas waved the soldiers back and picked up the rope that looped through the front of the sledge.

Dythragor worked on his knuckle. "What the hell . . .? Does he think he's going to move that thing?"

The sorcerer pulled. The sledge moved.

"*Damn.*"

Without visible effort, Tireas dragged the heavily burdened sledge toward one of the gaps in the peristyle. The force field that barred it flared brighter as he drew near, but he calmly raised his hand and allowed power from the Tree to flow into and through him.

The field gave a little. Alouzon understood. Mernyl had been without food since morning, without rest for some days, and he was weak and demoralized. By necessity, his control over the powers of the Circle would be slipping, waning, becoming more uncertain with each passing hour.

His hand a blue-white torch, Tireas moved a little farther into the gap, drawing the Tree after him. Mernyl was fighting, and had the Tree been at a distance, he might have succeeded in barring the way. But Tireas had brought the heavy artillery to his very doorstep, and at best, Mernyl could only delay his entrance.

Dythragor's voice made them jump. "Where's that fucking Dragon? Silbakor!"

It did not reply. When the phalanxes had overrun the Circle, it had disappeared.

"*Silbakor!*"

Alouzon grabbed his arm. "Shh! You want to have the whole damned army down on us?"

"What do you want me to do? Call collect?"

"Quiet." She shut her eyes, framed the thought. *Silbakor! I call you!*

I come. Alouzon heard the reply in her head. It held, she thought, a shade of reluctance, but the Dragon appeared, gliding silently and almost invisibly over the hills.

When it settled into the hollow, Dythragor stood before it. "Silbakor, you've got to stop that Tree."

"I cannot."

"Mernyl is going to get killed."

"I am powerless. I have told you: I cannot fight the Tree or the Circle. By doing so, I would be attacking the very existence of Gryylth, and that I am sworn against by the same oath by which you have called me."

Tireas was halfway through the gap by now. Mernyl was battling all the way, but the Tree's progress was inexorable.

Dythragor crouched down by the Dragon's head. "Silbakor, what's going to happen? Please."

"I do not prophesy."

Alouzon was afraid that Dythragor was going to weep. "And this is what I've brought Gryylth to," he said. His voice was shaken, bitter. "Everything I wanted, everything I dreamed of." He stood up and looked out toward the Circle. Tireas was through the gap, moving easily with the sledge, disappearing among the tall, standing stones. "I threw it all away. Even . . . even the Grail."

There was a higher hill to the north. Leaving the Dragon, the survivors climbed to its summit so as to see within the Circle.

At its center stood Mernyl, bent and worn, his feet resting on an oblong slab of white stone. About him was a tightly knit hemisphere of force that shone like a small star. Tireas made his way slowly toward him, and, working his way carefully around the stones, he positioned himself directly behind him.

His strategy was obvious: not only could the Tree now act without risking the focal path of the Circle, it could use that same path to attack Mernyl.

Wearily, the sorcerer of Gryylth faced about and raised his staff.

The first exchange blurred the entire central region into a haze of light. Outlines became indistinct and details were lost as power was flung and parried, caught and redirected. Ringed by the might of the Circle, though, the pyrotechnics were oddly quiet: only a faint rumble reached the Gryylthans.

Dythragor was muttering. "He's doing it . . . he's damned well doing it."

The battle went back and forth, the energies thickening the atmosphere within the peristyle into a pale, luminous soup. Standing waves of opacity and radiance formed nodes and peaks of brilliance. Silent blasts ricocheted off monoliths like billiard balls, but Mernyl did not budge. He was feeding at the center of the world now, and Circle and Tree were evenly matched.

An hour crawled by, two hours, but there seemed to be little change in the situation. When, at last, the exchanges dwindled in intensity, slowed, and finally stopped, the haze cleared to show the two men still facing one another, unharmed, power crackling about them.

"Right on, Mernyl." Alouzon found that she was gripping someone's hand tightly and discovered that it was Dythragor's. He met her eyes and looked away as quickly as she.

After some minutes, Tireas raised his hands, and Mernyl readied himself for a renewed assault. But, instead of a starburst of energy, there came a sudden, audible grinding of stone, that, though centered in the Circle, seemed to reach out to the distant horizon. The ground trembled and bucked, the monoliths shuddered, and Mernyl was almost knocked off his feet.

Now, instead of a surface battle of coruscating energies, the sorcerers were virtually struggling over the ground on which they stood. Mernyl was no longer fighting for his life: he was fighting for the Circle, for his source of power. The trilithons about him rocked, and the bluestones vibrated with the intensity of the energies that Tireas unleashed.

The Circle could not last. Alouzon saw the monoliths loosening. Tireas had merely to continue his efforts, and it would eventually fall.

Dythragor shook himself into action. "We've got to move. We've got to get that Tree. If the Circle goes, I'm willing to bet that every bit of constancy in Gryylth goes with it."

She was still holding his hand. "Something else goes, too."

"Don't remind me."

"And you're assuming something that . . . maybe you shouldn't."

He dropped her hand, shook a finger in her face. "I know damned well what I'm assuming, girl. And maybe you'd better start assuming it too."

"And how the hell do you think you're going to get the Tree, anyway?" she countered. "Mernyl can't do it, and he's got the Circle backing him. Weapons won't work. You might do something if you threw a monolith at it—" She started, looked down at the right upright of the trilithon directly behind Tireas. "Jesus . . . that thing's buried less than a yard in the ground."

"The trilithon?"

"The upright. Do you know about it, Dythragor?"

He thought for a moment, shrugged. "I seem to recall something about one of the trilithons being weaker than the others. Stonehenge wasn't my field any more than yours."

"But we've all read the literature on the subject. There's Petrie's book, and Lockyer's, and Hawley's. Did you read Niel?"

"Of course I did. Supermarket stuff, though."

"Supermarket? It's the best condensation you can get!"

"Sure . . . whatever . . ." The ground shook again, and Dythragor grabbed Alouzon to keep from being knocked off his feet.

But she thought she saw the upright shift with the vibrations. "That one's called 57 in the standard texts. For some reason the people that made Stonehenge didn't sink it as deep as the others. It was one of the first to fall, and it brought the trilithon down." Inches from hers, Dythragor's face was suddenly hopeful. "If you read the usual stuff," she continued, "there's a good chance that you've incorporated it into the Circle. And the fighting has loosened it: I saw it move. If we can get some people inside with some rope, we might be able to pull it down. It'll fall—"

"Right on the Tree." Dythragor stared his own death in the face, but he smiled. "Marrget," he called, "we have sword work ahead of us."

They made their plans quickly. One group would create a diversion out along the Avenue so as to draw men and material weapons away from the vicinity of the Circle. A second party would attempt to enter through the peristyle. Alouzon contributed what she knew about the construction and idiosyncrasies of Stonehenge while trying not to think of the decision she would have to make if the plan succeeded.

Selecting the proper trilithon and upright was critical, and Alouzon went with those who would actually enter the monument. Marrget was with her, and Relys and Wykla. Santhe and the men left from the Second Wartroop rounded out the party. The rest accompanied Dythragor and Vorya and Cvinthil so as to ensure that the diversion was adequate.

Alouzon was not even certain that it was possible to get inside the Circle, since the monument was walled off by forces that had even given difficulty to Tireas and the Tree. But amid rumbles and the screams of tortured rock, her group crept through the darkness and made its way through the low hills. Moving carefully, they took up a position in the shadows just beyond the ditch.

I don't want it. I don't want Gryylth. Isn't my life screwed over enough?

She peered over the embankment, her eyes dazzled by light that blazed with actinic ferocity. True, she did not want responsibility for the lives of others. But did she want responsibility for their deaths? Their negation? And then, behind everything, was the Grail. Did she want that?

She turned around, her back against the grassy bank, slid down, and put her face in her hands. "Oh, God . . . I want it."

The screams and shouts in the distance were barely audible over the rumbles and grindings from below. Dythragor and the rest were attacking, and the Corrinians moved off to meet the threat. Marrget touched Alouzon's shoulder, and Santhe straightened up and drew his sword, his eyes turning from mirth to calculation.

When they topped the embankment, they found but one guard left, and he was dispatched silently with a single thrust from Marrget. In a moment, the women and men had dashed quickly across the open area and dropped to the ground at the base of the peristyle.

Alouzon and Santhe examined the force field. It seemed impenetrable. With some hesitation, the Dragonmaster tried to put her hand through it, but could only compress it a few inches before it turned adamantine. Santhe shook his head. "If we use force, we will only bleed Mernyl."

She peered through the swirling light into the interior. Dimly, she saw the sorcerer of Gryylth standing on his slab, his staff upright and inclined toward Tireas. His eyes were open, and he was facing in her direction.

"He might see us. I can't tell."

Two Corrinians suddenly appeared, and Wykla threw herself at them, backed up by Relys. Before the men could call for help, they were dead.

But Mernyl had seen Alouzon, or perhaps the flash of swords had attracted his attention. The humming that emanated from the Circle altered in pitch a trifle, and the field between the uprights of the peristyle seemed to soften under the Dragonmaster's hand. At the same time, though, the underground rumblings became louder.

"We bleed him nonetheless," said Santhe. He gestured to the others, and boldly led the way.

Marrget followed, and the captains hurried the men and women in, then motioned for Alouzon. The field yielded reluctantly to her, as though she were pressing forward through thick cotton batting, but Marrget and Santhe took her arms and dragged her through.

The interior was a hell of sound and tumult, with gusts of air blasting from all sides and a reek of ozone that struck like a fist. Coughing and gagging, they staggered through the inner ring of bluestones and approached the horseshoe of great, freestanding trilithons. On the other side of the stones, the two sorcerers battled from within blue hemispheres of force.

And, turned as he was to face Mernyl, Tireas had not noticed the entrance of the Gryylthans.

Alouzon stopped at the base of the target trilithon, indicated the shallowly buried upright. "This one."

Marrget regarded the structure. It glowed with energy, flickering in response to the conjurations that sought to bring it down. "I am loathe to have my warriors touch this."

Alouzon shrugged helplessly. "We're going to have to."

Marrget nodded, gestured. Relys hurled a small ball of twine over the lintel so that it fell on the inner side of the trilithon. Santhe tied the thick rope they had brought to it, and Relys hauled it over.

An end of the rope now dangled on either side of the trilithon, and Relys was on the inside, working directly behind Tireas. If the Corrinian became aware of her presence, she would doubtless die instantly. But her movements were quick, deft, silent, and Mernyl allowed not a trace of emotion to cross his face that would indicate that he saw anything save the inhuman gaze of Tireas.

Steeling herself visibly, Relys reached an arm through the trilithon, and Marrget passed the outer end of the rope to her. Relys knotted the ends together. At a nod from Santhe and Marrget, the Gryylthans passed to the interior, seized the double rope, and pulled.

Upright 57 weighed in the vicinity of twenty tons, and its lintel added another twelve—an immense amount of inertia to overcome. Under other circumstances, the task would have been a fool's errand, but this particular trilithon was top-heavy, and the concussions that had been rocking the Circle since the battle had been joined earlier that day had already succeeded in loosening it.

As they pulled, the conflict of magics went on. Tireas's earthquakes and tremors were actually helping them, easing the upright back and forth in its shallow socket. They were indeed bringing down the Circle, but not in the way the Corrinian had in mind.

The upright shifted slightly, then jammed. Alouzon's hands were raw. The others were panting, sweating, bleeding. Marrget was breathing in short, harsh gasps, staring fixedly at the trilithon as though she would bring it down by sheer force of will.

But, having yielded a little, the upright refused any further entreaties. Their feet dug furrows into the grass as they fought for a better purchase, but even though they strained until tendons cracked and muscles turned to lumps of fire, the stone would not move. Retching from the ozone, Alouzon shook her head and gestured for the others to stop for a moment.

She realized then that the shaking had ceased. Startled, she looked back, right into the hot, seething eyes of the Corrinian sorcerer.

"He's seen us! Pull!"

Expecting at any moment to feel a killing blast at her back, she shut her eyes and heaved on the rope. Grim, frightened minutes went by. Now that discovery was no longer a concern, Santhe called out a cadence, his voice ringing through the odd silence and echoing off the stones. The upright remained obstinate.

But no blast came.

Alouzon risked another backward look. Mernyl had locked Tireas into inaction by refusing to allow him to disengage from the magical combat. He was diverting Tireas's energies, taking their full brunt on himself, gambling that Alouzon and her party would be successful before his strength gave out. Held fast, the Corrinian could deal neither with the Gryylthans nor with the potential impact of thirty-two tons of rock.

Minutes dragged by, minutes measured in raw hands, rope burns, and straining muscles. The upright shifted a little more, but not quite enough to overbalance and fall. The air was growing thicker, the efforts of the Gryylthans weaker, and Alouzon had all but decided that they were going to fail.

Then she looked up at the sky framed by the trilithons. There, sailing across a sea of stars in the light of a newly risen moon, was Silbakor the Great Dragon, carrying Dythragor on a steadily rising course.

❖ CHAPTER 25 ❖

❖

IT WAS A LOVELY NIGHT FOR FLYING.

Though the sun had set hours before, the air was still tepid from the heat of the day, and the fragrance of midsummer lingered sweetly even at the altitudes sought by the Dragon. Dythragor held to its neck as the great wings beat rhythmically, massively, and the flow of air on his face and in his hair was bracing, the wash of moonlight cleansing. The odors of mortality and the dust of the land were, he felt, leaving him, laved away in a ritual bath of light and wind, preparing him for what lay ahead.

But, for now, he did not think of the future. That was Suzanne's affair—or Alouzon's—and in any case, he was content to watch the stars, to breathe the clean air, to relish the sight of the land that had been his for the last decade.

The years had been filled with battles and with what passed for glory. Men had fallen: friends, enemies, trusted comrades. Even Helkyying that red-bearded giant who had led the First Wartroop, had died fighting the Dremords on the great plain that lay to the south of Ridgebrake Forest. It had taken four men to carry his body to the grave, and all the captains of the wartroops had let their blood for him.

Dythragor shook his head sadly. Helkyying. His place had been taken by Marrget. And he had failed . . . her.

Her face had been drawn with fatigue and with the strain of an interior battle fought more valiantly than any waged with sword and spear, and yet he had run from her. But she had, in the end, extended her hand to him in friendship, and had allowed him to fight once more beside her. If there was any glory in Gryylth, any at all, it was hers.

Marrget . . . And what would happen to her afterward?

He put his hope in Alouzon. He did not understand her, doubted that he ever could, but he knew the Dragon had chosen well. She had helped Marrget and the wartroop, had inspired Vorya and Cvinthil and Santhe, and had won the admiration and respect of most of the soldiers who had fought with her. If anyone could break down the ramparts of social structure and custom so that the women could live freely, it was Alouzon.

Ironic. Here he was, rooting now for the student radical. Everything that he had wanted was gone, and he had actively embraced what had once revolted him. Helen would have laughed.

He shut his eyes at the thought. Her laughter was too cruel to comfort him tonight. But, nonetheless, he wished that she could see. He was doing something right for a change, and he wanted her to know that.

"Silbakor," he said. "Old friend."

"Dragonmaster."

"Will Suzanne accept the Guardianship?"

The Dragon was silent for a moment. The wind rushed by. "I do not prophesy."

"I'm not asking you for that. I want to know what you think about it. I've got to know. I need someone to tell me that Gryylth . . . will continue. I . . ." He voice caught, and the stars blurred into vague nebulae. "I can't do this without knowing."

The Dragon's voice was laden with regret. "Solomon," it said softly, "I cannot tell you that which I do not know. Suzanne Helling is an individual like yourself. Her movements and decisions can neither be predicted, nor even guessed at." It drove ahead through the sky, its yellow eyes glowing like lamps. "Nor can she be judged, regardless of her choices."

"I don't want to judge her."

"That is wise."

"I just want to know if there's any hope."

"There is always hope."

Dythragor sighed. The Dragon was as difficult as ever. He put his hand on his sword, leaned against the wind, and peered down. The Circle was a cauldron of light, the figures of the sorcerers tiny and deceptively insignificant. To one side of the conflict, the Gryylthans struggled to pull the trilithon down onto the Tree.

From the beginning, he had known that they would have trouble. It had taken thousands of years to topple even the weakest of Stonehenge's members, and the Circle was barely ten years old. Despite the stresses of magical battle, it was essentially stable and intact. Given time, given more people who had not been fighting since morning, Alouzon's party might have succeeded. But when the diversionary attack on the Corrinian forces had continued on and on with no sign from the Circle, he had summoned Silbakor.

Now he patted the great, iron-colored neck. "It's time, old friend."

"It is well." The Dragon circled rapidly out to the southwest, reversed its course, and began to descend. Far ahead and far below was the trilithon that contained upright 57. It had tipped, but it had not fallen. It needed one extra jolt, but Alouzon and the rest were too tired to supply it.

The wind turned cold as the Dragon gained speed. It roared in Dythragor's ears. "Silbakor!" he called above the noise, "I think you must be pretty sure that Suzanne will take the Guardianship. You wouldn't fight the Tree like this if you weren't!"

"I but bear you, Solomon Braithwaite, Dythragor Dragonmaster. I carry you. In doing so, I do not oppose either Tree or Circle with my own being."

The Circle was directly ahead now, growing quickly, upright 57 leaning crookedly . . . refusing to fall . . .

He readied himself for his spring, just as he had prepared for his first exultant entrance into Gryylth. He had tensed, then leaped into the thick of battle, his sword flashing, a smile on his face.

The Dragon leveled out. Dythragor drew his sword. "Silbakor," he said suddenly, the question overwhelming him, "was I wrong? Was I so wrong?"

The trilithon bloomed in front of him, and just at the proper moment, he sprang from the Dragon, falling freely as he crossed the outer peristyle. His timing was perfect, his form flawless, and, arms wide as if seeking the embrace of an old lover, he hit the top of the upright at something over seventy miles an hour.

Alouzon guessed what Dythragor was doing the moment she saw the Dragon, and she nearly lost her hold on the rope. For an instant, she thought of running, fleeing the Circle, putting as much distance between herself and Gryylth as possible. But that choice was gone, she realized. She could no more leave Gryylth than she could have left Wykla, or Marrget. She had other choices now, and other strengths.

Though her hands were slick with her own blood, her palms raw and burning, she sought a better hold, pulled, shouted encouragement to the others with what breath she had to spare. Eyes narrowed with her efforts, the trilithon blurring into a phantom doorway into night, she put her back and shoulders into her efforts, calling inwardly on the Grail for help.

For most of its approach, the Dragon was hidden behind the stones, and yet she knew precisely when it was going to arrive. She did not want to see, or to hear, but there was a sudden blast of rushing wings, a fleeting shock wave that penetrated the unyielding barriers surrounding the Circle, and, finally, a dull, muffled thump. The rope gave in her hands.

The trilithon was falling.

The others were already moving, Marrget and Santhe brutally shoving their warriors toward the peristyle as the upright ground slowly down. Alouzon had one glimpse of Mernyl before she was half dragged toward the rear of the monument: the sorcerer was standing straight, facing toward the Avenue, his staff pointing out along the axis of the Circle. Tireas was looking at the trilithon, helpless, his face white.

The warriors had moments to escape. Amid the rending of nearly sixty thousand pounds of rock, they reached the peristyle. No force field barred their way now, and they passed through without slowing, fleeing out along the flat expanse of grass that surrounded the monument.

The first explosion threw them to the ground. Alouzon slid for several feet, propelled both by her own momentum and by the shock wave that ripped through the air. But that was only from the lintel striking the ground. Upright 57 turned slightly as it fell, reared as though in surprise, and crashed down directly on top of the Tree.

A moment of silence as though life and time had been suspended. A coffin lid might have been screwed down on the world. Then, with a crack that seemed to reach from the sky into the foundations of existence, Stone and Wood detonated.

Light burst as though a star had kindled within the peristyle. Blue white, white blue, it flared into incandescent life, expanded hugely, and enveloped the monument. Alouzon had put her head in her arms and clenched her eyes, but the brilliance dazzled her still. It mounted unbearably, continued to mount, and threatened to grow forever and ignite the universe with unquenchable flame.

One terrific blast, one flash that must, she thought, leave her blind, and then it was all over, dying away suddenly without even an echo, the light vanishing as though turned out by a switch. Dazed, fighting for the breath that had been crushed out of her, she rolled over on her back. At first, she could hardly focus her seared eyes on the sky, but when she did, a scream forced its way out of her.

Calmly, without any visible cause, the moon was disintegrating. And the stars were fading, one by one.

As though it were bleeding into a vacuum, the air turned thin. Crawling to her hands and knees, Alouzon looked around frantically, saw, a short distance away, her companions lying sprawled on the ground, unmoving. Marrget was closest, her face serene and tranquil, delicate and lovely . . . shimmering, beginning to turn transparent.

"Marrget!" She scrambled toward her. But the transparency was even more pronounced when she drew near and bent over the captain, afraid to touch, afraid to move.

. . . should your successor be found . . .

The sky was an empty darkness steadily lightening toward white. The ground began to ripple. Marrget was fading, and Wykla, and Relys, and all the rest. Deprived of a Guardian, Gryylth was ending.

"Please . . ." she whispered. "Someone . . .?"

Out beyond the broken and scattered remains of the Circle, a golden light flickered into being, grew. For a moment, she saw the Grail. It held within it everything that she wanted, everything that could reassemble her life from the fragments into which it had fallen. It held life, and wholeness, and an end to yearnings and pain.

And, as she watched, it, too, shimmered, faded.

"No . . . No, don't . . ."

The light went out. The sky was a blank piece of paper.

She was alone, bereft of friends, world, Grail, hope. The choice was inescapable. It was, in fact, no choice at all, and with the toppled monoliths of the Circle beginning themselves to waver, she sat back and screamed at what was left of the heavens:

"All right, you bastards! I'll take it!"

She clamped her eyes shut, fell on her side. "I'll do it. I'm crazy, but I'll do it. Just . . . bring it back. Put it back together again. I'll do it . . . please . . ."

She did not know whom she so entreated. Perhaps it was the Grail, perhaps the nameless gods in whom Mernyl had put such trust. But the grass was soft and fragrant, and the breeze that sprang up was fresh and clear, smelling of wheat and forests and the sea. Suddenly and incongruously, she remembered the yellow flowers she had seen at the Circle: buttercups and dandelions.

Alouzon sobbed, her hands clutched tight over her face. Marrget and Wykla found her that way, and together they held her, as they themselves had each been held, while the Dragonmaster dealt with her own racking, blinding grief.

Mernyl was dead. So was Tireas. The Tree and the Circle were both utterly destroyed.

In his last moments of life, the Gryylthan sorcerer had apparently done his best to focus the blast he knew was coming. Using the remaining trilithons as reflectors, he had sent much of the detonation out along the Avenue, directly into the massed ranks of the Corrinian phalanxes that had been gathered together by Vorya's diversionary attack. A swath of earth fifty yards wide and nearly three quarters of a mile long had been fused into green glass, and only an occasional charred remnant of weaponry or armor was left from those who had encountered the terrible heat.

There were a few survivors. Much of Vorya's party had been clear of the blast, warned by Dythragor to flee the moment the Dragon began to descend. Twenty or thirty Corrinians had also escaped, but they were in no mood to continue a fight that had exterminated most of the young men of their land.

Age and loss of blood had brought Vorya down shortly after Dythragor had left, and Tarwach had perished in the blast. Cvinthil and Darham were the rulers now. The councilor of Gryylth had wept bitterly when informed that his king was no more, and Darham, summoned back from his journey to Benardis by the incredible light and explosion, had come to him bearing his own grief, for he had lost a brother.

Neither man was any more interested in continuing the war than were his soldiers and warriors, and after they had together raised a single mound over both their kings, they swore peace to one another, offering friendship and what aid was theirs to give.

Alouzon stood by, watching and listening as Cvinthil and Darham made their oaths and promises. The scribes would come later, and parchments would be written on, sealed, and signed with the monograms of the new kings, but here in Gryylth, one's word alone was binding. The war that had raged since the beginning of the world was over.

Her arms around Marrget and Santhe, she wept and turned away. The war might have been over, but other matters were just beginning. Gryylth was her land now.

The captains led her to her blankets, and she slept for twelve hours, bathed wearily in a nearby stream, and slept again. When she awakened, the sun was bright on the tumbled and blackened remains of the Circle, and it sparkled on the river of glass that stretched out along the Avenue, but she still felt a numb weariness, and her hands still felt the tackiness of blood.

Clad in fresh garments, she sat in the shade of a makeshift canopy and watched the survivors of both armies making ready to leave for their homes. Marrget was beside her, once again wearing an oversized robe. The captain looked tired, and the lean hauntedness that had left her eyes in the thick of battle had returned.

"Dragonmaster," she said, "I do not know whether to thank you or not."

"Marrget?"

Marrget looked away to the activity on the slope before them—men and women gathering and bundling belongings, calling horses, Corrinians and Gryylthans making tentative shows of camaraderie and trust—but did not seem to see any of it. "When we entered the Circle, I was looking for death. An honorable death, to be sure, but a death nonetheless. I had hoped that the destruction of the Tree and the Circle would be so all-consuming that we would all die."

Alouzon hung her head. Were it not for her choice, Marrget would have gotten her wish.

"Instead," continued the captain, "I am alive, and . . . unchanged." She regarded the soft roundings of her body, sighed. "I cannot say that I am grateful. Forgive me."

"Your place is among the honored of Gryylth."

"I am a woman. My place, in the opinion of my people, is over the cooking pots, and tending children." She grimaced, snorted defiantly.

"I take it you're not inclined to follow custom."

She lifted her head, and her voice was even. "We are the women of the First Wartroop. We have fought before. We will continue to fight."

A deeper voice came to them. "Is there need for more fighting, my lady?" A tall Corrinian stood before them. "Forgive my interrupting. I am Karthin, from Rutupia . . . on the eastern coast." He was a big man, his hair gold and his eyes clear and blue, but he blushed suddenly like a schoolboy.

"Marrget of Crownhark," said the captain. "And Alouzon Dragonmaster beside me." She peered at him, shading her eyes against the sun. "What do you wish, sir?"

"King Darham has ordered me to assist with the sharing of food between our two peoples. I will be accompanying King Cvinthil back to his seat."

"You do us honor, sir," said Marrget.

Karthin fidgeted, still blushing furiously. He held something behind his back.

"Is there something more?"

"Forgive me, lady," he said. "I fear you will think me ill-advised and hasty."

"Nay, sir, pray continue."

He would not meet her eyes. "When we fought one another, captain, I swore that I would rather be your friend than your foe. I find that my desire has been granted." He brought his hand from behind his back. In it was a small spray of buttercups gleaned from the torn grass about the Circle. "I bring you these, lady, in token of our friendship. In token of peace."

Marrget stared. Then, slowly, almost without thinking, she reached up and accepted the flowers from him. "My thanks, Karthin. The . . . the gods bless you."

"And you also, Marrget."

The silence grew, both captains speechless with embarrassment. Marrget was white, Karthin red.

Alouzon broke in to save her friend. "What will you do in Kingsbury, Karthin?"

At her words, they both seemed relieved. Karthin passed a hand over his face and took a deep breath. "As you know, much of Corrin's wheat was destroyed. Cvinthil informs me that Gryylth has some surplus that he is willing to give in aid. And there are methods of forcing an additional crop before the winter. I am

. . . I was a farmer before I found myself with a sword in my hand. I have some skill with planting. I can advise."

"The harvest will be ready soon," said Marrget. "But we have few hands available for a single gathering, much less two. I am afraid that the wheat will rot in the field for lack of men to cut it."

Karthin folded his arms thoughtfully, stroked his cheek. "What of the women of Gryylth?"

She swallowed, paled again. "Women do not labor in the fields. By custom they are . . . confined to their homes."

He looked sympathetic, as though he understood her plight. "You spoke of fighting, captain. Perhaps you find your fight before you." Marrget looked grim, but he smiled. "Have no fear. You will not fight alone." He bowed and strode away. Alouzon noticed that he moved stiffly, as though he were in some pain.

Marrget looked down at the buttercups in her hands, then at Karthin. "I remember him, Alouzon. I believe I broke his ribs in the battle at the Circle."

"That's one hell of a guy."

"Indeed." She stared after him. "We were so wrong about Corrin . . ."

Wykla approached respectfully, glanced at Karthin, then bowed to her captain and the Dragonmaster. Her hair was loose, and it gave her a girlish air. "The king wishes to know when you will be ready to leave for Kingsbury," she said.

Alouzon could not meet their eyes. "I . . . won't be returning to Kingsbury with you."

Wykla looked stricken.

"I've got to go home for a while," she said. "I'll be back, though." She could not but return. Gryylth was hers. She might as well have tried to run from her own soul. "I'll help you. I mean it."

She felt empty and drained, as though her words had run out through a hole in her heart. There was little that she loved in Los Angeles, but it was familiar. She needed the familiar now—cars and college, telephones and cans of soda pop. She needed the sound of traffic cruising by outside her apartment, and she needed her own bed . . . to herself. Joe Epstein was out of a roommate.

"My lady," said Wykla. "I . . . would wish you to know . . ." She blinked in the sunlight, her hair bright and unbound, looking for all the world like a coed from long ago. One who had not died. " . . . that I will continue. For your sake." She knelt, bent her head. "With your blessing."

Alouzon put her hands on Wykla's head. "Wykla, you have it. Do you think you can make it?"

The girl straightened, nodded slowly. "At first I thought I must die of shame . . . or fear . . . or . . . I know not what. But then I fought at your side, and I decided that, if the Dragonmaster can be a woman, then so can I. I am afraid still, and shamed, but I will live. Someday, maybe, I will heal."

Marrget murmured beside her: "I understand." There were clear drops on the buttercups that were not dew.

Healing. Alouzon wanted it also, but she could not be as confident as Wykla. Could her hands, so bloodstained, ever hold the utter purity of the Grail?

She felt hollow, but she could not allow herself to show it. She was a Dragonmaster. Trying to look encouraging, she took the hands of the other women. "Fight valiantly," she said. She could think of nothing else to say.

❖   ❖   ❖

Silbakor bore her to the north, beating the air with heavy wing strokes. Below, the land unrolled as though it were a brightly painted canvas.

Preoccupied with her thoughts of Guardianship and her worries about the people she had left behind, Alouzon did not notice for some time that there was still land beneath her. But eventually she looked down, frowned. "I thought you were taking me home, Silbakor."

"There is something I would that you see."

She shrugged. "You're driving."

The Dragon continued north in silence. Behind, and far away now, the peace was lengthening, hour by hour, and friendships and alliances were forming. Karthin's gift to Marrget was perhaps an emblem of the assimilation that would follow, a blending of two not dissimilar cultures. After years, or decades, a new society would evolve. The women of Corrin were not kept at home, and Alouzon hoped, for the sake of the First Wartroop, that the custom would spread quickly to Gryylth.

Silbakor altered course slightly and flew toward the coast. Soon they passed over a shore of blue waves and white sand, and the Dragon swung north to follow it, its shadow flitting among the breakers and foam.

"Silbakor, I . . ." She rested her cheek against the adamantine scales. "I need a friend. You're all I've got now. What do I do? How do I keep going?"

"You are Alouzon Dragonmaster. You have both taken life and given it with honor. Live as befits your status."

"That doesn't help much, guy."

"I will help as I can."

There was an unfamiliar note in the Dragon's voice. Longing? Sorrow? Did it miss its former master? Did it grieve over the passing of a familiar world?

Silbakor angled out over the water and began to follow a rocky promontory. "I will help as I can," it said again.

She suddenly realized that it was sorry for *her*.

"Look, Dragonmaster: out to the west."

She strained her eyes against the afternoon sun. The horizon was misty, blurred, but a definite form lay behind the clouds. Land.

"Behold," said the Dragon. "The world continues."

"I thought it ended." She knew what had happened, but she hoped to hear otherwise.

"It did, once."

Alouzon sagged, wept.

"The Grail is there." The Dragon's voice was gentle.

"Yeah . . . and what else?"

Silbakor said nothing.

"How bad are things there?" she said. "How many people am I going to have to kill there?"

"I am sorry. I wished to give you some hope."

She wiped her tears on her forearms, her eyes still on the distant land. Like Gryylth, it seemed fresh and new, with high mountains rising up behind a broad, fertile plane. Her land. "Maybe . . ." The wind was a cool torrent that whipped her hair into a bronze cloud. "Maybe I did better than Braithwaite. I hope so." She leaned forward toward the Dragon's ear. "Did I . . . did I despair that much?"

Silbakor was silent for a minute. It began to gain altitude, and the blue sky shaded into starless black. "At Kent State," it said softly. "Then and afterward. In Dallas. In your own apartment with each rising of the sun. The bullet that missed you wounded you nonetheless. You are Guardian of Gryylth, Suzanne Helling, but your own land awaits you."

"And you, Silbakor?"

"As I said: I will help as I can."

The sky had faded, and void was about them. For a time, she felt the sensation of incredible velocity without apparent speed, and then all motion ceased. With a soft thump, the Dragon alighted on a floor that should not have existed, that stretched off into infinity on all sides.

"Dismount, Suzanne Helling."

She found that her hands were, once more, plump and soft, her skin white, her hair long and dark. Clumsily, unused to the sluggish responses of her old body, she slid from the Dragon's back. As her feet touched down, she noticed that the floor began to take on the characteristics of institutional linoleum.

Silbakor shrank, dwindled, and a nimbus formed about it that solidified into the appearance of glass. With a momentary flicker as of a projected image being brought into sharp focus, the paperweight returned, and Solomon's office reappeared.

He was sitting in his chair before her, slumped to the side, dead. A soft smile was on his face, as though his last thoughts had been pleasant ones.

"In this world," said the Dragon from the paperweight on the desk, "Solomon Braithwaite has died of a myocardial infarction."

"What do I do now?"

"Notify the proper authorities. No time has passed since you left."

Suzanne hesitated.

"Take the paperweight," said the Dragon.

Still, she did not move.

"Put the paperweight in your handbag."

At last, mechanically, she did so, and the rounded shape nestled against her hip. When she put her hand on the doorknob, sounds started up outside. Type-writers. Conversation. Dr. O'Hara was passing by, talking to someone about fifteenth century warfare.

"Then we got into gunpowder," he was saying, "and it was a whole new ball game."

"Yeah," she muttered. M-1s and magic, and a Dragon, and the timeless sprawl of dead men. She gulped down some air and glanced once more at Solomon's body.

Gritting her teeth, she swung open the door and tried to look as though she had never seen death before. "Someone call the paramedics! Braithwaite's in trouble."

Faces turned toward her, conversations stopped in midsentence.

She faltered out the words. "I . . . I think it's his heart."

About the Author

Gael Baudino grew up in Los Angeles and attended collge at the University of Southern California. She now lives in Denver.

Beside her writing, she maintains a busy teaching schedule as a minister of Dianic Wicca; and in her alter-ego as a harper, she plays every Sunday at a local mtetaphysical bookstore. She also performs with the Maroon Bells Morris Dancers of Boulder.

She lives with her lover Mirya, a lumbering adolescent named Michael, two ferrets, and a cat.

Her stories have appeared in AMAZONS II and in THE MAGAZINE OF FANTASY AND SCIENCE FICION.